THE EXILED KING

T0033933

By Sarah Remy

THE BONE MAGIC SERIES
Stonehill Downs
Across the Long Sea
The Bone Cave
The Exiled King

THE
EXILED KING

SARAH REMY

HARPER

VOYAGER
IMPULSE

An Imprint of HarperCollinsPublishers

THE EXILED KING. Copyright © 2017 by Sarah Remy. All rights reserved. Printed in the United States of America. No part of this book may be used or reproduced in any manner whatsoever without written permission except in the case of brief quotations embodied in critical articles and reviews. For information, address HarperCollins Publishers, 195 Broadway, New York, NY 10007.

Digital Edition SEPTEMBER 2017 ISBN: 978-0-06-247376-9
Print Edition ISBN: 978-0-06-247377-6

Harper Voyager, the Harper Voyager logo, and Harper Voyager Impulse are trademarks of HarperCollins Publishers.
HarperCollins is a registered trademark of HarperCollins Publishers in the United States of America and other countries.

FIRST EDITION

17 18 19 20 21   HDC   10 9 8 7 6 5 4 3 2 1

For Aidan

PURSUIT

The moon, fat and silver in the night sky, was no friend to the small party of soldiers hunkered low in the dubious shelter of late-blooming gorse bush. The night was bright as a summer afternoon, and hardly cooler. Moonlight set white sand dunes ablaze and threw every shadow into stark relief. A staggered trail of footprints disturbed the smooth sand up and across the dunes away from Whitcomb to the north, clear as day even at two hours past midnight.

Russel used the back of her hand to swipe sweat from the tip of her nose as she considered the trail.

"He's not far ahead," Lory said, his voice a whisper in the sluggish, salt-laden breeze. "And look there—blood on the sand, if only a little. Martin's arrow struck true."

A miracle in itself, Russel knew, as Martin's skill

lay with the sword, not the bow, and they'd been riding hell-for-leather through Whitcomb's narrow streets when he'd loosed his arrow in a last attempt to slow their quarry. Russel thought Martin had been aiming for the man's horse; instead the arrow had stuck in the spy's leather-clad calf.

"Bleeding steadily," Martin agreed. The gap-toothed man lay on his belly in the sand. The gorse bush did little to shield his bulky form. "Pulled the arrow right out, looks like. Guess the desert breeds 'em stupid."

"Managed to lose all three of us in a village the size of my granny's herb garden, and I know Whitcomb better than most," Russel retorted. "Mayhap not so stupid as all that."

Lory grunted agreement. The Kingsmen stared mournfully at the trail of blood and footprints in the moonlight. In a moment Russel would give the order to stand and charge, but none of the three were eager to rise. It wasn't that the job was difficult—they were highly trained soldiers in a well-schooled army—but that it was impossible. They'd been chasing the desert scout along Wilhaiim's coast for near a day and a half, having promised their betters to bring the man in alive. But it had become apparent that the fellow intended to die.

"Wishing you'd stayed behind, are you, Corporal?" Lory guessed. He'd shaved his beard against the summer heat. He looked ten years younger without it. "Prefer dogging the pirate prince about the palace to getting dirty with the likes of us?"

It was a good-natured jab, said to pass the time while they caught their breath and considered their options, but it smarted. Wilhaiim didn't much care for Admiral Baldebert, not since he'd first stolen their magus away and then engineered a betrothal between their king and Baldebert's own royal sister. Russel, as the admiral's part-time bodyguard, was not as immune to the chiding tossed her way in the barracks as she'd like. Her fellow soldiers didn't blame her for the assignment—she'd sworn to serve the throne, as had every man and woman in the king's scarlet uniform, and the throne desired Baldebert alive—but it was possible they wished she'd show some resentment for the task.

"Fuck you, Lory," Russel said amiably. She squinted through the gorse at the moon. It would be setting soon, but not before the sun showed its face. Tonight, like the night before, they wouldn't be able to rely on the cover of darkness.

"Ayup?" Martin prompted, which meant he'd caught his breath and come to terms with their certain failure.

Russel nodded. "Stay low. There's naught but bracken and dune north from here till next week. Bleeding or not, he'll be waiting. Up!"

As one they rose and drew their swords, jumping the gorse and scaling the dunes, like hounds on the scent. They ran quietly but for the rattle of leather and the soft clink of Martin's chain coif. The sand was uneven and made the going difficult, but Russel had hours ago grown used to aching muscles. She hadn't slept since they'd left Wilhaiim's gates on word that there was a yellow-eyed sand snake holed up in Whitcomb. She hadn't bothered with food since a sparse breakfast of dried ham and spring wine. Her belly was hollow, but her pulse was racing, her teeth gritted in fierce joy, her entire being focused on pursuit.

Russel was a Kingsman, sworn to the throne, and she'd do whatever Renault required of her without complaint, even if that meant saving the kingdom's most hated man from himself, but she wouldn't pretend she hadn't missed this, this rush of danger, this dance on the knife-edge of possibilities.

She came up over a dune the size of a small house, howling challenge, and the desert spy waited on the other side, curved blade glittering in the moonlight. He swung his sword as she fell upon him. She twisted away, barely avoiding its bite, rolled in the sand, and was up again even as the blade sliced the ground near her feet, sending up a small shower of grit.

He pivoted, blocking her strike. Their blades crossed, steel sliding against iron. He was larger, but she was stronger. Martin was right; the man had made a mistake in pulling the arrow from his leg. The sand around him was dark with his blood. He was surely dying.

"Yield," she said, as blade kissed blade. Lory and Martin came around the dune together, intending chaos. They stopped when they saw Russel and stood still but for the heaving of their chests, watching.

"I yield," the sand snake said in the king's lingua. He smiled.

He had very white teeth in a narrow face. His yellow eyes were limpid, his skin turning gray under a desert tan. He'd pulled the arrow because he meant to die. He was quite young, she saw with a shock of muted distress, younger even than Liam. The beard on his face was naught but peach fuzz.

War tended to turn boys into men before their time.

"He's all but dead," Lory said, disgusted. "Lord Malachi will have our hides. Martin, you shit."

"I was aiming for the horse," Martin said, aggrieved.

The boy dripped blood on the sand. The scimitar wobbled in his hand then fell from his fingers. He slumped sideways.

"By the Aug!" Russel swore. She kicked the curved sword out of reach as she sheathed her own. "Lory, grab him. Martin, staunch the wound. Quick! Mayhap it's not too—"

But the spy bucked in Lory's grip, gurgling his last. The dunes drank his blood; the scent of iron mingled with the salt in the air.

Russel swore again and kicked the scimitar until it pinwheeled in the sand. Then she took a breath.

"Go through his pack," she ordered. "Turn out his pouch. Mayhap there's something of use to the king."

But there wasn't.

Russel and Lory were both theist enough to protest when Martin suggest they strip the boy's corpse and leave it for the crabs and birds and coyotes. Martin, vociferously pragmatic, pointed out that no good could come of hauling a dead desert spy in full view back along the King's Highway to Wilhaiim, that considering the end-of-summer heat the corpse would soon begin to stink, and that if Lord Malachi wanted to interrogate the boy's spirit, Martin would be happy to show the necromancer exactly where the lad had bled out—but only after the lot of them had a chance to eat, sleep, and explain their failure to the king.

Lory objected and the two men almost came to blows. Russel backed them down with a few well-chosen expletives.

"We're burying him," she decided. "Here. Cut the feathers from his hair, take his belt. We'll keep those, and the sword. The pouch and his pack. Everything else belongs to the god."

Martin pressed his lips together in disapproval, but did as she ordered, using his belt knife to cut feathered ornaments from the boy's long sun-bleached hair. He set the collection carefully to one side, then added the boy's belt and curved sword.

Digging in the dune was much like walking on the dune: awkward and irritating. Sand slid back into the hole almost as soon as they scooped it free. Lacking shovels, they dug with hands and pieces of gorse bush. Lory, struck by inspiration, kicked off one boot and used it as a makeshift spade. Russel and Martin soon followed suit. Grit coated their mouths and eyes and settled in worse places.

They tipped the spy into the ground just as the moon sank behind Whitcomb. Russel closed his yellow eyes before they pushed sand back into the hole. The dune rolled easily over his cooling corpse. When it was done, Lory marked the grave with a sprig of blooming gorse and two smooth ocean stones they'd freed from the sand in their digging.

"In case we *do* need to find him again," he said, although they all knew the shifting terrain would consume the small monument in a matter of days. Then even Mal, she thought, would have difficulty finding the grave.

Russel crossed herself, right shoulder to left, brow to groin, and said a silent prayer to anyone who might be listening that when someday she went to ground it would be in cooler weather and into damper soil. The sand made her itch.

"Right, then." She picked up the scimitar, slung the boy's belt and pack over her shoulder, and tossed the feathers and embroidered pouch at Martin. "Let's go home."

CHAPTER 1

Master Paul was laid to ground with quiet ceremony in the temple's private sepulcher. King Renault stood attendance as four tonsured priests carried the Masterhealer's casket into the narrow gray stone building where Paul would sleep forever with the boxed bones of his predecessors. Wilhaiim's Masterhealer, it turned out, was favored even after death. The sepulcher was an elaborate edifice, the lintel carved all over with birds and saints. The temple's chalice and barbed spear glittered above the door, delicately rendered in colored glass.

Avani, standing to the left and two paces behind Renault, couldn't help but recall the window in the Masterhealer's private sanctuary. That window bore the chalice and the spear in all its glory. Paul's sanctuary was now declared desecrated, defiled by bloodshed and violence. The new Masterhealer would have to set up office in a different part of the temple; the old sanctuary was even now being sealed, the door ensorcelled, marked with the theist sigils that would keep it securely locked.

Avani could feel the temple magic at work—a shiver in her limbs, come up from the grass beneath her feet all the way to her teeth. The strength of it made her sigh. The yellow gem in Andrew's ring winked against her breast.

"A powerful incantation," Mal murmured from where he stood at Renault's right hand. The magus looked idly up at the old fruit trees planted to shade the tomb. Sparrows fluttered in the branches, disturbed by the commotion below. "Whatever the priests think remains in that room, they're desperate to keep it behind closed doors."

"I told you—Paul's ghost is well and truly banished," Avani breathed. Between them Renault mouthed the words of the burial ritual with placid solemnity. A small contingent of senior priests, standing in the shade against the sepulcher, did the same. It did not escape Avani's notice that they watched the king closely as they did so.

The temple and the throne, allies for generations, were lately suffering a painful fracture.

"I saw to him myself," she added, watching the theists watch the king. Brother Tillion, the priest who appeared to spend most of his waking hours railing against Renault's recent betrothal, was the only one of the group who seemed more interested in the burial rites than the king's party. He leaned against a heavy staff, yellow eyes fastened on the door of the tomb, expression so rapt as to be almost feverish.

"That one will be the thorn in our side," predicted Mal, following the direction of Avani's gaze. "The genuinely pious always are."

Renault grimaced. Avani, who knew the king was a devout man, frowned. Mal only smiled blandly in Tillion's direction.

And they say I'm mad, the magus whispered in her head, as the four priests, relieved of the Masterhealer's casket, stepped back out of the sepulcher and into the garden. *At least I have an excuse. I wager Tillion burst raving from the womb.*

As one, the pallbearers fell to their knees in the grass before the tomb. The congregation of priests beneath the fruit trees did the same. Renault bowed his head but remained standing. The theists began to sing in unison, voices ranged from deep to shrill. The canticle was unfamiliar, the words foreign to Avani's ear, but the poignancy of the call made her heart squeeze.

When they finished, the last low syllable quieted, sigils previously obscured by the carving around the sepulcher's door burst to life, burning indigo before fading to pale silver. The ritual was over, Master Paul safely entombed.

Look how he holds himself, Mal added, irreverent. When Avani pushed disapproval across their link, his mouth curled at the edges, but he continued, *Look how he checks himself, how he grips his stick. As if he fears his joints will shatter. Notice the tick in his jaw, the way his left eye rolls away from his right. Mayhap that disfunction of the brain the healers call glass syndrome. Possibly of the waxing and waning variety. I've seen it before, but not for many years. In truth, I believed it bred to dormancy—*

"Malachi," Renault interrupted mildly, "you grin as if it's Ceilidh night and you've been given a gift to rival all others. Mayhap recall where you are and school your face appropriately before I'm accused of engineering Paul's demise amongst my other trespasses."

Chastened, Mal subsided. Avani wondered if it was possible Renault suspected the illicit connection she had, all unknowingly, forged with his vocent. It would mean her death, and Mal's, if ever Renault did more than suspect. The king's great-grandfather had ordered magi burned at the stake for much less. Renault, realistic as well as devout, would bend precedent for the good of the throne, but not so far as to put his people at risk.

He loved Mal, but he loved Wilhaiim more. If the truth came out, Renault would sacrifice the one for the sake of the other.

As for Avani, Renault was kind to the foreign witch who stood now at his side, but that, she knew, was for Mal's sake as much as for his own. She was a useful tool in the throne's armory, her worth proven, but not so valuable that she could not be put aside, even as Wilhaiim charged headlong toward war.

Renault would blame her, she thought. For the link, which grew stronger daily even as she pretended otherwise, and for the tenacious darkness lurking just behind Mal's green gaze.

Renault—devout, practical, yet unbowed by the weight of his crown—would likely weep over her loss even as he set the first flame to her pyre.

"Goddess have mercy," Avani said as the king and his dissenting priests crossed themselves a final time. She hoped Master Paul, at least, had left all fear behind.

"On every one of us," Mal, who did not believe in god or goddess, agreed. He'd switched his focus from Tillion to Avani. She raised a brow. His distracted smile sharpened to real amusement.

"Brother Orat," Renault said, alerting his companions to the approaching contingent of robed priests. The theists were gathering for a chance to nip at the king. Avani hoped they would not blacken the beauty of Master Paul's farewell with fiery words. Their discontent was a palpable force. Theists drew their magic from books of spells and ancient liturgy; they could not claim the innate power of vocent or witch. Even so, temple magic was a not a trifling thing. The garden seemed to grow chill as they approached. The birds in the branches of the fruit trees quieted. Avani cupped her hand around Andrew's ring to mute the gem's angry glow. Mal's signet, twin to Andrew's, flashed a warning from the index finger of his left hand, a small yellow sun.

Brother Orat did not appear put off. He'd been long enough in Renault's service to retain some confidence that Mal would not smite him where he stood simply for the robes he wore. Avani was less positive. Mal's fury simmered in her head, bright as the ring on his finger.

Brother Orat bowed from the waist. "Majesty," he said. The other priests milled at his heels. Tillion, taller by a head than the others, leaned hard on his staff.

"Brother Orat," the king replied. He did not so much as incline his head in greeting. Before the Masterhealer's death Orat had been Renault's spy in Wilhaiim's temple, another tool in the throne's collection. But now, as a senior priest, he was wanted at the temple.

Just as Renault will always choose Wilhaiim, she thought, *Orat will choose his god.*

Wrong, corrected Mal. His derision rang in her skull, but it was not for her. *Orat will always choose himself.*

"Thank you for coming, Majesty," Orat said. "You honor both the god and Brother Paul with you presence."

"I am sorry for the temple's loss." Renault did not

say he would miss the Masterhealer because he would not, and he preferred to speak the truth whenever possible. "Paul deserved better than Lane's sword in his heart."

"Lane was your dog," Tillion said. He did not look at Renault when he spoke, but at the grass and the sky, the roses and the sky again. Avani, who had seen the priest performing in the town square, could not quite reconcile this restless form with that of the charismatic preacher on his box. "Was she not?"

"She was not," Renault retorted. "I do not condone the murder of innocents. I regret she was not taken alive, to face my judgment."

Tillion's wild gaze flicked to Mal and away again. Mal, whose task it was to see the king's justice carried out.

But Lane was not alive to face Mal's inquisition because Avani had killed the armswoman, stabbing her through the throat, twisting the blade as she'd been taught to make sure the job was done well. She'd done it to save Baldebert's life, and it was possible Lane deserved to die as she'd lived, in battle—but to Avani it was still a life taken, and a life taken, innocent or otherwise, was a life wasted.

Tillion asked, "And the other one? Is not he yours, also, Majesty? Himself, his father, and his father's father before?"

"Only," replied Renault coldly, "in so much as is any other man, woman, or child who lives upon my land. As are you, sir, so long as you shelter within my walls. Best not forget it."

The priests shifted on the grass, robes whispering. A cloud blew across the sun, sending shadows along the sepulcher wall. A cool breeze kicked up. Summer was waning.

"Holder will be recovered," Mal promised. "Sooner rather than later. No one escapes His Majesty's attention indefinitely. He can't run forever. To whom here shall I send word when it's done?"

It was a subtle way of asking whether the temple had yet selected the next Masterhealer. Avani thought Mal's outward tranquility impressive. She could feel how desperately he wanted to berate the priests for daring to implicate Renault in Lane's corruption.

"The decision could not be made until our brother was laid to rest," one of the pallbearers replied. He was younger than the rest. His cheeks were still wet with tears. Avani did not know his name, but she recognized him from time spent in the temple fighting the Red Worm. "Tonight we will celebrate Paul's life. Tomorrow we will begin to pray that the god will quickly show us his replacement."

"There is no time to waste," Tillion agreed, looking at his own bare toes, at the garden wall, and up at the gathering clouds. The wooden staff quivered in his fist. "Our indecision only angers the god further." His teeth clicked suddenly together and he winced, eyes narrowing in pain.

"I can help you with the tremors," Mal said mildly. "Mayhap even the cramping. There is a method I've seen used—"

"Malachi," Renault warned even as Tillion reared back, insulted.

"Healing is the temple's work," Brother Orat said quickly. "While we appreciate your offer, Lord Malachi, bone magic is anathema and best left to those who are desirous of your specialized talents. Brother Tillion has no need of them."

A bird called from the branches of a fruit tree. Renault shifted. Avani saw from the flick of his thumb against his sword belt that the king's patience had at last run out.

"When Brother Paul's successor is chosen," he ordered, "let him present himself before me. There is a war to discuss, and I cannot wait upon the god's decision to make my own."

Brother Orat bowed again. The rest of the theists followed suit. Renault turned on his heel and strode away from the sepulcher, Mal in his long black vocent's cape plunging after. Together they were imposing. Avani knew it was by design. She brought up the rear, pausing to admire fading rose blossoms. The cooler air chased her from the garden, through a narrow gate, and out onto the city streets. She reveled in the chill, grown weary of the long, sultry summer.

An escort of six Kingsmen stirred from where they stood outside the temple. Pikes in hand, they surrounded Mal and the king. The streets were slowly filling with people. Wilhaiim was waking. Farmers, housemaids, tradesfolk, and court attendants all gave the Renault and his soldiers a wide birth. They bowed as they passed. Many smiled. Renault was royalty and still well beloved. Avani, watching as the scarlet-liveried troop ushered the king away toward the palace, couldn't help but worry that theists meant to turn that old, comfortable affection into something poisonous.

"People fear what they don't understand," she mused aloud, as her own small escort detached himself from a patch of morning shadow thrown off by the temple walls. "To most of Wilhaiim, Roue is an unknown, its people no less ominous than those of the desert."

Liam shrugged. "Wilhaiim will be glad enough of Roue when Baldebert's ships arrive carrying the Rani's elephant guns."

Liam wore his own version of the king's colors: a simple red tunic over gray shirt and hose. The red was a new addition to the page's uniform and marked him as a senior squire. A brindled hound, tall as Liam's hip, waited at his side. She panted affably as she watched people pass to and fro, great strings of saliva dribbling from her strong jaws.

She had been Holder's dog, before Holder disappeared. Now she seemed attached to Liam, who had an uncanny way with animals. He fondled her large ears, staring after the king's party until it disappeared from view. He seemed mostly unaffected by his ordeal in the Bone Cave, despite the bruises still purpling one side of his face. The discoloration made the old scars on his cheeks and brow more pronounced: a trellis of white seams carved into his flesh by jagged *sidhe* blades.

"Any news of Jacob?" Liam demanded. He'd asked Avani the same question each of the past five mornings, ever since she'd made the mistake of worrying out loud that the raven had gone missing.

"Nay." She reached to ruffle Liam's dark hair but he ducked away from her hand, making her laugh. "It's not the first time he's gone off on business of his own, nor will it be the last." She could still feel Jacob on the edge of her senses, a faint but reliable impression of ruffled feathers and distemper, less intrusive than Mal's serrated wit and more familiar. She'd lived with pieces of the raven in her heart—a blessing and a curse—since the Goddess had seen fit to tie Jacob to her, back when Avani had first arrived on flatland shores.

"Aye, well. Jacob had best be careful." Liam scowled as he followed Avani into the street. Passing strangers gave the dog at his side a large berth. "It's not safe as it once was outside the city walls. The days are growing longer and strange things are stirring after dark."

"*Ai*, Holder will have to show his nose sooner or later." Avani spoke with more assurance than she felt. "And when he does the Kingsmen will have him. There are more scouts riding the King's Highway of late than even Deval can recall from years past."

Liam shook his head. "There are worse things in the fields and on the road than Holder," he muttered. "*Dire* things."

Avani glanced around. They both recalled the dire things that had once walked the Downs, and the destruction left behind.

"Not *sidhe*," Liam said quickly. He met Avani's gaze before glancing away. "At least, I don't think so. Wythe's horse guard talk over supper of wolves in the fields, whole packs of them, and great, frenzied elk stampeding in herds from the red woods, afraid of no man. Riggins says he's seen an enormous eagle with eyes like flame circling over Whitcomb. Big as a pony, he said it was. More than big enough to swallow a raven entire."

"Big as a pony, was it?" Stopping, Avani quirked her brows. Liam flushed but lifted his chin in challenge. Wilhaiim eddied around them, becoming noisy as the morning ripened. The blacksmith's hammer rang out from three streets over. A fishmonger called her wares while a man selling summer squash out of woven baskets played a jolly tune on a small silver flute, vying for attention. Avani's stomach rumbled. She'd skipped breakfast for the Masterhealer's interment.

Once she would have soothed Liam's worries with

spiced cider and a pasty roll. Once, when a full belly had been a luxury for the pair of them, an indication that all was right with the world. But now Liam was stretching toward manhood and he no longer looked to Avani for comfort. Lately, he kept his counsel close as any treasure, doling out companionship as parsimoniously as coin.

It struck her that his concern for the raven had sent him to her side five days in a row, a rarity and a boon, and so she checked her amusement before it could do either of them harm. She gripped his shoulder as she had seen Renault do Mal's, equal-to-equal, and let him see the honesty in her face.

"I cannot tell you what mischief Jacob is about, but wherever he is, he is alive and not made meal for eagle or wolf. I would know," she promised, "if it were otherwise." She touched the place on the edge of her perception that was Jacob, gingerly as a tongue probing a bad tooth, and felt the raven's distant irritability in reply. Whatever the bird was up to, he wanted no part of her interference.

Liam released a breath. The brindled hound wagged her massive tail, neatly knocking a man in a feathered cap sideways. The man swore. Avani awarded him an apologetic smile.

"Come," she told Liam, "I've a desire for cider before the day warms to unbearable."

CHAPTER 2

Eight days after Lane's death Avani was startled from her loom by a sudden pounding on the chamber door.

"My lady!" As Avani rose from her stool a sharp cry joined the drubbing. "My lady! Are you there?"

Puzzled, Avani crossed the room and opened the door. The scent of honey wafted from the corridor without. Even so it took her longer than it should have to recognize the woman hovering impatiently on the threshold. She'd learned to distinguish the lords and ladies of Renault's court out of recent necessity; she did the throne little good if she could not pick out the king's advisors from his detractors.

The lass standing in the corridor and smelling of honey was no titled aristocrat. Avani almost did not recognize her away from her brightly colored tent and toothsome wares. But her remarkable alabaster hair—now bundled off her face beneath a patchwork scarf—and delicate features made a lasting impression on most who met her. Villein and soldiers alike were drawn to her tent, intent on sampling more than honey. In Avani's experience the lass had a bold wit and a talent for flirtation and seemed to enjoy wielding both.

"Beekeeper?" Avani inquired, puzzled. She was not unaccustomed to patrons knocking on her door at odd hours in search of her favors as weaver and seamstress, but rarely did a client seem so intent on beating in her door.

"Cleena," the beekeeper said, and Avani was abashed to think she'd never bothered ask the lass's name. "Come with me. Hurry."

"Is something the matter?"

"You're wanted, my lady, at once." She looked past Avani's shoulder, dark eyes scanning the chamber. "Faolan said to bring your healing tackle—your teas and ointments and such."

"Faolan!" Avani ducked out of the doorway and swiftly gathered up the odds and ends she kept close in case of illness or injury amongst the more reticent of the king's subjects. Despite temple rhetoric, there were many who preferred magus over priest when it came to ailments of the body, and more than a few of those who favored Avani's quiet competence over Mal's brusque bedside manner.

"Faolan is in Wilhaiim?" she demanded, scooping equipment into her sturdiest sack. She knotted it neatly closed, then slung it over one shoulder. "Is that wise? Is he injured? Sick?"

Cleena grimaced. "Mulish and hardheaded," she said. She plucked at her patchwork apron with long, pale fingers. The apron, like the lass's scarf, was all the colors of a wheat field at sunset: gold and yellow, lavender and rose, and black and silver where pieces of damask were sewn into the hem. "Are you ready?"

"Aye. Where are we going?"

"Down," replied Cleena.

Avani's chambers, while not so luxurious as Mal's, were nevertheless situated high enough above the bailey as to indicate her worth to the king. Even during the heat of midsummer, with her windows cracked, she was rarely troubled by the sound of city traffic. The rest of the floor was deserted but for an elderly viscountess who, for the most part, kept to herself, preferring sleep to company. Locked doors guarding empty rooms ran the length of the twisting corridor between torches smoldering blue mage-light.

Cleena darted unerringly toward the back staircase used almost exclusively by Avani and the palace servants. Avani's pack bounced against her spine as she jogged to keep pace, the worn carpets muffling their footsteps. The servant's stair was hidden behind a discreet tapestry featuring a spearman, a hound, and a rearing stag. The striped hound called to mind Liam's brindled companion.

Cleena twitched the tapestry aside. She slipped into the staircase, gesturing for Avani to follow. The steps were wide, square-hewn, slanting at right angles into the depths of the palace. More mage-light kept shadows from encroaching, but Avani still brushed the knuckles of one hand along gray stone walls for balance as they descended. The stone was pleasantly cool and dry to the touch, the air crisp no matter the season. For all the times she'd traveled up and down the staircase Avani had not yet found a magus's sigil but she knew it must be there, hidden high above her head near the tower eves or carved in the old stone near the bottom-most stair, mayhap anchored with a sliver of bone to keep the temperate spell strong as time unspooled.

A pinched-face lady's maid passed them on the stairs, slippers whispering on stone as she hastened upward, a bundle of clean linen pressed against her chest. She eyed Cleena warily but awarded Avani the briefest of curtsies before rushing on. The labored puff of her breath echoed as she disappeared upward.

"How far down?" Avani queried when the Cleena led her past floor after floor with no sign of slowing. Avani knew from experience that the stair eventually led to the sewers beneath the castle foundation. She'd gone swimming in the Maiden's Spring once and wasn't inclined to repeat the experience.

Cleena didn't look around. The beekeeper's long, silvery hair cascaded down her shoulders almost to her waist, shimmering in the dimness. Even in haste her hips undulated provocatively. Her simple shift bared strong calves and delicate, sandaled feet. In the close stairwell she was redolent of lavender and honey.

The friendly, flirtatious nature Avani remembered from the Fair seemed now too pronounced, her allure exaggerated into ripe sexuality. The back of Avani's neck prickled warning even as her mouth went dry in late understanding. She stopped on the stairs and reached for her wards. Her fingertips throbbed as protective magic burst around her, sparkling silver.

The beekeeper whirled. Her dimpled smile turned derisive.

"There's no call for disrespect," she said, "little witch."

"What are you?" Avani challenged.

Cleena pursed her lips in irritation. "You know," she said. "You've seen, always. I've never bothered to hide more than the edges of the truth. Humans are so easily beguiled by merriment and sweets."

"*Sidhe*," Avani accused. She drew her wards tight, wondering if she dared reach for Mal.

"*Sidheog*," Cleena replied, terse. She eyed the glittering perimeter of Avani's spell. "Mind your manners; I mean you no more harm now than I did when last we exchanged gossip over my wares."

Avani swallowed. The *sidhe* were a clever folk

fond of word games. The beekeeper's promise was no promise at all.

"What is *sidheog*?"

Cleena dimpled. "When the *ban side* dance above our barrows, it is the *sidheog* who calls the steps. And when the hag calls warning beneath a dying man's window it is the *sidheog* who tempers her song. Before iron and magi forced my people into the depths of the earth, it was the *sidheog* who sent *sidhe* disguised as the fairest of maidens to warm mortal beds and suss out flatlander secrets."

"But I closed the all *sidhe* tunnels beneath Wilhaiim!"

"And I rode through the east gate with my hives in a wagon behind, a farmer's lass proud of her bees." Cleena scoffed. "Did you suppose Faolan the only *aes si* intent on passing amongst you? Rumors of war have penetrated even our deepest dreams; the elders are stirring in their sleep."

"Faolan," Avani prompted through gritted teeth. Her wards crackled, sending sparks into the air, echoing her alarm. She was confident she could keep the *sidhe* woman at arm's length for the moment, but she couldn't help regret the sword she'd left behind in her rooms.

Cleena whirled on the step, apron fluttering. "Two more turnings," she said over her shoulder. And then, as an afterthought, "Your master is with him already.

He'd be a pretty piece for my bed, that one, if not for the rough-healed broken nose and the shattered heart. What a waste of fine flesh."

Mal was visibly relieved to see Avani. He waited on the staircase just inside a narrow door deep enough into the castle foundation that Avani thought she could smell the sewers below. From the layer of dust on the stairs and on the threshold itself, it was apparent the door was rarely used.

"This way." Mal waved Avani through the door. A rudimentary passage waited beyond—packed earth floors and imperfectly cut gray stone walls.

The only illumination was the green-silver sheen thrown off by Mal's mage-light and the entirely natural torch he held in one hand. He offered Avani a second smoking torch, waiting until she snuffed her angry wards before leaning close.

"Be careful," he murmured into her ear before straightening.

"You took your time," he accused Cleena, sweeping the *sidhe* with his green gaze. "Or you ran into trouble."

Cleena replied, "Neither. Your student was distrustful." She pushed past Mal, quickly disappearing down the gloomy passage.

Mal looked thoughtfully after. "They see in the dark easily as any night bird."

Avani grabbed his sleeve. The Hennish leather warmed between her fingers. "What is this place? What has happened?" She uncurled inquiry along their link but Mal quickly shook his head.

"Not here," he warned. "Don't be fooled. *That one's* strength is deceptive. Best not give her any reason for suspicion." He folded gloved fingers over Avani's on his sleeve and chivvied her forward. "Nevertheless, Faolan has done us a great favor, whether he intended it or not." He made a sound of dry amusement as he sent his mage-light ahead along the tunnel. "And he refuses succor from any but you. I am, apparently, unworthy."

Avani appreciated the lightness of Mal's tone. Since returning to Wilhaiim he was more often bitter than not, seemingly jealous of Renault's regard. The king had done little to bolster his vocent's flagging confidence, professing to distrust the changes that capture, imprisonment, and deep water may have wrought in the magus. Renault relied more often on Avani's judgment, even as she sought to distance herself from the roll of advisor, and Mal had grown sour in the face of the throne's distrust.

She found solace now in his levity. Mayhap, she thought, the Mal she'd first met on the Downs was finally beginning to revive.

"What is this place?" she repeated, reclaiming her fingers. She held her torch up until flame threatened to brush the ceiling. "It's cold." Colder than the staircase. Close to the curve of the ceiling, droplets of condensation stretched long before contracting into spatters of rain. "Not a *sidhe* tunnel, though it has the look of one."

"Nay," Mal agreed, pacing behind. His mage-light bobbed merrily overhead. "This particular passage was dug out by mortal hands. Craftsman used it for the laying of the castle catacombs, passing blocks of gray stone man to man along the way. See—" He waved his torch to his right. Past the flame Avani caught the impression of a dark archway and another tunnel. "The dungeons are just that way, although no one ever uses that entrance anymore. It's unpleasant and dangerous."

Avani refrained from pointing out the catacombs themselves were the very definition of unpleasant and dangerous.

"The beekeeper approached me this morning while I walked in Kate's garden," Mal continued. His vocent's cape whispered around his ankles. "With word of Faolan. She's a canny one, with designs of her own, and offered me a tidy little bargain."

"You'd do better on Whore's Street for that," muttered Avani. "If you must sample her wares, stick to the honey."

Mal choked back a laugh. "Not that sort of transaction. Nay, she offered up Faolan's prisoner in exchange for mine own. And I've accepted."

The tunnel rose abruptly, making Avani's legs

ache with the effort it took to ascend the slope, then dead-ended at another door, this one tidily free of dust. Avani followed Mal over the threshold, wagging her head in resignation when she recognized the drafty hallway and the long line of identical wooden doors, many of them secured with locks both magical and solidly physical. After the blackness of the tunnel behind, the ensorcelled ceiling, higher and much brighter, dazzled Avani's eyes.

Blinking moisture from her eyelashes, Avani snuffed her torch in a bucket of sand waiting against the wall for just that purpose.

"*Ai*, I should have guessed," she said. "All roads lead eventually to your lair."

"Not every road," Mal replied. His torch hissed when it met sand. "Despite my efforts."

Their footsteps rang on the stone floor. Avani tucked her hands in her armpits to keep from shivering. Mal cocked a brow in her direction but didn't offer the warmth of his cape as once he might have. He'd learned she preferred not to be coddled, just as she'd come to understand that for all his outward austerity he was often gripped with inconvenient empathy.

"If I'd known you'd secreted Faolan in your laboratory," Avani said dryly, glaring at frost-covered walls while Mal deftly separated two keys from the ring on his belt and used them one at a time to unlock the complicated latch guarding his cold-room, "I would have dressed for winter."

"Do you always tolerate this one's insolence?" Cleena asked, materializing next to the door where an instant before there had been only frost and stone. Avani's teeth clicked together in surprise. "I'd drop her in a deep hole until she remembered respect, were she mine."

Avani glowered. Cleena smiled, showing pointed fangs that had not before graced the beekeeper's lush mouth.

She's clever with a glamour, Avani realized, recollecting the subtle *sidhe* magic used to cloak barrow around Stonehill. *Is anything about her truly as it appears?*

Careful, Mal cautioned again, the barest of whispers in the back of her head. Then he opened the door, sweeping Cleena a mocking half bow as he ushered her through.

"They are here," he said, "and safe, exactly as I promised."

CHAPTER 3

Avani had expected Faolan. She hadn't anticipated five feral barrowmen poised with knives and spears, nor the angry, kilted woman bound wrist and ankle and propped against the foot of Mal's marble worktable.

The lesser *sidhe* hissed. The bound woman snarled past a length of dirty fabric tied several times around her mouth. Cleena laughed, delighted. Faolan exhaled painfully as he rose from where he'd been sitting cross-legged on the floor. Avani, seeing the savage red-and-purple mottling his face, winced in sympathy. She slung her pack to the floor, and dug through its contents. The barrowmen quivered and spat.

"Cease," Faolan ordered. The barrowmen lowered their weapons. The five were different than any

Avani had yet encountered beneath Stonehill or outside Wilhaiim, distinctive for their colorful, disparate garb and the ease with which they held their blades.

They regarded Mal and Avani with flat, black-eyed hatred but backed into the depths of the room when Faolan clicked his tongue.

"They are frightened," the *aes si* explained. "Trapped here in this largest of flatland cities and in a necromancer's den, of all places. They are very loyal, but this tests their allegiance to me in ways you cannot possibly fathom."

"Wicked," one of the lesser *sidhe* said in clear king's lingua. Clawed fingers flexed at its side. "Wicked, wicked spellbinder."

Mal stiffened. Faolan rubbed at the torque locked around his neck.

"Please excuse Halwn," he said with weary courtesy. "It speaks out of turn."

"Halwn *speaks* so out of anguish," Cleena corrected, turning to Mal. "We had a bargain. Faolan's desert prize in exchange for Tadhg. And here is the woman within your den, but where is Tadhg?"

"Patience," counseled Mal, even as Avani asked, "Tadhg?"

"Halwn's kin." Faolan beckoned Avani closer. "The one kept in your dungeon on the king's whim."

"Holder's barrrowman?" Avani narrowed her eyes. "What did you do to your face?"

"You'll recall the sun dislikes my kind," Faolan replied with dignity. "Nor was the wind off Skerrit's Pass gentle." He touched his cheek. "The bruising was misfortune. I remembered the ointment you carried always on the Downs for similar afflictions."

"Rose and calendula." Avani unscrewed the lid of the battered tin. "Calendula for healing, rose for soothing. Take off your headscarf."

Faolan complied. Avani blanched. The chapping and patches of red that afflicted the *aes si's* face continued along his scalp. He'd lost hair in places; the bald skin was blistered and weeping.

"Wind," Faolan said, watching as Avani scooped a dollop of salve from her tin and warmed it between her hands. "Up in the mountains it sneaks beneath one's clothes and leaches the moisture from one's flesh." He startled when Avani touched his face but sat still while she massaged the cream carefully across his brow.

"I'll leave this with you," Avani said, dipping her chin at the pot. "Calendula is not so difficult to come by here in the city as it was on the Downs. I can easily make more. Use it often and thoroughly."

Faolan's eyes drooped shut beneath her ministrations. If he were a cat, she thought, he would be purring. The lesser *sidhe* drifted close, watching with dubious fascination. They, too, had suffered beneath the sun's kiss, faces burned to peeling, lips cracked.

They were a motley bunch, shapeless beneath layers of badly stitched, variegated fabrics. They stank of wet earth.

"They won't let you touch them," Cleena warned from across the cold-room. "Nor accept your medicines. Halwn's kin keep their own healing magics."

"Black soil," one of the lesser *sidhe* acknowledged. It was not Halwn who spoke, but a smaller, dirtier bundle of rag and fur holding a short, sharp blade. "And feathered mushroom."

Avani finished her ministrations. She wiped her fingers clean on her salwar, sealed the tin, and passed it to Faolan. "I know the mushroom he means," she said, surprised. "Kate kept bundles of plumed toadstool in stock, for strengthening the blood."

"They are neither he nor she," corrected Cleena. "And prefer to be called by name."

"They speak the king's lingua," Avani said, turning from Faolan to frown at Mal, "are capable of self-identification, and keep healing magics of their own. Did you know this?"

"I had begun to suspect."

"And yet throughout the kingdom, they are regarded as little more than mute beasts," accused Avani, "hunted and extinguished like mice amongst the grain."

"They are dangerous," Mal returned calmly. "Have you forgotten Stonehill so soon? They would do the same to us here, if they had the numbers and the strength."

"You are the mice amongst the grain," agreed Cleena. "But for the iron you wield, we would have our lands back." The barrowmen shifted restlessly, muttering assent.

Avani was saved from answering by a brisk knock on the laboratory door. At Mal's urging, Baldebert hastened through, Holder's prisoner clutched tightly against his side. Baldebert was dressed in his best court finery, head-to-toe emerald velvet and silk. His black boots were buffed to a shine, his golden curls braided into one plait down his back. Jewels decorated his earlobes. True gold circlets stacked his arms wrist to elbow, chiming as he moved. Avani thought he looked quite the harmless courtier, if not for the poniard he kept pressed firmly beneath the barrowman's chin.

"This had best be worth my time, Doyle," Baldebert complained. "I was attending important business when your messenger interrupted." His yellow eyes flicked disinterestedly across the group of *sidhe*, until they came to rest on the woman sitting bound beneath the vocent's table. His expression shifted subtly. "Oh," he said. "Now, isn't this interesting?"

Faolan stepped around Avani. In a single heartbeat he'd grown somehow more imposing, consumed more of the space in the room than his slight form allowed for. The soft, spelled glow off the laboratory ceiling flickered ominously. Mal's mage-light, floating forgotten near the door, spat green sparks, disap-

peared, then snapped back into existence. Mal's jaw
bunched; he lifted a hand.

"I wouldn't, were I you," said Faolan. "The stone
on your finger is no match for the gem in my collar,
and all of you together are of no consequence to *sidhe*
and *sidheog*, unless you thought to bring your iron
blades, which of course most of you did not, being
magi and conceited."

Baldebert showed his teeth. The point of his poniard left a mark on the lesser *sidhe*'s pale throat. The
barrowman shuddered. Only then did Avani notice
it was manacled in the old ivory cuffs that Roue had
used to subdue Mal.

"Stop," Baldebert warned. "Happens *I* came with
iron. Give me a reason to use it; I don't mind."

Faolan stilled. Cleena said something unintelli-
gible and musical to the lesser *sidhe*. They, too, froze.
From her place on the floor, the bound woman began
to make a harsh, breathless sound. It took Avani a
moment to realize she was laughing.

"I did what I could to keep the wounds from fes-
tering," said Mal, "while it was under my care. But
damaged hands are a knotty problem." He managed
to give the impression of looking down his nose at the
much taller *aes si*. "We found it mutilated so. Can you
say the same of yours?"

"It was a matter of honor," said Faolan dismis-
sively. "We let her live, for your sake. And 'twas not
only for my own self I wished Avani's curative herbs."

The woman's harsh laughter muffled to sobs. Avani grabbed up her sack and marched to the table, pushing past lesser *sidhe* as she went. The prisoner turned her face away, stubborn even as tears tracked along sharp cheekbones. Avani went to her knees on the cold stone floor and held out her hands in entreaty.

"Let me help."

Face turned into the table, the woman bit her lip until the rosy flesh turned white. She was lithe but not bony, muscular as any warrior. Her dark flesh was marked here and there with old scars, and covered with elaborate tattoos. The snakeskin vest she wore above her kilt was stained with sweat. Her hair was a bird's nest, long and tangled, her yellow desert eyes bright with fever.

Someone had bandaged her hands, wrapped dirty, makeshift rags around her palms and fingers. Dried blood crusted the bandages. Avani had a healer's nose. The woman's hands had gone putrid; the air around her smelled sickly sweet. Her wrists beneath the rope bindings were sticky with blood, old and new.

"Free her hands. I cannot help her like this."

"Not yet," Cleena said. Mal shook his head in agreement.

"She's hostage to the throne," he told Avani. And then, more gently. "Be patient."

"Patience is wasted on the desert," Faolan warned. The *aes si* did not look away from Baldebert. The amber stone in the collar around his throat smoldered yellow menace. "That one tried to cut Everin's throat, and nearly succeeded. We would have killed her, but Everin convinced me you would find her useful." His smile was cold. "Whatever magic you've attached to Halwn's kin, it is nigh wicked as iron. Take them off. At once."

Mal nodded at Baldebert. Slowly, Baldebert sheathed his poniard. The lesser *sidhe* did not react. Where sword point had kissed its throat, veins stood red beneath white skin, inflamed.

"Don't move," Baldebert advised the roomful of *sidhe*. "I've a volatile nature and a rapid draw." He reached around, brushing his fingertips across old ivory. At his touch the bracelets split each down the middle. Baldebert snatched at the pieces before they fell, then tied the four slender half-moons to his belt with a piece of satin ribbon.

The freed barrowman swayed in place. Then, with a preternatural speed that made Avani gasp, it darted across the cold-room past Faolan and Cleena, into Halwn's arms. The lesser *sidhe* closed around their returned kindred in a protective group, whispering.

She'd not thought to feel sympathy for the barrowmen, not since she'd watch them score Liam's flesh over and over again with claw and knife. They'd tasted Liam's blood as they flayed him, and taken feral joy in his suffering. But as she watched the broken *sidhe* return to the comfort of its kin, she could not help but feel a twinge of compassion.

"They were under your dead wife's thrall," Faolan said. "Siobahn compelled them with threats and promises. Do not judge what you cannot understand."

"Enough," said Mal sharply. "You have your man, Faolan. The exchange is made. Now get out of my city."

"Wait," protested Avani. "What of Everin?"

Mal grunted. "The throne will thank him for his foresight, when next he deigns to show his face. And I'll admit I'm glad he's not lying dead on the mountains, throat cut. But that man's a walking misadventure and I've no interest in spending time second-guessing his next folly." He bowed in Faolan's direction, chill and correct as the *aes si*'s smile, then turned on his heel. "Admiral?"

Baldebert did not bother to draw his blade as he approached the weeping woman.

"Servant of the desert," he said. "Will you walk or shall I throw you over my shoulder?"

Avani jumped to her feet in protest. She stepped in front of the prisoner.

"You summoned me here to help her," she reminded Mal through clenched teeth.

"I did not. You are here because Faolan asked for succor."

"She cannot walk! She is feverish and afflicted with wounds gone foul."

"Not over your shoulder," Mal ordered Baldebert.

"Remember compassion. Snarling at me will not help, Avani. Come, if you want to help—or don't. It makes little difference to me."

He strode from the room. Baldebert scooped the desert woman up off the floor, cradling her close. Her head lolled. At some point, as they'd been arguing, she'd lost consciousness. Avani suffered a pang of guilt. Baldebert's mouth twisted in disgust. Avani grabbed her pack and followed him to the door. She could feel the *sidhe*'s dispassionate regard like the scrape of a poniard along her spine.

Pausing on the threshold, she glanced around. The barrowmen, intent on reunion, paid her no attention at all. Faolan continued to smile.

"Thank you for the salve," he said. "You have questions. When you are ready, Cleena will know how to find us. Cleena?"

"As you wish," promised the beekeeper. "When she's ready."

"Mal won't let her stay in Wilhaiim," argued Avani, "now that he knows what she is."

Cleena's dimples flashed. "But he's known all along," she said. "He came to me at once, said I stood out: a sun of surpassing beauty against insignificant stars. He's known since the very beginning."

They laid her out on Mal's four-poster bed. Avani upturned her pack on the velvet coverlet. Selecting a pair of small silver scissors from amongst tins and bundled herbs, she began to cut away the woman's bandages.

Wrinkling his nose at the smell of infection, Baldebert eschewed the bed for the chamber's mullioned windows. He stuck his head through an open pane, inhaling deeply, before sighing in relief. He turned around, sweeping Mal's rooms with an attentive gaze.

"I expected more drama and less clutter," he said then gave the mantel a second glance. "Are those my earrings?"

"Jacob's a bloody thief." Mal kindled the hearth with a word before Avani had a chance to ask, setting water from a nearby pitcher to boil in a small pot over the flames. "If they belong to you, take them. Even if they don't. I can't move about anymore without tripping over pieces of his stolen collection."

Baldebert retrieved the golden baubles, secreting them up his sleeve before joining Mal near the mattress.

"Well?" challenged the bastard prince of Roue, looking down on the supine woman. "Will she live? We've yet to catch one alive, for all Russel and her friends are wearing themselves to the bone in effort."

Avani pressed her lips together. "You're blocking my light."

Mal lit a taper from the hearth and held it over the mattress, carefully away from the folds of the embroidered canopy. Avani felt a swell of appreciation for the man's attentiveness, then remembered Cleena and squelched friendly feelings with a growl.

"Someone splinted her fingers," she reported after a moment of careful examination. "But before that someone else broke them beyond any chance of proper healing. I think I can beat back infection, given time, and save the hands, if I'm very lucky. But she'll not have use of them again."

"Don't waste your medicines on knitting bone," advised Baldebert. "She's desert ilk. Wounds like that and captured to boot—she'll let herself die, or find a way to hasten the end first chance she gets. They have no interest in living with failure."

"She's employable to me dead or alive," Mal reminded Baldebert wryly. He touched Avani's shoulder before she could protest. His reluctant empathy ran warm through their link and in her veins. "But let's do what we can to keep her alive. I'll arrange a guard to keep watch once Avani's finished."

Avani paused in undoing splints. "She's to stay here, in your chambers?"

"This is the safest place for her. If what Faolan told me is at all true, we'd best keep her a secret from the temple a while longer."

"The barrowman was in no better shape," said Avani, baffled. "In fact, nearly identical. But you kept it in a catacomb cell from the very beginning."

Mal's fine dark brows rose in confusion.

"A barrowman is not human, Avani," he said. He held the taper over the woman to better see her face. "She may be our enemy, but as of yet we cannot assume she is a monster."

"Once she wakes," Baldebert predicted, selecting a plump fig from the bowl of fruit on Mal's writing desk, and cleaning it on his sleeve, "you'll soon change your mind."

CHAPTER 4

Everin waited a day on Skerrit's Pass.

Come dawn he studied the desert from the top of his great-grandfather's watchtower, trying to learn about the army camped below as daylight painted the eastern side of the mountains white and yellow and gold. He knew a few things from time spent in service on the sand, and so the legion on the wasteland alarmed him.

He knew, for instance, that the sand snakes were a proud and independent people, distrustful of change. Fiercely loyal to family and godhead, rarely did they stay long under a single lord's banner, preferring to wander the vast badlands in small, unruly tribes, trading amongst themselves, enrolling in service only when coin was of short supply.

"Are there cities?" Drem asked. The lesser *sidhe*

had not attempted to hurry Everin in his contemplation, instead spending hours rooting about the rocky cauldron that was Skerrit's Pass and nosing around the depths of the old tower. It still wore the form of a desert woman—long limbed, dark skinned, and yellow eyed. Everin found the facade disconcerting.

"Aye. Cities of canvas, tent post, and brick. Up for a generation, moved on in the next. A lord reigns where her banner flies—sooner or later she will grow bored of the same sand and brush and move on to the next place."

Drem propped its elbows atop the tower battlements. Midday sun gilded the sand, obscuring the desert floor in lambent haze.

"And now they wish to see the other side of the mountains," it predicted.

"It happens." Everin cringed at the sound of his butchered voice. Thanks to Faolan's skill the wound across his throat was all but healed, the flesh knitted into place. But his speech had yet to fully recover; the best he could manage was a rough whisper. He took some hope in that it no longer hurt to make words, but that seemed flimsy solace when a man could not make himself easily heard.

Drem waited, head tilted in invitation.

"The last time was in my grandfather's age," Everin continued, scuffing his foot meaningfully against tower stone, "the time before that, *sidhe* still walked above ground and helped beat them back. That was in advance of Wilhaiim's white walls; flatlanders were farm folk, more intent on surviving than laying claim. Or so I was taught in my youth. You don't remember?"

Drem demurred. "I am not so old as that," it said. "Faolan might recall. The elders certainly would, should they ever stir themselves to care."

"Time, and time past, the sand snakes have tried and failed. Roused, routed, and returned to their desert." He pursed his lips. "There were not so many of them before."

"Once there were not so many of *you*," Drem retorted. "Mortals breed like rabbits."

It stalked off, Desma's kilt swinging, bare feet slapping angrily on stone. Everin hoped it retained enough of Faolan's magic to conjure sandals before they braved the burning sands.

"**C**ome eat," said Drem, returning later to the top of the tower, a small brace of fat fish looped over its elbow.

A deep, blue lake at the center of the cauldron provided the fish as well as fresh water for drinking. Drem was a clever swimmer, impervious to the icy temperature, and able to stay submerged for much longer than any mortal. Everin, who knew the *sidhe* barrows were crisscrossed with underground springs and rivers, was nevertheless impressed by Drem's fortitude.

Still, he couldn't help but grimace at the fish. "Once I promised myself I'd never again eat raw meat." He meant *On the day I escaped* sidhe *tunnels for the open air.*

Drem was not sympathetic. "Optimistic," it said. It gnashed its teeth, the *sidhe* pantomime startling on a human face. Then it grinned. "Come down," it coaxed. "I've made a fire."

Everin started to protest the wisdom of risking a fire when an army lurked nearby, the mountainside no doubt lousy with scouts, but Drem cut him off.

"A small one," it said. "In a place meant for hiding. They will not notice our smoke when so many other fires burn below." Drem glanced over the battlements. The cliff side was now painted with the colors of midday—brown and green and amber—morning haze clearing from desert sands. Campfires were indeed plentiful, plumes of gray smoke visible in blue sky.

The fires were disturbing, not for their quantity, which Everin had expected, but for their consistency. There was an order to those gray plumes, camp fires burning in groups of exactly ten, that suggested everything he thought he knew about desert warfare had changed.

"Someone has your sand snakes in hand," Drem agreed, noting Everin's expression. "Can you discern the banners?"

"The color. Not the device."

"Red starburst," said Drem. "On a white background. Each of them, more than there are false stars beneath the skin of the earth."

Everin frowned. Red starburst was not a device he remembered. As for false stars—the *sidhe* barrows were freckled with shards of mica and chunks of glittering yellow crystal. Drem was exaggerating, but not by much.

"Come eat." Drem shook the fish, spattering Everin with cold lake water. "More wisdom in scheming on a full belly, or so Bail always said."

Bail, one of Drem's ferocious kin, had been killed on the way up the mountain, trampled by frightened horses beneath a stormy sky.

"I'm sorry," Everin said. He turned away from the desert. "About Bail."

"You said so once before." Drem led the way into the tower. "Words won't bring Bail back. Stop talking and walk faster. I'm hungry."

The keep was not a comfortable place. It was spare, modestly constructed of gray stone and mountain boulder for the simple purpose of guarding the pass. A narrow stair ran up the very center. Animals and traveling tinkers had made use of the ground floor since its abandonment. Dried leaves, old embers, and broken crockery littered the packed earth. A macabre black vine, branches thick as a man's wrist and petals large as trenchers, wrapped the building from top to bottom, obscuring old loopholes and most of the front entrance. Rot or scavengers had decimated the gate; heavy iron hinges, still attached to the stone lintel, were all that remained of once sturdy portals.

"Don't touch the branches," Drem advised, ducking past low hanging vine. "They're sticky, and the sap burns. Dark necromancy birthed that creeper. It's foul."

Everin didn't doubt the *sidhe's* assessment. A charred lumber cross stood witness in the cauldron near the edge of the lake, the rocks around it forever blackened. At least one necromancer had been executed there above two kingdoms, likely more than one. Before they were declared dangerous and ordered extinguished, the magi had been as much a king's weapon as his Kingsmen. They'd lived and worked side by side with Wilhaiim's best soldiers to keep the flatlands safe, from coast to mountain peak.

How surprised both soldiers and necromancers must have been, Everin thought, glancing sideways at the looming cross, to wake one morning and discover friend was now foe.

"This place exudes sorrow. I'll be glad to be clear of it."

Drem sidestepped the dampened earth outside the tower where Faolan had saved their desert captive by smothering her and then reviving her again. Streaks of the muddy potion the *aes si* had used stained the ground. Everin avoided the splotches with care.

Once out of the tower he could smell the smoke of Drem's secret fire. Intrigued, he followed the lesser *sidhe* around the back of the building, turning sideways between vine and rock. There he discovered a pleasant hollow between tower wall and cauldron edge. The black vine provided leafy roof, hiding the niche from view. Someone had enlarged the hollow by digging into the side of the cauldron, excavating small boulders before using the rocks to line a little fire pit. A neat pile of tinder was stacked against the tower: sticks and scrub from the valley floor.

"This place is new," Drem said. The lesser *sidhe* squatted near the fire. It went quickly to work on the fish, slitting all three head to tail and emptying their bellies with its fingers. "It stinks of men. Not tinkers. Tinkers know better than to collect yew for burning." Drem made a face at the stacked kindling.

"Yew grows west of the mountains." Everin peered about the hollow. "Every flatlander child knows better than to burn it for warmth or cooking."

Drem skewered a fish on the point of its spear and passed the weapon to Everin. "Not too close to the flames," it warned. "I'll not lose my spear to your foibles."

So saying, it bit the head off a second gutted fish, chewing with dramatic relish.

Everin ignored the *sidhe*'s mockery for the puzzle of the yew.

"This is a sand snake's hole," he hazarded while the meat on the spear began to smoke and spit. "They've gone back and forth over the mountain more than once. Gathered wood for kindling along the way, not knowing enough about western stock to avoid the poisonous variety."

Drem grunted agreement. "Best sleep with one eye open tonight," it advised. "A cozy lair like this one means regular traffic. They'll be starting to wonder what has become of the two we took," it added, licking grease from its fingers.

"Sleep now if you're in need," replied Everin. "Once the sun sets we move on."

Drem rummaged the tower while Everin walked the cauldron's perimeter. A shallow bowl scored into the mountain's peak when some long-forgotten cataclysm had reshaped the surrounding pinnacles, Skerrit's Pass provided an important vantage point from which to view the land east and west of the dividing range. The ground was stony, uneven, broken here and there by stubborn mountain grass. Fat white clouds raced over the lake's placid surface, mirroring the busy sky above. While unforgiving wind scraped over mountaintops, the crater provided protection from all but the most wretched of storms.

Everin selected a stone from the ground between his feet. He flicked his wrist, skipping the pebble across the surface of the lake. Rings formed and expanded, breaking apart reflected sky. With a quiet plop the stone sank.

He'd seen the pass for the first time when he'd escaped *sidhe* imprisonment on the back of the winged *dullahan*. It had been a difficult task to convince the monster to flee the mounds. The creature—an *aes si* so ancient few remembered its existence—had extracted a promise in return. Everin, desperate for a taste of freedom, had agreed to the *dullahan*'s terms without much thought for consequences. He already belonged to the *sidhe*. At the time of his escape a second life debt atop the first seemed negligible.

Besides which, from boyhood he'd planned to die a hero the desert, had constructed a narrative in his head to rival even his tutor's best tales.

But the *dullahan* had refused to take Everin into the desert. Their arrangement ended at the pass when the creature alighted on the edge of the crater, black wings beating beneath an angry moon, whip-like tail snapping against the rocks.

Here, it said in Everin's skull, silver-bell tones a marked contrast to its grotesque form. The *dullahan* most commonly wore the head and torso of a mailed knight above the body of a large winged serpent. It smelled of leather and dust, and when it breathed it sounded like bones breaking. *No further.*

"This is not far enough," Everin had protested. "I'm not safe here."

The *dullahan* threw him off with a shake of its body. Everin landed hard on rocky ground, the air knocked from his lungs. The *dullahan* stretched its wings, blocking out the moon.

Get up and run, little king, it advised. *The path is there: it winds down onto the sand. Don't stray off the trail. The drop will kill you.* Then it sprang into the sky, shedding scale and feather, leaving Everin alone at the top of the world.

The path was still there, if much disguised. Everin left the lakeshore for the eastern edge of the cauldron and perched atop a flat boulder near the trailhead. The sinking sun cast purple shadows across the cliff face. For the moment he had no fear of discovery. He could make out the high end of the trail for several leagues before it snaked down between two large rocks, dropping toward the desert floor. Until the sun shifted again, he'd glimpse anyone coming up the path long before they espied him in the shadows.

Evening turned the army into squares of light and dark, bare sand and tent lodges. The lodges were large enough each to sleep ten warriors pressed thigh to thigh. Everin recalled the close quarters clearly, but also the security he'd felt knowing the men and women in his tent would protect him with their lives.

A thrush whistled. Everin, who knew there were no such birds high up on the mountains, recognized the warning for what it was and didn't jump when Drem scuttled up the side of the crater, settling on a nearby rock.

"'They'll see through you immediately," Everin said mildly. "If you creep and scamper on all fours like that."

Drem folded long legs beneath Desma's kilt. "There are no eyes here but our own," it said, "none to fool but you, and you know the game so there's no pleasure in the fooling. As for eyes, I've found you an ensorcelled one."

It tossed a short, narrow tube into the air between them. Everin caught the cylinder before it fell onto rock. It was light in his hand, made of bronze but for a thumb-sized silver knob set halfway down its length. When Everin turned the tube in his hands he saw that it tapered gently, narrowing at one end.

"Put that end to your eye," said Drem. "Look through the glass."

Everin did so and puffed surprise. He took the cylinder away from his eye, examining both ends. Then he peered through it again, enchanted and uneasy both. The metal tube showed him a slice of life half a league away as if it happened instead a finger's breadth from his nose. When he swept it down the mountain along the trail, he saw a ground squirrel foraging for supper at the base of a stunted tree. The squirrel's long whiskers twitched as it sniffed the dirt. Everin could count the tufts of hair on the tips of its pointed ears.

When he took the tube again from his eye, and looked down the path, he could not make out even the distant tree.

"Point it at the sand," Drem suggested wryly. "Turn the knob until the image is clear. You'll make out the very flecks of amber in their ugly yellow irises."

Everin narrowed his own yellow eyes at the *sidhe*. "*Hsst!* Go take a look at yourself in the lake: you'll see an amber stare reflected back."

Drem shrugged, unrepentant. Everin directed the tube at the army below. Drem hadn't exaggerated. It took Everin three turns of the small silver knob to make the image come clear, but when at last it did he nearly fell off his seat in shock.

"A powerful mortal magic," Drem intoned as Everin swept the cylinder back and forth over the desert below. "I found it in the tower kitchen, beneath a broken wine jug."

The image jumped as the tube passed over white sand, then steadied when Everin pointed it at a darker square of desert encampment. Canvas snapped immediately into focus, as did several kilted warriors seated on their heels in the shade of the lodge.

"Not magic," mused Everin. "This is a compound lens. The Black Coast whalers use such devices, I'm told, though I've never seen one. This is worth your weight in true gold."

He moved the tube gingerly this way and that, counting heads. Four large tent lodges to a square, ten men to a lodge . . .

Frowning, Everin direct the lens at the next encampment, and then the next.

"They're the same," he said, when he was certain. "Each the same. Four lodges—forty warriors—stationed in a single camp." He set the lens carefully on the rock near his thigh before regarding the mosaic of darkening purple below.

Drem appeared taken aback. It rubbed a finger along Desma's lower lip, gaze hooded.

"Very many angry scorpions," it grumbled, borrowed yellow eyes flickering back and forth over the vista. "Even Faolan would not have guessed so many."

"Ten thousand warriors," Everin agreed in growing disbelief. "All of the desert in one place—impossible."

"Obviously not. But there is good news."

Everin quirked a brow.

"There are far too many to come up and over," the lesser *sidhe* said. "I am right. Faolan was wrong. They plan to go under. And we shall stop them."

"There are two of us," Everin said, in case Drem needed reminding. "Against ten thousand. We need a plan of our own, I think." He added wryly, "No matter how skillful, your disguise will do us little good in the face of so many if we but wander in circles looking for a *sidhe* gate that may or may not be nearby."

Drem rolled onto its knees and then all the way upright, balancing on the edge of the crater over the cliff face as if it planned to sprout wings and fly. Fingerling breezes picked at the edge of Desma's kilt, made the blue feathers in Desma's long hair dance, brought goose pimples to lean arms. The desert woman had been lovely, a wild but earthly creature. Drem wearing the woman's skin was frighteningly preternatural.

"By the Aug!" Everin croaked. "Get down before they see you!"

"They won't," Drem said. "Look, point the tube there, do you see? It's there."

Everin clenched his jaw to keep from swearing but did as Drem asked, aiming the double lens at the southwest corner of the army.

"What am I looking for?" He held his breath to keep the lens from shaking. Ripening evening softened the landscape. Dusk pooled in the alleyways between tent walls, softened the jagged lines of three-armed cacti, stained sporadic rock formations indigo.

"You've survived amongst us longer than any other mortal the elders favored," replied Drem in oblique answer.

"Hidden in plain sight," Everin hazarded. On first inspection, the southwest corner appeared no different than any other stretch of desert. Until he noticed a patch of rock and cactus where twilight flickered subtly in and out of existence, and eventide shadows slipped sideways across the sand only to reform and dissolve again. If he squinted, the *sidhe* glamour thinned to a gauzy veil. Beneath he glimpsed white stone and a soft, rosy glow.

"Too many blades," Drem diagnosed. "So many sand snakes wielding iron fangs. The glamour is failing. Or it started to collapse all on its own and in doing so drew unwanted attention. The gate is there."

Everin took the lens from his eye. Drem ignored his sudden scrutiny.

"There are no *sidhe* in the desert," Everin said slowly. "Magic does not thrive east of the mountains. Most tribesmen discount sorcery entirely. They should not recognize that glamour for what it is, even less so understand what it hides."

"There is more going on here than I first thought." Drem rolled bare shoulders in a resigned shrug. "Best hope your king gets out of Faolan's charge what information he can. I fear you and I will be of little use to him now."

Drem pivoted and pointed, not in the direction of the army, but over Everin's shoulder in the direction of the lake, the watchtower, and the western mountain path. Everin turned and caught a glimpse of fat ponies coming up over the rise, lean riders bristling with spear and scimitar. Then Drem struck him hard in the side, knocking him off his rock and onto his back on the stony ground. Breath left his lungs in a painful gust. The gloaming sky whirled overhead. A sharp blade pricked his ribs through the fabric of his tunic.

"You're late," said Drem to the newcomers in the guttural desert tongue while Everin gasped for air. "I had begun to think you weren't coming after all and I'd have to haul him down the mountain myself."

CHAPTER 5

Liam was outside the armory, carefully chopping Old Pumpkinhead and his straw brothers into manageable pieces with a borrowed hatchet, when Morgan and Arthur found him. Bear noticed the two lads first, drawing Liam's attention with a sharp bark, rising from her haunches. Long strings of drool puddled in the dirt. Her wagging tail sent bits of straw and burlap every which way.

"Bear," Liam scolded. "Sit."

The brindled hound obediently sat but her tail continued to buffet the dirt.

"Captain Riggins wants you, sir," Arthur called as the lads approached. His features were screwed up in excitement, his dark hair sweat-damped and matted to his skull. It was no longer so unbearably hot outside as to excuse Arthur's swelter nor Morgan's more subtle flush, and both pages were panting as if they'd just run a foot race 'round the bailey. Liam immediately set aside the hatchet and reached for his sword. Bear, alerted, began to growl.

"What's happened?"

"Naught, yet." Morgan, the young earl of Wythe, nudged a butchered piece of burlap with the toe of his boot. He tossed an envious glance Bear's way but knew better than to pet her wedge-shaped head, no matter how he itched to do so. "But if you don't come now, Riggins is threatening to shoot your bird out of the Mabon tree."

"Parsnip's trying to talk him down," Arthur added, bouncing in excitement. "Not the bird. Captain Riggins, I mean. Captain's in a right rage and Parsnip's stayed behind to calm him, but you know how he is about that particular tree, and he said iffin' you don't hurry he'll be having crow for his supper tonight. Begging your pardon."

Liam didn't waste time on a reply. Hatchet and straw men forgotten, he raced away across the practice yard, around the backside of pages' dormitory, and down a grassy incline toward the thick wood edging the Royal Gardens. Bear ran at his side, tongue lolling.

Summer had begun the slow turn toward autumn, but the birch and maple in the wood were not yet displaying harvest colors. The Mabon tree, transplanted from the king's scarlet woods as a sapling by a gardener long forgotten, was easy to spot even from a distance, its needles a brilliant orange amongst all the green.

"Captain!" Liam shouted, spotting Riggins with his compact bow poised beneath the old tree, arrow nocked, string drawn. "Sir! Don't shoot!"

"He promised to wait!" Arthur gasped, running hard on Bear's heels.

"Riggins!" Morgan passed them all in a burst of speed. "Stay your hand, man!" He managed to sound every inch the nobleman even as he slid to an unwieldy halt at the base of the tree, almost crashing into the wide trunk. "I say, stop!"

Riggins, a temperate man who rarely broke to anger, was wild of eye and quivering. He glanced at Liam then lowered his bow, inclining his head Morgan's way in grudging acceptance.

"My lord. I'm sorry. But that crow's a fiend disguised, shrieking and screaming like a mad thing, and all up in the branches of the *Mabon tree*."

"Liam," Parsnip called from up the tree where she clung to a low branch. Bear, suspecting a game, snapped playfully at her limbs. "You didn't tell me someone's taught it to speak. And the vilest things you can imagine." Even half upside-down with twigs caught in her short hair, she sounded censorious as an old maid.

"He doesn't—" Liam said. "You must be mistaken, Jacob doesn't speak."

"Fire!" screeched the topmost boughs of the tree. "Bring the torch! At once!"

"Doesn't speak?" Parsnip wrinkled her nose at Liam. "What's that bloody noise, then?"

Captain Riggins had his hand on his bow again. "You won't burn this tree!" he shouted. "This is His Majesty's tree! His Majesty's *Mabon tree*!"

"I'll have his head for this!" shrilled the branches. "Bring the torch!"

"Treason," Riggins muttered, fingers clenching arrow and brace. Morgan soothed him with a murmur. Bear growled low in her throat.

"Liam," the young earl demanded. "*Is* that your bird?"

Baffled, Liam approached the Mabon tree. Parsnip peered down at him from her branch.

"Climb up. You can't see him from down there. He's sitting in the very crown, way up at the top."

Liam craned his neck. The tree was a healthy specimen, blessed with a spreading canopy and plentiful branches of every size. A man could easily hide himself up against the trunk, shielded by fanning orange needles. A bird might reside in its branches indefinitely.

"Jacob!" he hollered. "Is that you? Come down!"

"The torches!" retorted the tree in shrill tones. "I'll make a chalice of his head bones!"

"By the Virgin," sighed Liam, sighting a promising-looking branch. He toed off his boots and, shedding his new squire's tunic, slung an arm over bark. He braced his feet against the trunk, and began to climb. Parsnip, lounging astride her branch with the same ease she sat a horse, watched his progress with interest.

"Keep close to the trunk," she counseled. "The branches are strongest there."

"I've been climbing trees since before you were whelped," Liam said, stepping from limb to limb, choosing toe and finger holds with care.

It wasn't a fib. His first clear memory was of scaling the single tall tree in Stonehill, an ancient pine that had somehow learned to thrive on the inhospitable Downs. He remembered clambering to the very top, laughing at the cold on his cheeks. Joy had turned to terror when he'd reached the pinnacle and glanced down to see how far he'd come. He'd sat in the old pine for a day, embracing the trunk tightly to keep from falling, listening to the sound of birds and squirrels in nearby branches and, later, a family of marmots digging for truffles near the base of the tree. His shouts for help had gone unheard. Alone and wracked with self-pity, he'd watched lights kindled in nearby Stonehill against the coming night. It had been dark when he'd finally found the courage to climb down again, but he'd managed without falling.

After, the Widow had scolded him for being late to supper and smacked him for the rips in his trousers. But he'd never been afraid of heights again.

"You climb like a cat," Parsnip allowed. "Or a *sidhe*. Have you claws on the ends of your fingers in truth?"

Liam said a rude word he'd recently learned from a grizzled Kingsman in the dining hall and purposefully shook a waterfall of needles down onto Parsnip's upturned face. Parsnip squealed. Liam could hear Arthur's resounding laughter from down below.

Scars disfigured the tree's otherwise smooth trunk, old wounds where branches had been cut away for Mabon. Liam hadn't been long enough in Wilhaiim to witness the harvest celebration, but he knew that the burning of carefully selected, bright orange branches was an important part of the ritual. The tree had been moved from the scarlet woods for just that purpose; the forgotten gardener had been acting upon royal decree. It seemed a foolish thing to Liam, the transplanting of a tree from forest to city for the color of its foliage, but he was coming to understand how dearly the theists valued ceremony.

Something moved in the branches overhead, causing Liam to stop and look up. He glimpsed a flutter of black behind bright needles. Hugging the tree for balance exactly as he had done as a child, Liam bent backward for a better look.

"Jacob!"

A mess of twigs rained down from above. A chestnut struck the top of Liam's head. The Mabon tree bore no fruit; the chestnut had to be a purposeful weapon gathered from deeper in the woods. Suspicion woke in Liam. He climbed more quickly, ignoring Parsnip's cries of caution.

The Mabon tree was taller than any other within the confines of the Royal Gardens. Liam doubted anyone had expected it to grow so high or spread so wide, or why not give the tree pride of place at the center of the king's flower field? Away from the palace its beauty went mostly unnoticed. The soldiers who looked upon it every day soon grew used to the tree's startling height and color, its charm overlooked in the daily routine of barrack life.

Liam climbed above the garden canopy and into bright sunlight. He paused while his eyes adjusted to the new brilliance. When he could see again, the sky overhead was a blue to rival the deep sea off *The Cutlass Wind*'s bow. The palace towers pierced the horizon across the gardens, dwarfing Wilhaiim's housetops. Only the temple was as impressive, levered roof open wide to receive the day.

"Burn him," muttered Jacob in surly greeting, peeking at Liam from a hole in the tree trunk. "Cast him out."

"Look at you. That's a nice home you've made yourself, you churl. Have you been here all this time? Avani's worried sick, you know."

Jacob turned his head sideways to better regard Liam with one black eye. The raven was not a small bird, but he appeared somehow diminished, hunched deep in a nest of needles and old sticks. He seemed disinclined to move, even when Liam stretched out a gentle finger and stroked his inky head.

"You're full of tricks, aren't you?" Liam praised. Relief made him grin. "I never knew you could talk."

"Tricks," agreed the bird. Jacob clicked his beak, and rattled his feathers, and it was only then Liam noticed the raven was injured. One wing drooped from his shoulder, useless. The wing was missing great clumps of feathers in patches; the exposed flesh looked raw.

"God's balls!" Liam blanched. Avani called Jacob her goddess's avatar, and whether there was truth in that claim or not, Jacob always seemed unusually wily and resilient. Liam had grown used to believing the raven was invulnerable and took his presence for granted. He saw now that he'd been indulging in a lad's happy superstition and regretted that the time had come to let that comfort go.

"It's fine." He soothed the wounded raven. "It *will* be fine. Is the wing broken, do you think? Poor fellow, you must be hurting."

In his nest Jacob grumbled and sighed. He watched Liam attentively. A breeze came up, rustling the crown of the Mabon tree. Liam heard Riggins and Arthur calling from below but didn't dare answer for fear of startling Jacob deeper into the tree.

"Come down with me," Liam coaxed. "We'll get you help. Avani will know what to do."

Jacob retreated deeper into the trunk, away from Liam's hand.

"Tricks," he scolded, pecking dully at a clutch of needles.

Parsnip popped her head above the canopy, making Liam squawk and Jacob croak. The raven backed into the tree as far as he could go, disappearing but for the gleam of one watchful eye.

"Sorry," said Parsnip, although she didn't look it. Ducking around one branch and shimmying across two more, she reached Liam's side. "Isn't this a grand view! Heard you talking," she confessed, peering into the trunk. "That's him, is it?"

Parsnip, instead of being cowed by their shared experience in the Bone Cave, had instead grown newly bold as to be almost cocky. Liam appreciated bravery so long as it did not ripen toward stupidity. In the small handful of days since Avani and Baldebert had rescued Liam and Parsnip from Lane's grasp, she seemed intent on proving her mettle. She'd been the first to volunteer when the king's constable called a hunt on Holder and his rogue straw men, even though Liam knew she was terrified of the magically quickened dummies. She'd tendered her name when Beaumont had passed his hat for extra patrols on the king's road even though Beaumont was looking for commissioned soldiers and Parsnip was not yet made squire.

"I can ride as well as anyone," she'd argued when

Beaumont balked. "I'm stout and, now I've got my ax back, I'm deadly. His Majesty needs Kingsmen on his road. I've proven my worth. Let me help."

"His Majesty requires Kingsmen," returned the old soldier, "not pages still in uniform." But Parsnip had insisted on tossing her ax in demonstration, hitting her target dead center at twenty paces. Beaumont had been grudgingly impressed. His Majesty's army was stretched thin after plague season, and so in the end Parsnip was awarded a place on daylight patrol.

"Has he hurt his wing?" she asked now, leaning close. Jacob clacked his beak but Parsnip ignored the warning. "We might send for the royal falconer. She's the only one I know who can splint a bird with doing it more injury."

"We need to convince him to come down," Liam said, exasperated. "The royal falconer is of no use up here. Jacob, come out and let us help you."

"Tricks," retorted Jacob. And then, "Torches!"

"I met a man with a talking bird, once," Parsnip said. "A sailor on break come through town, and he'd taught his parrot to say a few words for pieces of apple. 'Row harder!' and 'cut the jib,' and the like. Birds are smart. Yours found his way up here, built himself a cozy hidey hole. He looks healthy but for the wing. He found his way up. I suppose he'll find his way down when he's ready."

Liam stared at Jacob. Jacob stared back, unblinking.

"He's safe up here," Parsnip added. "Riggins has terrible aim." She winked. "And naught but you and I are daft enough to climb so high above the world."

Riggins waited for Liam to grab up his boots and tunic then marched him back across the practice yard into the pages' barracks. He strode ahead, waving for Liam to follow, not up the stairs into the dormitory as Liam expected, but straight out again onto a swathe of grass at the backside of the armory. Bear trotted after but kept her distance. She'd assessed Riggins and decided he wasn't a threat.

"Sit," the captain ordered, jerking a thumb at the grass. "Put on your boots before you step on a thorn." He'd slung his bow across his back but still fiddled with one arrow, passing it from hand to hand.

Bear sat first. Liam pulled on his boots one at a time. Riggins wasn't an unfair sort, nor did he take any pleasure in pulling rank.

"What's yon bird doing shouting insults from His Majesty's tree?" he demanded of Liam. A vein pulsed in his forehead. "What does it want?"

"I don't think he wants anything especially." Puzzled, Liam looked up from lacing his boots. Then he recalled that many theists believe black-feathered birds were ill luck. He chose his words with more care. "Jacob is Lady Avani's pet, sir. He's a rascal, but not dangerous. I wager he's atop the tree for shelter;

one of his wings has been badly wrenched by the look of it."

Some of the tension eased out of the captain's shoulders. "Lady Avani's pet, you say? My lady's a good sort, for all her strangeness. I've no doubt she means well. Still." His scowl returned. "A talking bird. Those were not benedictions it was screaming from on high."

"Ah." Liam scratched his nose. "Birds are clever mimics, sir. I believe as a wee hatchling, before my lady took him on, Jacob belonged to a Black Coast raider." Silently he thanked Parsnip for the lie. "He doesn't know what he's saying."

"Aye, of course it doesn't. It's just a bird, after all." Riggins furrowed his brow. "There's been carrion birds above the city lately, looking for a last fat mouse before the fields go fallow. Mayhap yon crow ran afoul of one of them. Poor thing. Shall I send a runner, let my lady know her pet's up the Mabon tree?"

Liam hesitated. It occurred to him to wonder why Jacob hadn't gone first to Avani for help.

"Sir. I'll go." The second lie was more difficult than the first, and Liam worried his expression would give him away, but Riggins had no reason for doubt.

"Aye, good." The captain brightened. "Tell her the king's got a fine falconer on hand for just these sorts of injuries."

"Yes, sir."

Pleased, Riggins ceased fiddling with his arrow

and sheathed it with its fellows in the quiver he wore on his back. The arrows were fletched with the red-and-black-barred feathers taken off special hens bred by the royal bowyers for just that purpose. Liam eyed the arrows with ill-concealed yearning. He was a competent rider and could shoot a bow from the ground with reliable aim, but as a mounted archer he was just as reliably inaccurate, and not even practice would earn him a spot in the king's cavalry. He knew he'd make a capable foot soldier. He didn't regret the path he'd chosen, but he couldn't help admiring the arrows and the status they described.

Riggins offered Liam a hand up. "Give Lady Avani my regards," he said. "And when you're back, finish chopping those mannequins. We'll burn the pieces tonight, feed the bonfire until the flames are lofty enough for Holder to see. Wherever he's hid, he'll know his creatures will never walk in Wilhaiim again."

CHAPTER 6

Brother Tillion was a dangerous man.

Mal, lounging cross-legged on an upturned beer barrel across the bailey from the priest, studied Tillion with clinical interest. The theist, balanced upon an empty casket almost identical to the one Mal had claimed, was the image of grace and stamina. Gone were the tremors Mal had noted in Tillion's hands only a day earlier; absent was the staff required to ward off vertigo. In the temple garden Tillion had walked with the hesitancy of a man who feared each step would be his last. In the bailey, an adoring crowd spread at his feet, Tillion was lithe and confident as any acrobat, quick to turn and challenge a detractor or bend low and bestow blessing on the brow of a zealous devotee.

"Opion," Baldebert suggested from beside Mal's barrel. He, too, watched the priest, but with an expression of open disgust. Tillion's entire purpose in preaching was the defamation of Baldebert's older sister—Roue's queen and Renault's newly betrothed. Mal appreciated Baldebert's acerbic scowl, as Tillion had just finished loudly promising the one god would blast the Rani to ash should she dare set one foot on flatland soil.

Mal said, "Opion dulls the senses. Does he look dull to you?"

Mal had clothed himself in a disguise of villein's shirt and trousers. A rimmed farmer's hat obscured face. He'd put lifts in his boots to hide his small stature. Fingerless gloves shielded the ring on his finger from view. He'd not gone so far as to change the shape of his broken nose with clay putty, although he had been sorely tempted.

Baldebert's deceit was of the magical variety. Pinned to his breast he wore a shiny new silver brooch in the shape of branch and sapphire berries. The original bone pin had been part of the royal treasury for generations. Its concealing sorcery allowed kings and queens to walk amongst their subjects undetected, a rare freedom and a carefully kept secret. The theist spells protecting the Bone Cave had proved too much for that brooch; the silver had smoked, nearly burning Baldebert in his attempt to rescue Liam from Armswoman Lane. The bone hidden within had shattered, necromancy dissipating along with the spirit that had kept the spell alive.

Much later, Mal had searched the ground outside the cave, sifting through a detritus of toys and flowers laid in memorial as well as a scattering of well-gnawed sheep bones in the hole where Holder's brindled hound had lingered for a time waiting for her master. He'd found the damaged, misshapen silver and all but one of the fifteen faceted sapphires that had decorated the brooch.

He had carried the pieces back to his laboratory, hoping to learn something of spell crafting from a necromancer long dead. But when he'd laid the pieces out for examination he'd seen the way of it with startling clarity. While the spirit tied to the sliver of bone the old magus had used was fled, impressions of the vocent herself remained still in the metal, like fingerprints on a dusty tabletop.

It had been the work of an afternoon to remake the brooch to Mal's own specifications. The new bone he took from the foot of a Kingsman who'd dropped dead of liver failure not two days earlier and whose spirit still haunted Mal's cold room, unwilling yet to move on. Despite an unhealthy appetite for Whitcomb wine, the soldier was a good man—a strong, bright star in Mal's head. It took little convincing to bind the haunt again into the throne's service. The bone of the man's smallest toe, disguised in the brooch as a sapphire-flowering silver twig, anchored his spirit to the bauble. The strong, bright star would fuel a new concealment spell for more generations to come before at last burning to nothing.

"Craft a hundred of these," Baldebert said, and Mal realized he'd been staring at the brooch now pinned to the prince's tunic. "You'd have an invisible army."

"And what would I do with an invisible army?" Mal pulled his gaze from the silver bauble. It was difficult, lately, not to shelter in his head. The world around had grown strange since he'd suffered deep water madness. Where once he'd tolerated the useful shine of a dead man's spirit, now the living also sparked, tantalizing. Vitality tapped seemed a far more efficient use of sorcery than a haunt slowly unspooled.

"I meant for His Majesty, of course," replied Baldebert. His face still showed the damage done him by Avani's magic. One eyebrow was all but burned away, the flesh about it reddened.

"Of course." Brother Tillion's life force was no brighter than those surrounding him on the street below: he was as human as his admirers. Nor was his star in any way diminished by the brain malady Mal was certain he suffered.

"You've been staring at the man like you'd enjoy opening up his skull and taking a peek inside," said Baldebert. "And that absurd brimmed hat does nothing to hide your inclination. Mayhap *you* should have worn this damn jewel after all."

"I'm not the one needs protecting," Mal retorted. He hopped onto the street, pausing to stretch kinks from his legs. "That mob would be *inclined* to tear you to pieces if they saw your pretty face, and I'm not sure our priest would do anything to stop them. Brother Tillion is a dangerous man."

Baldebert blinked, puzzled. He touched the ivory manacles hanging on his belt. Then he sighed. "I'm not torn to pieces, so your new jewel must be as potent as the old. Am I now excused from this experiment, Doyle? I'll admit, I begin to dread your increasingly more frequent summonses. I have political machinations of my own to attend to. I don't need to be drawn into your mischief, as well."

"You are not excused." Mal adjusted his hat to better shade his eyes. "Not yet. We're going hunting."

"**H**e's not here." Hands on hips, Baldebert studied Holder's farm from the road. To either side of the dirt path wheat had begun to lie down in the final throws of summer. On the hill above Holder's land the crop had been left to go to seed. "Why would he be here?"

"Someone's been feeding the animals," Mal told Baldebert. Baldebert, shielded by the bone pin, stood safe from unfriendly eyes in full view of Holder's barn. Mal slouched out of sight in the uncertain shade of a stunted oak tree. "Those we passed in the lower pastures, and those cows there."

Baldebert contemplated the black cattle with vague distaste. "Probably the same Kingsmen who pass by here on patrol twice a day, just to keep an eye on the place. He's not home. If I were him, I'd be riding for the northern steppes fast as humanly possible."

"Go down and take a look," suggested Mal. He plucked a ripe plum from a pocket in his trousers and took a bite, watching Baldebert while he chewed. The juice burst across his tongue, tart.

Baldebert's eyes diminished to thoughtful yellow slits. "Is this some sort of test?"

"Aye. Of the pin on your breast. If Holder's down there, I'm hopeful he'll not see you coming."

"Hopeful, you say. And what will you be doing, while I flit in and out of a cow barn all unseen?"

"Walking the perimeter," answered Mal. He flashed Baldebert a grin. "Shout if you need help."

Baldebert snarled. Mal ate his plum, waiting for the admiral's curiosity to overcome his pride. It did, rather more quickly than Mal had expected. Gritting his teeth against words better left unsaid, Baldebert whirled away. He strode down the gentle hill toward the barn. Mal finished his plum, spat the pit into dirt, then slunk the back way down the amber knoll through the failing crop. Holder's cattle watched him approach. They were all four fine specimens, their black Hennish coats buffed to a shine beneath a new layer of dust. Mal hopped the paddock fence. The cows followed him around the modest turnout while he checked the level of water in their trough and then kicked over a mound of fodder.

It was possible the patrolling Kingsmen had been told to toss the beasts hay, and fill the trough. Just as possible a neighbor was tending to their needs—although Holder's closest neighbor was not close at all. And yet—Hennish cattle were a rarity, valued by the throne for their unusual black skin. Hennish leather was a luxury reserved for Wilhaiim's magi.

"Not so much demand now as there once was." Mal pulled the gloves from his hands. He stroked the wet nose of one bold cow, enjoying the animal's curiosity. "I imagine you're glad of that." The cow had intelligent brown eyes and an abundance of life pulsing in her veins. How effortless it would be to borrow just a thimbleful of that energy, a few days off her life, and use it to ease the ache in his back leftover from a long night sat in an uncomfortable chair by the bed of their uncooperative desert prisoner.

The cow wouldn't know to miss the stolen hours.

Mal scrubbed the palm of his hand gently up and down her muzzle.

A shadow passed overhead, blotting blue sky. Mal dropped his hand and looked up. Not the black raven wings he half expected, but a white-tailed hawk drifting on sluggish breezes. The relief he felt made him puff out a breath in bitter self-mockery.

He'd never been afraid of Jacob before. He didn't intend to start now.

He jumped the fence on the other side of the paddock, leaving the cows to their own devices, and continued along the property's edge. He'd visited the site twice since Holder had gone missing, but always in the company of soldiers and in his role as vocent. It took a clever man to hide his secrets from Mal but Holder had been born into a family long associated with magic, and it was possible the farmer had help.

Down a steep incline from the barn the remains of a burned-out cottage smudged the earth black. A single stone chimney stood proud at one end of the broken edifice. Saplings grew up out of the cracked foundation, green leaves turning to yellow. Mal stepped around them, ducking low to keep the chimney between himself and the barn. Baldebert had disappeared from sight. The barn door was closed. But for the soft lowing of the cattle and the distant scream of the hawk overhead, the day was quiet.

He crouched, bending to peer into the ruined hearth. It housed an abandoned mouse's nest and a collection of pebbles. Bracing to stand, he pressed his palm against stone, and when he turned he had company. Consternation made his pulse jump. He had to clench his fists to stop spitting green sparks from betraying his agitation.

The man stood naked in the rose-gold light of winter twilight. His flesh was stippled from shoulders to groin with the bleeding stripes of recent punishment. An iron chain wrapped about his waist and thighs, shackling him to a sturdy sapling. Mal could smell freshly cut pine boughs and smoke. The man's head was bowed, long hanks of gray hair obscured his face. He coughed, and spat, and turned his head, and saw Mal.

His eyes were the color of good beer—not a haunt's fiery blue. He wasn't dead. Nor was he still living.

"Brother," he said, peering at Mal from beneath beetled brows. "What are you doing here? Run, you fool, you cannot help me—"

Mal jerked. The apparition vanished. In the paddock a cow slapped her sides with her tail, disturbing a cluster of flies. Mal glanced over his shoulder. The barn door was still closed. The hawk circled overhead. Only the briefest of moments had passed.

This time when he crouched, he did it with concentration, blowing dust and dirt from the chimney stone. He took his dirk from his belt and used it to scrape ash from the stone, careful not to touch the rock with his bare hands. He found the trick stone halfway down the chimney: a brick made of mortar and crushed bone cunningly crafted to resemble gray stone. The brick was clean of ash; it had been placed in the chimney after the gutting fire.

Mal steeled himself, pressed his hand flat against the false stone, and looked around.

"Brother," the apparition begged, looking straight at him. "My brother. What are you doing here? Run, you fool, you cannot help me—" He gasped, faltering as a lash came down from above, ripping flesh beneath. "Run, run!" Another tearing lash, and Mal choked on gathering smoke. The chained man looked up and away, challenging an enemy Mal could not see.

"We have done nothing to deserve this!" he screamed. "Nothing! We are your neighbors, your cousins! Arden—Arden Cooperson, I see you there!" Coughing, he withered against his fetters. "Beau Lovett! I see you both! Who was it, then, who kept the *sidhe* from your daughters and your doors? They'll rise again, Arden, Lovett, and who of us will be left to save you?"

The stench of burning flesh and heated metal was overwhelming. Eager flames licked at the tethered man's feet. His screams turned to shrieks.

Mal snatched his hand from the chimney. He bent double, gasping. Smoke made his eyes smart and run. The taste of charring flesh lingered on the top of his tongue. He swallowed hard to keep from vomiting.

Mal, Avani slipped through the cracks in the walls of his mind. Effortlessly, she bolstered his failing courage. Together they were so much more than they were apart.

What is it? What is that you're seeing?

It's not real. He knelt in the dirt, eyes closed. *It's not real.*

It felt real, horribly real. Is it a vision? Put your head down between your knees until it clears. I can still hear the poor man's screams.

I don't have visions. But her practicality eased some of his shock, made it possible for him to open his eyes and catch his breath. The cows had wandered away and were nosing at their fodder, backs turned. The sun warmed his scalp. The hawk had vanished from the sky. Bees buzzed in the clover near his feet.

You've had two that I know of, Avani replied tartly. She resented his cavalier dismissal of all things spiritual. Mal had an impression of her loom, the sound of her shuttles at work, the aftertaste of Baldebert's black tea in her mouth.

Not a vision. A memory. He recollected the golden spires growing out of Roue's verdant forest like great jeweled flowers, the "memory keepers" erected to honor the beloved dead. *A private remembrance. I triggered it by mistake.*

A monument to a burning man. Avani's shuttles stilled. *His murder. Was he magus?*

Mal didn't answer; there was no need to confirm what they both already knew. Avani glanced up from her loom.

What are you up to, Mal? Where are you? Somewhere pleasant, under blue sky—are those cows?

Holder's place. He felt like a lad caught with his hand in the pie plate, but he didn't try to hide his discomfit, hoping she wouldn't see past superficial guilt to deeper secrets.

Not for the first time he wished he'd had the strength of heart to sever their bond before it rooted.

Holder's place? She left the loom for the Goddess on her hearth. When she buffed the idol's golden skin with her thumb, he felt phantom metal against his own flesh. *Well. Let's see it again, then.*

Are you certain? He was no stranger to the grotesque. He'd long ago learned, for the throne's sake, how to be stoic in the face of another's suffering. But this was different. Whether or not the man deserved it, this was execution for the sake of extermination, a uniquely flatlander crime.

A uniquely human crime, mayhap. Or not. The sidhe would rid this world of mortals, had they the means. Whoever he was, he was one of us, Mal. Someone thought enough of him to seal his death in stone. He deserves our witness. Her grief crept into Mal's heart and nested there. *Mayhap we'll learn his name.*

As you wish. Resolved, he turned back to the chimney. When he pressed his palm against the false stone, Avani stood within him. The magus appeared at once, flames superimposed over honeybees and clover.

"Brother! My brother. What are you doing here? Run, you fool, you cannot help me—"

The door to Holder's barn hung from a metal track. When Mal pushed, it slid open along small cogs, an elegant contraption. The barn was cool and dry, the inside tidy as any cottage. The earthen floor was swept clean. Stacked hay filled the loft above. Sunlight filtered through uneven slats in the peaked roof, pooling on the floor. Three of the original box stalls remained but the rest of the barn had been cleared to make space for Holder's handicraft. Augurs, chisels, rolled burlap, pieces of brass and iron, and a collection of miscellaneous cogs covered the surface of a long wooden table that ran the length of one side of the building. A bucket of water stood beneath the table, the water murky with dust and disuse.

"There's an anvil and forge out back," Baldebert reported, from just inside the barn. "Forge is cold. His wagon's there and two more oxen. Cellar beneath the barn—the larder's been rummaged. He's lit out, just as I said. And I wager he's not coming back any time soon."

Mal chose a spiral of shaved wood from Holder's worktable. It was a fine white walnut, the sort used to craft a wardrobe or a jewelry chest. More white curls dusted one corner of the table. Mal brushed them aside, baring a large pair of carpenter's sharp-edged pincers.

Baldebert took a step back, fingers hovering near his dirk. The sapphires in the ornament on his shirt sparkled in the gloom. The spell tied to the brooch would hide Baldebert from unfriendly eyes if he so wished, but Mal did not need to see the man to know where he stood. The pulse of Baldebert's life was beacon enough.

"If I meant to do you ill," said Mal. "There are more convenient ways and means in Wilhaiim. Ground Curcas nut in your tea, for example, and you'd be dead of purging—just like your mother. Viper's Blossom applied to the inside of your boots to bring on a fatal palsy. Or mayhap I'd slit your throat on Whore's Street and tip you into the Maiden. Of a certain I wouldn't resort to skullduggery and pincers."

"I'm a difficult person to kill," Baldebert cautioned. "Even for the likes of you. But if you didn't intend my murder, why the wild goose chase, why bring me out this way? Holder isn't here. You never really thought he was."

Mal pointed overhead, drawing Baldebert's attention to the rafters. "The theist sigils there and there, over the doors. I noticed them when last I was here. It's the same blessing as was cast on Bone Cave, and by the same priest. That's our late Masterhealer's work."

Baldebert was a quick study. He slapped a hand over the sapphire brooch as if he thought to keep it from bursting into flame.

"You sent me in here expecting the pin on my front to catch fire exactly as the last one did!"

"I sent you in here trusting I'd improved upon the old spell, and I was right. Where the old could not withstand the temple's interference, the new does. Renault will be most pleased. His anonymity is once again assured."

Baldebert strode forward, exasperated. "You had

no need of me. You might have tested it on your own, magus."

"On the contrary." Mal smiled faintly. Hefting the pincers, he grabbed the bucket of water from under the table, and marched past Baldebert, deeper into the building. "To conduct the experiment to my satisfaction, I needed to stick as close to the original variables as possible. You were wearing the first brooch when it failed; it seemed prudent to have you on hand when I tried the second."

Only three stalls remained within Holder's barn and those had been changed, the box walls built up high as the loft floor. Tall, sturdy doors had been added where once horses would have looked out onto the aisle. There were bars of iron across each of the doors, with chains and thick-shanked locks to hold them in place. Theist sigils decorated both lock and iron bar, but that temple magic was cold and harmless now, long used up.

Mal approached the first stall. Setting the bucket by his feet, he squatted, and examined the complicated lock. "Furthermore," he told Baldebert, "if my suspicions are correct—and they usually are—I expect you'll want to see what Holder's been keeping in his barn. A practical man like you, Admiral—why, I do believe you'll be happily surprised."

"I'm a realistic man," retorted Baldebert. "You'll never cut through the locks, even with those pincers. The shanks are wide as my thumb."

"Nay, not the locks," Mal agreed. "But the chain's another matter." He handed the pincers to Baldebert. "I imagine you've done your share of lock cutting, pirate prince."

Baldebert didn't deign to reply. Humming, he inspected the chain link by link until he chose one seemingly at random. "Here, if anywhere," he decided, running a thumbnail over a depression in the metal. "The seam shows promise. Even so, it would take a great deal of force to crack it. This is no clinker on a ship's catch. Whatever your man's stowed, he means to keep it safe."

"Work the cutter," Mal ordered, smiling faintly. "I'll take care of the rest."

Baldebert complied, aligning the jaws of the pincers against the seam in the link. He gripped the handles with both hands. "Go on, then."

Mal set two fingers on the chain link. He spoke the basic cant he preferred for kindling flames in a cold hearth or striking fire to a candlewick but embellished the spell with word and intent, directing incandescence through the tips of his fingers and into iron. The metal began to warm. Mal's fingers did not, though heat pulsed in heady bursts from his pores.

"'Ware the sparks," said Baldebert. "Recall we're in a barn beneath a bloody hay loft. Catch the walls and it will be our funeral pyre."

For two heartbeats Mal smelled burned flesh within the perfume of hot metal, heard the phantom screams of the murdered magus. The chains lashing the necromancer to his post were similar enough to those on the stall doors that they might have been made by the same hand—in fact, they most certainly were, and forged on the anvil behind the barn.

"This is an ill-fated place," said Baldebert. Mal glanced his way, wondering if he had spoken aloud, but the other man was frowning down at the pincers in his hands and the glowing metal beneath Mal's fingers, a wrinkle between his yellow eyes. "If your priest meant to cleanse it with his signs and spells . . . aye, well. Someone might want to give it another try."

The heated iron spread in veins of orange and red along the link. The metal was not so molten as to bulge and drip, but the insides had become dangerously close to flaring.

Mal snatched his hand from metal, breaking the cant. "Now!" he ordered as he reached for the bucket of water.

Baldebert clenched the pincers. Iron grated in protest. Effort bent the wiry man nearly in two, but effort paid off: the overheated link yielded to the pincers, rupturing along the weakened seam, falling to the ground in two refulgent pieces. Mal dashed the pieces with water from the bucket before the smoking metal set the floor alight, splashing Baldebert's glossy boots in the process.

"Hsst!" Baldebert chided, dancing away from the mess. He set the pincers to the side while Mal pulled lock and chain away from door. Then it was only a matter of pushing the weighty bar free and trying the latch. The door gave readily, opening outward when Mal pulled.

Baldebert coughed. "Oil," he said. "Gone rancid. And gunpowder? Like one of my cannons in need of a cleaning." He peered around Mal. "Dark as a tomb. Witch up a light, why don't you?"

"No need." As soon as Mal stepped over the threshold soft white light set the narrow space aglow: bone magic roused. Mal didn't need to glance up at the sliver of bone mortared into the stall's furthest wall to know it was there. It was timeworn necromancy, the spirit nourishing the magic so depleted Mal could make out only the faintest of impressions. The sliver had once belonged to a femur, the femur of a young woman killed in battle by *sidhe*. Her bones had guarded Holder's barn for so long she'd forgotten what it was to be alive; her spirit was so long diminished by the spell she'd never learn what it meant to die. Another year, at most, and she'd be completely devoured. The spell would fail, her light gone out.

"Old Man Mountain take us and save us," Baldebert breathed, gone stark in the white light. "Ferric soldiers. The king's iron army."

"In fragments," confirmed Mal. Excitement kindled behind his ribs. He stepped further into the makeshift vault, turning in circles to better see Holder's treasure—shelves of clockwork limbs and clawed, birdlike feet. Rods and pistons and delicate, tensile chains. Four helms set one next to another, visors closed. Breastplates and vambraces decorated all over by a forest of wicked, curving metal thorns. And in one corner, uprooted, jointed clockwork spines tangled with detached iron tailpieces.

Fragments that would, once assembled, make more monstrosities like the one drowsing now in the Bone Cave, waiting only upon Mal's attention.

"Not quite seven." Mal frowned as he counted helmets and breastplates again. Armswoman Lane, before he'd used her to charge the first Automata, had bragged of Holder's seven more.

"Seven?" Baldebert, grown bolder, stalked back and forth in front of the shelves, apprehensive as a cat expecting rain. He reached toward a spiked vambrace three times the size of his own forearm but paused midstretch, cowed. "Seven is too many. I've read your histories, Doyle. Even Khorit Dard feared the walking machines, and Khorit Dard was a man who adored vile things. These should not be here. The Automata were destroyed alongside their masters."

"And yet here I am," replied Mal. "And here *they* are." He smiled coldly. "Grab up the pincers, admiral. There are two more doors yet to look behind."

CHAPTER 7

"**M**aggots, m'lady?" Hitch-Step Harry was less than impressed. The old man bent over the shallow bowl Avani held in her hands. He squinted at the clutch of wiggling white larva inside. "Are you sure?"

Harry dwelled on squatters' row, the makeshift and oft-changing ghetto grown up outside Wilhaiim's walls. He made a living busking outside the Maiden Gate, on the days he could walk. Today was not one of those days. His twin, a thin woman with worry lines graven deep around her pinched mouth, had sent to the temple for help days prior, but the temple priest had come and gone and Harry was no better for theist prayers and possets.

"The infection's gone deep."

Harry propped his foot, bare of shoe and stocking, on a low stool. The small tent he called home was redolent with sickness. Harry had already lost three toes to the gout, but now his entire foot was rebelling, swollen to twice its normal size and beginning to ulcerate in several places on the sole.

"Hasn't been this bad for years," Harry agreed, morose. "Burns like a hot poker between my toes. The good brother wanted to take it off at the ankle, but Gwen wouldn't let him."

"Three toes gone and still not cured," Gwen told Avani. "What's to say taking the rest of his foot will do any good? Besides, I need him fit. Can't walk the rabbit traps all on my own, can I?"

"Gwen's in the cony business," Harry explained. He seemed unable to look away from the maggots in Avani's dish. "Makes hats of their skins and stew out of the rest. We do all right, come winter."

"Summer, not so much." Gwen shrugged. She sat on a low stool twin to the one Harry used as a footrest, but near the flap of their tent, as close to fresh air as she could get. The tent was one of the largest in the ghetto. Besides the two stools and Harry's chair, there was room enough for a bedroll and a chamber pot, but not much else.

"We get by," Gwen continued. "Can yon grubs save my brother's foot, Lady Avani?"

"Ai, they're His Majesty's own best grubs," Avani replied lightly, stretching the truth just a little. She set the bowl carefully on the floor alongside Harry's foot. "Used just this past week on a royal friend whose hands were in worse shape than your toes. Lord Malachi keeps clean maggots always on hand, for cases such as yours, Harry."

As she'd hoped, making the larva royal eased Harry's nerves. He relaxed back into his tattered chair with a pained sigh, closing his eyes. "His Majesty's grubs, you say? Aye, well, if they're good enough for him who sits our throne . . ." He waved permission. "Go ahead. Will they hurt?"

"No more than the wound does already." Avani sat on her knees on the bare earth floor. Anticipating a lack of hot water, she'd brought a flask of medicinal alcohol with her from the palace, and used it now to sluice her hands. "Maggots, like leeches, are sometimes more useful in healing even than herbs." She tilted her head at the theist's posset near Harry's elbow, the small linen bag empty of all but a few crumbles of dried leaf. "Yarrow will tamp down the fever, but it's the fever that fights the sepsis."

Gwen fidgeted near the tent flap. "I hope His Majesty don't expect payment for his grubs, my lady. We've naught to offer since I traded my last bit of silver to Tilly down the road for opion."

"It helps me sleep," confessed Harry. "I hain't been sleeping much. And Gwen doesn't sleep when I'm up all night."

Avani bent over the old man's foot to hide her expression from Gwen. Opion was as dangerous as septic gout. Too much of the black tar—swallowed as a tonic or rubbed in a paste on the gums—could poison a man beyond saving. It was also a scarce and addictive cure, and was meant to be carefully regulated by the theists. But of late it seemed to have found its way out of the temple. Avani knew Harry wasn't the first on squatter's row, or for that matter in the city proper, to find relief in an opion stupor.

"Be cautious," she warned as she turned Harry's foot gently. "Opion is a western cure and many flat-landers find the dosage tricky."

"No matter." Gwen twitched back the tent flap, helpfully letting in more light along with breathable air. "We can't afford no more, can we, brother?"

Harry grumbled assent. He swallowed convulsively when Avani stirred the grubs with one finger, waking them to movement. She patted his ankle in reassurance, then shifted his foot on the stool until the ulcer on the sole was better exposed. Harry's grumble turned to groans. He bit hard on his lower lip to keep from crying out.

"Gwen," said Avani, "come and hold the leg still. If he shifts while I tend the wound I'm like to lose some of the maggots." Harry shuddered and closed his eyes. Gwen rose and did as Avani asked, leaning hard on Harry's calf with both hands. She looked down into the now-wriggling contents of Avani's bowl.

"Them's a lot of grubs," she pronounced. "You'll not get all of them to fit in Harry's foot."

"As many as possible." Gently, Avani picked a white larva between thumb and forefinger. Moving quickly, she began to pack the maggots one by one into the ulcers on Harry's foot. The sores were deep, most of them no larger than a walnut. It took some doing, but she managed without dropping even one of her tiny charges.

"You'll have to keep the foot up." She shook a roll of fine linen bandage from her sleeve and wrapped Harry's foot deftly from toes to ankle. "The bandage will keep them in place."

"How long?" Harry demanded. "I can feel them moving about." He was green beneath sweat-damped cheeks.

"Until the wounds bleed clean red." Avani sluiced her hands a final time then climbed to her feet. "A few days. I'll come back in one." She looked at Gwen. "No more yarrow. I don't mind the fever, so long as he stays lucid. Make him drink—water, not alcohol— and eat what the fever lets him keep down. Send for me if there's a change for the worse."

"Aye, m'lady." Gwen retrieved the bowl of maggots from the dirt floor. "We're in your debt, I'm sure." She shook her head as she passed the bowl to Avani. "I never thought as I'd be grateful to grubs."

"They are an unlikely remedy," Avani agreed, thinking of the desert prisoner lying incoherent in Mal's bed, her hands packed, wrapped, and splinted, an attendant stationed on each side of the mattress to keep the unconscious woman from harming herself further.

"Goddess willing Harry will be feeling much better in the morning." She tossed the man a wink but he was staring in queasy fascination at his bandaged foot and didn't see. Gwen ushered Avani through the tent flap and into the sunlight, bidding her farewell.

The sun was still high in the sky. Most of the unlucky souls who made their home in the ghetto were away for the day, busking or laboring or, as Avani well knew, spending precious coin on a day's drinking in one of Wilhaiim's less savory taverns.

The King's Highway bisected squatters' row. In daylight hours traffic was heavy. Avani made a point of counting liveried soldiers as she picked her way back toward Wilhaiim's northernmost gate; since Faolan's unexpected appearance with word of war looming east of the divide, mounted patrols were more prominent than ever and tempers were running hot. The average villein or tradesman had no way of knowing for certain what manner of threat lurked over the mountains. Coming so soon after the Red Worm's devastation, whispers of war must seem twice as disturbing, and Renault showed no inclination to address his subjects' growing unease. Instead, and to Avani's growing unease, he ignored his council's call for immediate action in lieu of Baldebert's promise that the Rani's ships would arrive in time to avert disaster.

Renault, she worried, was loath to further alarm a kingdom already stirred to apprehension by his refusal to take a temple-sanctioned wife. But Wilhai-im's court could count as well as their king, and those few who now knew of Faolan's report knew also that any ship sailing from Roue would not arrive soon, no matter how fair the weather on the Long Sea. Avani suspected Renault's hesitation was doing more harm than good.

A group of six Kingsmen thundered by on horse-back, splitting just in time to narrowly avoid a tinker and his pony-driven wagon. One of the soldiers kicked out at the wagon's running boards as he galloped past, shouting imprecations. The tinker made an ugly gesture in response then blushed when he caught Avani looking.

"I didn't see you there, my lady," he said by way of excuse, reining his pony. Foot traffic streamed to either side of his cart, making pots and pans stacked in the back rattle. "Or I wouldn't have—But they've grown quarrelsome, lately, His Majesty's soldiers. Ever since the armswoman was convicted of treason and blasphemy both, and buried without ceremony."

"*Ai*, is that so?" Avani awarded the man a friendly smile.

"'Tis the truth. I've been stopped twice on the road in that many days, just so they can take a peek in my cart for barrowmen." Smiling back, he knocked the running board with a fist. "Would you like a ride into the city?"

Avani suppressed a snort. "*Ai*, man. Me sitting behind your pony won't stop them checking your wares on the way in."

"There're no barrowmen hiding in my cart, mistress." The tinker, red of head and feisty with it, waved Avani up. "They can look all they like, so long as I'm through in time for supper at Packney's Tavern. Come and sit. It must be lucky to give a pretty lass such as you a ride."

He didn't recognize her, Avani realized. There was no reason he should; she'd eschewed vocent black since Mal's return, if not completely her role as king's magus. For her visit outside the city she'd dressed in a gray cotton salwar and her favorite pair of battered boots. She wore Andrew's ring and her barrow key on a long gold chain, tucked safely beneath her shirt. Kate's string of rubies she'd left behind in her chambers.

The tinker would take her for a noblewoman—cotton was a luxury and her boots, while scuffed, were made of fine leather—but he had no reason to believe her anything other than she appeared, had no reason to know she kept the king's counsel and could, if provoked, let loose her magic and char a person near to death in the process.

"You're very kind," she thanked the man. "But

I prefer to walk." If she climbed onto his cart, she would have to explain the maggots and she couldn't be certain of her welcome after that. "Now that the weather is turning."

"Mabon threatens," he agreed, accepting her refusal with good grace. "And I'll not miss the heat. Good day, my lady." He touched his forehead with the butt of his whip in cheerful farewell. Avani stood in a rut between the road and a sagging clapboard hut and watched him go.

Mabon threatens. The tinker, like most of the people traversing the highway, looked ahead only as far as the change in seasons.

Avani had lost that comfort the day Stonehill fell.

"**D**isgusting," Cleena said when Avani stopped at her tent. She wasn't sure whether the beekeeper meant the maggots or Avani herself. The Fair was busier than she had seen it in weeks, customers coaxed out of chamber by the pleasant weather. "You're scaring away my clients."

A string of patrons lingered over Cleena's wares, sampling honey, exchanging coin for sweets. Cleena flirted with them all, from the grizzled nan with a basket of bread on her arm to the young footman with Worm scars on his face and neck, and everyone in between. She was doing fine business and the exchange of coin didn't slacken even when Avani set her bowl down with a thump amongst a display of honey sticks and lavender sachets.

Cleena refrained from showing her teeth in threat but Avani caught the enraged flex of her delicate hands.

"Honestly," the beekeeper said, sotto voce, "I'm not above spelling you into salt and stone."

"*Ai*, I misdoubt you could," retorted Avani smoothly. "As far as I can tell your talents lie in creeping and sneaking and seduction."

"Sex," Cleena confirmed, making the footman blush over his shopping. He did a double take when he saw the contents of Avani's bowl.

"Are the grubs for sale?" he wondered aloud, blinking bemusedly Cleena's way.

"Nay, love. Not the grubs." The *sidheog* petted his arm before walking around her table and grabbing Avani by the elbow. With her other hand she removed the bowl of maggots from her display.

"Get away from my place, witch," she said, steering Avani backward into the crowd. "Get away and stay away."

"You're hurting me." Avani tried to wrench her arm from Cleena's grasp, but the beekeeper was inhumanly strong and she couldn't break free. So she stepped hard with the heel of her boot on Cleena's instep, grinding past slipper to bone. Cleena swore and let go, jerking away. The bowl fell from her hands. It broke into pieces when it hit the ground, sprinkling maggots.

Both women stared down at shattered crockery and writhing grubs. The Fair bustled about them, unaware. Avani rubbed her smarting flesh. Cleena took a deep breath then sighed it out.

"Oh, that's hard luck," she said in flat tones. "The bowl's lost but the crawlers might still be saved. Let me get a pot."

She spun in a flurry of colorful skirts and was back in an instant, crouching to pick the fallen maggots one by one from between Avani's feet.

"They'll survive my temper," she promised as she worked, then cajoled: "Dipped in honey they'll be a sweet treat."

"They're not for eating." Avani chose her next words carefully. "That was unfair of me. Your business is not my concern."

Cleena wrinkled her nose. "The sex, you mean? I'll take my pleasure when and where I like." She rose and restored the maggots, motionless now in the bottom of her jug, to Avani. "But you've no reason for jealousy. Malachi Doyle is not a customer. Nor would I have him. And I'll not apologize for hurting you. Not after the damage you and yours did Halwn's kin. To think mortals call *us* monsters."

"It wasn't us who took a cleaver to the barrow-man's fingers—"

"Not its hands." Cleena leaned in until her breath warmed Avani's collarbone. It was not flirtation: it was threat. Avani did not doubt a few inches more and the *sidhe* might rip out her throat. "Its mind. Smashed like your bowl, turned over until there's nothing left worth saving. At least we kill your people cleanly."

Avani stood her ground. "I want to speak to Faolan. I have questions, just as he supposed."

"Oh, is that why you've come sniffing about my tent? Faolan's busy trying to undo your damage. Go away." Flapping a hand, Cleena returned to her wares. Her patrons, patient and devoted, bloomed under her increased attention.

Avani rubbed at the back of her neck to soothe prickles of unease.

"You'll tell Faolan," she said. Andrew's ring under her salwar flickered amber inevitability. "You gave him your word."

"Go away," Cleena repeated, her back still to Avani, "before I set Thomas on you for disturbing my peace. You'll make her go away, won't you, Thomas?"

The footman, lips sticky with traces of sampled sweets, turned a baffled stare in Avani's direction. He was not a big man, but he was young, strong, and heavily muscled.

"My lady magus," he said. Unlike the tinker, he knew well who Avani was but did not care. "You're not welcome here. Please go." The tendons in his neck corded as if he struggled to make the words come. "I don't want to compel you, but I will, if Cleena asks. Go. Take your little grubs and go."

Avani went.

She returned the maggots to their small chest on a shelf in the back of Mal's cold room. The chest was half filled with cornmeal but in the chill environment the larva were more likely to sleep than eat. Eventually they would die and Mal would replenish his store. She knew he used the maggots for stripping flesh from corpses more often than for healing; he preferred to leave physicking to the priests whenever possible. For all his reputation as a sophisticate, Mal fraternized with the dead more easily than he did the living.

A corpse was laid out on Mal's worktable: a middle-aged, sparsely bearded man. He was naked but for a modest sheet pulled up and under his armpits. Avani couldn't tell from a cursory look what had killed him. His flesh was very white, Mal's neat stitching where he'd opened the body up and then sewn flesh back together was very black.

The man's ghost was not there. The empty laboratory and the lone corpse made Avani shiver; it was a lonely place.

Avani closed the door firmly on the way out, resisting the increasingly invariable urge to reach out and find Mal. She hadn't seen him since he'd given her permission to use his maggots on the desert woman, and while he'd watched with honest interest as she'd packed and bound the prisoner's wounds, he'd hurried off without explanation soon after.

It would be a matter of little effort to unfurl a finger

of magic and find him across their link. But Mal had been reticent since his encounter with the phantom magus on Holder's farm, shocked small and quiet, his presence a vague chill one didn't dare examine too closely for fear of a blossoming fever. But she longed to turn toward him for comfort, and give comfort in return. The knowledge that he was there, an antidote to isolation, was as enticing as whatever *sidhe* glamour Cleena used to lure and keep her patrons.

Avani thought it possible the executed magus, whoever he was, might have relied on a similar solace. Had he died for that indulgence?

So as she climbed the stairs out of the palace depths and onto more lively levels, she distracted herself from temptation by reaching instead for an old friend.

Jacob was also there, as he always was, but lodged in her heart instead of between her ears. Jacob belonged to the Goddess as much as he belonged to himself. He'd tolerated Avani from the beginning because the Goddess had willed it. Years of partnership had shaped forbearance into love. Avani and Jacob were family. For quite some time after she'd first begun to live as a flatlander and was still mourning parents and siblings lost to cataclysm, the raven had been the only family Avani could tolerate, the Goddess's grace given wings.

But for all Jacob was goddess-blessed, he was also a bird, a wild thing, more at home beneath the sky than between four walls. As of late he'd been spending as much time indoors as without, but Avani had not been surprised when he'd gone missing from his usual perch above Renault's throne. Jacob had a finite tolerance for human idiocy.

He was never away for very long, and she was glad of it, because she missed Jacob when he was gone even as she understood his bid for independence.

Above the stairs the palace teemed with life and color. Avani idled against a tapestried wall as she sought Jacob behind closed eyes, letting the sound and scents of a late summer Court soothe away the chill she'd carried with her from below. Through windows open overhead she heard the ring of a blacksmith's hammer, the bored bleat of a goat, and the rise and fall of Brother Tillion's preaching. Closer by a housemaid carrying a dusting rag whistled a pretty tune as she navigated the crowded corridors. The rag smelled lightly of lemon juice and pine oil.

But, nay. The scent of pine was fresh as needles recently crushed beneath reckless hands, needles that tickled the bottom of her feet where she stood balanced precariously. Her wings were spread in appreciation of pleasant breezes, but the right did not want to work as it should. Her shoulder ached with the wrongness of bones wrenched. Far below a dog barked excitedly. She'd spent the morning pelting the animal with walnuts and stones from her hidden cache but was growing bored of that small amusement.

"Jacob," Avani said, dismayed. "What are you up to?" She could see the Royal Gardens through the raven's eyes, and the top of the barracks' towers. "You're hurt. Come home."

He was not pleased by her invasion. She felt his affront, sharp as if she'd given insult. It was not his usual fractiousness. She could feel his repugnance as her own; he wanted her gone.

"Come home," she said, but Jacob chased her out by force of will. His indignation stung. Thrown back into her own body, Avani sagged against tapestry, pressing her thumb to the new tenderness between her eyes. "*Ai*, you bastard."

"Lady Avani." A firm hand kept Avani from falling. She opened her eyes, blinking to clear away a double image of orange needles and blue sky over palace rugs and gray stone walls.

"Lady Avani," the king's constable repeated, concerned. Avani recognized the other woman from her increasing presence in Renault's council chambers, and from the marked resemblance she bore to her son, the young earl of Wythe. "Are you ill?"

"Nay." Avani straightened. The Countess Wythe took a step away, smiling affably. She was dressed for riding, her leathers polished to shining. She wore the silver-and-onyx starburst, a sign of the king's favor, on her breast and rare black Shellshale pearls in her ears.

"It looked as though you were caught short of

breath," explained the countess. "It's always close in these corridors, not matter the weather. Walk with me?"

It was more command than request. Avani hesitated.

"Your lad mentors mine own Morgan in the barracks," the king's constable explained. "Morgan's a good boy, but his head is often in the clouds. There are so few of our children left. I lost my eldest boy to the Worm. Morgan's all I have left. I worry."

Avani, prepared to dislike Wythe for Renault's sake, suffered a pang of sympathy. The woman, for all her stiff posture and proper uniform, seemed genuinely concerned.

"It's been difficult, letting him go." Wythe glanced everywhere but at Avani. "He's striving toward manhood and I have responsibilities of my own. I should not interfere. But it seems only yesterday Morgan learned to walk in his brother's footsteps. Impossible that he lives now in the barracks and trains for war. That was meant to be Michael's role, before we lost him. I worry Morgan's not suited to soldiering."

"I used to think the same about Liam." Avani schooled her face to friendliness. The ache between her eyes throbbed protest. "I'm headed for my chambers, Countess. But you're welcome to walk with *me* along the way, if you like. Liam's a good man. He'll take fine care of your Morgan and better yet, teach Morgan how to take fine care of himself."

Wythe walked as though she were heading into battle: upright and forward. Her leathers creaked with every step. The pommel of her sword sparkled. The silver spurs on her boots jingled. Avani, who preferred to walk in quiet contemplation, nevertheless thought her gallant in a stern, overly forthright way.

"Liam was an orphan," she began, as they made their way forward toward the gathering court. Nobles adorned with dyed pheasant plumage in celebration of summer's end mingled with men and women in farmer's kit and merchants with samples of their wares in hand. The throne room's double portals were closed to audience, but a line of supplicants nevertheless twined back and forth on the edge of the great hall in anticipation of Renault's reappearance.

"Abandoned on the Downs," Avani continued, picking her way through the crowd. "He was too proud even then to let me take him into my house, but I kept his belly filled when I could and gave him the castoffs from my loom, and in return he gave me his trust."

"Possibly more valuable even than a full belly," the constable mused. "But let us cut to the chase. Tell me, Lady Avani, do you believe the lad retains human sensibilities despite his *sidhe* background? Or need I warn Morgan to be on guard?"

Avani stopped and swung around. They'd walked beneath one of many great arches, and into the main hall. The low rumble of many voices quieted as the court took notice. A vagabond tinker might not know Avani in a crowd, but her days of anonymity in the palace were past. And the king's constable in her stark leather and silver was a shining blade in a forest of gaudy silk and fringe. Heads turned as courtiers took notice.

"Liam is a good man," Avani repeated coldly, deciding it was easy to dislike Wythe after all. "Morgan is lucky to know him. I'm sure you don't wish to imply otherwise." She could hear the room begin to buzz again in anticipation. Renault's court would take entertainment where they could find it.

The countess's stare was thoughtful. She did not appear to notice or care that they had become the center of attention. She said, "You're an islander."

"Aye. I was."

Wythe nodded. She knocked her heels together in another precise bow. "My condolences. My sister worked aboard a Knotcreek trawler before she married. She said on the day the islands sank, they brought up so many bodies with the fish in their nets that the ropes snapped."

"I was only a child. I clung to a piece of flotsam and was washed free of the maelstrom. The flatland ships arrived not long after, and I was pulled, scarcely alive, from the sea." Avani didn't care to dwell on that long night in the roiling water.

"This world is full of unforeseen dangers. My sister, and my father—they were drawn to the sea.

My grandmother and my great-grandsire—they had a talent for horseflesh. They rode together with the Aug against the *sidhe*. They also had stories, of barrowman coming from nowhere out of forest and rock, crippling the cavalry with claw and fang until our own fell down dead in the dirt. They said that so many Kingsmen were lost that the flatland springs were fouled by rotting corpses and the king's necromancers could not lay all of their spirits to rest.

"Your orphan may now be a good man—" Wythe held up a sympathetic finger, forestalling Avani's protest "—and I do not doubt he is, if you say it's so. But he cannot change his past any more than I can change mine or you can change your own. So you will understand, I think, if I warn Morgan to keep watch."

CHAPTER 8

Avani slammed the door to her bedchambers closed behind her. She stripped off her boots and sword. She left the boots where she dropped them just inside the door but took care to lay her sword in its place before the Goddess.

"The countess is an ugly piece of work," Avani told the idol in Jacob's stead, shedding salwar and trousers. Naked but for the chain around her neck, she bent over the wash basin she kept always near the foot of her bed and splashed squatter's row dust from her face and throat. "And she may be handy with the bow and arrow, but I wager she's cold as ice beneath all that pretty polish."

The idol did not reply, nor did she expect it to. Avani snatched up a washrag and used it to blot dry her cheeks. The spot between her eyes still hurt but when she checked her brow in the square of mirror she kept on hand for vanity's sake, she saw no sign of injury.

"And *that one's* no better. Playing hide-and-seek when it's obvious he's in need of care. What were you thinking with him?"

She sighed. She'd seen Jacob's roost from his point of view. He was holed up very near the barracks; she thought she could find him without much difficulty. But would he forgive her the interference, when he so obviously intended to be left alone?

She dressed as efficiently as she'd undressed, choosing soft red silk and a pair of open-toed slippers. Both were gifts from her friend Deval and brought her happiness. But it was a bittersweet comfort. Wythe's tale of island bodies in Knotcreek fishing nets threatened to wake buried sorrow.

She twisted her long hair atop her head and pinned it into place, then looped Kate's string of rubies twice around her neck. That was another sorrow, more recent; a new-made friend murdered for the barrow maps she'd hidden in her herb garden. Kate's loss was still raw. In the short time Avani had known the king's beloved, Kate had always extended her sincere kindness.

"And you know there's not enough of *that* to go about in this city," Avani said pointedly before stomping again out of her room.

The two Kingsmen stationed outside Mal's chambers thumped the butt of their pikes on stone in salute as Avani approached. They were members of Renault's elite guard, meant to serve in the throne room. That the king had assigned them watch over his newest prisoner said much about his state of mind. With Brother Paul murdered and the role of Masterhealer not yet filled, and Brother Tillion preaching dissent in the castle bailey, Renault and the temple were in disharmony. The spy in Mal's bed was a close-kept secret, which meant also that she had been saved from the dungeons but also denied the theists' healing magics.

It was twilight in Mal's chamber, heavy velvet curtains drawn over all but one of the floor-to-ceiling windows. Embers glowed on the hearth. Fat beeswax candles burned in the multicolored lanterns Mal so loved, and in a bowl on his desk. The two Kingsmen tasked with keeping the spy from damaging her bandaged hands stood on either side of Mal's mattress, almost hidden by swathes of the bed's ostentatious canopy.

"No change, my lady. She's uncomfortably warm, but not dangerously so. The fever abated for a time this morning and returned an hour ago. She's not woken but the once to drink water. For the most part she's laid still as a stone."

"*Ai*, thank you." The soldiers were plainly dressed, out of uniform. Both had been chosen for their competency in the sickroom and their attachment to the throne. Avani was not certain what connection they had to the king, but it was apparent from the affectionate way they spoke of Renault that they knew him personally and held him in the highest regard. Both had gray in their beards and a capable glint in their eyes.

Avani pulled the drapes back from the window, letting in light and air. She stoked the fire until flames crackled, cleaned her hands from fingertips to wrists with the wedge of lye soap Mal kept on his mantel near a broken penknife, a raven's dark feather, and a mountain cat's fractured jaw bone. Then she climbed the sleeping dais and examined her patient.

"She's a wild specimen, ain't she, my lady? All shank and sharp chin and knotted hair. When she dreams, it's not the king's lingua she's speaking, either. Strong, too. Even with her ruined hands. You won't want to be alone with her when she wakes, begging your pardon."

"I'm not afraid." Avani checked the spy's right hand, and then her left. She'd soaked the ruined flesh in a solution of vinegar and honey before resetting what bone she could and strapping each splayed hand flat on a piece of wood borrowed from the palace cooper.

She hadn't awoken to voice protest, not even

when Avani introduced the maggots to her wounds and loosely wrapped each hand. Then, she'd been wracked with high fever. Avani pressed the back of her fingers against the unconscious woman's cheek. She was warm, but not dangerously so. Like Harry on squatter's row, the desert woman would do better in the end if her body managed to burn out infection.

The pulse in her neck beat steadily.

"She needs to keep drinking." Satisfied that the dressings did not yet need changing, Avani checked the level of water in the bedside pitcher. "Mayhap soon some broth. Salt would do her good." She wrinkled her nose. "And a bath. Will you send for hot water?"

The Kingsmen shared a dubious glance. "No servants, my lady. His Majesty's orders. Not until she wakes and we've determined the extent of the temple's treachery."

"Well, she cannot lie here flaking dried blood and mud onto his lordship's linens. Go and fetch broth and hot water from the kitchens, the both of you. Use the servant's stairs. Be clever about it and none will be the wiser."

"But, my lady—"

"Go!" Exasperated, Avani clapped her palms together. The Kingsmen paled as if she'd conjured lightning from the ceiling. "Make sure the water is steaming."

The old soldiers moved with the alacrity of men

used to obeying orders. When they were gone, Avani took a turn around Mal's chambers, poking absently at his eccentric collection of bits and bobs—a chunk of red-striated gray stone near the wardrobe, a pouch of loose emeralds on the windowsill, a weathered iron cog no larger than her fist being used to weigh down miscellaneous papers near the inkpot on his desk.

She settled into the large leather chair he used as his own private throne, shed her slippers, and folded her legs beneath her. On the desk next to the odd iron cog and the stack of illustrations and the inkpot lay a thin book, upside down and open spine cracked. Avani winced for the badly treated binding. She turned the book over. She'd anticipated a treatise on war, weaponry, or dissection. Puzzled, she discovered instead a thumbed-over volume of poetry. A lovely etching of Selkirk's rose device graced the front plate. Beneath the etching was a scrawled and brief dedication: *For My Son Rowan.*

The Kingsmen returned swiftly with wash water. Avani heard their footsteps in the hall, the quick pat-pat that came of balancing an awkward burden. They came with company, although she did not think they were aware of their companion. Mal's footsteps made no sound, yet she knew he was there; his nearness made the hairs on the back of her neck stand up in recognition.

She rose and opened the door, saving the Kingsmen the task.

"Near the bed, please," she said, holding the door wide as the soldiers carried a steaming bucket and a covered tureen over the threshold. "And then you're dismissed until suppertime. Wait outside the door if you like, but I'll not have you hovering over the bath. Let's spare her that indignity if we can."

The Kingsmen swallowed protest and bowed their way back through the door. Avani knew they would take up position with their brother and sister in the hall, close at hand in case of trouble. She closed the door but for the sake of their pride left it unlocked.

"*Ai*, then, I take it you've fixed Renault's handy little bauble to your satisfaction," she said as she rolled up her sleeves in preparation for the task ahead.

It was like watching a ghostie materialize in front of the hearth, but Mal's eyes were a wicked, diverting green and for all his small stature he was more solid than any wandering spirit. He unpinned the sapphire brooch and set it on his desk.

"Better than fixed." He sighed and stretched; Avani could hear his back pop. "Improved upon. Take it with you when you go, if you like. Study it. When you've learned how the spell works, we'll return it to Renault. It's not the sort of knowledge we want lost."

A sponge had come along with the bucket, the sort farmed near the Black Coast, collected by seal-sleek divers in baskets and later sold to royalty for more coin than Avani would earn in a lifetime. She cast a suspicious look door-ward, wondering if the Kingsmen had bypassed the kitchens and gone straight to Renault with her request.

"Of course they did," Mal said. "Or did you think Cook keeps the broth in his kitchen warming in an embossed silver tureen?" He shed his dark vocent's cape, tossing it over the back of his chair. Beneath he was clad in the Hennish leather tooled for his office. His curls, recently shorn, barely brushed his collar. The amber jewel on his finger shone subtly.

Avani saw the moment he realized she'd been sitting at his desk and braced for his displeasure. But he merely picked up the book of poetry, closed it, and set it aside without comment. Then he stepped onto the dais and bent over their patient.

"Still sleeping, I see. Good. The body and brain protect themselves. She'll stay so for a time longer, I think." Mal brushed his fingers, whisper-quick across the woman's brow. "No longer burning up. Much improved, I suspect. I envy your healing magics; I doubt I'll ever grasp the knack of it."

"It comes of knowledge, not magic," Avani corrected, ladling hot water into a shallow bowl, then adding the sponge.

"You don't truly believe that." Mal lifted one of the spy's bandaged hands, sniffing. "She may indeed retain the use of her hands, if only minimally." Straightening, he nodded Avani's way. "Your little friends aid in fighting the infection, certainly, as do your potions and ointments. But it's not only island recipes that saved my life in the forest almost a year ago, nor again chased away impending brain fever upon my return from Roue. You've saved my life twice, and vanquished the Red Worm in between." He took the bowl of water from Avani, freeing up her hands for the sponge. "I didn't bring you to Renault's attention for your skill with the mortar and pestle, but because you are quite literally overflowing with potential. Using bones to knit sorcery, or sorcery to knit bones. It's the same principle."

"Is it?" Avani dunked the sponge and wrung it out over the bowl. The water was hot enough to chap her hands. "What you do is called necromancy. Healing magic is the temple's dominion. What I do is only by the Goddess's will."

"Only?" Mal's fine black brows rose beneath his curls. His crooked nose gave him a rakish mien. Avani was hard-pressed not to smile. Mirth fizzed across their link, headier than the finest wine.

"Stop," she chided quietly. Then, as she gently blotted the sleeping woman's torso. "You're in a fine mood. Much less sour than last we . . . spoke. What's happened? Did you find Holder after all?"

"Nay." He reined back overflowing amusement. "But I imagine we'll tree him soon enough. Ah, now. Look at that. Interesting."

The prisoner wore the same scant snakeskin vest and long kilted skirt the *sidhe* had found her in, short her sandals that Avani had removed before tending to her hands. Long feathers, crushed from capture and confinement, were sewn onto the sleeves of the woman's vest and woven into her tangled hair. As Avani sponged away filth tattooed onto the woman's arms and belly, revealing more feathers by way of individual azure pinpricks.

"Family narrative," Mal said, taking the sponge from Avani and setting it and the basin aside. He leaned in for a closer look. "They're a wandering people and take their history with them by way of self-decoration." The woman sighed in her sleep, turning her head minutely on the pillow. Avani froze but the woman slept on. Mal tested the woman's brow again for fever but shook his head, unconcerned. "Whoever she is, the design and number of the tattoos indicate rank and bloodline. According to Faolan, Everin believed she had some status. I'd have to agree."

"You've spent time on the other side of the mountains." It wasn't a question.

His good mood ebbed. "The desert has always been Wilhaiim's enemy. I've had occasion to do business on the other side of the divide, but not since before Andrew died, when I was quite young."

Avani emptied the dirty water out the window, refilled the bowl, and returned to her task. She worked without speaking, trying with little success to imagine Mal as a young man—a king's assassin, ridding Wilhaiim of a distant enemy by poison or blade or sorcery. A cruel errand, she thought, as much for the assassin as the victim.

"It wasn't," said Mal. He'd taken his knife from his belt and was meticulously separating a broken pinion from snakeskin. "I lived only to serve Renault, and Andrew. The ways and means may have been less visible, but it's no different than sending any other lad or lass off to war. Liam will go this time around. In the infantry, I imagine. Best prepare for it."

He took the rescued feather from the dais and placed it on his desk. Avani, intrigued, followed. In the colored lamplight the barbs shifted from white to orange and red. The shaft was bent in several places. Mal reached around Avani, plucked the raven feather from his mantel, and set it alongside for comparison. The raven's was longer, although not by much. Avani frowned.

"Jacob's found mischief," she confessed. "At first I thought it was only his usual sport, but now I'm not so sure. He's injured, and holed up in a tree near the barracks." She set down the washing bowl. "He wants nothing to do with me, which is not like Jacob at all."

"Jacob?" Attention caught, Mal inclined his body almost imperceptibly in Avani's direction. *Show me*, he said, granting permission.

So she let him see blue sky past swathes of orange needles, the barrack's tower top, the hollow boll in the tree trunk where Jacob had made his temporary nest. She let him feel the wrongness in Jacob's shoulder, the dull, spiraling ache in his breast.

Something broken, or torn, she hazarded. *Something I could fix, if he'd let me help. Not so different from finger bones, I think.*

I wager our spy is an easier patient.

Mal experienced the bite of Jacob's repudiation as Avani had. He retreated and then returned full force, snatching the recollection and turning it over between them, a puzzle to be solved. Mal wasn't gentle. He had no experience in visions or the sharing of secret things. Avani had learned that dance by her Goddess's grace, and Jacob's interferences. It didn't do to step without finesse into that space inside another's skull. But Mal, dexterous when it came to spell craft or intrigue, boiled across their link without subtlety, overwhelming to the point of pain. He sorted through the record of Avani's morning one experience after another, from breakfast alone at her table before sunrise, the dusty walk out of the city, Harry's rotten foot and the tinker's cheerful wave goodbye. Cleena and her threats, Thomas the footman with his empty, lust-bedazzled smile, Jacob, and then the Countess Wythe, the king's favor sparkling on her breast while she called Liam less than human—

"Stop!" Avani cried aloud and in her head both, shoving at Mal with all her strength. He would consume her and she would let him because the ardor that was his complete absorption felt like worship.

Avani forced open eyes she didn't remember closing. Mal was a hairsbreadth away, his lips brushing one corner of her mouth, his breath apples and heat on her tongue. She thought he'd kissed her as they tangled hearts and minds together. She knew he wanted to kiss her again. His heart was leaping in her ears, her arousal pooling in his gut.

Why not worship? demanded Mal, gently soothing reverence and adoration over the insult of his intrusion. *There are none left like us, none so powerful or precious in all the world. Are we not worth worship?*

She closed the scant distance between them. When he took her mouth a second time they tasted Mal and Avani in equal parts. It was headier than anything they'd ever experienced, as powerful as giving life, as addictive as taking it.

The door to Mal's bedchamber crashed open. They might not have taken notice if not for the sudden influx of life force, a cloud of singular mortal stars behind closed eyelids, and then the crier's ringing shout:

"His Majesty the King has arrived—make way!"

They broke apart, one being sundered again into two. Avani was left reeling. Mal, always more adept at hiding his feelings, straightened at once, the only evidence of his discomposure a slight stain of darker color on his cheeks.

"My liege." Mal cleared his throat. "Apologies. I was not expecting—"

"In truth, neither was I," replied Renault. He stood in the middle of the room, Brothers Orat and Tillion two steps behind, while Kingsmen and priests took up position along the walls, making a large space feel tight. The pinched look around Renault's mouth might have been embarrassment.

Ignoring Orat's glower and Tillion's whispers, Renault plucked the circlet of his office from his head, handed it to a hovering attendant, and scrubbed gloved hands through his hair and beard, hiding his face as he did so. When he remerged he was calm again, no longer thrown by the sight of his two most trusted advisors caught midembrace.

"The new Masterhealer and I," the king explained, indicating Brother Orat, "have sadly reached an impasse. I see only one way through it, other than throwing the entirety of his temple in my dungeons on suspicion of treason. And my dungeons are not so large as that. I need you to wake our spy, Mal, and I need you to wake her now."

At Mal's request, Avani busied herself with snuffing the lanterns and opening wide those windows she could reach. The fresh air was a welcome antidote to her heated skin. She lingered for a moment with her back to the room, watching the bailey below. If she pressed her hands on the sill and leaned out into daylight she could just glimpse treetops between the

Royal Gardens and the barracks towers. Somewhere amongst the bristle of green a ruddy tree grew.

It was easier to think on finding Jacob than on the ache of Mal's absence.

"No matter his faults—and there were many—I cannot believe Paul would treat with any enemy of the throne, and especially not with sand snakes." Behind her the new Masterhealer came perilously close to shouting. Avani, without turning around, could tell the unforeseen responsibility of his new position lay uncomfortably on Orat's shoulders.

"Our ancestors followed the one god west over the mountains to escape persecution, to build our temples and spread his word," he continued. "Surely, Majesty, you have not forgotten your theist catechism."

"I have not. Mayhap Brother Paul did."

"He would not," Orat reiterated. "He sought to restore the god's good will to the throne in a time of trial. He wished to see you properly returned by marriage to the temple, not cast down from your seat. I tell you: I would know if it were otherwise."

"You are not infallible." Renault did not have to shout to make his point. "It is possible he affected treason under your nose. And now that you have contrived to take his place in power, my old friend, his mess is yours."

"Wake her," Tillion urged. "Make her tell the tale. If there is treachery under our roof, we must smoke it out."

Avani hugged her ribs as she turned back into the room. Tillion, leaning on his staff, towered over everyone else. His hands and jaw trembled faintly but his yellow stare was stone—steady as he watched her from the other side of the chamber.

He knows, she thought, feeling all at once as if she would be violently sick.

"Avani," said Mal sharply. "A hand, if you will? Torn from sleep without the body's natural coping mechanisms to rely upon, she'll be confused, frightened, and in pain. This is not a sympathetic magic."

One foot in front of the other, she walked around Mal's writing desk and approached the sleeping dais. Priest and Kingsmen alike fell back as she drew close. She wondered distantly if she looked as ravaged as she felt, or if they were merely reacting to long ingrained superstition. Renault gave her a hand up onto the platform, squeezing her elbow.

"Water, to ease her throat," Mal ordered as she crossed to his side. "Keep her from tearing off her splints; I expect she'll become violent once she realizes what we're about. She'll need calming. Can you do that?"

He could do it himself with a word and a twitch of magic, Avani knew, spelling the spy immobile as he woke her. He didn't need anyone's help. He intended only to distract Avani before her face gave them both away.

"Nay," he said quietly but plainly. "I am better with

you by my side." It sounded like an apology, but they both knew it was too late for regret. "Are you ready?"

"Almost." She looked past the crowd in the room to the two veteran soldiers standing on the threshold and beckoned them in. Solemn, they took up their stations again on either side of the mattress, braced to keep their patient still. "Now," she said.

Mal shed his gloves and laid them neatly aside. The magus ring on his hand warmed to amber. He set his bare palms to either side of the spy's face, cupping her cheeks as he might a lover's. He spoke softly. Avani recognized the cant for summoning sorcery, meant to call a departed spirit into attendance. She hadn't seen it worked on the living. On the dead, it was coercion, on the living it was grisly anathema.

When Mal finished speaking, the woman's eyes snapped wide. It was a harrowing thing to witness, a body ripped from healing sleep and made at once awake and aware. Her pupils swelled and then shrunk again at an alarming rate, going from black pinpricks to near as large as her yellow irises and then back again. Her muscles protested, shaking her on the mattress. The Kingsmen held her arms immobile while she thrashed. Her teeth rattled as she shuddered.

"*Ai*, watch her tongue!" But as she'd suspected, Mal knew what he was doing. He pressed the woman's jaw closed as she shook, preventing her from bloodying tongue or lip, until the seizure passed.

Avani saw the moment the agony of forced consciousness brought the woman around. The spy groaned and sat up off the pillows. Mal shifted his grip to her bare shoulders, restraining. Realization chased awareness across her face; she blinked and her pupils returned to normal. She was awake, but without her body's consent.

"Galenos!" Her voice cracked. She struggled briefly against constraining hands then slumped, panting. Sweat sheened her brow. She shivered.

"There is a reason the body retreats to sleep when pushed past all limits," Avani warned Renault. She reached for water, filled a small tumbler, held it to the desert woman's mouth. "Drink," she said. The woman took a grudging sip, enough to wet chapped lips, then turned her head away.

"It cannot be helped," the king replied. "My scouts are returning with word of more desert wolves come over the mountain, singly or in twos and threes. They are testing our borders, learning the land. A first foray toward war, much earlier than anticipated. So you see, it is not just for the Masterhealer's honor we must use her thusly. I need to hear what she knows. Believe you me, I take no pleasure in her suffering." He joined Avani and Mal on the dais. "What is Galenos?"

The spy twisted her mouth in keen disgust. She looked as if she intended to spit in Renault's face, or at Mal. But Mal's spell was still within her, compelling, an irresistible force. Instead of spewing the vitriol as she so clearly desired, the desert woman opened her mouth and told Wilhaiim's king what he desired to know.

"Galenos was my brother." She spoke heavily accented king's lingua.

"And what are you called?"

"Desma, daughter of the sand guard."

"Where is Galenos now?"

"Dead," she replied. Fury drained color from her face, leaving behind the hectic red spots of returning fever. "Killed and eaten by the same who brought me to you."

"Mal," chastened Renault.

"She speaks her truth," Mal replied mildly. The jewel on his finger continued to glow, a merry accompaniment to the ugly magic holding Desma in thrall.

"Ask her," prompted Tillion from the foot of the dais. "What does she know of the temple?"

Desma stared past Renault at the priest. Her breathing quickened again, becoming shallow. Then her eyes rolled up in her head and she fell back, limp. Alarmed, Avani reached for the pulse in her neck, but the Kingsmen were faster, shouldering Avani to one side just as Desma came off the mattress. Mute, muscles coiled until they stood taut under her tattooed flesh, she fought the soldiers forcing her prone her even as she battled Mal's mastery.

"Have a care!" Orat shouted at the Kingsmen. "We need her whole!"

Whole, thought Avani, was exactly what Desma would never be again. The woman beat her broken hands against the mattress despite the soldiers' attempts to keep her from harm. Desma welcomed the pain, embraced it as a harbinger of death, as an escape from violation.

"Stop!" Avani told Mal, dodging past the Kingsmen. She grabbed Mal's wrists, tried to wrest his hands from Desma's face. But a third Kingsman dragged her away, apologizing as he pulled her back. Avani brought up her knee but the soldier blocked her strike. Catching her arm up behind her back, he forced her still. It was the first time Renault's soldiers had treated her with anything but respect, and the shock of it rendered her breathless.

"If you die," Mal told Desma, ignoring the commotion in the room, "I am duty bound to bring your shade back. Again and again, until you have answered His Majesty's questions. Living or dead, you will not win this."

"Monster," Desma whispered. She collapsed again onto the mattress, beaten. Avani's dressing had come loose from her hands. The cooper's boards were broken. One of the old soldiers lay across her thighs. The second held his forearm against her windpipe. Mal, implacable, cupped her chin.

"I am," Mal agreed, "a fine honed weapon, and one far beyond your ken. Now speak."

"It was a sham," she replied hoarsely. "Your priest

wanted mercy for his temple in return for his service." Her grin was a rictus, savagery directed past Mal and Renault at the theists behind. "It was the work of a summer, his diplomacy. Pretty words and pretty gifts sent up the mountain, all for the sake of sparing his robed brothers."

"What service?" Orat demanded.

"Living so long amongst farmers has made you soft," she accused the theist. "You have forgotten the courage of your desert forefathers." She took a halting breath. "We meant to kill you anyway. Mercy is a flatlander concept. We will kill you, and when we take the white city we'll have the priest's gold as our own."

Renault turned abruptly away. Orat braced as if he'd suffered a physical blow. Tillion's whispers had grown to mutterings, he gripped his staff with both hands as he called on the one god for forgiveness. The Kingsman's breath stuttered in Avani's ear. Her arm, twisted back and up against her spine, was beginning to go numb. The sickness that had struck her when the king's party first entered Mal's chambers threatened again. She thought she might vomit.

"Desma," Mal said, "tell me. What service did the Masterhealer do the desert?"

Desma fought him as best she could. She was sand stock, born to wind and sun, scorning compassion and unafraid of death. Had it been a fair fight, she might have won. But Mal didn't skirmish with sword or spear. He took her mind, flaying knowledge from hidden places, exposing truths irrelevant and pertinent. Desma, who had no experience with sorcery, couldn't conceive of how to keep him back. Avani felt the woman's shame and despair as she failed beneath his onslaught, gave up everything to his demand.

"*Smashed like your bowl, turned over until there's nothing left worth saving,*" Cleena had said of the damage done to Halwn's kin. "*At least we kill your people cleanly.*"

"Mal?" Renault barked, impatient.

"Horses," Desma said, throat working. Green sparks fell from the tips of Mal's fingers. The soldiers, pale-faced, snuffed the sparks one at a time before they could set bedcovers alight. Tillion crossed himself shoulder-to-shoulder and throat to groin before falling on his knees in supplication. Orat stood amongst his slack-jawed priests, hunched.

"Strings and strings of ponies, led over the pass by this priest or that. Supplies, so we would not starve. Water, so we would not thirst." She gasped, groaned, and gasped again. "And the key! They gave us the key! The key to open the demon gates kept locked against invasion. We will rise up and—"

Mal silenced her with a twist of magic. She sagged on the mattress, eyes rolling in her head. Brother Orat had put his hand on the wall to keep from falling.

"We're doomed," he said. "May Paul rot; he's doomed us all for the sake of his pride."

CHAPTER 9

Three sturdy coastal ponies of the sort the *sidhe* had stolen from Galenos and his small party crested the west side of the cauldron near the tower. Four riders sat astride the ponies, looking as unsuited to their stout mounts as Everin had been. Horses of any sort were almost unheard of east of the mountain divide. Horses could not tolerate the desert's extreme temperatures or paucity of water. Instead tribes domesticated large, three-toed animals they called camels. Everin had ridden his share of camels in travel and during battle. He'd also seen a fine flatland stallion slaughtered for meat when the warrior who had won the animal in a game of dice decided the beautiful, high-strung beast was not worth the cost of upkeep.

"Desma!" The foremost rider, a lithe young woman with a bow strapped to her back and a long, fringed veil over her nose and mouth, whooped as she kicked her pony down into the bowl, racing along the lakeshore toward Everin and Drem. A lad no older than five or six rode behind her, clutching the back of her kilt for balance. The child was naked but for a loin-wrap and sandals. "You're alive! Bless!"

"Of a certain I am," Drem replied in the desert tongue. Drem's spear dug painfully into Everin's side, an admonishment. The magic that turned the lesser *sidhe* into the desert woman's twin through the bit of cord and stolen hair would provide Drem some insight into its role as doppelganger, but aside from language and a few, hazy, stolen memories, Drem's success relied on Drem's wits.

A lucky thing, Everin thought, as his own seemed to have fled in the face of a few desert snakes on fat coastal ponies, and he was unable to do more than stare at the approaching riders. But also concerning, for although the *sidhe* made regular study of mortals, the desert was outside their province.

The riders pulled up in front of Drem. The ponies' hooves scattered scree. Their leader wore a look of exasperated concern. Her grown companions, two men of—from the scant feathers in their hair and on their vests—low rank, watched impassively from the backs of their mounts. Spears and curved blades they had in plenty. Flaccid water skins hung from their saddles. One of the ponies had a twig of flatland scrub tangled in its blond tail.

A scouting party in truth, Everin thought.

"We were concerned when we found only corpses at the gathering place. What has happened?" The warrior and her small companion leaned forward, eyeing Everin through identical yellow eyes. "And what have you got there?"

"It went wrong." Drem twisted its spear until Everin grunted. "Galenos is dead, murdered. And the others."

There was silence, but for the wind above the edge of the cauldron whistling against the guard tower. The sky was growing dark. In the lake, something splashed. The lad stuck a fist in his mouth. The riders stared at Drem, mute.

"I killed them all," the *sidhe* continued calmly. "The priests, for their betrayal. It was a fine blood sacrifice. The ground ran red. Galenos would be pleased. I killed all but this one, he who dared end Galenos."

"The priests?" One of the men sputtered. "The priests killed Biton and Deon? *Iros?* The priests carry no weapons—they are cowards."

The Aug's sword still hung on Everin's belt, stuck now beneath his hip. He thought he could reach it in time to unhorse the closest rider. Mayhap the closest two. But the sand snakes were armed and wary. And the lad, now grinning toothlessly, was problematic. Everin wasn't a child-killer. Drem might be.

"Disguised as priests, but not all priests in truth," lied Drem. Any other time, Everin might have appreciated the irony. "Underneath their robes, some were like this one. Dangerous." Drem kicked Everin forcefully in the thigh.

The second silence weighed heavier than the first. The child gurgled. Everin counted weapons: three scimitars, two spears, and the small but powerful-looking bow on the woman's back.

"We found the remains of a demon on the trail. One of the *sidhe* beasts." The man could not quite make his mouth fit *Tuath* vowels. "Trampled into the mud like so much dung."

Drem said nothing.

"What weapon is that," asked the woman, "in your hand, Desma? Where is your sword?"

Shit, thought Everin. Drem's spear was pointed bronze on a wooden shaft, clear even in the fading light. It was not a desert weapon, nor even a flatlander's iron pike. He braced himself.

"Mine was lost," Drem replied, unmoved. "In the slaughter."

"Lydus," snapped the leader. On her order one of the warriors stretched forward, offering his own curved sword to Drem. Steel glinted. It was a lovely piece of craftsmanship: embroidered horses ran the length of the silk wrapped pommel and, engraved, onto the blade.

Even Faolan's magic could not protect Drem from the threat of iron.

Drem refused the blade.

"Flatlander sorcery. Kill them," the warrior said, triumphant. She plucked free her bow and nocked an arrow with a speed that rivaled *sidhe* haste. The child clutched her middle. Her arrow struck the rocky ground where an instant before Drem had been standing. She snarled at the bounding *sidhe*. "Desma and Galenos pledged to die as they were born: together. She would never walk away from his corpse. Whatever you are, you are not our Desma."

By the time Everin rolled to his feet, sword drawn, the one called Lydus was already unhorsed, Drem's spear through his chest, heart's blood running along the slope toward the lake. Drem, weaponless, dodged the second man's attack, ducking down and around the startled pony, which snorted affront but did not spook.

Iridescent fletching whistled through the air. Everin rolled in time to avoid a volley of arrows. He came up in front of the snake and her lad, grabbing at the thin saddle. She rode the pony in the way she might a camel, without stirrups for balance. She kicked at him as he clung, dropping her bow and reaching for the gleam of steel on her belt. The child began to cry. Everin could not make himself cut her down; the Aug's sword was useless in his hand.

"*Tá sí ár n-namhaid,*" Drem shouted. *She is our enemy.* The lesser *sidhe* moved on the edge of Everin's vision, inhuman speed turning the Desma masquerade grotesque. "*Bhaint amach a ceann!*" *Strike off her head!*

The warrior looked into Everin's face as he clung to her stocky mount. She laughed. "Fool," she said, and brought her dirk down.

He let go at the last second, sliding in scree. The pony, stumbling, struck him a glancing blow on the thigh where Drem had so recently kicked him. He swore. When he sat upright, the woman and her child were galloping away down the mountain, the pony's tail flagging as it maneuvered the steep trail.

"You," said Drem, coming to squat at his side, bloodied spear again in hand, "would have made a laughable king. Faolan did the flatlanders a favor in negotiating your exile."

Everin looked at the two men who now lay dead on the rocks in the gathering shadow. Their mounts, nonchalant, nosed dangerously close to the necromancers' black vine.

"She's gone for aid," he guessed, rising and sheathing his sword. "Time to move." Limping, he approached one of the dead men. "Help me strip him."

Everin rolled the warrior's kilt and vest and sandals into a bundle and tucked it under his arm. He retrieved the heavy veil from around the man's neck then grabbed the horse-etched scimitar from the ground.

"You'll need that." He indicated a feather-hung spear. "Your own won't do once we're below. I'll carry it for the nonce. And also the lens, and the veil, there, from her head. We'll want it all, I think."

Drem complied without comment, snatching up the steel-tipped spear and tossing it Everin's way. Thus laden, Everin stepped over the eastern edge of Skerrit's Pass and onto the mountain. Drem followed. The trailhead had not changed since last Everin stepped upon it. Wide enough for a single horse pulling a tinker's cart, a camel hauling a bundled tent, or two men side by side, it pitched straight down the side of the mountain. An uninformed traveler might balk at the precarious course and look for a more gradual way down the cliff face but Everin knew better. Repeated use over time had culled loose rock and pitfalls from the path; scorpions, serpents, and boar tended to avoid places regularly tainted with human spoor. And the mountain to either side of the trail was unreliable, subject to rockslides and hidden fissures.

The *dullahan* had not been wrong. Any wayfarer so foolish as to step off the trail was likely to meet a precipitous end.

"And when she returns with companions?" asked Drem. "What then?"

"It will be full dark very soon." Already Everin had to step warily. The worn path was becoming a stripe of silver in flat black. "Time is on our side. Even once the moon rises, they won't dare the mountain. We're not worth the risk. A man on these cliffs after sunset? He risks reliable death."

"Reliable death," echoed Drem, dry. "Have you no fear of falling, yourself?"

"Unless I have forgotten: sun or moon, it makes no difference to the people of the mounds."

"You have not forgotten," replied the *sidhe*. "We prefer the dark to the light, and blame the flatlanders for it."

"Blame can be shifted." Everin waved a hand. "Go on ahead, then. I'm trusting you to keep me safe."

One quarter of the way down the mountain, on a relatively level outcrop Everin recognized by an old rock formation in the shape of a broken arch, they stopped to rest. The place on Everin's ribs where Drem's spear had left a bruise, and on his thigh where Drem's foot had left another, ached fiercely. His knees and ankles, no longer so spry as when he'd first attempted the ascent some thirty years earlier, protested the sharp incline. And his voice, capricious in the aftermath of his cut throat, had retreated to a grating whisper. Every time it failed him for longer than a short while, he worried it was gone for good, in spite of Faolan's restorative magics.

He was not a vain man, but he thought he would not like to live the rest of his life so silenced. And he cursed himself for a coward.

An indolent stream trickled alongside the trail before falling beneath the arch to unseen depths below. While Drem refilled their water skins, Everin changed out of flatlander tunic and trousers and into

purloined desert kit. The kilt fit him as it was supposed to, hanging low on his hips and falling in pleats
to just past his knees. He had to loosen the laces in the
vest, and the snakeskin chafed uncomfortably along
his ribs, but it would do. He tied on the dead man's
sandals and slung the scimitar in its embroidered
sheath over one shoulder.

Down below, the tribes were alive in the night,
campfires twinkling, the far-off sound of many voices
rising and falling with the wind. The air was warming as they dropped out of the pass, although not
by much. The desert, viciously hot during the day,
cooled rapidly after sunset. Everin paused to stand
still and listen; when the wind ebbed, bush crickets
sang from the dubious shelter of scrub and rock. He
could hear the stream splashing down along the cliff
face, the scratch of something small, likely a squirrel, crossing sand ahead of them on the trail, and the
warble of waking goatsucker birds.

"The moon will show its face soon," Drem said. "I
would like to be on the ground before there is enough
light to shoot us off the cliff face."

Everin grunted. Anticipation made the hair stand
up on his forearms. The promise of white sand again
beneath his feet after so long a time woke a song in
his heart to rival the stirring night birds.

Drem, who could come and go unnoticed in daylight, was an adroit guide. The lesser *sidhe* never
strayed more than four steps ahead of Everin on the

path, and often reached out to direct him around a rough spot in the ground or away from a precipitous edge. Drem's fingers were cold on Everin's wrist and did not linger long. It did not speak; it did not need to. Everin's body recalled an endless eventide spent in *sidhe* barrows, the ways and means of living in a twilight world, often with only a *sidhe* guard to lead him safely from place to place under the earth.

He was not afraid. Drem would not let him fall. Drem *could* not let him fall, any more than Drem's kin could have let him wander at will in the hidden kingdom.

Halfway down the mountain, the moon rising in the east, they hit a patch of loose sand. Drem leapt straight into the air as the ground slid beneath their feet. Everin managed to keep his balance, but only by the skin of his teeth. The sand became a small torrent, ankle deep, and he could not seem to find purchase beneath. Swearing, he slipped inexorably forward down the cliff face. There was just enough light now to see where the ground was, but not ahead to where it was not. He plunged his spear point-first into the mountain to one side of the sliding earth. The spear stuck. Everin clutched the haft. His feet went out from under him.

"Don't let go," Drem advised helpfully. The *sidhe* clung spiderlike to the sheer rock face above Everin's head. Everin lay on his back as the sand hissed around him, a landed fish in a rushing river, the muscles in his arms straining. "You neglected to mention the way down was snared."

Everin waited until the avalanche had passed them by before responding. "It wasn't last I walked it." There was sand in his mouth, between his teeth, in his ears and hair, in his eyes, and in places beneath his kilt he preferred not to think of. Slowly, he let go of the spear and sat up. The ground, thankfully, stayed steady beneath his arse. "Why would it be? Tinkers and traders come this way regularly."

Drem dropped off the wall. It dusted sand from Everin's head and shoulders, then helped him stand. "Someone's been telling the tinkers and traders where not to tread, I think." It wiggled Everin's spear out of the mountain, avoiding the steel tip. "Hand on my shoulder, now. The rest of the way, you step where I step."

They moved at a slug's pace after, both testing the ground ahead with spear point as they descended. The horizon brightened to gray. The moon was a silver orb over the desert, blotting stars above and campfires below. The trail gentled as the mountain became less steep. Everin glimpsed the foothills not far ahead. The stream, having followed them most of the way down the peak, dried up. They edged past the remains of a tinker's cart, smashed to pieces, buried in sand. Dragged off an overhead bluff, Everin realized, by the same sand trap that had tried to spit him off the cliff. A skeleton lay on its back nearby, picked-over bones shining in the moonlight.

"Bad luck," said Drem, deadpan, and it inched on.

The wind picked up as they left the heights, blowing sand in spirals around their knees and, on the occasional angry gust, into their faces. Everin tied the sand snake's veil over his nose and mouth, and low over his eyebrows for protection. His hands still knew the way of the complicated knots.

"At least," he said, "the wind will prevent their shooting, if they're so unwise as to leave their tents in this weather for two strangers on a mountaintop. We are two against ten thousand, and as apt to fall prey to snares as the tinker." Drem's head was bowed against the flying grit; Desma's strong shoulders rounded in defiance, blue feathers fluttering in dark hair. "Be grateful it is night and cool. In the heat of day, I'd fear sandstorm."

"Sand, sun, heat," replied Drem, droll, "scorpions. I fear them each equally." The lesser *sidhe's* self-mockery looked out of place on Desma's stern features.

The foothills were more extensive than they appeared, and a longer climb than Everin had let himself recall. He remembered the dangerous descent down the cliff face as being the worst of it, but in truth it was the gradual unfurling down to the desert floor that made him regret Skerrit's Pass. The moon set and the horizon turned orange with incipient dawn. They lost the path in scrub and blowing sand. Where the mountain met lowlands the ground was a series of jagged ribs, a march of shallow canyons one after another until, at last, fissures lengthened into desert. The tribes called the foothills Shoat's Wash, for the wild pigs that ran there in the summer season. During the winter rains the Wash often flooded and was unsafe for habitation, but when the weather was fine, the canyons were busy with huntsmen in search of boar.

Everin doubted there were boar enough in all the desert, let alone Shoat's Wash, to feed the army squatting nearby. He could hear camp sounds clearly now—shouts and laughter, the call of camels disturbed by the rising sun, the rattle of teakettles and feed buckets. The canyons obscured much of the desert floor, but the wind blew rising smoke overhead, and with it the stink of many people living in close quarters: sewage, sweat, smoked meat, animals, and the too-sweet perfume of opion gum smoked in pipes.

"Riders," said Drem suddenly. "Coming up the hills."

Everin saw only crag and low-lying brush, but he didn't doubt the *sidhe*'s exceptional senses. They ducked into a gulley behind a large growth of sage broom plant. Little more than a trench scraped into the earth by repetitive flooding, the deep crack was one of many along the wash. An acacia tree shaded the depression. Dawn had not yet reached the bottom of the trench through its twisted branches. They lay on their bellies in blue shadows, breath held. Everin felt the beat of hooves through the sandstone and up into his teeth, a growing thunder.

The riders passed in a sprint, ponies held back from a gallop to a fast trot, kicking up a shower of sand and pebble. It was not a small company: fifteen sand snakes wrapped against the wind, veils and kilts trailing, indistinguishable from one another. They charged up the foothills toward the cliff face, contesting the rising sun. Two long-legged, slender hunting dogs ranged in the rear. Their handler, horseless, jogged at the end of leather leashes. The leashes, like the warriors, were decorated with trophy feathers. Strips of fabric shrouded the dogs' eyes from grit; they relied on their sensitive noses and their handler's whistled commands for navigation. Although not blind in truth, the dogs were trained up from pups to hunt as if they were.

The company passed quickly. The dogs did not. They stopped abruptly, curly tails waving in excitement. They snuffed the ground, weaving from side to side along the trail, chasing scent. When they drifted inexorably toward Everin and Drem and the shaded gulley, Everin knew the game was up. Many a desert scoundrel had been brought to justice by a sand lord's well-trained coursing pair.

The dogs paused on the other side of the sage broom, noses pointed at the gulley. Their tails stilled. They grumbled, but without conviction. Drem growled back. The dogs jumped away, tails pressed between their long legs. Their handler tugged on their leashes, whistling them on up the mountain, sparing little thought for what might lie beneath the acacia tree. Dogs sent to hunt down a man would not be distressed upon finding his scent and were expected to react with caution in the presence of scorpion, serpent, or fox. Their handlers would have no experience with the nervous aversion most animals displayed when confronted with *sidhe*.

You'll be glad of me, Drem had said. Twice in a span of hours that prediction had proven sound.

When the sound of hoofbeats faded and the dogs were well out of sight, Drem stirred, sitting up out of the sand. The veil over Desma's mouth puffed outward on a sigh.

"They seem overly concerned with two strangers on a mountain," it said, borrowed yellow eyes glinting. "What now?"

Everin heaved himself out of the gulley. They had been walking a full night. He was weary. Where his body didn't hurt, it itched from sand. Anticipation had left him. It was occurring to him that they were unlikely to reach the *sidhe* gate without the need for bloodshed. The possibility that they would reach the gate intact seemed less certain than it had at sunset. He felt his age as he had not since his last days living with the *Tuath Dé*.

"The ponies are a puzzle," he worried. "They haven't made sense from the beginning. Coastal stock, ridden by an inland people who would eat a horse before wasting water on its upkeep. The ponies make no sense to me at all."

Disturbed by their presence, a dust-colored serpent slithered around acacia roots. Drem blinked, and took it through the head with the point of its spear, exactly as Everin had taught the *sidhe* and its kin, Bail, days earlier. The serpent was dead before Drem plucked its body from the blade. Drem brushed cloth from its mouth and neatly bit off the snake's head. Juices ran down Desma's chin. It chewed vigorously, then ran a startlingly blunt human tongue over Desma's even teeth, cleaning away bits of meat.

"Skald's balls," Everin groaned.

Ignoring Everin's tired revulsion, Drem snapped down the serpent in three more bites, then wiped sticky hands on its kilt. "What now?" it repeated.

To Everin's embarrassment, his stomach grumbled hollow protest. Raw serpent was no better than raw fish, but they'd not eaten since they'd fried lake trout in the tinker's hollow, and his gut cared only that it was empty. It didn't escape his notice that Drem had, this time, neglected to share.

"We continue on," Everin replied grimly. "But as sand snakes, desert warriors in truth, no more dodging, no more hiding. Which means you cannot be Desma. Not if Desma is recognizable." He stalked Drem, circling once around the *sidhe*, and then again, brows lowered. "Wrap your face again, all but your eyes. I'll do the same. No one will question covered faces, not in this wind." He demonstrated, winding the veil across the crown of his head and then three times over his face, securing it at the back of his neck and tucking the ends into the sleeves of his vest. "The feathers have to go." Using his belt knife, he cut the plumage from Desma's tangled hair. The matted locks and pinions felt tangible under his fingers, but each time he severed a dark strand from Drem's head, feather and hair disintegrated in his hand, an illusion broken.

"Also the tattoos." Everin frowned at the family marks on Desma's arms, belly, and thighs, wondering if they, too, could be scrubbed away like so much smoke. "Even more than the feathers, they signify household and rank."

"Touch my flesh with your iron and I will cut off your hand for the offense." The thrice-wrapped veil did little to muffle Drem's swift animosity.

"*Sidhe* justice," Everin agreed. "I have not forgotten Desma's broken hands. But I have a better idea, and one that does not require retribution." Sitting on his heels in the sand, he used his blade to scar the acacia, cutting through bark and into soft wood to the viscous brown sap within. He scooped a thimble-ful of the gummy substance onto his palm, added sand, and spat twice into the mixture before blending it rapidly with the tip of one finger. The end result was a satisfying, sticky potion slightly darker than desert dust.

"Acacia gum," Everin explained. "One hundred uses. A potter I knew used it in his glaze. Cover the marks." Everin scooped the mess into Drem's hand. "I'll make more."

They worked quickly, wary of interruption. Drem painted Everin's glaze over the tattoos on Desma's dark skin. Everin daubed the stain where the *sidhe* could not reach. It was a temporary solution, and left Drem looking begrimed and displeased, but it did the job, obscuring Desma's markings completely.

"If it itches," Everin cautioned, smearing more of the gum on his own skin to match, "leave it be. They will not question an unwashed traveler—when one is away from home, water is for drinking."

"They?"

"The first tent we come to, that I deem safe to ap-proach." Everin hefted the steel-tipped desert spear. "This is your weapon now. We are not *sidhe* and flat-lander, we are two weary scouts looking for shelter from the sun before we make report to our lord. Speak little; let me ask and answer questions."

Drem accepted the spear. Faolan's illusion shivered briefly in the proximity of steel, but held. Everin did not dare wonder if it would continue to endure amongst a forest of similar weapons. Drem, too, would suffer. Iron sickness was an inescapable curse, an affliction that brought even the strongest *sidhe* elders to their knees.

"We won't tarry," Everin said. "Gather what information we can and then back over the mountain."

Drem smiled, twisting Desma's mouth into an enthusiastic leer. "And mayhap," it said, "some amusement in between."

CHAPTER 10

Mal sprawled in the chair behind his desk, eyes closed, head tilted toward the open windows, and walked with Avani as she tossed her most precious possessions into the old journey bag she had carried all the way from Stonehill. A jug of good red wine sat on his desk next to a fine silver goblet. The goblet was empty. The jug was mostly so.

The aftertaste of drink lingered on his tongue, and on Avani's, although if she were as tipsy as Mal—and he thought she might be—it was his fault, for she had consumed nothing but spring water from the goblet near her loom.

Running solves nothing, he said, as she spun about her chambers, wadding her favorite salwar and slippers into a tidy ball for packing. *I never took you for craven.*

I am not craven. She didn't want him in her head, but Mal thought they had moved beyond the point where they could force each other out, and he was selfishly glad of it. *I am not running. I'm leaving. While I still can; while I still recognize right from wrong.*

She was thinking of violation as she stuffed her medicinal kit into her bag. Mal's wine-addled stomach rolled.

I am no rapist. The force of his indignation made them both flinch. He took a deep breath. *I thought . . . I know . . . you wanted that as much as I.* It had been a long time in coming. Longer, mayhap, then they wanted to admit.

She didn't pretend not to understand. Avani strived toward honesty, even when she was livid. She stood in the middle of her chamber, a length of silk hanging between her fingers. She closed her eyes and they were alone in the darkness behind her lids.

You and I, yes, she granted him. *But the woman— Desma—had no choice in the matter. Nor the sidhe. You turned them inside out, took everything they had, and left them in pieces. It was evil.*

It was necessary. He did not understand her renewed distaste even as it became his own. Not understanding made him surly. Her repugnance became his self-revulsion. *I thought you had come to realize, while I was away, when you worked in my place. We are born to serve the throne.*

You've been telling yourself that, have you, since your

*father sent you away for setting Selkirk's temple afire?
Wilhaiim needs you, so Wilhaiim comes first, no matter
the consequences. You're so desperate to be needed, Mal,
you can't see past the empty hole in your heart. Damn
your father for that. He ruined you before you were even
begun.*

*Deep water didn't turn you mad, you were born an
abomination.* His self-revulsion became her con-
demnation. They were caught together in a ring of
acrimony, unable to escape, unable to separate themselves from the tangle of Mal's regrets.

Mal snarled. The wine jug crashed from his desk
to the floor. Several chambers away, Avani yanked
too hard on Kate's strand of rubies and the string
broke, sending raw stones showering over her feet.

Avani sucked in air, let it out again. "The wine
doesn't help," she said out loud to the empty room.

If he were less drunk, he thought he could get
around those last standing walls, have every final
piece of her for his own. If he were sober, he knew he
could make her give up those final pieces willingly.

"Shit." He opened his eyes, saw the rough surface
of his desk instead of Avani's cozy bedchamber. "I am
not . . ." *That.*

*Is there any way to end this, this thing we've woven be-
tween us?*

Between his hands the surface of his desk was pep-
pered with red droplets of spilled wine. "I don't know.
If there were, could you?"

Her answer was a long time coming, although he saw the truth of it right away.

"Nay," Avani confessed, bundling the Goddess idol in silk for travel. "It's too late for that. For better or for worse, we're bound. For worse, I think, and they'll come for us with torches."

"I won't let that happen," Mal promised. Wine and relief made him bold. "I'll keep us safe."

I don't want your help. She wasn't lying. She slung her bag over her shoulder, cradled the Goddess in her arms. *I won't be your excuse.*

"Where will you go?" It was hard, so hard, not to seize the answer before she offered it. He clenched his teeth and reached for wine, then recalled the jug was on the floor.

You'll know when I do. She wasn't quite good enough to shield him from her bitterness. He thought she was being unfair. Why was he any less welcome than Jacob, who nested always in her heart?

You're tipsy and making no sense at all. Her flash of temper said he'd hit a nerve; he felt very clever for the success. *I've no wish to share in your intoxication. Go away.*

Avani pushed him out of her head. The spell was well done, a variation on one of his own vanishing cants. Probably she didn't realize she'd taken the crafting of it from his internal repertoire, and without his permission. If she did know, would she be as ashamed of her own violation as she was his?

Pot, he thought loudly, rubbing the bridge of his nose, *meet kettle.*

Avani didn't answer.

Mal dozed for a time at his desk. He dreamed of the sea and of screaming gulls and of Rowan, his brother, piloting a ship full of dead children. When he startled awake again, his head ached viciously. He cursed the good red wine even as he mopped its remnants from his desk and the floor. His joints popped protest at the work, his body objecting to years of long hours and ill-use.

Desma lived, but just barely. He'd used her spirit to sustain the spells that forced her to speak truths she meant to keep secret. Her life force was badly depleted, her star fading. It was Faolan's tampering that kept Desma breathing. Whatever *sidhe* magics the Faolan had used to repair her broken body on Skerrit's Pass was older and stronger than necromancy. Even her hands, so terribly damaged, were growing whole again, bone knitting and flesh scabbing, a curative made stronger by Faolan's enchantment and Avani's healing sorceries. Mal had loosened the bindings and splints, recaptured Avani's maggot friends, but too late. There was not enough spirit left within Desma to appreciate the continuing marvel. She was dying as her body recovered.

"Desma, daughter of the sand—" Mal looked

down on her pallid form "—an evil man would cut you open to see what sort of enchantment keeps a lifeless husk breathing. As I am *not* an evil man. I'll wait you out and give your body to the wind with proper blood sacrifice, as befits your rank." The tattoos, he thought, were quite impressive. As were the memories he'd purloined for Renault's sake. Desma had been brave, and accomplished. She'd loved her twin more than she'd loved any other, and she'd been ready to join him in death.

He'd taken that from her. There would be no afterlife for Desma, no haunt left to walk the halls or be welcomed by the god she favored. Except for a feeble, struggling ember, Desma was gone. He could take that spark, too, use it to ward off the aftereffects of too much wine drunk too quickly. She'd never know to miss it. Temptation made him lick his lips.

He hesitated, then turned away. Abandoning the dais, he flung his cape around his shoulders and pulled on his gloves. He snuffed the last of the lanterns as he left the room, securing the door with a cant behind him. He expected he'd find a cooling corpse in his bed whenever he returned.

Upon Baldebert's arrival in Wilhaiim, Renault had ordered Roue's admiral and his royal contingent housed in one of the palace's more ancient wings, as far away from court as workability allowed. There were many in the city and beyond who wished Baldebert executed for kidnapping the one man who might have stopped the Red Worm plague at its beginnings and prevented the loss of a generation. In stealing away Wilhaiim's vocent for Roue's use, Baldebert had committed an act of war. Because Baldebert had—albeit unknowingly—left Wilhaiim without an experienced magus during plague season, the decimation of many a flatland family lay squarely on his shoulders. Avani had done her best in Mal's absence, but the Red Worm had taken more victims than Avani had saved.

Baldebert's pledge of troops and artillery to aid Wilhaiim against the desert meant nothing to parents mourning their dead children. And the theists, who themselves feared a foreign queen, were doing their outmost to fan the flames of hatred. Brother Tillion's impassioned rhetoric had taken hold during summer months, as inexorable as any plague. The Rani, if she ever dared cross the Long Sea to her new husband's side, would not be celebrated—far from it.

Mal hoped Baldebert had taken it upon himself to warn the Rani of Wilhaiim's discontent, but he suspected Roue's queen, like her brother the admiral, would not be kept form any duty she believed essential. Baldebert had not survived years on dangerous waters through timidity. The man was, at his core, a pirate and a fearless romantic—willing to sacrifice all for the good of his sibling and her tiny principality.

Which, as far as Mal was concerned, made Balde-bert a near-perfect conspirator in roguery.

The palace's oldest corridors were quiet, empty. Torches burned without heat or smoke. Carpets and wall hangings were clean but visibly worn. Renault's great-great-grandmother, Queen Elodie, gowned all in silver brocade, looked down on Mal from a mouse-eaten tapestry, clutching a posy against her breast. Elodie was remembered as a queen who loved her station more than her people, intelligent but quick to anger and slow to forgive. Mal, who knew her as the mother who had traded her firstborn son to the *sidhe*, was not surprised to find her likeness hidden away in a vacant part of the castle. Renault did not speak of her often.

A Kingsman stood guard outside Baldebert's rooms. When she saw Mal, she straightened, her mouth tightening in resignation, and stepped squarely in front of the door.

"Russel." Mal awarded her a mocking bow. "Back on nursery duty, I see. Renault told me you had some trouble in Whitcomb. Too bad."

"He's busy," Russel snapped. She was one of few in all Wilhaiim who believed Mal contemptible instead of frightening. Most of the time he found her refreshing. "Not to be disturbed."

Mal let his eyebrows rise ceilingward. "Not lost him again, have you? He's snuck out the back, mayhap?

I swear the man's impossible to keep track of. Doesn't make your job simple, does he?"

Russel wouldn't be baited. "He's safely within, my lord. Only he asked not to be disturbed by any but the king's private messengers."

"Not sent to Whore's Street again, has he? A princely appetite indeed. No matter. I assure you, I'm not easily shocked." Mal stepped toward the door. Russel blocked him with her pike, expression determined.

Mal laughed. "Corporal, I *am* the king's messenger, in every way that matters."

"He isn't expecting you. I'll tell him you stopped by. My lord."

Mal rocked back on his boot heels. This wasn't Russel's usual game of one-upmanship. She had been tasked with keeping him out. And not just any visitor knocking up Baldebert's chambers, but Mal specifically.

"Corporal."

"Aye, my lord?"

"I can make you let me in."

Russel swallowed. The helm she wore hid her eyes but not her clenching jaw. "I'm aware, my lord. But without the admiral's permission, or His Majesty's missive, it's my duty to try to stop you. In case, my lord, you mean Admiral Baldebert harm."

"Move aside, Russel." Mal summoned a wisp of power. Behind him in the hall the ghost of a long-forgotten groundskeeper, ambling along the wall, insubstantial garden trowel in hand, winked out of existence. Mal curled a finger. Russel's sword, untouched, rattled angrily on her hip.

Russel didn't flinch. "Do as you like, my lord. I won't be forsworn. I've given oath to the throne and, for the throne's sake, to Baldebert, but I've never sworn any oath to you that I recall."

"I can see," said Mal, "why Avani likes you."

"I can't," returned Russel, "in all honesty say the same of you, my lord." She clapped a hand on the pommel of her sword to stop its furious dancing.

The door to Baldebert's chamber burst open, saving Russel from Mal's affront.

"Corporal! What's all the bloody racket? Oh. It's you, is it, Doyle?"

Mal crossed his arms over his chest. If he'd ever learned the redheaded sailor's name, he didn't recall it now, but he well knew her face. She shared his own curse of a broken nose healed crooked. She was an officer, once in charge of the living engine in Baldebert's *The Cutlass Wind*, and a slave. She wore gold in her ears, on her fingers, and her toes, and the iron torque of servitude around her neck. Mal had set her broken collarbone on shipboard, and later she'd sat on his chest when, raving, he'd murdered Baldebert's first mate and tried to do worse after.

"You look awful," the officer said. Mal couldn't tell whether she was pleased or sympathetic. "Come in, then, but don't make any sudden moves. My men haven't forgotten what you are. Best not meet anyone's eye too close, eh, necromancer?"

Dismissing Russel with a jerk of her chin, she led Mal into a room more window than stone. Three of the four walls and the rectangular, slanted roof were naught but a latticework of glass. The panes were clean, clear as to be almost invisible, a wall of light. The brilliance did nothing to help Mal's aching head. The sky above the glass ceiling was cloudless. For all that the room should be an oven, no heat breached the glass. The air in the orangery was artificially mild, kept so by a shard of bone mortared into the floor and the old magic attached to it.

"This way. Captain's spent the morning on correspondence, but I've just brought him a spot of tea in the garden. Can't say he'll be glad to see you. I suppose you guessed that."

Baldebert's mariners had made the glass room their own. Bedding and rucksacks cluttered the floor, obscuring antique, azure-tinted tile. Two men sat together, cross-legged, on a battered chaise, a map spread between them. A third crouched nearby, idly rolling dice. They looked up when Mal entered the orangery. The dice player crossed himself. His two companions looked away.

An incongruous collection of thick rope, scarves, and sashes hung from myriad hooks on the interior stone wall. Someone had been mending leather armor. A small pile of cuirasses, smelling of oil, sat atop a table. A single white conch shell crowned a stack of books. A keg of Rouen beer waited, untapped, next to a picked-over platter of meat and cheese.

The redheaded officer led Mal through a door cleverly concealed in the glass wall. Outside in the attached garden sparrows darted between the branches of two old sycamores and landed on the manicured lawn. Late season flowers still bloomed in beds along the periphery: coneflower, blue aster, and phlox. A Selkirk rose, pink blossoms withered to fat black rose hips, grew along a tall hedge. Mal was surprised to see the specimen alive and thriving so far from the coast.

Baldebert sat on a rug spread beneath the trees, legs crossed in the fashion of his men. A silver pot of tea steamed at his right hand, an inkpot and scroll stand rested at his left. He did not appear pleased at the interruption.

"Sorry, Captain. This one made enough racket at the door to raise the kraken and I feared he'd boil our corporal where she stood if I didn't let him through the door."

Mal flashed his best baleful glare the officer's way.

"Thank you." Baldebert stabbed a silver-tipped stylus into his inkpot. "You're excused." He waited until the redhead had returned to the orangery then leaned back on his palms, regarding Mal with displeasure. "What do you want?"

"I think you know," replied Mal. He nudged the edge of Baldebert's rug with the side of his boot, stirring scrolls. "Best not speak it out loud; these days even the hedges have ears."

"If I'm to believe my own spies, the hedges are full of temple conspirators." Baldebert poured out dark brew into a pretty tea cup. He sipped, watching Mal through hooded yellow eyes. "She was of use, I'm told, our desert wolf."

"Thanks to Brother Paul's machinations, they've access to *sidhe* ways under the mountains and incentive enough to make the journey. The tribes have rallied under a single banner—for the moment they're of one mind. They've no reason to wait out winter on the pass. As we've suspected, they're coming now."

"Demon roads eschew mortal laws. 'Now' could mean today or in a fortnight." Baldebert swirled his drink. He tilted his head, indicating ink and scroll. "*The Cutlass Wind* is the fastest of my ships, and she is here. My sister writes that she has sent our three second fastest, heavy with elephant guns, gun powder, and many good men, but they will not make land for another six weeks, at the earliest."

"There is more," Mal confessed. "Desma's uncle and cousins are traveling north and west to join troops marshalling again near Roue. Khorit Dard is dead, but the desert has not yet given up on gold and opion."

Baldebert flapped a dismissive hand. "Four seasons, mayhap five, before they are number enough to attack Roue again. We will be ready."

"If you say so. Best write the Rani now and let her know she'll be handling the next invasion without you. If ten thousand desert warriors come swarming out of the ground tomorrow, Wilhaiim will be nothing but a memory, and your sister will be without allies or admiral."

Baldebert pressed his lips together. He set down his cup. "I begin to regret the day I decided stealing away Wilhaiim's magus was a clever idea."

"Reap what you sow, Admiral. We saved Roue once. We'll do it again, but first mine own people."

"Your solution is no solution."

"It will work. We have five. Parts for more. I know a capable blacksmith who could be convinced—"

"I think, Doyle," interrupted Baldebert harshly, "that Brother Paul might have said much the same thing to your dead armswoman and her farmer friend when convincing them to commit treason. For all the right reasons, I'm sure."

Mal loomed but intimidation did not work on Roue's pirate prince. Entreaty might.

"Paul was no magus. The Automata are my birthright. I can make them walk again. One iron man is worth one thousand living soldiers. Eight, nine may save us."

"You've never been to war."

"Which is why I need you."

"Even if it works, they'll burn you alive, after."

"Let them. Your redheaded guard dog was not wrong when she said I was a breath away from taking Russel out of this world. I am not the man I was a year ago. Easy to blame a journey over deep water, but I begin to think a magus is born flawed. It takes only time to strike that fracture all the way through."

"And what am I, if I agree to a madman's cockeyed plan?" demanded Baldebert, scrubbing his curls in exasperation.

Mal smiled. The game was won. "Prudent. You trusted me to save your ship, and your sister's kingdom," he said. "Trust me one last time."

Baldebert rose from his blanket. He made a show of dusting off his sailor's trousers and loose shirt. His fingers lingered on the ivory cuffs hanging always from his belt. Then he essayed a half bow and held out that same hand for Mal to shake, a promise made.

"Your 'capable blacksmith' takes Orat's coin," he said, lips curving. "I've a man on my ship knows his way around forge and anvil, and we can trust him to keep our secret safe."

The Mabon tree was a beautiful specimen. Almost as tall as the nearby barrack's tower, it wore its years in the circumference of its wide, smooth trunk and in the spread of its boughs. Mal stood in the shelter of its branches, orange needles fanned above his head and spread, dropped, on the ground below his feet, colorful as one of Avani's rugs. He retrieved a handful of shed needles from around the trunk, crushing them in gloved fingers, inhaling their pungent scent. It was the perfume of harvest festival, when day and night hung in balance, and every villein prepared for winter. The orange-needled branches were burned in iron baskets outside the palace, and on the king's hearth, and in the Wilhaiim's temple; the tree's sap made the flames jump with uncommon rainbow color.

Poorer houses burned evergreen or sheaves of wheat as an appeal to the one god, in hopes that he might keep the coming longer nights at bay. The dark hours came anyway but the memories of a good Mabon festival might keep a person warm until Winter Ceilidh came around again.

Mal had recognized the tree through Jacob's eyes. It hadn't been difficult to find, one ruddy tree growing tall above a green canopy. He'd come on it through the Royal Gardens, avoiding the barrack's entrance. The knot of woods where Liam and his young friends had been chased by Holder's straw men was calm now, birds and small animals dozing in the waning afternoon. Mal's feet made no sound in the thick underbrush. He was practiced at sneaking. Thanks to a concealment cant, even the fox drowsing under a gorse bush didn't notice his passing.

But Jacob was no longer in the Mabon tree. A vole

nested in the trunk near the tree's crown, and many tiny insects made homes in its branches. If Mal closed his eyes he could track their scurrying in his head, streaks of light, insignificant glimmers compared to the greater flare of the fox under the gorse and the small suns that were three pages playing at stick fighting in the barrack's courtyard. Wherever the raven had gone, he was no longer anywhere close. It would be difficult, although not impossible, to separate the bird from the buzz of radiance that was Wilhaiim entire.

Mal uncurled his fingers and let aromatic needles fall from his hand.

One meager spirit out of the many refused to be ignored. It had followed Mal from the bailey and through the Royal Gardens at a distance, always chary of coming too close, but tenacious in pursuit. Human, and unusual in that it faded and then dazzled, only to ebb and burst forth again. Mal, gripped by curiosity, had done nothing to end the chase. He'd increased and decreased his pace through the gardens, stopping beside a burbling fountain when the distance stretched, or lengthening his stride when the stalker grew too near. It was an exercise in patience, a distraction from disquiet. Mal had been trained in the contest of cat and mouse; his adversary obviously had not.

Now, standing under orange branches, Mal decided to bring the diversion to a close. He left the

Mabon tree, circling back into the woods, verdant shadows conjured close, further cloaking his shape. He reversed his track. Sunlight filtered through the canopy above his head. A pheasant, long tail bobbing, dashed across his path. It did not notice Mal.

He heard the faint thump of wood on brush before he saw the man. He thought he knew then. He breathed air through his nose, testing, and scented temple incense. The flicker and fade of his opponent took on new significance. He stepped out into the open, let the concealment spells drop, met Brother Tillion in a widening patch of sunlight.

"Oh!" Tillion gasped. He froze midstride, one bare foot lifted off the ground, and would have toppled had not Mal grasped his shoulder. "Oh. You startled me."

"Surely not," replied Mal. "You've been following me since I left court. You must have supposed I'd take notice eventually."

Tillion gathered his dignity. He stepped away from Mal, leaning instead on his ever-present staff. The theist was sweating although the day was mild and it was cool within the woods. He stared everywhere but at Mal's face, blinking owlishly as he considered his bare toes, a nearby thicket, a squirrel watching from an overhead branch. Mal, who had seen the priest address rapt crowds from atop his makeshift pedestal, could not quite equate the frightened man before him with the vivid preacher in the bailey.

Despite himself, he felt a pang of empathy. Tillion

might be a self-proclaimed enemy of the throne, but it was apparent he suffered adversity of his own.

"What can I do for you, Brother Tillion?" Mal began again, this time with as much gentleness as he could muster. "You've walked a distance to find me."

"Aye." Tillion's agitated gaze came to rest on Mal's hand where beneath Hennish leather he wore the vocent's stone. The theist swallowed audibly, then straightened his shoulders and lifted his chin. Almost, he met Mal's eye.

"My lord," he proclaimed over the top of Mal's head, "I've come to bring you word of the one god's displeasure."

Mal's patience evaporated.

"I assure you." He stepped around Tillion, already dismissing the priest from his thoughts. "I am quite aware of your god's unfavorable regard toward the throne and the throne's current policy. How could I not be, with your trap flapping outside His Majesty's windows all the day long? Good afternoon."

"Magus." Tillion darted after Mal with unexpected speed, blocking his retreat. "You misunderstand." The priest straightened, regard newly hawkish. Mal caught a glimpse in his changeable expression of the impassioned preacher. "This chastisement is for you alone and you alone will suffer the consequences if I cannot make you take heed and reform your transgression."

Mal scoffed. "Transgression?"

"Oh, aye, Lord Malachi. My god knows a thief when it's his own cupboard emptied."

"You're not making any sense." Mal choked back irritation. His headache had returned with a vengeance. He'd run a fool's errand to the Mabon tree when that time was better spent on more pressing matters. Avani, like Jacob, had flown the nest without any concern for consequence. And by now there was, most certainly, a corpse in his bed. "Get out of my way."

"The dead belong to the divine, my lord. It's your duty to send them on, not feed on their vitality to bloating."

Mal felt cold. "I said, get out of my way." He shouldered Tillion aside, making the taller man stumble. But Tillion recovered at once. He hurried after Mal, staff thumping on the forest floor. Birds startled from the branches at their passing, and the fox woke under the gorse. Mal walked faster, spurred on by rage, and eventually Tillion faltered, but he did not give up.

"'From the one god we are born and to the one god we must return!'" he boomed, preacher's voice at odds with his lurching step. "The spirits of the dead belong to the one god, Malachi, and are not your playthings. 'A man who thieves just one sheep will give up four in final reckoning.' Reform, magus, or he will have his retribution."

Mal stretched his pace near to jogging.

Loud with derision, Tillion called after: "No one escapes my god's wrath indefinitely; you can't run forever. He is watching you, Malachi! You cannot hide!"

CHAPTER 11

"The falconer said it wasn't broken," Liam assured Avani. "Just wrenched. She's seen a few like it in her time at the royal mews. Rest and time, she said, for the healing."

Together they looked up at Jacob where he perched in the rafters of the pages' dormitory. The raven was pretending to be asleep, beak tucked away under glossy feathers, eyes closed. He did not appear to notice Avani at all, but Liam thought he was shamming. Jacob, he knew, wasn't the sort to let anyone creep up unnoticed.

"*Ai*, well." Avani's grin was relieved. "Thank you for taking care of him. He's a stubborn fellow, prone to ignoring misfortune."

"'Twas Parsnip's idea." Liam winked at the lass. Parsnip hid her blushes by examining the toes of her boots. For all she'd recently grown bolder, it was apparent she held Avani in very high esteem. "The falconer, I mean."

"He came down from the tree all on his own," Parsnip demurred. "I think he wanted the help. He must have been hurting."

"He'd never let you know it, if he were." Avani left Jacob to his pretext. Returning to her cot, she went about the business of unpacking. "When we were first living on the Downs, one of my ewes kicked him for getting too close to her lambs." Unwinding silk from around the Goddess statue she carried with her always, she set the idol on the floorboards between the cot and the window, in a patch of sunlight. "It was days before he'd let me peek at the wound, and even then, he was mulish about the whole thing." She took a small bowl from her pack and laid it at the statue's feet. "Animals, like people, prefer not to show any weakness."

Parsnip crouched, watching with interest as Avani filled the offering bowl with smooth round river pebbles taken from a leather pouch.

"Is it magic?" the lass asked. "The bowl and the stones and the gold lady?"

"It's not magic." Liam snorted. "It's *religion*."

"Oh." Parsnip's mouth collapsed in disappointment. "My mum made us do religion, in the temple. I don't see the point. All the prayers about the Red Worm and everyone still died."

"You didn't." Liam thumped Parsnip on her shoulder. "Time to go. Riggins is expecting you, and I'm wanted in the stables." The recollection threatened to sour his joy over Avani's company. He tamped worry down.

"Are you certain it's no problem?" Avani glanced about the room. "My staying here for a time, I mean?"

"No one will notice," Liam promised. "With Lane gone, no one comes up here but us."

"That will change." Parsnip predicted, scratching her nose thoughtfully. "Now that His Majesty has signed the draft and sent Kingsmen to villages west and north. The plague can't have reached everywhere. Soon this place will be full of conscripts, and I'll be glad of it."

"Farmers and seamen and outcasts make shift as far away from the city as possible to avoid forced service," Liam grumbled. "Riffraff and rabble."

"Liam." Avani widened her eyes in rebuke. "Have you already forgotten where *we* come from? It's a lovely new tunic you're wearing, but you're a Stonehiller underneath, and just as valuable for it."

"Don't go belittling farmers," Parsnip added. "Those that work the land will spill blood to keep it safe."

Liam threw up his hands in mock defeat then surprised himself by leaning in to kiss Avani's cheek. "Doesn't matter. It will be weeks yet before the conscripts show. Stay. I'll keep you safe."

Avani's lips twitched but she did him the favor of pretending his promise held weight. "Thank you."

Liam left Avani to her puttering, Jacob still feigning sleep in the rafters, and delivered Parsnip to Riggins in the barracks' schoolroom for her daily struggle with reading and writing. The lass was determined to someday become an officer like her father, but a soldier who couldn't read would not travel far up the ranks. Captain Riggins was a patient man, but Liam could tell by the man's subdued greeting that Parsnip's inability to make sense of letters was a growing frustration.

Or mayhap the captain's sour mood was because of Morgan and Arthur, whispering together over their open books. The schoolroom was windowless and drab, and possibly the last place any young lad or lass would choose when the weather outside was at last turning fine.

"Sir!" Morgan sat up straight. "Parsnip, you're late. Captain said we couldn't learn Ra'Vadin's *Five Verses* until you came."

"I said after mathematics." Riggins tapped the pages of Arthur's book with the flexible wand he used both as pointer and incentive. "Which you've barely started. Get back to work, young man. Liam, are you staying? I seem to recall your understanding of geometric equations is shaky, to say the least."

"Sorry, sir. I'm wanted in the stables," Liam told Riggins, ignoring Arthur's muffled amusement. Morgan, the young earl Wythe and the only remaining child of the king's constable who in turn headed the royal cavalry, became immediately somber.

"Very well." Riggins dismissed Liam with a wave of his baton. "Tomorrow, then, and no excuses. When I said your understanding of geometry is shaky, I meant nonexistent. And what, my lord Wythe, is one of the uses of geometric equations on the battlefield?"

"To direct the siege engines, sir," Morgan replied promptly. "Or the canons."

"Exactly," Riggins said as Liam fled. "And furthermore, once the elephant guns arrive as promised . . ."

Liam took the stairs down from the schoolroom two at a time. He didn't mind learning, when he had the time for it. Reading history in particular could often be entertaining and, to Liam's mind, beneficial. A man learned from the mistakes of his forefathers and was better for it in his own time. That Liam understood.

But he'd seen Roue's elephant guns in use, been knocked off his feet with the force of the gigantic canons. He didn't believe geometric equations had anything to do with that destruction. As far as he'd been able to tell, the gunners had simply chosen a target, pointed the canon, and set the flare. There had been no time between attacks for mathematical calculations.

The royal stables were located behind the barracks, between the north-most tower and castle's rear bailey. It was possible to reach the stable shed rows through shallow tunnels that ran beneath the towers, but Liam—like Morgan and Arthur—preferred fresh air over confinement. He stepped out of the barracks into the practice courtyard and took a lungful of evening to settle a rising attack of nerves. Bear woke from where she'd been dozing under a nearby archway and came to join him. Liam took comfort in her warm, wedge-shaped head under his hand. She was a good dog, and seemed to have survived her separation from Holder without any lasting side effects.

He stroked her ears, recalling Avani's speculation: *Animals, like people, prefer not to show any weakness.*

"You're a brave lass," he told the hound. She wagged her tail. "I'd do well to take your example." To Bear he could confess what he hated to admit to himself, the worry he'd held close to his heart since receiving the constable's message upon rising. "She won't send me away; she can't afford to."

But he knew the Wythe didn't trust him, for the scars on his body and the whispered rumors that followed him everywhere he walked. With Lane dead, and Avani having fled the palace, there was no one left to champion his cause. If Wythe had at last convinced the king that Liam was in fact a *sidhe* spy, he doubted Mal would care to intercede on his behalf.

And drumming out was the least of his worries. He'd seen what happened to the last barrowman captured.

"No weakness." He gave Bear one last pat. "I won't be afeared of a wicked old hag. Whatever happens, I'll stand tall."

Countess Wythe did not at all resemble a wicked old hag when she met Liam in the hay barn just inside the royal stables. She'd traded her uniform and shining boots for dungarees and villeins' clogs. There was mud and worse on her hands and on her face. She smelled of horse shit and hay, and her cropped hair and dirty knees made her look nearly as young as Parsnip.

"You're late," she said, sounding just like her son. "I expected you before supper."

"Apologies, my lady." Liam essayed his best courtly bow. "Something unexpected came up."

"Did it? With me, also." She gestured behind her at groomsmen working through stacks of hay. It was a large barn, sturdily built to withstand summer's heat and winter's cold. Grain barrels and empty buckets lined one wall but most of the vaulted space was taken with new-cut hay. "Rot's got in, and before the rainy season. Some fool packed damp grass in with the good, and now it's spread." Absently she knocked manure from the bottom of her boots. "The bad needs to be carefully picked out, or we'll have colicky horses come winter." She left the barn, crooked a finger at Liam. "Follow me. Can you pick rotted grass from good, boy?"

"Nay." Liam glanced back at the groomsmen working in the barn, puzzled, before hurrying to keep pace. "I only know sheep, my lady, and on the Downs they grazed out no matter the weather."

Wythe made an inelegant noise. "Sheep are not horses. A horse is a delicate creature, Liam. Mess with his gut and you're like to lose the rest of him." Wythe led Liam into the shed rows. Covered box stalls lined either side of a wide, sandy walk. Horses of differing colors and sizes stuck their heads out over half doors, nickering and blowing or watching without comment. It was apparent many of the animals knew the constable by sight; most pricked their ears in greeting. Several pawed their stall floors in a bid for attention. The throne owned several hundred head, every animal trained to battle, although none had seen war in their lifetime.

Wythe stopped to acknowledge a rawboned bay gelding. Liam recognized the horse.

"My son's courser," Wythe confirmed. "Called Wilde. He's worth his weight in silver; he'll take care of Morgan come the desert."

Liam searched for a response and found none. He'd seen Morgan ride the horse across Holder's fields and knew the young earl had a solid seat, but he couldn't image delicate Morgan charging into battle with much success. Morgan, who knew his equations and could pierce a straw man through with his sword so long as it was secured in place, and who always fell hard beneath the quintain.

Wythe fished in the pocket of her dungarees, retrieving a carrot. "Can you ride?"

"Aye."

"More than a carthorse, I mean. Have you learned the tilt?"

Liam was hardly better at the quintain than Morgan, but he wouldn't admit it in the face of the constable's keen attention. "Aye," he hedged. "I've been practicing."

Wilde nickered. Wythe handed Liam the carrot. "Go ahead," she said. "The yellow ones are his favorite."

It felt like a test, but Liam couldn't grasp the rules. He fed Wilde the carrot, smiling despite the knot in his gut when the horse smacked lips and tongue together in appreciation.

"He likes you." Wythe crossed her arms. "I can count on one hand how many people this horse tolerates. I've seen you with the hound and the raven. You've a knack. Animals like you."

"The sheep always did," Liam replied, hoping he didn't sound as defensive as he felt. "And the Widow's old cat, Tom." He shrugged. "I'm kind to them, is all."

"Everyone knows neither horse nor hound will tolerate the barrow folk. Birds grow silent when they pass. Even the fish in the lakes and ponds retreat before their shadows. I wager even sheep on the Downs would shun their unnatural company."

"I've heard no such thing," replied Liam, the challenge come clear. He refused to shout or stomp or punch Wythe in the nose as he had Baldebert for once implying the very same thing. He bit the inside of his cheek instead and let the pain of it cool his shame.

"Good lad." Wythe awarded him a quick nod. "Got a hold on your temper, have you?" She reached into her pocket, fed Wilde a second carrot. "People ask you about it a lot, I suppose." She nodded again, this time at Liam's scrolling scars. "Whether you're *sidhe* or mortal man or something in between. What those scars are all about."

"A few ask. More just stare and whisper. My lady, if you've brought me here to prove I'm barrowman, you've wasted both our time." He started to turn away, dread making his steps heavy. "If you're planning to drum me out, my lady, just say so. I can't prove to you I'm not a threat, and I won't try."

Wythe stopped him with a click of her tongue. Wilde, startled, pulled his head back inside the shed row.

"You don't know, either," Wythe realized. She put her hands in her pockets and pushed off the stall door. "What you are. And you've got more self-confidence than I expected. Well. I can work with that."

"My lady?"

Wythe looped her arm in his. She was taller, but not by much. Liam froze, dismayed by the breach in station. If Wythe noticed his discomfort, she gave no indication. The constable started walking, and Liam was forced to keep stride. Groomsmen, soldiers, and stable hands were busy in the shed rows, but none paid Wythe or Liam any attention.

"I've worked around animals all my life," Wythe confided. "They never lie. Men and women, not so forthright, although Renault's witch doesn't seem the sort to equivocate. She said you are a good man, and I am inclined to believe her."

Liam's relief sounded like ringing in his ears. "Thank you."

"Thank Wilde. That horse can smell a villain two villages over. Some people trust their instincts, I trust Wilde. If he'll take a treat from your hand, it's because he likes you. So. I'm willing to take a chance on you, Liam, but just the one. Don't make me regret it." They'd left the shed rows. Wythe paused before the stable gates, a wonder of ironwork embellished with bronze horse-head medallions and the throne's silver starburst. The gate stood open. Outside a farrier worked in the evening and a groomsman grazed a spotted mare on a patch of grass. Past the farrier, the setting sun touched the palace's lowest spire.

Wythe released Liam's arm. "Day after tomorrow Morgan's moving out of the page's dormitory and into the cavalry's. He's far too young, but he can sit a horse and throw a lance. He'll go to war one way or another, and I want him under my wing."

A chill dripped along Liam's spine. Wythe gave him another of her brusque nods.

"Word came down this morning. The sand snakes are mobilizing and Roue's ships are nowhere near Low Port. We're to prepare to move. A week, maybe two, if we're lucky."

"The draft," said Liam.

"Aye."

"Morgan—"

"Is an earl and so must ride out with our house. I want you to ride out with him, as his companion and his squire. You're handy with a knife and capable with a sword. You say you know how to ride. And I'm betting my last son on the chance that a good man who is neither entirely mortal nor completely *sidhe* may have a few tricks up his sleeve."

"Parsnip and Arthur?"

"Will stay behind in the palace," replied Wythe. "As will any other children dredged up in His Majesty's draft, god willing. It is the throne's opinion that our surviving young must be kept close and safe. I can't say I disagree."

"They'll be very angry." The farrier's hammer was an echo of Liam's thumping heart. He'd assumed he would see the war from the ground, in the infantry. He'd not thought to see it so soon.

"Anger is a privilege of the living. Let them be

angry, so long as they are protected. So." Wythe cocked her head. "Will you do it? It's good pay, and good company. And if you keep Morgan safe, I'll be in your debt. Wythe is an old, strong house and we'd do well for you, I think."

The groomsman and his charge walked back through the stable gate, the mare dancing on cobble-stones. He nodded a greeting, his curious gaze linger-ing on Liam's face. The setting sun turned the white palace red. Pennants flapped on the highest tower but on the ground the air was still. Breath held, Liam imagined, waiting on his decision.

"Well?" prompted Wythe.

In the end, it was a simple choice.

"I will," he said, "on one condition."

"**T**o war?" Avani wrapped the woolen blanket taken off her cot more securely about her shoulders. It was well after dark, and while not frosty, the night felt like impending fall. Avani, for all the years she spent on the frigid Downs, was not one to suffer cold easily.

"It's coming," Liam said, "sooner than expected." He couldn't read her expression in the great caged bonfire that burned in the yard through the night. They had come outside to talk quietly, away from Parsnip and Morgan and Arthur, each of whom were intent on questioning Avani about life in court.

"*Ai,* I know." Avani pulled her knees up beneath

her chin. They sat together on the steps beneath one of the yard's impressive white stone archways, looking out onto the woods beyond and the Mabon tree, a brighter stripe in a forest of shadows. "I have no quarrel with the desert."

A loose thread already marred the line of Liam's new tunic. He worried at it with thumb and forefinger, thinking. He'd spent the entirety of his short life relying on Avani's greater wisdom. He knew he owed her his survival at least twice over, and she'd never called that debt in, nor would she. He also knew that, in this, he was right, but she wouldn't like to hear it.

"Your goddess is a peaceful sort."

She watched him over the swell of her knees. "And I serve Her in all things."

"I wouldn't ask you to change that," he promised. "Only, I don't think the people of the desert are. A peaceful sort, you understand. I don't think they've any interest in coming to an understanding. From what Riggins says, they never have done. There are far more of them than there are of us, and they're desirous of our good land, our cities and ports. They want what we have and they've no interest in leaving flatlanders alive."

"Mercy is a flatlander concept," Avani murmured.

Liam blinked. "Just so." He tugged on a corner of her blanket, stealing a bit of warmth for himself. "Wythe isn't asking you to fight. She wants you to come along as magus, and healer."

"There are priests for that."

"And to lay the dead," Liam told her. "In Roue they had no magus to do so, after battle, and the dead walked in circles on the fields, without ever stopping, Mal said. It was like in the Bone Cave, only worse. I couldn't see them but I could *feel* them and it was wrong."

"Mal—"

"Will be kept in Wilhaiim near His Majesty, to see the throne safe. Besides—" he tried for a knowing look but faltered "—the barracks aren't far enough away from that one. I don't like to say it. I know you've admired him from the beginning. I think you admire him still. But . . ." The words stuck.

"I know," Avani said quietly. "You don't have to explain. I've seen it in his head. As he sees in mine. We're often inseparable now. I suspect that's why Jacob shuns my company. I'm no longer only myself."

Liam half rose in distress, dragging Avani's blanket from her shoulders. Shock rattled his bones in a shudder. "Avani! Skald's balls, if anyone were to find out—"

"Hush," she interrupted him quickly, raising a hand. She looked toward the woods and the Mabon tree. "Someone comes."

Liam, recalling the walking straw men who had appeared in the night and snatched him and Parsnip away, drew his knife. Avani rose slowly, retrieving the blanket and wrapping it once again about her torso.

"Be calm," she told him. "It's only Faolan."

They came up out of the woods in a group of three, Faolan and a pale *sidhe* woman and a barrowman dressed in multicolored rags. Faolan was exactly as Liam had last seen him, much older than he appeared, long limbed, his skull bare, a gleaming torque fastened around his neck. The woman had long hair and dark eyes and her skirts matched the barrowman's motley. The barrowman scuttled past the bonfire in the way of its kind, a bronze-tipped spear held in one hand.

They all three crossed the courtyard with remarkable boldness. Liam clenched his fingers around the hilt of his knife, comforted by the weight of it against his palm.

"Faolan," Avani rebuked when the small group was within speaking distance, "the barracks are patrolled. Any moment now, the Kingsman on duty will come around that corner, and how will I explain *sidhe* in the heart of the city? I'd hoped you were safely without."

"We have been without," replied Faolan, smiling small. "And now we are within."

"Halwn has tracked your rat." The woman eyed Liam. Her black gaze was unfriendly. Her sultry features were familiar, but he couldn't quite place her. When he tried, his head buzzed unpleasantly. "The one you call Holder," she continued. "We know where he's hiding, and it's time for a Hunt."

"I'll send word to the palace." Avani swung toward the barracks, but the *sidhe* woman stopped her with a hiss.

"Holder belongs to Halwn," said Faolan. "To do with as it likes. As reparation for Tadhg's death. Tell Renault the problem of his traitorous farmer is dealt with."

"Tadhg is dead?" Firelight made Avani's expression stark, stricken. "Its wounds were healing."

"Tadhg died of shame," said Halwn. Liam twitched in surprise. He'd not thought a barrowman could know the king's lingua, but Halwn spoke it as clearly Faolan did. "For becoming less than whole. Maimed heart and hands."

"The barrowman." Liam's own hands went clammy with shock. "Tadhg is the captured barrowman? I saw it, in the fields, and then later, when my lord walked it through the gates. My lord—*Malachi*—did Malachi *kill* it?" He thought he might weep.

Avani wouldn't meet his eye. The *sidhe* woman showed Liam her pointed teeth. The barrowman stared, flat black eyes reflecting bonfire flames. Only Faolan paused for thought.

"Liam," he said slowly. "You are welcome to join our Hunt."

Avani made wordless protest, reaching to pull Liam close. The *sidhe* woman snarled, bestial sounding as Bear. The barrowman showed no reaction at all.

Liam's tongue tasted sour. "Why would I?"

"It is your right, if you want it." Faolan touched his torque. "Have you never wondered what it means to be *sidhe*?"

"He is not *Tuath Dé*! He is the very opposite!"

"Hush, Cleena," Faolan warned. "It is not for you to decide."

"Last Liam was alone amongst the *sidhe* they meant to kill him," Avani said. Her arm around his waist tightened.

"It's not for you to decide, either. The choice belongs to Liam, should Halwn agree to have him."

"We don't eat tainted meat," replied the barrowman. "The farmer did Liam damage as well as Tadhg." It rubbed its pointed chin, claws gleaming in the night. "It would be a tale to tell. Tadhg enjoyed a good tale. If he can keep up, we will have him."

"Well." The corners of Faolan's mouth curled. "Liam. What do you think? Can you keep up?"

Cleena began to laugh. Her merriment echoed off flagstone, unpleasant. Avani was rigid against his side. The barrowman, standing across the bonfire, waited.

"Aye," said Liam. His lips were numb, but unlooked-for excitement sang in his veins. He hadn't meant to accept the invitation, not at all. Yet the minute acquiescence slipped out, the sourness in his gut and mouth eased. Relief felt like joy and made him shiver. He sheathed his knife. "I can keep up."

CHAPTER 12

They gathered in the moonlight outside Wilhaiim's Maiden Gate: Faolan and Cleena and twelve barrowmen. Faolan and Cleena overtopped the lesser *sidhe* by at least an arm's length. To Liam, standing awkwardly on one side, it seemed a bizarre family gathering, and Faolan the patriarch. Only, Halwn's kin were the very opposite of rambunctious children with their spears and sharpened sticks and dagger-like claws. Cleena played a resentful wife, glaring often in Liam's direction and refusing to look Faolan's way. It was very apparent she begrudged the *aes si*'s decision to include Liam in the night's activities. Liam, who had finally placed her face, believed her vexation more than a little bit unfair.

Pride stung, he sidled around waiting barrowmen

until he could catch her eye. "You used to delight in taking my coin," he said. He was pleased to note they were of a height, when in early spring she had been taller. "In exchange for your sweets."

"Business," Cleena said, folding her arms beneath her breasts and raking him head to toe with a scathing glare. "I take coin from all sorts."

She was more voluptuous than Liam remembered, her lips full and inviting in the moonlight. She smelled of the honey she worked with, and of something else he couldn't quite place, a perfume as alluring as promises whispered in private.

"Cleena," said Faolan. "I promised Avani we'd bring him back in one piece. Not banshee stricken."

"Banshee?" Liam reared back. "The keening hag?" Even the Stonehillers had feared the banshee, the wandering old woman who appeared in the night to foretell a person's death or a family tragedy. The Widow had avowed she'd seen one of the banshee peeking through her bedroom window two nights before her husband succumbed to the dropsy.

"*Sidheog*," Cleena corrected. "The *ban side* are to the *sidheog* as the sapling is to the deep-rooted oak." She swiped the pink tip of her tongue along her lower lip, and as she did so Liam saw underlying her pretty, freckled face a white-bone skull and lank, parchment-colored hair. The skull's eyes were empty holes, the hair stuck to the moon-washed skull in thin hanks.

The heat that had been gathering in Liam's groin

dissipated so quickly as to be painful. Cleena's laugh sounded like dry bones snapping.

"By the Aug." He backed away.

"Come," said Faolan, sweeping Liam beneath one arm. "Halwn is ready."

The Maiden Gate was not a busy portal even in daytime, nor was it often deserted. A fat moon made for easy travel. Kingsmen guarded the gate itself; more rode out on a patrol, calling out to each other as they went. The horses snorted at the *sidhe* gathered near the wall, but the soldiers payed no attention. Nor did a lone farmer, leaving the city with empty produce baskets hanging from a pole across his shoulders. Nor a fishmonger, pushing his cart home for the evening, whistling mournfully as he went.

Halwn waited amongst its kin. It watched Liam as he drew near. The barrowmen, although uniform in size and shape, were unique in dress and weaponry. The four standing nearest Halwn wore furs and patchwork tunics. They carried spears tipped with bronze. The rest were barrowmen as Liam had come to know them—emaciated, barely clothed, and holding sharpened sticks instead of bronze. Each of the twelve had painted their faces with dark soil. Muddy swirls darkened their cheekbones and chins and looped across their foreheads. A few wore the same vining designs painted on their forearms and bare calves.

The swoops and loops were familiar to Liam. They disfigured his own hands and face, and his torso and thighs beneath his clothes. The barrowmen had decorated him in a like manner, not with mud or paint, but by drawing the patterns into his flesh with claw and knife.

He lifted a shaking hand to his chin.

"Halwn will lead the charge," murmured Faolan. "Do not get in their way. I see you wore your knife, though I asked you to come unarmed. I will not dishonor you in front of them by taking it from you now. But do not draw iron against them, Liam. Even I cannot protect you against their wrath, should they see you as threat." The gem in Faolan's torque glowed a muted yellow beneath the scarf he wore. The stone was a larger version of the matching carbuncles in Mal's ring of office, and in Andrew's ring that Avani now wore on a chain around her neck. Liam had seen Faolan's collar before. The bronze was aged to green, the pale flesh beneath calloused. It marked the *aes si* as acolyte, servant to sleeping *sidhe* elders.

It was not at all dissimilar to the iron chokers worn by the human engines in Roue's ships, a badge of indentured servitude, slavery in disguise.

"There are no gods but us," Faolan said before Liam could remark on the resemblance. "Everything mankind knows now sprang first from the *sidhe*, when we walked above ground and mortals looked still in our direction for answers." He beckoned Halwn close. The barrowman stepped obediently forward. Between its hands was cupped a small earthenware bowl. Steam curled off a simmering black mixture within.

Faolan dipped a finger into the bowl. "Close your eyes," he bade Liam. Liam glanced between Halwn and the *aes si*, wondering if he'd made a terrible mistake. He couldn't refuse without appearing small. He wished he knew whether the catch behind his ribs was from terror or elation.

He closed his eyes.

Faolan's finger pressed firmly against Liam's brow. The muck on his fingertip was warm, slimy. His skin tingled where Faolan traced it, circles around both of Liam's eyes and a sweeping stripe down his nose.

"There." The night air stirred as Faolan retreated. "It's finished."

Liam opened his eyes. At first the world seemed unchanged. The Maiden Gate was as it had been a heartbeat earlier. The Kingsmen standing guard talked quietly together beneath the portcullis. The barrowmen milled in a restless knot, waiting. Faolan and the banshee stood side by side in silence. A cloud crossed the moon, briefly blotting out light.

He took a step in Faolan's direction. Moving was a mistake. Cobblestones flowed like river water under his feet. The Maiden Gate receded in a blur of unwinding white wall. Trees and grass and a soldier returning from patrol washed past in a lengthening cloud of color.

Liam froze, both arms helplessly extended to

either side for balance, like one of Renault's jesters stuck halfway along his tightrope. His surroundings came back to order: The King's Highway, rolling fallow fields, a copse of trees lit bright as tapers by the moon.

Slowly, he turned his head. He could still make out the Maiden Gate for the impression of flickering torches set on either side of the opening, almost half a furlong distant. Carefully he pulled his arms back against his chest.

"Everin fainted the first time he attempted a Hunt," said Faolan, materializing at Liam's side where before there had been only moonlight. "You kept your feet. Congratulations. But the leader of the Hunt must always go first, or you'll find yourself lost."

"One step." Halwn and its kin, absent one minute and there in the road the next, measured Liam with a dubious glance. "A child could manage as much."

"Exactly that." Cleena joined them, pale hair rising off her shoulders on a breeze Liam couldn't feel. "Let us see how he runs."

"Holder has hidden himself away in the red woods," Faolan told Liam. "It's not far. Keep your eyes on Halwn's back as we go. Don't look away, or you might get lost. I'll keep you safe as I can. Are you ready?"

Liam nodded. Halwn raised its spear in a salute. The barrowmen began to caper in place. Even the scrawniest of the group, those more sinew than flesh, began to hop and yelp, rattling together spears and sticks. Liam heard Faolan inhale. So warned, he pinned his gaze between Halwn's fur-draped shoulder blades. When the barrowman scuttled forward, crowded by its kin, Liam trotted after. The King's Highway vanished from beneath him. Moonlight and shadow ran together in smears out of the corner of his eye. He thought he heard the barrowmen singing, in sweet silver-bell voices. He knew he heard Cleena laughing.

The *sidhe* Hunt had begun.

It was more frightening than sneaking into Khorit Dard's army camp and wetting his blade on the first taste of war. It was as breathtaking as hanging upside down from *The Cutlass Wind*'s bowsprit, the sea splashing in his face while Baldebert steered the ship toward home. It was like waging battle, only the skirmish was between heart and head. Or dancing a sailor's jig to a familiar but mostly forgotten piper's tune.

There was no sound at all, not footfalls or words exchanged or wind in his ears. Even the *sidhe*'s singing had dwindled to nothing. An unnatural silence, and one that Liam feared to break, if even it could be broken. But if his ears had failed in the *sidhe* spell at least his eyes still worked, though it was difficult not to look away from Halwn. The oddities fluttering on the edge of his vision became stranger as time passed. Bright colors, some of which Liam had no proper name for, tantalized from amongst passing shadows. Once he thought he glimpsed the trailing end of a gilt-tipped scales. And once, a darting rabbit ten sizes too big. More of Riggins's dire things come out of the red woods, he puzzled, like the gigantic eagle or the rampaging wolves? The muscles in his neck twitched to peek, but he hadn't forgotten Faolan's warning. The very last thing he wanted was to be left behind.

Liam could feel breath pumping in and out of his chest, and the flutter of his working heart. His body thought it sprinted when in truth Halwn kept them at a light jog. His nose and mouth had gone uncomfortably dry; it was difficult to work up enough spit to swallow without choking. Then he did cough, and as if that soundless gasping was a signal, Halwn stopped. Liam rocked to a halt, stumbling into the barrowman.

They fell out of the spell. The world summersaulted. The fat moon rolled under Liam's feet and then resolved itself overhead, shining in silver triangles through a high, sparse canopy. The king's red woods were around them and above them, thick, springy grass beneath their feet and a glittering spring bubbling up from the ground nearby. Night animals drank from the spring: a young stag and his white-tailed doe, a spiny hedgehog, and a yellow-breasted bird. When the *sidhe* appeared, the animals started and fled.

Liam's ears popped in time to catch the sound of their frantic departure.

"Drink," said Halwn. Liam realized he was leaning on the barrowman's thin shoulder for balance and quickly let go. Halwn indicated the spring. "The water is good."

Halwn's kin were already drinking, on their knees in the grass, scooping up handfuls of spring water. Liam had never been so thirsty in his life, even after days aboard ship under the pounding sun, dependent on Baldebert's rationed beer. He lurched forward, dropped alongside the barrowman, and drank. His cupped hands trembled. The water was the sweetest he'd ever tasted.

Faolan knelt at Liam's side on the forest floor. He scooped water from the spring with more dignity than the rest, but with equal concentration. When he had taken several swallows, he smiled at Liam.

"The body doesn't like it, the stepping through time. Even the *sidhe* suffer some effect. Parchedness is one. Sit and rest for a moment; you'll recover quickly."

Liam sat. It seemed as if he had woken from a particularly vivid dream, and his wits were still trying to catch up. For a time he was content with watching the spring froth out of the earth where it bubbled up between cracks in a moss-covered stone. Then he became aware that the stone was too round and too flat, man-made and ornamented around the edges with hatch marks and spirals.

He took a final drink, swirling cold water around

his teeth, then rose to his feet. His knees were steadier. His hands had stopped trembling. He took stock and saw that Halwn had led them to a modestly sized grove, a break in the trees that allowed for clearer sky overhead and thicker grass underfoot. The surrounding evergreens grew tall and close together. Wildflowers decorated the grass around the spring, a carpet of red stars.

It was a tranquil spot, and isolated. When last Liam had been inside the forest, he and Avani had relied on Everin to guide them along safe, well-used tracks. He did not think Halwn's spring was near any of those commonly trod paths.

"We're close," said Halwn. The barrowman sniffed at the night air. Intrigued, Liam did the same and caught a whiff of hearth smoke. "This way." Gripping its spear, the *sidhe* slipped between evergreens.

This time when the world lurched and his senses went awry, Liam was better prepared. He'd lost Halwn in the muddle of shifting, bounding barrowmen and almost he panicked, but then he found Cleena, tall and spectral amongst her lesser kin, and concentrated on the swinging plait of her colorless hair. If she noticed his attention, she gave no sign and he was glad of it, for if Liam was certain of only one thing that night, it was that the banshee hated him.

By all appearances it was a shorter sprint. When the hunt ceased, Liam was neither out of breath nor panting for a drink. His ears popped while the evergreens stopped spinning. He could hear a cow lowing in quiet distress.

"Be still," Faolan warned from beside Liam. He reached across and erased the mud-painted sigil from Liam's brow with his palm. "This place is not unprotected."

It was a crumbling stone hovel surrounded by red flowers and enormous ferns. Smoke rose from a crooked chimney. A candle flickered in the single square window. A large cresset on an iron pole shed light over densely packed trees, the nervous black-coated cow, and four misshapen guardsmen made of straw and metal and gourd and stick.

The cow turned tail and fled, crashing through the trees. Two of the *sidhe* detached from their kin and skittered after in chase. The barrowmen made no sound at all. The cow made enough noise to wake the sleeping forest. The candle in the window went out.

"Get to the cresset!" Liam whispered. "They don't like fire!"

"Who?" demanded Cleena, but at that moment the straw mannequins began to move.

They were larger than Holder's original creations by at least a head, and thicker around the middle and arms. Where the monsters that snuck into the barracks were meant to resemble practice dummies, these new creatures need fool no one and Holder had spared no addition. They retained gourds for heads—carved eyes and gaping mouths—and the odd mincing walk of knees that bent backward instead of forward, but their torsos and limbs were bundled wood and stone, all wrapped about with thick strips of leather, and their hands were many dagger blades welded into deadly, shining bouquets. More iron hung all around their upper bodies, chains and rusted cogs and bristling awls, arranged sharp end out.

"By the Aug," Liam breathed. "He's tried to make his own."

"Own *what*?" Cleena snarled as she backed away. The barrowmen stood motionless. Liam could not tell whether they were frightened or only confused. He was too young to have seen iron sickness at work. He wondered if they were feeling the effects of it already.

"Automata," growled Faolan. "The magi's servants, conceived for the singular purpose of destroying a *sidhe* army. Bane of the *Tuath Dé*. But this farmer is no necromancer, to conjure life into insensate things. How is it possible?"

"He's a cunning bastard, that's how."

The stick-and-stone mannequins were not as quick as their predecessors, weighed down by iron and tree branch. But it was apparent they could see in the dark as well as any *sidhe*, even with empty pits for eyes. Their pumpkin heads swiveled in the direction of Liam and the *sidhe*, and their shuffling picked up speed. They split in two directions around the crowded clearing, intending, Liam supposed, to hem the barrowmen in.

Cleena began to snarl in earnest. The lesser *sidhe*, still silent, retreated into a tight cluster, pressed back to back.

"Nay, you've got it wrong." Liam made a desperate shooing motion with his hands. "It's the fire that stops them. Get close to the cresset, don't let them catch you up."

The closest mannequin was almost within striking distance. Its dagger fingers clicked together. It made a snuffling noise as its head swung back and forth. Two more of the barrowman broke, flitting away into the evergreens. Halwn shouted angrily after his kin, but they did not return.

Faolan began to speak slowly and loudly. Liam did not understand the words any more than he ever did Mal's recitations, but the intonation and the increasing glow around the *aes si*'s torque suggested a powerful magic about to be unleashed, so Liam did the most prudent thing and got out of the way.

He knew from experience that Holder's monsters preferred big, swinging movements to small. So when the first mannequin struck out, knife-hands slicing down and together through filtered moonlight, Liam ducked and darted, yawing right and then left. Dagger fingers cut the air near his head, but he dropped to hands and knees, scrambling through fern toward the roaring cresset. Glancing over his shoulder Liam saw the mannequin turn, clumsy as a drunken sailor, and give chase.

Whatever magic Faolan worked sent a second creature to the forest floor, cut off at the knees, arms flailing. The remaining barrowmen, startled into action, swarmed over the fallen mannequin, Halwn at their head, striking with spears and sticks.

The forest floor was chill and damp against Liam's hands and knees. Red flowers, crushed in his scramble, discharged puffs of pollen into the air, making him sneeze. The cresset was not far away but the straw man behind him was gaining ground, its tree-branch legs working frantically. As it grew close, terror struck Liam to the core, turning his insides to liquid and making him falter. The mannequin lashed out. Daggers sliced Liam's leg, puncturing flesh and pinning his trousers to the grass. Gasping, he struggled, but pain and fear made him impotent. The mannequin leaned close. Liam could hear the clicking of knives as it reached for his head.

Cleena yanked him out from underneath the monster, tearing his pant leg and the flesh of his knee in the process. "Quickly!" Her eyes were dark holes in a white face, her hair a writhing nest of snakes. She had a spear in her hand. Ichor smeared the shaft: *sidhe* blood. "The cresset! Go! I'll keep it back!"

Liam was moaning. Not for the fire in his leg but for dread. The forest echoed with the sounds of battle: wails of pain and fear, snarls of the dying.

He longed to curl up in the grass and close his eyes. Cleena booted him, hard. "Go!"

He went, staggering upright and weaving the last few paces toward the cresset. Pain scalded his right knee but the leg held. So did his fractured nerve. As he moved further from the mannequin, his courage began to return. By the time he stood in front of the fire, he'd regained determination. He snatched up a pair of long tongs lying at the base of the cresset and reached within the basket for a burning log.

"Not so fast." A sword point kissed the back of Liam's neck. "That's the only thing keeping the wolves at bay."

Liam knew the voice. He heard it still in his nightmares. He could see Holder out of the corner of his eye, just as he'd glimpsed shifting oddities on the *sidhe* hunt, a short man made larger by the changing firelight.

"Move away," Holder ordered. "Slowly."

It was possible Holder didn't recognize him. In the night Liam's scars were less visible, his features obscured. And Holder was looking at the ongoing struggled beyond the cresset, not at Liam's face. The tongs were growing wretchedly warm in Liam's bare hand; the flames licked at the cuffs of his sleeves.

In the clearing the *sidhe* were failing against Holder's straw men. Two barrowmen, sharp teeth bared, propped Faolan between them as they attempted to fend off a mannequin with their spears. The mannequin had somehow lost its pumpkin head in the fray but it did not seem at all impaired. As Liam watched, aghast, it hopped a man's length forward and took one of the barrowman through the gut with a bladed hand. The barrowman fell. Faolan tumbled after onto fern and red flowers. The headless mannequin squatted, knees bending birdlike in the wrong direction, and raised both arms for a second strike.

Liam grabbed the tongs with both hands, captured a burning log, and flung it at the creature's headless torso. The point of Holder's blade left a searing line from the nape of Liam's neck to behind his shoulder blade, a twin agony to the throb in his calf. Holder shouted in surprise, then furious, struck out again. Liam was faster. The heated tongs took the shorter man in the temple, spinning him sideways. The sword slid from Holder's lax hand as he fell. He lay still where he dropped.

The headless monster was burning. Fire licked its entire right side; its tree-branch limbs caught in conflagration. It tottered in place before collapsing in a shower of metal and spark.

Two straw men still walked between the trees. They wreaked violence with mindless concentration, slashing and stabbing at anything that moved, crushing those that didn't. And there were many more bodies lying still on the forest floor than up and struggling. Liam saw Halwn, bloodied about the face and chest, still on its feet, and two more of its kin, both barely standing. Of the eight barrowmen who had braved the clearing, only three remained upright.

He didn't see Faolan or Cleena at all.

A straw man turned suddenly in his direction. It walked over *sidhe* bodies without taking notice, smearing ichor in the grass. As it came near, so did that black cloud of horror. Liam let go the tongs. He took a step backward, shaking.

The straw man crouched, readying to spring. Liam looked in its empty, hollowed-out eyes and saw nothing. He heard a strange, choking sound and knew it came from his own throat. He was more afraid of the mannequin than the death it carried.

The straw man jumped. Liam rolled onto the grass next to Holder. The farmer's chest still rose and fell, though his eyes were open and staring. The mannequin landed amidst scattered kindling. Liam scrambled sideways, barely avoiding its deadly hands. As he did so, he plucked his knife from his belt and used it to slit Holder's throat. Blood gushed. The straw man hesitated, missed a step, and fell. Liam scrambled backward but the creature lay still in the ferns.

In the clearing the last mannequin faltered and slowed. Holder's death broke the spell that animated its body. Listless, it sagged.

Liam rolled onto his back. The canopy above was too dense; he couldn't see the moon. He closed his eyes, near to passing out. His leg had finally gone numb, which was a blessing, but the pain his neck had grown to agony. Everything smelled of Holder's blood.

"Up you go." Cleena bent over him. She snatched Liam up out of the fern without any effort at all. Her cheek was split open, freely bleeding ichor. She smelled like death. "We're finished here."

"Are they stopped?" Liam asked. For all that Cleena despised him and likely wanted him dead, for all he knew she was banshee and less than human beneath whatever glamour she wore, she would never be as frightening as Holder's creations. "You have to burn them, or chop them, or kill their master. He's dead. Are they stopped?"

"They're stopped," Cleena assured him. Her dark eyes were flat, her mouth fierce. "*Sidhe*'s bane." A growl caught in her chest, vibrating against Liam's ribs. "Vicious, ugly, conniving mortal magic." She took a breath. "Brace yourself. There are strange things sniffing about this place. I'm not inclined to linger."

"Wolves." Liam remembered. He felt woozy, exactly as he had when Mal had tried to murder him aboard *The Cutlass Wind*, draining away his life one gulp at a time. "Am I dying?" He hadn't planned on it so soon.

"Not yet," Cleena promised. "Hold tight."

The canopy overhead twisted into a whorl of evergreen bough and disappeared.

CHAPTER 13

Avani dozed in a spot of sunlight. Her half dreams were full of comfortable sounds: a lass's low cadence, Liam's smothered laugh, a raven's calling. There were spring lambs playing on the Downs, a tasty stew simmering on her stove, and when the last of the snow melted off, she would begin to plant her garden.

"Ten soldiers wide and sixteen rows deep," said the lass quietly. "Like a square."

"Aye, or a rectangle." Liam was still hoarse, a holdover from the *sidhe* Hunt. Mortals, even mortals so unusual as Liam, were hardly meant to traverse as barrowmen. "I think it looks more like a rectangle."

Eyes squeezed shut, Avani turned over on her cot. She clutched her blanket up against her chin. She thought she should tell Liam to drink more of the water she'd left in a jug beside his bed. She knew she should get up and check the sutures in his calf. But the gash was healing nicely and the slice across his neck and shoulders hadn't needed much tending at all.

He'd been lucky. Faolan hadn't. Nor had Halwn, nor any of its kin.

Wakeful, Avani shifted again, chasing after pleasant dreams. Of late her sleep had been full of nightmares: the old dreams of drowning but in the depths of the sea there were frightful, hungry things waiting to drag her into darkness and suffocation. Sometimes, when she turned her head on a scream, her last bubbling exhale rising to the surface, she saw Mal sinking alongside her.

"In the infantry Kingsmen are ordered so," said Liam. Avani heard the shuffle of pages in a book turning. Up in the rafters Jacob sneezed. "Shield men and then spear men—"

"Or women."

"Aye, or women," Liam agreed. "Tell me this word."

"I can't. It's too long."

"Try," urged Morgan from where he was perched near the window, industriously wiping down his leather jerkin, boots, and gauntlets with a rag and flaxseed oil.

Parsnip groaned. Avani pressed her face into the mattress. Children preparing for war through words and diagrams on the page seemed a hopeless thing when they'd had so little preparation out of the schoolroom. Parsnip, at least, would have relative safety inside the city walls, but Liam and Morgan would be lambs to the slaughter.

Despair felt like being pulled into the depths of the sea.

"Cast him out!" Jacob shrieked from the rafters, making everyone in the room jump. Avani sat bolt upright. Jacob glared down at her, head cocked, black eye bright. "Cast him out!"

"Goddess," Avani swore, heart in her throat. "By all that's sacred, *what*—"

"Oh, aye." Liam and Parsnip looked calmly over the top of their book. They had pushed two cots together and were cuddled close so Parsnip could turn the pages. "He does that now. The talking. I thought you knew."

Avani threw off her blanket and rose her feet. "That's impossible." She arched her brows at the bird in sour disbelief. "Jacob doesn't speak."

"I knew a parrot once—"

"Cast him out!" Jacob clicked his beak rudely. "Bring the torches! Burn him!"

Avani's heart dropped from her throat to her gut. Jacob shat on the dormitory floor as if to punctuate his point, then paced back and forth on the rafter, head bobbing, injured wing dragging. Parsnip clapped her hand over her mouth to muffle a snort. Avani sat down again. She let her head drop into her hands, then looked sideways at the idol resting peacefully in the sunlight.

For all the rudeness of her chosen messenger, Avani thought, the Goddess couldn't have made Herself more clear.

The dormitory door slammed open. Avani lifted her head. Arthur burst across the threshold, wide-eyed. "The king!" he reported, through gasps of air. "The king's coming! They're on the main road; I cut through the forest. Riggins says straighten up, neat as a penny!" He made a dash for his cot, hastily scooping up strewn papers and empty honey pots from the floor and shoving the entire mess unceremoniously beneath the mattress.

Liam caught Avani's eye across the room, a silent question.

"*Ai*, I imagine he knows I'm here," she said. "What will he do, drag me back in chains?'

"Might try," Parsnip said, struggling to push her cot back into place, "after he finishes whupping Liam for running wild with barrowmen."

Liam grimaced. He pulled his coverlet up around his chin, concealing his bandages beneath. Avani rose to help Parsnip with the cot. Jacob ran back and forth across his rafter, screeching. Arthur stood by the windows, watching the courtyard beneath. Only Morgan seemed unconcerned, folding his rag and capping his jug of linseed oil without hurry.

By the time heavy treads shook the dormitory

stairs they were well in order, the pages standing at attention in the middle of the room, Jacob's shit scrubbed off the floorboard with Morgan's rag. Liam sat stiffly beneath his blankets. Avani stood near the windows, hands folded placidly behind her back, braced for conflict.

She knew before Riggins entered the room that Mal was not with them. His attention was turned inward, his thoughts fragmented, consumed with bone dust and rust and old manuscripts and candle wax. Sometimes, when she blinked, she looked briefly out through his open eyes, fleeting impressions of his laboratory or his chambers. Sometimes he waved a hand over his head as he worked to shoo her away. Sometimes, when she woke hungry in the middle of the night, it was because he'd forgotten to eat.

She'd hurt him by running away to the barracks; he was doing his best to ignore her, and she her best not to draw his distracted attention. They were both, she thought, shamming freedom.

"Stand for His Majesty King Renault," Riggins proclaimed. His pleased smile said that he was relieved to see his young soldiers already on their feet and tidy. His worried look Avani's way said he hadn't expected to find her in the dormitory.

Four Kingsmen entered first, two at a time, arranging themselves on either side of the door. The dormitory was a narrow room. Their bulk and ceremony seemed to suck much of the light air from the space. Avani moved closer to windows.

Renault entered next, Brother Orat two steps behind. Parsnip, Morgan, and Arthur immediately took the knee, heads bowed. Liam scooted upright against his pillow, trying for dignity. Orat was no more pleased to see Avani than Riggins had been. But Renault had expected to see her there; he inclined his head in her direction. She returned a half bow for his courtesy, but did not kneel. The simple silver circlet he wore on his brow caught sunshine. Above their heads Jacob chortled.

"There he is, the troublemaker." Renault cocked an eye at the raven. "I hate to confess it, but I've missed his company. The throne room is less engaging without his mischief. I suppose you'll be taking him with you."

Avani blinked. "Your Majesty—the choice is Jacob's. He's recovering from injury, and of late he and I have suffered a—" to her horror she felt tears threaten "—a falling out."

Renault rubbed a hand over his close-cropped beard. "The battlefield is no place for alienation," he said gently. "Whether Jacob goes or stays, best repair your quarrel before riding out."

"And when will that be, Majesty?"

"Three days, mayhap four. No more." Renault took his hand from his face and she saw that his mouth was resigned. "Jacob is not the only patient in this room, I'm told. Liam, attend me."

"Your Majesty—" Avani took a step forward in protest. The nearest Kingsmen put his hand on his sword in warning. Renault held up his hand.

"Well, lad, can you stand or no?"

"I can." Liam pushed away his coverlet and sat up. Carefully, he swung his injured leg to one side of the mattress. The bandages around his knee and calf made his trousers bulky and walking awkward, but he limped to the center of the room without hesitation. "Your Majesty."

Orat clicked his tongue and wagged his head in professional dismay.

"Well." Renault sighed. "Can you ride, lad?"

"Aye."

"Your Majesty," Riggins interjected. "Aye, *Your Majesty*."

Liam stared at his feet. Avani dug her fingernails into her palm to keep from speaking out. Mal's curiosity stirred. She looked out the window and counted clouds in the sky until, distracted, he forgot her again. Jacob cackled.

"Liam," said Renault, ignoring Riggins. "Are you still my man? Or do we, also, have a quarrel between us?"

"Your Majesty." The crack in her lad's voice did nothing to staunch Avani's traitorous tears. "I burned down your woods."

Renault coughed. The sound was a laugh smothered. "Not all of them, lad. Perhaps an acre, no more.

The smoke has cleared; the skies are blue again. It happens, more often because of lightning strike than *sidhe* mischief. Orat."

Brother Orat reached beneath his robes and pulled forth a heavy circlet of bronze accented in the middle with shining amber. The bronze had been cleaned of smoke and blood. Liam stifled a soft cry. Avani stopped trying to quash her tears.

Renault took the torque from his priest and presented it to Liam. "I didn't know what to do with this, at first, when my soldiers laid it before my throne. 'Twas Malachi who suggested you might like to have it. The priests have made sure it is free of any *sidhe* taint. I cannot pretend I will mourn Faolan, but he risked much to bring me word of rising threat, and then again to rid my kingdom of a more immediate danger. He was more loyal than Brother Paul or my armswoman or Holder, whose grandfather knelt before mine own."

"I don't think it was for loyalty he did it, Majesty." Liam's mouth trembled as he regarded the torque. "I think it was for family." He took Faolan's collar in his hands and clutched it to his chest.

Renault nodded. "I fear you have to choose, lad. Are you my man, for loyalty? Or does your heart turn now to family and darker places? I will not blame you for your birthright, Liam, but I cannot keep you if it is *sidhe* trumpets thrilling in your ears."

Liam bit his lip. His knuckles were white around

Faolan's torque. He was no longer the child Avani had first encountered in the Widow's kitchen, dirty and starving, scrawny. And he was not the lad who had survived *sidhe* knives only to emerge forever disfigured. She'd thought him a man when he'd returned from Roue, but now she realized she'd been mistaken. He'd been growing, but not quite grown.

Liam heaved a sigh. Then he set the torque aside and sank gingerly to his good knee. And it was a man Avani witnessed kneeling before his king. The disastrous *sidhe* Hunt, and Faolan's death, had at last put an end to Liam's childhood.

"Your Majesty," he said. "I am yours."

"Thank you." Renault's mouth softened. From his own breast he unpinned a narrow silver bar: a private's insignia. "Rise," he ordered, and when Liam did, Renault fastened the medal to Liam's tunic before moving to one side to allow Orat room. The theist sketched a sigil over Liam's head and murmured a simple blessing. Andrew's ring, hung on its chain beneath Avani's salwar, warmed in response. So, too, did the thumb-sized gem in Faolan's torque. Jacob flapped awkwardly from the rafters to investigate, effectively shielding the waking *sidhe* gem from view before king or Orat took notice.

Renault beckoned again to Brother Orat. Together they walked down the line of pages, stopping before Parsnip and then Arthur to bestow on each a silver bar and the temple's blessing. Parsnip's grin was wide and proud. Arthur was somber and pale, his expression disbelieving.

"Wythe," the king said, pausing at last in front of the young earl, "rise."

Morgan rose nimbly to his feet. Of all the new-made Kingsmen he would be the smallest. Even Parsnip was taller, her body already becoming compact and muscular. Arthur had begun to fit his large feet and hands. But Morgan seemed caught in that strange youthful twilight between nursery and first beard.

No wonder, Avani thought, his mother was afraid. Even hidden away in the cavalry the young earl was at a disadvantage.

Renault pinned the silver bar to Morgan's breast. The lad's title trumped his new-made military rank, but by the way his fingers shook when he reached up to touch the bar, Avani knew without question which honor mattered more.

"I'm told Wythe brings one hundred good soldiers to the cavalry and infantry each," said Renault. "Men and women who should by all reason instead be settling their land and livestock for winter's sleep."

"Yes, Majesty." Morgan's cheeks were pale as milk. "It's an honor, Majesty."

"Wilhaiim is grateful. Your mother says you will ride out ahead of her horsemen. As earl you will require attendants on the field. I daresay you will be pleased to hear that amongst those chosen Liam has agreed to ride at your side as squire and swords-bearer."

Morgan swayed. Avani thought he might faint but Orat caught his shoulder before he could go down. Arthur caught at his other arm, holding him upright. But Morgan regained his own. He shook Arthur and the theist off, and lifted his chin.

"Thank you, Majesty," he said. "Liam is my friend, and a brave companion. I am . . . grateful."

"Good," Renault said. He clapped his hands together. "Tonight you'll be sleeping with the cavalry. Liam, are you up to the task of settling your new master at once in the north tower?"

"Aye, Your Majesty."

"Majesty," Arthur interjected before Renault could turn away. "For Parsnip and me? Is it the infantry?" His eagerness was in stark contrast to Morgan's set face and Parsnip's more wary countenance.

"Not quite yet," replied the king. "Captain Riggins will be settling you and the lass in the palace, with my personal guard."

Parsnip stiffened. Arthur's excitement deflated. "You're keeping us back."

Riggins blanched. "Young man—" he placed a hand in warning on Arthur's head "—remember to whom you are speaking. His Majesty has given you a great honor today. Do not—" his fingers flexed "—make me regret your training."

Arthur's face fell. Parsnip's hands were fists at her sides. Renault hesitated.

"You are children yet," the king said bluntly.

"Children are always precious, but as of late more so. You are also not wrong; I am keeping you back. I prefer not to send children to war, whenever possible. Even blooded children. If you believe your friend has seized the better end of the stick, you are wrong. He sees the truth of it, if you do not." Renault tipped his chin in Morgan's direction. "Now, say your goodbyes and make them count."

Riggins ushered his charges away from the king. Liam limped after. Morgan accepted their embraces with aplomb, although his smile faltered and threatened to slip.

"You have decided I am cruel," said Renault, joining Avani by the windows. He waved Brother Orat away, irritable. "Nay, don't deny it. You've run all the way to the barracks to hide yourself. Didn't high yourself back to the empty Downs and tuck away amongst your sheep?"

"Liam was here."

"Liam doesn't need you anymore."

Avani met his mild stare. "Aye," she said. "I think you're cruel. For what you ordered done to Desma, and to the barrowman in your dungeon. For sending that lad all unprepared into war. For using Mal as you do."

"He is a willing tool. He would find your suggestion otherwise deeply offensive." Renault peered out the dormitory windows. Avani didn't think he was seeing the blue sky or the Mabon tree, or even the retinue of palace guards waiting patiently below. "I did not suppose he'd find a woman's comfort again, not after Siobahn. I was glad for him, when we startled the two of you midembrace. Pink-cheeked as two children caught stealing from the larder, the both of you. I was pleased." Renault turned his back on sunshine. "Now I am not so certain. You say I am cruel; I say the same to you."

Fury turned the edges of the room white. Avani's wards crackled into existence, sparking silver. She hadn't meant to summon them into being. She was distantly dismayed.

Five blades hissed from their scabbards, five swords pointed in her direction. Riggins, despite his age, was almost as quick as the king's guard. Any other time she might have been impressed.

"I'm not a threat." Renault hadn't moved. Silver netting sparkled a hairsbreadth from the toe of his boot. "I am your king."

"You were never that," denied Avani through gritted teeth. Jacob hopped across floorboards, stopping just beyond her wards. Orat, too, drifted close again. "Mayhap, you were my friend."

"Do you plan to go to war under my banner," asked Renault, "or have I misunderstood?"

"To tend the injured, at your own constable's request."

"Healing is the provenance of the temple," Orat said. "There will be theists aplenty in amongst the troops to do so."

"House Wythe asked for Lady Avani. In particular."

Orat scowled at Morgan. Renault scrubbed his hand through his beard. Avani thought this time he was hiding a smile. She quenched her wards with an effort. Jacob, mercurial as ever, launched himself to her shoulder where he clung, sharp claws piercing the fabric of her salwar.

"My mother trusts Lady Avani," continued Morgan. "A rare thing, as I'm sure Your Majesty is aware. She's not wont to trust many, my mother. And, as I suspect Your Majesty is also aware, ofttimes it's better to indulge a mother's whims."

Wythe is no friend to the throne, Mal reminded her.

Go away. This is my business.

When were you planning to tell me? You're no more fit for warring than those children. Am I so abhorrent you prefer certain death to my company? His bitterness made her throat ache. She pushed at him and he retreated but not so far she didn't feel him there, bearing witness.

"It would be a boon indeed, a magus riding with your house," said the king. "There are only two left alive in my kingdom. Apart worth more than all the treasure in my vault, together priceless. Why would I grant Wythe that honor?"

"Your Majesty," retorted Morgan, "it would seem that gift is not yours to give. Lady Avani?"

"I will go," Avani told Renault. "As and when I

like. *Ai*, unless you mean to clap me in manacles and lock me in the catacombs."

"Don't tempt me." But he nodded and as one the Kingsmen sheathed their blades. "Imagine, if you will, what might happen should you fall into the hands of the desert lords. You say Mal is my agent. What prevents you from becoming a weapon against me, in the wrong hands?"

"I am not Mal," Avani replied coldly. "I serve the Goddess first and myself second and there is no room for a third."

"You are dangerously naïve." He unpinned a final silver bar from his breast and flicked it onto the nearest cot, where it bounced on the mattress. "Wear a uniform, at least, so you draw less attention. And the bar, there, or one of my soldiers may skewer you for a spy. I care not that you refuse to swear allegiance, but promise me you'll think of your friend before you step rashly into battle."

"My friend?"

"Aye," Renault agreed sharply. "Me." He cast her one last sour glance before making for the door, Orat and the Kingsmen hurrying after.

Well done, said Mal from a distant, dusty barn, sleeves rolled up to his elbows, fingers sooty. His sarcasm was equally black. *You and I are not so different as you like to believe.*

CHAPTER 14

The mystery of the coastal ponies was quickly solved: camels were terrified of the *sidhe* gate.

Their first day on white sands Everin and Drem passed without notice through the temporary city that was the desert army. Two sand snakes in a nest of thousands drew no undue attention. Their trickery held, although often Everin caught Drem scratching absently at the dried acacia gum concealing Desma's tattoos. Each time he warned the *sidhe* off with a low whistle or an elbow in the ribs. Everin didn't blame Drem; the dried solution itched worse than the dune fleas biting at their feet and ankles. At least the fleas let up during the hottest part of the day and the coldest hours of the night. The acacia prickled constantly.

In the beginning, they moved toward the gate, choosing those well-trod lanes between encampments that seemed most direct. The lanes were busy. Nomadic living meant whole families settled in one lodge and tribe members camped side by side. Dogs, livestock and children ran wild. Chickens roosted atop the tents or in the bundles of hay kept behind each lodge for the ponies. Tradespeople set up shop in the lanes, hawking everything from fresh cactus fruit and dried khaim jerky to warriors' kilts and sandals to comfort of both the medicinal and sexual sort.

"Disgusting," said Drem in its mother-tongue, low, muffled by the folds of its veil. It stepped over a pile of steaming manure. "Humans stink."

Everin didn't bother to point out they both smelled worse than any person they passed. "I told you not to speak," he said instead.

"You promised we'd be out of the sun, in a tent, with water," Drem retorted, turning silken *sidhe* vowels sharp. "We've been walking for more than a day, half of that time now beneath burning skies." It stopped, forcing traffic around them both. A woman dressed in a linen chiton instead of snakeskin glanced their way as she trotted past, a large jug of fermented mesquite beer balanced on her shoulder. Six kilted warriors, faces wrapped against the wind, passed three to either side. They gave Desma's strong thighs a cursory, appreciative glance before moving on. Drem didn't notice. "I am *fatigued*."

Everin adjusted his veil. Between the lodges the wind was lesser but a sandy grit still hung in the air, making his eyes water. He'd been so intent on weaving his way through the temporary city toward their goal he had forgotten that, in the heat and surrounded by steel, Drem did not have a mortal's endurance. He saw now what he'd ignored and what the passing sand snakes had not noticed: behind Desma's stern desert beauty, Drem was beginning to droop.

"Water," the *sidhe* said, twisting Desma's mouth into a sneer, "and a sit down is all I require. Don't look so eager. The iron hasn't got me yet."

Everin squinted past lodge poles at the horizon. He'd lost track of time. The sun hung midsky. Awareness made his stomach wake and cramp on emptiness. Blisters stung between his toes where sandal leather rubbed. The skin on his shoulders felt stretched from too much time in the heat.

"This way," he decided, choosing a promising tent from amidst a forest of similar. "Don't speak."

Drem scoffed but followed.

The encampment Everin approached flew two flags from its highest tent pole. The topmost was a crimson starburst on white background. Below that flapped a smaller pennant: two black scorpions on a field of red. Three lodges were pitched side by side, canvas doors fastened shut against wind. A large pot hung from a tripod over a banked cook fire. Sisal rugs covered the ground between the tents, the cook fire, and two hobbled camels. The rugs kept the sand from blowing into the lodges or the food or onto the camel.

They were weighted down at each corner with elaborately woven capped baskets.

Two men sat in the shade cast by the lodges, talking softly. They looked up when Everin and Drem stepped off the road and onto their rugs. Their faces were wrapped and they wore feathers in their long hair and sewn into the pleats of their kilts. They did not seem alarmed by the intrusion.

"How much," asked Everin, "for one of yon beasts?"

One of the men uncurled and rose to his feet. His chest and feet were naked in the heat. He pulled away his scarf, baring an amused smile. The camels stirred as Drem came near, squeaking uneasily. Their master hushed them with a sharp word.

"Not for sale," he replied.

"Everything is for sale," said Everin. "At the right price. We've come a long way. Our camel died east of the fissure. One is all we need to carry our tent and our baskets."

"A long way indeed," the man said, "and late to news. Those are not beasts of burden any longer. They are supper."

The second warrior laughed at Everin's surprise. He stayed seated but also pulled down his scarf. He was older, his yellow eyes clouded. Gray salted his brows and beard, and age lines pulled down the corners of his mouth.

"Join us," he offered formally, "before you fall

down. We have beer, and some meat to share. Then we will talk camels."

Everin accepted the invitation, squatting on his heels in the shade. There the wind was nonexistent. He freed his nose and mouth from folds of cloth. The shade was only marginally cooler than direct sun but it was a relief to sit.

"You, also," their host told Drem, who hadn't yet moved. "I am Myron, and this is my son Pelagius. The others are resting after a night in the saddle." He nodded at the tents. While Drem settled on the rug, spear laid carefully beside Desma's knee, Pelagius fetched a pitcher and four cups from within a basket. He poured out a round of beer before sitting again in the shade.

"Erastos." The old name fell easily off Everin's tongue. "And my sister, Demetria." For courtesy's sake he toasted Myron before taking a healthy swallow of beer. Unlike flatland ale, the liquor was sweet and syrupy, and warm. One cup refreshed the body. Four could send a man into a drunken stupor. To Everin, the beer tasted like home. "May your enemies fall before you."

Myron chuckled. "It's been a good year," he conceded, "and not just for the scorpion tribe." He sipped his drink before raising gray brows in polite enquiry. "From east of the fissure, you said? I had family east. They were not so late as you to war. They arrived a full season past, with the rains."

Drem had not touched the beer. Pelagius watched the *sidhe* minutely. Everin could not tell whether the young man was admiring Desma's beauty or affronted by Drem's abysmal manners.

"Sister," Everin chided. "If you fall asleep over your drink you will offend our hosts."

Drem glared, through the folds of its veil. Then it plucked aside silk, raised its cup in a succinct toast in Myron's direction, and downed the drink in one gulp. Myron's smile deepened. Pelagius's mouth twitched.

"Good," Drem said, smothering a cough. "Thank you."

"My family serve in isolation," Everin continued, hoping Drem was not about to vomit all over Myron's rugs. "As brick makers, in the mudflats. News always comes to us several seasons too late."

Myron puckered his lips in sympathy. "And which lord is it that you serve, Erastos?"

Everin took another swallow of drink to hide vacillation. It was possible, although not probable, that in his absence titles had shifted or been lost. Like the white sands, desert hierarchy was oft changing, prey to familial schism or tribal feuds. There was no guarantee the man he had served ruled still.

"Nicanor," he ventured.

For a heartbeat Everin thought they were lost. Myron closed his eyes in thought, brow wrinkled. Drem shifted, one hand alighting on the rug very near its spear. Everin rested his own casually on the pommel of the Aug's sword. Then Pelagius nodded.

"Nicanor is here," he said. "They are much closer to the gateway, near Black Crom's lodges. Remember, father. We saw his flag when he came in."

"Ah, yes." Myron's eyes snapped open. "But that was moons ago, *before* even the rains. You are quite tardy, Erastos. Nicanor will not be pleased."

Everin finished the dregs of his beer to hide his face.

"Tell us," Drem said after a moment of silence. "About eating the humped beasts."

Everin coughed. Drem arranged Desma's mouth into a bland expression, deliberately not looking Everin's way.

"New orders from the top," replied Pelagius. He licked his lips. "Camels, they will not go near the demon gateway. They spit and moan and fall in the sand. The ponies are not so smart, and do much better, as promised." He propped his chin on one fist, regarding the two dozing camels with fond resignation. "I will be sorry to put old friends to the slaughter, but who knows what we will find on the other side of the mountains? I would rather eat gamy camels than starve."

"I have heard," Myron added, "that the flatlanders are forced to catch their suppers in river waters, or in the sea."

"Fish," said Drem with relish.

"Demetria has spent time on the other side of the divide," explained Everin hastily. "Scouting the west face of the mountains."

"Ah!" Pelagius leaned close. "Demetria! Tell us! Is it as they say? A land bursting with true gold and opion and plenty of fields for a man to make his own? Greener than scrubland after a hard rain?"

"It is," replied Drem, "a green and gold land, also black as dusk and red as dawn. Plenty of rain on root and leaf, and sweet meat to fill an empty belly. If," the *sidhe* added, "one is willing to kill for a piece of it."

Myron busied himself with refilling their cups. "I look forward to sweet meat," he said. "I grow tired of famine. Every year is harder than the last. The rainy season is shorter each turn: the crops turn to dust, the animals die. We all suffer for it." He swirled the beer in his cup. "For a little while longer we will make do with khaim and camel meat. So then. You were not wrong. Everything under Two Scorpions is for sale—at a price. I am willing to sell to you a piece of my beasts. Say, a quarter of a haunch. If you are interested."

"I am more interested," replied Everin, "in talk of ponies. We would rather ride proud through the gateway than run behind."

"That is your Nicanor's business," retorted Myron. "Whom of his tribe shall ride and whom shall walk? Take it up with him."

Everin flicked two fingers in acceptance. Desma's

head was lolling; Drem was not pretending weariness. Pelagius looked dangerously close to laying his head in her lap.

"A place in one of your lodges," Everin decided. "Until sun down. So my sister may sleep."

"For the telescope," answered Myron. "You may each share a sleeping fur in one of my tents. Also—" he wrinkled his nose "—water to wash. For the sake of my family."

"Telescope?" Baffled, Everin followed the other man's gaze to the lens hanging on his belt. "Of course. But we are hungry. And this telescope is very fine, indeed."

"Water to wash. A place to sleep until sundown. Khaim and a jug of beer. For the rest, you'll have to find your lord. If you are lucky, he will not whip you for being tardy."

Everin spit in his left hand and then offered it, palm up, in the manner of a desert bargain sealed. "Done," he said. "And thank you."

Myron's cloudy eyes danced. "Pelagius will show you to the water cask. Mind he keeps his hands to himself. He is of an age for a second wife, and your Demetria is a rare jewel."

They left Two Scorpions after sunset. Pelagius was visibly disappointed to see them go. Myron, busy taking apart his new telescope near the cook fire, was less so. His family, forsaking bed for the evening's activities, gathered to see them off, inquisitive and solemn.

"May your enemies fall before you," Pelagius said. "But if they do not, may you find the god's cradle in good time."

"I will look for you there," Everin responded, bowing from the waist. Drem, gnawing a strip of khaim, said nothing. Everin ushered the *sidhe* away from the lodge and back onto the road. Light was coming up all throughout the encampment; torches burned near each lodge and at every intersection, smelling heavily of animal fat. Cook fires were fed fresh tinder until the flames leapt high and hot. Laughter rang out as day-sleepers stirred. The wind had abated at last. The army was waking, singing praises to the gloaming.

"Is it the same god?" Drem wondered around a mouthful of jerky. "Pelagius's god and the one on the other side of the mountains?"

"There are no gods but the *sidhe*," Everin recited. He meant it as mockery. Drem shrugged.

"The gate is directly that way," the lesser *sidhe* said, jabbing khaim at the twilight. "'Twould be simpler to cut across."

"Simpler but hardly expedient. Every lodge we crossed would play host. We'd soon be too drunk to find our own feet. These are a congenial people, Drem. They value allegiance."

"When they're not fighting amongst themselves."

"Which they are not, for the moment." Everin stopped at a crossroads to find his bearings. Drem was right. The tent city was a maze. He could not be sure the correct turning was the most obvious and they did not have time to waste. Already they'd been off the mountain two days too long. Drem might claim no ill effects, but there was no certainty Faolan's magic would hold up indefinitely under the weight of so much surrounding iron.

"Nicanor?" he asked, stopping a lass before she could hurry by. "Nicanor's lodge?"

"Lord Nicanor?" She pointed opposite the path he would have chosen. "That way. Next to Black Crom's lodge, you can't miss it. The demon gate shines upon his tent flap."

"Shines?" Everin asked Drem when the lass had trotted away.

"Black Crom?" Drem frowned.

They walked on, stopping frequently so Everin might ask further directions. From Skerrit's Pass he'd assumed the army was exactly as it had looked: lodge squares laid out in a tidy grid. In fact there were as many sideways and byways as main roads, trails carved into the sand by necessity of use. Some squares had become rectangles as lodges were added to a family grouping, turning roads into dead ends as space ran out.

There were tinkers living alongside the sand

snakes, carts and wagons tied up near tents. From the depths of sand around the wagon wheels they were long ensconced. They whistled cheerfully as they set out their wares for the night, joking easily with the desert merchants who were their competition.

"They've been here some time," Drem said.

"The tinkers?"

"The army. Also the tinkers. The sun has faded the paint on their wagons. The tents, also, are more worn to the north, from whence the wind comes. Patched in places, do you see?"

"I see," Everin replied. "But I never thought it possible. To stop moving in the desert is to die."

"If you are a camel or a wolf or even a sand serpent," agreed Drem, "but these people have something neither the camel nor the wolf nor the serpent claims to know."

"And what's that?"

"Hope." For an instant sharp *sidhe* teeth flashed in Desma's smile.

Everin grunted. "Renault will never let go the flatlands."

"So we said, when the woods and waters and prairies belonged to the *sidhe*." Before Everin could respond, Drem lifted its spear, indicating with the tip. "Look there. It shines upon his tent flap."

In their circuitous ramblings, dusk had turned the sky to deep purple, and then to near black. The moon was not yet bright. A new brilliance bloomed on the horizon to the southeast, turning lodge roofs from white to rose. It shifted like a candle flame through wavy glass: expanding, retreating, and then burgeoning once more. Alarm made Everin's heart catch.

"Skald's balls." His feet stopped moving of their own accord. Drem dragged him off the busy road under the scant shelter of a merchant's canvas. The merchant, busy plucking spines from cactus fruit, looked up in welcome. Everin ignored him. "By the Aug—"

"Hsst," Drem interrupted. "Hush." The *sidhe* directed a scowl at the fruit merchant. "What is that? That light?"

The man walked around his counter to get a better look. When he glimpsed the rosy incandescence, he smiled. "Black Crom's grace," he said. "Isn't it lovely? Lately it shines often, as victory approaches and he graces us more often with his presence."

"Black Crom?" Everin paused in unhooking Myron's gift of beer from his belt. Drem snatched it away and stole a swallow. The merchant looked between them, puzzled.

"Yes, of course," he said. "Called Crom Dubh by his equals. May all his enemies—"

"Fall before him. Thank you." Drem placed a hand hard between Everin's shoulders blades and pushed him on ahead. Once out of the merchant's earshot, the *sidhe* began to laugh. Drem's laughter was as piercing as its voice, silver bells in a winter sky. It drew attention from nearby tents. Drem stifled the sound with one hand.

"Crom Dubh." Everin bit back more curses. "Not a tribesman, nor even a sand lord. I should have guessed. It needed something bigger to unite the desert." He looked bitterly at Drem. "Does Faolan know?"

"That a *sidhe* elder marshals mortal against mortal?" Drem's laughter subsided to musical giggles. "Would he have sent you, his best game piece, into the heart of it if he did? I think not." Desma's mouth curled, and that should have been warning enough, but Everin did not expect Drem's betrayal and so when the *sidhe* sprang, Everin barely missed being knocked to the ground. As it was, Drem's spear haft connected solidly with his ribs. Everin staggered, drawing his sword as he backpedaled.

"Hope," said Drem. Desma's spear whirled in its hand. "Until just now, you see, I'd mislaid it." Drem reversed the spear haft and struck at Everin's unguarded right side with the butt end. Everin blocked the blow, if not handily, then competently. The last time he'd had need to use a blade in earnest he'd been in Nicanor's employ. The irony did not escape him.

Drem slashed low. Everin hopped the spear haft, dancing forward. Drem scuttled sideways, evading Everin's thrust. Around them men, women, and children gathered, seeking entertainment. A few whistled approvingly and stomped their feet when Everin managed to dodge a third swat. The spear made Drem's reach much longer than Everin's own. Drem was faster, more agile. But Everin was unbloodied.

"You don't want to end me."

"Not yet," agreed Drem, closing their distance. "Not until I visit Crom Dubh and see how things stand." The *sidhe* leapt into the air, making spectators gasp. The spear butt came down with a crack on Everin's left wrist. The gathered crowd groaned sympathy. Everin grabbed at his falling sword with his right hand just as his left went numb, bobbled the pommel, and went down on his knees in the road to grab it again.

A warrior in snakeskin and wolf pelt clapped her hands, enjoying the show. "Your woman is good," she shouted cheerfully at Everin, "best apologize before she makes an eunuch of you." The people around her began to hoot.

"If Faolan didn't know, then things stand badly," gasped Everin, back on his feet. His left arm from his fingers to his elbow felt dead. In sword's play he was weaker with his right side than his left, but not incompetent. He clenched his jaw and set his guard. If Drem did not intend to kill him, all was far from lost. "Think. A new-waked *sidhe* elder? You'd be but a nuisance, an annoyance."

Drem's anticipation gleamed behind Desma's yellow eyes. "With you over my shoulder, I'd surely be welcomed."

Some things, Everin knew, were worse than death. He did not think twice. Sword in hand he wheeled and ran, plunging into the crowd, knocking unwary bystanders aside. Shouts and catcalls followed him off the road and into the nearest camp. He hopped a sleeping warrior, trod upon the cook fire, scattering sparks, and dashed on. From the sounds behind him, Drem was in fierce pursuit. In normal circumstances the *sidhe* would be far swifter. Everin could only hope the encompassing forest of steel and iron would deplete Drem's vigor.

The tent city was a maze, and Everin meant to use that muddle to his advantage. The night was a riot of sounds and smells. He pushed through one group of lodges to the next, and then the next. A sleeping camel rose upright out of the dancing shadows near a back road, startling him badly. He glanced over his shoulder as he ran. The camel hissed and spat, and struggled to break free of its tether: Drem was still too close.

Stars blinked in the desert sky. The rose-red glow on the horizon pulsed. His left arm was turning to pins and needles. The sound of his boots pounding on sand seemed too loud in his ears. He'd run from *sidhe* pursuit more times than he cared to remember in trying to escape the barrows. He'd never been fast enough. In the end, his strength always ran out.

A thrush called in the night, from mere steps behind. Everin recognized the whistle for what it was: Drem's sense of dark humor. Just as no thrush lived high on Skerrit's Pass, so also were the birds nonexistent in the desert. Everin leapt behind a tinker's cart, shoving it over into the road before he ran on. The tinker screamed outrage as her wares crashed onto the sand. Everin took advantage of the distraction to duck between a pyramid of stacked hay and a lodge tent. Puffing, he set his back to the stack, flexed his left hand as he listened for pursuit. A pony, hobbled near the hay, regarded him with suspicion.

Everin crouched, making himself as inconspicuous as possible. There was no purpose in moving on toward the *sidhe* gate any longer. He needed to get back up and over the mountains with word of the elder's interference. To do that, he needed to lose Drem. Alone in the dark, weary to the point of hysteria, and surrounded by enemies, escape seemed an impossible and frightening task. Drem, like all its kin, was bred for the hunt.

Everin reached for Myron's flask to ease his nerves, found it gone, and remembered that Drem sipped from it last. He choked back a snort of hysteria. The pony rolled an eye in his direction, clearly unimpressed. Everin sighed and sheathed his sword. A naked blade would draw notice, and he intended to blend in. He wrapped his veil around his face, rubbed the tension from his neck, glanced at the stars in the sky for orientation, and then stepped briskly out from behind the haystack and back onto the busy road, heading west.

None of the sand snakes paid him any attention at all. They were busy with talk of war and famine. He was one kilted warrior amidst many. The moon's silver face ripened, outshining every torch. In the night the desert was a place of beauty and promise, every man and woman united in survival. Almost, he was Erastos again, Nicanor's finest champion, a wolf running wild on the dunes. Almost, addled and sleep deprived, he believed he'd never left.

Almost, he made it to the western edge of the encampment. The mountains were again within sight; he could smell sage broom. He thought to hide himself in the wash, hole up in a gulley, and sleep. Relief made him lengthen his stride.

A thrush called from the road behind. Everin stumbled. He broke into a trot, pushing past a throng of opion befuddled, bare-chested men busy howling at the stars. The thrush called again, this time from the road ahead. Another answered. And a fourth, east and west and just behind. He stopped and drew his sword, surrounded and baffled by the trap.

Drem fell on him from above, as though from the moon itself, knocking Everin to the ground, pressing his face into the sand. Everin bucked, but when he inhaled, he breathed grit, and Drem, for all its child-sized frame, was heavier than it looked. He was pinned.

It had traded spear for dirk. It pressed the blade to Everin's pulse point and leaned close. "You'll be glad of me," it said into his ear, just as it had promised on Skerrit's Pass. Then it sat up and whistled. Everin lifted his head off the ground to better see his down-fall.

The bare-chested men were not so opion addled as they appeared. Nor Pelagius a love-sick fool in truth. They surrounded Everin where he lay, spears and scimitars shining, Pelagius at their head. He squatted near Everin.

"I have a message for you, little king," he said in the language of deep barrows and dark places. "The *dullahan* says your debt has come due."

They hoisted Everin onto his feet and took his sword and bound his hands behind his back with braided leather rope. When he struggled, Pelagius backhanded him twice across his face. Everin tasted blood. Dizzy, defeated, he stumbled ahead of their brutal encouragement. His captors surrounded him in a tight circle, using sword point and muscle mass to disperse curious spectators. Hardened warriors scattered before Pelagius's terse threats.

Everin looked for Drem but did see not his erstwhile companion anywhere.

Pelagius and his men marched him toward the rose-gold glow in the east. As they grew close to the gate, lodges became sparse. The encampments they did pass were lavish, tightly guarded by watchful warriors with ready swords. There was less noise; the energy of the common camp did not extend to this more private sanctum.

They rounded a corner and night turned to day. Here the torches were unlit, campfires banked low. Moonlight was nonexistent, subsumed by ruddy light. The world blushed. Everin lifted his chin and looked.

The gray stone arch was not a thing that belonged in the desert, between blazing skies and white sands, at the mercy of scraping winds. Impossibly green moss dripped in verdant swathes from its filigreed curvature, and down along two proud columns. Lush grass grew in an emerald sweep around its base. Blooming flowers scented the air; pink-budded saplings sprouted in the gate's shadow.

The saplings, the red-flushed flowers, and the emerald grass were not native to arid places. They were not, as far as Everin could tell, a flatland species, nor even coastal. He was certain he had never seen their like before.

"This way," ordered Pelagius, shoving Everin in the direction of a solitary lodge erected within striking distance of the gate. More armed warriors patrolled the camp perimeter. They carried scimitars and spears, bow and arrow. They took care not to step too close to the unnatural, flowering oasis. The rose-gold star within the gate turned their yellow eyes orange.

Pelagius propelled Everin into the lodge. Everin tripped on an edge of sisal carpet and went down. His bound hands were useless to break his fall. He landed on his shoulder and rolled onto his stomach, again facedown. There he lay still, a mouse hoping to elude the notice of a hungry hawk. It did him no good.

"Well done, Pelagius. Free his hands. He's beyond any chance for escape, and I wish to see what time outside the mounds has done to his face."

Everin knew that voice, he knew the lilting music of it. He smelled musty scales and dusty feathers and the odor of wet, fertile soil. Because he was not a better man, he cowered, curling in upon himself, hunching his shoulders.

It did him no good.

Pelagius was not gentle. He scraped Everin's flesh as he severed the leather rope. Then he grabbed him by the hair and hauled him up to kneeling. He grasped Everin's chin in unkind fingers, forced his gaze upward. "Crom Dubh wishes to see your face, mortal."

He seemed an ordinary man, to have the entire desert at his beck and call. Of average size, and average comeliness, his expression unreadable. He wore a snakeskin vest and wolf's pelt around his shoulders. There were many black feathers sewn onto his sleeves and kilt. His feet were bare of sandals, his dark hair pulled off a high brow into a loose tail.

He'd been standing near a brazier, warming his

hands over opion smoke and sage broom incense. He crossed sisal carpets without a sound, his movements sinuous and wrong, contrary as flourishing pink flowers in dry desert.

Everin heard invisible pinions dragging on sisal. Crom Dubh bent to better see Everin's face. A mediocre man with a mediocre smile, he huffed bland amusement.

"Little king," the *dullahan* said sweetly, his breath hot on Everin's brow. "Faolan is dead. Your debt to him is discharged. But you and I still have a score to settle. Stand."

Slowly, Everin found his feet. Pelagius's steel bit between his shoulder blades, a reminder. He stared blankly around the lodge, waiting for relief or sorrow and feeling neither. Faolan had been captor first, friend much later. He couldn't remember a time before the *aes si*'s interference in his life. It seemed impossible Faolan was gone, but the *dullahan* did not tell lies.

He glimpsed Drem standing alone against the tent wall. The *sidhe*'s shock made Desma's mouth tremble. When Drem saw Everin looking, it glanced away.

"You did not know? You did not feel the geis lift when he died? Ah, I see from your expression you did not. He was kind to you," the *dullahan* guessed. "You are an interesting plaything. Faolan enjoyed a tragedy. An infant princeling, traded by his mother to the *Tuath Dé* in return for her royal husband's life. The rightful heir to the mortal throne exiled forever beneath the earth because his progenitor loved him less. I imagine you suffered, knowing that. Faolan was attracted to human suffering, a moth to flame."

The *dullahan* stretched. It should have filled the tent to bursting. Its shadow did, darkening sisal carpet with an impression of wings spread and a coiled, lashing tail. Everin saw the shadow and Crom Dubh with his unremarkable smile, and his mind boggled. It was as if, he thought, the shadow cast the man.

"Human suffering is of no interest to me," the *dullahan* confessed. "Nor kindness. But I will be fair, so long as you fulfill your obligation."

Everin ground out, "What is it you want of me, monster?"

Pelagius hit him again for his disdain. "He is Crom Dubh. Show respect."

"That one," the *dullahan* said, regarding Pelagius fondly, "I caught the very night I left you on the mountain top. Tending his family's camels in the foothills. He was just a child, then. I recognized his ambition. No royal princeling, Pelagius, but he and his family have grown to be very useful. They appreciate malice and I reward each handsomely for his efforts. Almost, Pelagius's tribe is as useful to me as my lesser *sidhe*. Of a certain, they are more resourceful."

Everin did not respond. It crossed his mind then

that he might be wise in provoking his own death. Pelagius, he suspected, would be easily incensed. And it would not be a terrible end, so long as the sand snake knew how to use his blade.

Don't, said the *dullahan,* silver bells in his skull. *I will only bring you back, as many times as it takes. A painful process, a waste of time, and we both know you would not be unchanged. Die on the battlefield, if you like, but not until I'm done with you.*

"On the battlefield," repeated Everin. His head swam. He wondered what Pelagius would do if he fainted.

"You did well for yourself after I left." The *dullahan* padded across the lodge to the brazier. He spread blunt-fingered hands, warming them over the coals. "Erastos, desert wolf, hero of the dunes. Your enemies, I'm told, did indeed fall beneath your blade, easily as *sidhe* before iron."

The point of Pelagius's sword twitched against Everin's spine.

"When you vanished from the dunes, Nicanor mourned you as a lost brother," the *dullahan* mused. "And wept again when I told him just this evening that you were returned to us, alive and hardy, in the hour of our victory. He rejoices that you will lead the charge beside him with the rest of my heroes. These desert people are a courageous sort, but not unlike my lesser *sidhe,* they need incentive to take on a difficult task. The gate has been a task more difficult than most. Almost, it would be easier to convince them to move an army over the mountains than to convince one *warrior* to cross that threshold."

"It's the camels, Crom Dubh," Pelagius said with the air of a man who had explained this shame one too many times. "The camels will not go near it. In the desert, a man relies on his camel more so even than his sword."

The *dullahan* stretched again. Invisible pinions scraped. "No matter," he said. "We will make a show of it, and they will be convinced, from behind and ahead. It will not take much. They desperately want to believe. They've been so long without—" The *dullahan* blinked over the brazier at Drem.

"Hope," Drem offered quietly.

"So long without hope they're willing to follow anyone to greener fields."

"You want me to lead an army against my own people."

"The flatlanders were never your people. It was the desert you ran to when I flew you from the barrows. One last thing," the *dullahan* said, as if in afterthought. "Drem tells me Faolan taught you the ways of the tunnels beneath flatland fields and villages. I expect you can recall those youthful lessons. I trust you will make use of them for my benefit."

CHAPTER 15

"Here," said Mal, leaning over the old barrow map. He traced a finger along lines newly added to Andrew's original drawing. "And here. All of them, sealed. Avani and Russel took care of the entrances Andrew marked. I've closed twenty-seven more since, from Whitcomb to beneath the red wood and all the way again to the Maiden Cliffs." He met Renault's eye across the table. "The ones I've found, Majesty. I cannot guess how many I've missed."

Baldebert frowned over Mal's shoulder at the age-stained scroll. "It's a rabbit warren. How could you let it get so bad?"

"Let it?" Renault pressed his fingers together against his mouth. He regarded Baldebert bitterly. "They've been a long time underground, Admiral. I do not think anyone supposed they would survive their exile, much less prosper. In truth, we believed them extinct, old stories to frighten children in the dark."

"But will the sealed gates hold?" Orat demanded. He frowned at the map. Behind him in the oriel Tillion leaned on his staff and peered down through the panes at the street below, uninterested in the afternoon's proceedings.

Mal wished fervently that the new Masterhealer did not feel the need to bring his favorite lap dog to every parley. Tillion's presence did nothing to soothe already frayed tempers in the room.

"The gates will hold," he promised. "Avani and I have made sure of it."

"That one—" Orat shook his head "—belongs close at hand where she can protect His Majesty, not gadding about the battlefield like some green infantryman all afire for her first kill."

"Not her first," murmured Tillion from his place near the windows. "The armswoman was her first. Lady Avani came to temple after, and lit three candles in Lane's honor. She thought I didn't see her grieve. She thought I didn't see her at all."

Mal knew he could murder Brother Tillion on the spot and not feel inclined to light even a single candle. He cleared his throat.

"The gates that we have *found* will hold," he continued evenly. "But those that we have not? The palace, at least, is safe—we have made a thorough study of the catacombs beneath. I believe Wilhaiim, too, is shut tight against infestation. But outside our walls? Under the fields, beneath the villages, as far even as the coast—I will guarantee there are barrows not yet unearthed. If they have indeed found a way under the mountain, there is no telling from whence they might erupt."

"I had not thought to regret Faolan's loss," admitted Renault. "But he, at least, might have been convinced to our side, if only for the sake of peace. Surely the barrowmen do not want their warrens overrun with sand snakes any more than we want them in our fields."

"The other one." Baldebert glanced up from the map. "The beekeeper. Mayhap she could be of some help?" He tilted his head subtly in Mal's direction.

"Gone," replied Mal. "Her tent at the Fair, the hovel she called home, all cleaned out. If she's astute she'll have hidden herself well away until this mess blows over."

"'Mess,'" quoted Orat in disbelief. "By all reports we are outnumbered five to one. Our allies have come up short—" he curled a lip in Baldebert's direction "—and we cannot trust the ground not open beneath us and spit out the enemy at our feet. This is not a mess. This is a disaster. By the good god, what are we to do?"

"Pray," suggested Wilhaiim's king, resigned. He rose from behind the table, rolling up the map. "Or is that not the advice you've always given me?"

"In matters of state, certainly," Orat choked out. Almost, Mal felt sorry for the man. "And in time of sickness or drought. But this—we are facing certain slaughter—we are unequipped—"

"My new armsmaster will be distributing what reserve we have in the armory to the able-bodied," replied Renault. "If you hurry you may find yourself in possession of a sturdy sword."

"We are healers," Orat protested but stopped short beneath his king's cool stare. "You are quite correct, Majesty," he amended hastily. "Needs must."

"Needs must," agreed Tillion, peering thoughtfully in Mal's direction. "God will rise to the occasion and forgive us expediency. Or so one hopes."

Mal, catching the telltale signs of fury beneath Renault's dismissive gesture, did not think Wilhaiim's throne would ever forgive the temple for Brother Paul's contrivance.

"I think you dislike those two more than I," Renault said once the doors had closed behind the two theists.

Startled, Mal focused again on his king. "Orat is harmless. He served you well once and will do so again, assuming he finds his feet. It's Tillion I distrust."

Renault chuckled as he resumed his throne. "I've grown used to his preaching outside my windows. He's too fond of hyperbole but I appreciate his devotion to the cause." He accepted a goblet of ale from his newest page. The lass, dignified despite a preponderance of freckles and scabs on her knees beneath her thin hose, openly sized Mal up from beneath long lashes. He appreciated her hubris.

"Hello, Parsnip."

"My lord," she said after a glance at Renault for permission.

"You were paying attention? Listening carefully?"

"Yes, my lord. His Majesty said I might."

"Didn't frighten you, did we?" Mal wondered. He'd argued that it was unkind, exposing children to stark truths, but Renault had insisted on honesty.

"The Red Worm plucked those two from childhood without warning," the king had pointed out. "This time around, they deserve at least the illusion of control."

"You see, Parsnip, why I'd prefer to keep you close," Renault said now. "Within the city, where at least we can be certain our enemies won't boil up out of the ground without warning. You're safest here. Do you understand now?"

"Pardon, Majesty, my lords." She included Baldebert in her quiet disdain. "But me and Arthur, we'd make you better soldiers than both of those priests together. At least me and Arthur, we know which end of the sword is sharp."

At the back of the royal graveyard, closed behind a separate gray stone wall and an entirely mortal iron gate, Mal found Wilhaiim's hidden lich graves. Here, behind the sheltering wall, the bones of Wilhaiim's executed magi were interred. The gate was unlocked and not recently used. When he lifted the latch, flakes of rust fell from the iron onto the grass below. The hinges creaked as he coaxed the gate open, an eerie sound in an otherwise pleasant midday. Mal was no stranger to eerie sounds. He paid the squawking gate no mind as he picked up his spade and covered pail and hurried through the gate.

It closed behind him, latch clattering into place.

"Really, brother? Grave robbing?"

Mal didn't reply. Rowan wasn't there. Rowan was many years dead, lost at sea somewhere near the Black Coast. His ghost, if any such remained, haunted a grave fathoms deep. This thing, wearing Rowan's cheerful smile and floppy dark curls, was only a hallucination, Mal's madness taken form.

"Or mayhap your conscious," Rowan suggested, looking intently around the lich yard. "Trying to talk some sense. Do you really think stealing the bones of your murdered predecessors is a wise idea?"

Wistful reason or madness manifested, Rowan had kept Mal chattering company all the way from his quarters, through the cemetery where together they laid flowers first on Siobahn's grave and then Andrew's. It had happened once before, on *The Cutlass Wind*. Then not-Rowan had saved Mal's life. Today he seemed content with a lecture on morality, which

Mal might have found hilarious, given what he recalled of his brother's disreputable habits.

"Less humorous considering," Mal muttered. He, too, glanced around the yard, noting the temple sigils still shining up and down the wall, and on the obelisk set midpoint in the grass.

"Don't much like quarreling with yourself?" suggested Rowan. He wandered in a circle around the obelisk, buffing calloused fingers over the rough surface. "It's a bit not good, this going batty, am I right? Likely of the waxing-and-waning variety. What do you think we'd see, if we opened your skull and peeked inside? You and Tillion, side by side on the table?"

"Less humorous considering if I'm arguing with myself," continued Mal sharply over Rowan's disparagement. "And as I fear your very presence suggests I'm not fully committed." Mal tested the sod around the base of the obelisk with the toe of his boot. Choosing a likely spot, he began to dig. The spade cut grudgingly through grass. He lifted it up, brought it down again. And again. The force of it made his teeth jar.

"They'll burn you one way or another," Rowan agreed. He settled himself against the wall, crossed his legs at the ankles, prepared to wait. "If not for grave robbing, then at the end if you get yon monsters to walking. They'll hang you, or burn you, like the poor man on Holder's property, even if you do manage save your bloody king. Worth it, do you suppose?"

"It's what I do." Mal used the edge of his spade to peel back a square of grass. The soil was rocky beneath. He scraped and scooped then crouched to sift away larger stones.

"You never were so loyal as a wee lad." Years in court had suppressed Mal's seaside brogue. Rowan had it still.

"You never gave me the chance."

Rowan fell to silence while Mal shifted spadeful after spadeful of dirt from his hole to an increasing pile on the grass. He was not concerned with being interrupted; the wall afforded him plenty of privacy even if anyone wandered so far into the cemetery as to stumble onto the lich yard. When he'd left the palace, Tillion had been busy on his pedestal extolling the virtues of courage in the face of adversity while at the same time blaming Renault for the god's disfavor. And with Avani now having ridden out in the cavalry, there was not a person left who would willingly disturb Wilhaiim's vocent at work. He was still the most powerful man in the city, and now thrice as frightening for his growing air of eccentricity.

"Batty," Rowan corrected. "You would have been better off kept isolated at home."

Scowling, Mal wiped sweat from his brow. "I wasn't welcome, once our father realized."

"Not in the Rose Keep," Rowan agreed. "But there was nothing stopping you from setting up shop somewhere along the coast, brother. Driftwood cottage, a fishing line. A clever coastal man needs little else. You should have stayed a Serrano. Lord Malachi Doyle was always beyond your ken."

"Be quiet," Mal said, both hands clenched around the spade's handle.

"At least alone on the coast," Rowan added, "you'd do no one else any harm."

"Be quiet, I said!" Mal snarled, hurling the spade in Rowan's direction. It clattered against gray stone and bounced harmlessly away. Rowan wasn't there. He never had been.

Mal breathed through his nose. Blades of grass shed puffs of smoke around his feet where the embers of his temper had fallen. He stamped out the tiny fires, angrily collected his spade, and returned to his digging. Sorting stones from soil proved to be more time consuming than he'd planned. He paused occasionally to rest, leaning on the handle of his spade. In the darkness behind his eyelids a constellation of life sprang up. Lately he could not sleep for the brilliance in his head. In his very worst moments, he itched to quench each spirit, one at a time until he was alone and in peace.

The lip of his spade caught on something that was not dirt or rock, rousing him from a vivid daydream of tromping idly along a muddy water course, searching for arrowroot to the busy background of laughter and clashing sword blades. But he did not belong there; that was Avani's undertaking and she'd made it abundantly clear she wanted no part of him.

Mal dropped onto his hands and knees to better see what he had uncovered. A flap of old burlap, soil encrusted, disintegrating in patches. He worked his fingers in the dirt around it, trying to shift it loose. But the burlap was only a small square of a larger piece and no amount of gentle tugging would pry the whole free. He stripped off his tunic and lay bare chested in the dirt, digging now with his hands. Temple spells wreathing the lich yard kept the dead at bay, but Mal didn't need a spirit standing at his shoulder to tell him what he'd discovered. As he excavated more soil, he could feel the shift of intimate shapes inside the burlap: human bones.

When it came free it came all at once, falling into Mal's arms. Grunting, he hauled burlap onto the grass. Dirt and clumps of sod collapsed into the hole to fill the space left behind. Mal dusted soil from his fingers without much success as he considered his prize.

If the temple had spent time and effort to bind spells to the walls and to the obelisk for the sake of keeping executed magi safely entombed, they'd not put the same effort into interring necromantic remains. It was a large bag, heavy, and when Mal cut away the knots securing the top end, he discovered it was filled almost to bursting with a gruesome miscellany of bones.

Mal reached into the bag. He'd begun to think of them as his lost brothers and sisters, these anonymous magi. They'd shared his abilities, and likely shared similar joys and trials. They'd given their hearts to William's throne—up to a point. Possibly they'd been true to their obligation until the very end, possibly they'd been punished despite the depths of their loyalty. He was beginning to recognize intricacies he'd never considered as a younger man. For most of his life he'd been too bullheaded to see past the headiness of his office to darker implications. Self-importance had ruined his marriage and cost him his first love. He fully expected audacity would send him soon to join her in death.

There were three skulls in the bag amongst the bones. He set them side by side on the grass before dipping back into the collection. The bones were clean, cold, and smooth. The topmost layer showed no visible signs of charring. The smallest of the skulls was staved in at the top, by sword point or by halberd. That death at least would have been instantaneous.

Mal didn't believe in any god, but he crossed each skull for the sake of respect before placing them one at a time into his pail. He added a handful of phalanges and vertebra for good measure before covering the pail with a scrap of cloth. Then he began the process of reburying the burlap bag. With luck, no one would ever notice his thievery.

When Mal strode down the slope onto Holder's property, Baldebert was perched on the paddock fence, nose buried in the pages of a slim, silver-bound book. At the sound of his approach Baldebert shut the volume on one finger, marking his place. The sapphire-and-bone brooch glinted on his shirt.

Mal looked pointedly from Roue's admiral to the closed barn door. From behind the building came the clang of hammer on anvil: Baldebert's man hard work over Holder's forge.

"I don't like to be alone with it," said Baldebert, forestalling Mal's complaint. "It exudes dread and I believe it would like to tear me quite in half."

"I assure you, it has no inclination one way or another." Sighing, Mal set down his pail and spade. "It's spelled to respond to my commands. It has no free will, no more than sword or cannon."

Baldebert pursed his lips. "It moved. While I was working, it turned its head to watch me. It lashes its tail. If I accidentally venture too close my guts turn to water and my heart near stops in terror. It's as tall as the hayloft and covered in spikes and I know *it would quite like to tear me in half.*" He tucked the book under his arm and hopped off the fence. "Success?"

"In a manner of speaking." He was not sure the three ghosts who had followed him from the lich yard would agree. Two women and an elderly man, the magi had materialized as soon as he'd stepped out of the circle of temple magic. They'd followed him back through the city and out along the King's Highway without speaking. They stood silently now, waiting, blue gazes cast in the direction of their bones in his pail.

Baldebert executed a neat bow from the waist. "Then, lead on," he said. "I'll trust you to keep that *thing* from my throat."

There were new wards set about the barn's perimeter, tuned to Mal and to Baldebert and to Baldebert's ironmonger, but no other. They flashed silver as Mal and Baldebert passed through, then sparked savagely at the magi, pushing the spirits back. One of the women flinched away, covering her ghostly face with one arm. It was the first sign Mal had that the disinterred dead were aware.

He disengaged the wards. Baldebert slid the barn door open. Cogs in the frame squeaked. Inside the barn, shadows shifted. Mal conjured mage-light, sent it spinning up above the rafters. He slipped inside the building. Baldebert followed. The dead magi came after.

Lane's Automata waited, motionless, beneath the hay loft. It appeared no more alive than it had before he had kindled it in the Bone Cave, but Mal knew better. It had come at his command across the country in the night, breaking a hole in the back of the cave, earth and stone and theist spell of no consequence. It had loped across fallow fields to Holder's barn, leaving deep furrows behind wherever metal talons touched soil. He'd rejoiced to see it run, for the immense power of working pistons and wheels, and for sheer disbelief. He'd dealt in the realm of death for so long, he'd never imagined the thrill of conjuring life.

"Three skulls," Baldebert said, plucking the covering off Mal's pail. "That's but half of what we need, if we're to disregard the bones Holder collected."

Mal ground his teeth. In the corner the Automata lashed its iron tail. Both Mal and Baldebert pretended not to notice.

"Three for now," Mal said briefly. "More later. First I need to know if I'm going about it right. That fiend there required a coterie of children to wake. We cannot go around digging up whole boneyards in one swoop. Eventually someone is bound to take notice."

Together they had cleaned Holder's work table of detritus, sorting usable pieces of machinery from rubbish. The old tools lived now outside near the forge. There was space again on the long table to work, to puzzle out the ways and means of a clockwork beast. Baldebert's man was a capable blacksmith, blissfully ignorant of flatland history and the walking machines' deadly reputation, but he'd learned his trade with an eye toward shipboard maintenance. With Holder gone there were none left who knew exactly how to build the walking machines. Mal and Baldebert were relying on luck more than either liked to admit.

Mal placed the stolen skulls gently on a clear space at the center of the table. Upending his pail, he emptied the rest of the bones into a shallow pile nearby.

"It didn't occur to me until just last night that the most potent bones in the royal cemetery," he explained, "are buried in the lich yard. Lane and Holder were correct in thinking the ferric soldiers need a powerful magic to walk, but they went looking in the wrong direction. The iron in the framework countervails any benefit *sidhe* bones may retain." He picked up the damaged skull, turned it over in his hands. The three dead magi watched intently. "The straw men, the improved mannequins Faolan encountered in the red woods—those Holder and Brother Paul could stir to life, and even that magic, I suspect, was temporary. True Automata are the sole province of the magi, built purposefully of iron to *rid* the flatlands of barrowmen."

"That part, at least, worked as planned," commented Baldebert, eyeing the hole in the skull. "It was only later things got out of hand, if I'm to understand your histories."

Mal lifted the skull, gazed into its empty sockets. "Not this time," he said. "Then, magi were common enough to seem a threat. Now there are but two of us. Even with the Automata, we are a fraction of what we once were."

"Of late I find that reassuring," Baldebert confessed, touching the ivory manacles always on his belt. He nodded at the bones. "Potent spirits, then. And possibly very angry. Death by fire or noose was unlikely to improve what good temper they may have sustained amidst mass extermination." He picked up a phalange, restlessly set it back on the work table. "But do you think these will do?"

"Oh, aye," Mal answered, smirking not at Baldebert but at the three silent spirts. "I suspect these will do perfectly. Shall we see?" He passed the damaged skull to Baldebert. The barn's rear door was cracked open just wide enough for the ironmonger to move in and out with his work. Lane's Automata turned its head to watch as Mal and Baldebert passed. Its rust-stained chest, a welter of chain, cogs, and mismatched armor, rose and fell with a sound to rival the bellows beyond the barn door. Baldebert winced away.

As far as Mal could tell, the magi, drifting after, paid it no mind at all.

The blacksmith paused over his anvil to greet Baldebert. He was a brawny man, grizzled and weathered, his eyes blue as the sea. Mal did not remember him from shipboard but it was obvious from the way he refused to look in Mal's direction that he had witnessed the misfortune on *The Cutlass Wind*. The sailor quenched his hammer and tongs in a nearby bucket of water set aside for the purpose and arched a brow at Baldebert's burden.

"Ready to give it a try, are we, Captain?" he inquired doubtfully.

The ground behind the barn was strewn with segments of Automata carried from Holder's storage into the open for easier perusal. The smith, made orderly by a career spent on deck, had sorted recognizable pieces into quadrants on the ground around his forge: arms made of fragmented pauldrons, vambraces, and gauntlets. Fabricated cuirass torsos and overlong, stilt-like legs forged from pieces of delicately engraved greaves and thick iron chain. Clawed metal feet ten times as large as a man's own. Long, articulated appendages meant to be tail or tentacle. And, displayed on the fence posts of an empty pen, four polished helms of the barbute style, eye slits vacant.

Mal retrieved the skull from Baldebert. The ironmonger snatched up his bucket and poured water over his forge, extinguishing flames.

"If you don't mind, Captain," he said. "I'll just be taking a break while you endeavor." At Baldebert's nod he hurried off, slipping through Mal's rear wards and back up the hill away from the barn.

"Can't say I blame him." Baldebert squinted at a small mountain of long, deadly looking spikes, resigned. "I've read Brother Lino's journals front to back more times than I'd like to count and I still don't know how you intend to manage it. Shouldn't we . . . erect some sort of chassis before you begin?"

"Nay." The ghostly magi had wandered as a group between the blacksmith's neat piles and now lingered near the empty paddock, whispering amongst themselves. One of the women walked translucent fingers over a barbute, spectral eyes flashing blue. All at once Mal knew it was her broken cranium he held in his hands, and that his success was assured.

"Nay," he repeated, winking at Baldebert. Expectation was as intoxicating as good red wine. "You haven't looked closely at Lane's monster."

"I haven't," Baldebert agreed. "I can't get near it without wanting to weep and tear my hair. You don't seem to suffer the same challenge."

Mal's grin turned smug. "The Automata don't frighten me. The founding pieces of that skeleton are not forged together," he explained. "The head, the limbs, the fingers, the tail. Those are very loosely attached to the torso by chain and cog, aye. Enough to hold together while standing. The living body is a flexible and delicate miracle, Baldebert. No machine can obtain that balance of its own accord." He tapped his fingers on the skull. "It's the magic that keeps it together, allows it movement. Holder and Lane started with sparring dummies, man-sized dolls sewn together for the purpose of training young lads and lasses to recognize the enemy and his physical weaknesses. And mayhap, like a doll, Holder's predecessors loosely pieced together each ferric soldier to a certain specification. But I suspect not. I suspect there was more *imagination* involved in each creation."

Baldebert scoffed. "Lino suggests nothing of the sort in his writings."

"Never mind Lino," snapped Mal. "When we can go straight to the source." He indicated the dead necromancers. Baldebert blinked vaguely in their direction, unperceiving. Exasperated, Mal waved him off. "Get back, Admiral. Against the barn, if you will, and out of my way. We have three new allies. They were there, they know how it was done and you weren't wrong—they're not inclined toward forgiveness."

"Fantastic." Baldebert retreated. "Just so long as they understand you're in charge."

"They're dead." Amused, Mal selected a helm from the fence, fit it tenderly over the wounded skull. "I am not—yet." And there in the open air, evening settling by way of purple shadows waking autumnal breezes, power sparking in his blood and setting aflame the yellow stone on his finger, Mal silently exulted. Life, he thought, had never been so sweet. "Let us begin."

At his request one of the magi separated from her whispering companions. She stopped in front of the cooling forge, watching Mal expectantly. For the first time he noticed her phantasmal form wore a wound on the back of her head to match the hole in her disinterred skull. Dried gore crusted the shoulders of her black cape. Blood and brains matted her short hair.

He suppressed a shudder. Her blue flame eyes flickered mockery.

You must tune the bones, she reminded Mal when he hesitated. *Speak the binding cant and I shall do the rest. Or have you forgotten how the spell is worked, young man?*

He didn't appreciate her arrogance. "This spell hasn't been worked for generations." Near the paddock fence the magi stopped their whispering.

What, he wondered, had they expected would happen to the world once their kind was extinct? Did they suppose their secrets would be preserved?

"What are you called?" he asked.

Sensha, of the Black Coast. She appeared suddenly less certain. Absently, she put a ghostly hand to the back of her head. *I am Queen's Elite.*

"Were," Mal corrected. He placed the helmed skull in the dirt at her feet. She took a step away but then steeled herself and stood firm.

Remember to hold the boundaries, she said, blue stare riveted to the top of the helm. *Else you'll snuff me to oblivion. Better to be bones in a bag than nothing at all—*

"Be quiet," he ordered, stopping her mouth with a twist of power. Her brother and sister began to mutter again. They were uneasy, edging toward fearful.

"Now," he continued, releasing Sensha's tongue. "Speak the words to me."

She did because he commanded it, though resentment made the words harsh when he thought they should have been musical. He committed the cant to memory—it wasn't difficult, no more so than binding witch-light to a shinbone set in a cold room ceiling or wards to a sliver of femur buried beneath a cottage keystone, yet infinitely more elegant than the provisional spell he'd worked in the Bone Cave to bind Lane. It took more strength, much more than he had expected, but that was easily remedied. He fed Sensha to the working, bolstered her essence with what living magic he had to spare, and when that wasn't enough, fed her the ghosts of her brother and sister, and for good measure added what remained of the burned magus tied to the cottage chimney on the other side of Holder's barn. The magi struggled against his pull but the dead were nothing against the living. In an instant they were obliterated, and the Sensha machine stronger for their annihilation.

It was all Mal could do not to steal Baldebert's living essence and add it to the mix. How much easier it would be to work the magic with more vital energy, how much more powerful the result?

Mal resisted temptation, though barely. He collapsed to his knees. The vocent's ring on his finger dazzled his eyes. While he knelt on the ground, struggling to regain use of his senses, Sensha began her work.

Plucking components seemingly at random from the ironmonger's piles, she began to build an Automata. Metal whirled through the air, dangerously close to Mal's bent head. Talons walked themselves through crushed grass below his nose, soon followed by a length of heavy chain link, winding over the ground. A flock of finger-long spikes tumbled through the evening, rattling as they bounced off each other in flight. Near the barn door Baldebert's steady swearing became a terrified moan.

When she was finished, the barnyard stood still and too quiet. Mal pressed the palms of his hands flat in the grass, lifting his head. The wards he'd placed around the forge were fallen, their glow demolished. He wondered if Sensha had taken their energy, as well.

Bracing himself on a fencepost, Mal rose to standing. He confronted his creation.

The Automata was beautiful in the way of unknowable things—the efficiency of the human heart, the vibrancy of plague through a lensed scope, the rush of deep water beneath a ship's prow. And it was ghastly in the way of unbearable secrets—the whimper a man made before death when garroted from behind, the scream of a mind irreparably broken, the echo of a young man's prayers for godly forgiveness gone unanswered.

Almost he could understand Baldebert's prostrate terror.

But Mal did not indulge in fragility.

He clenched his teeth and crossed to stand within touching distance of Sensha's ferric soldier. It was taller by a head than Lane's monster, but less bulky.

While Holder had strung together an original chassis in the likeness of a man, Sensha had pieced her form together with the enthusiasm of the demented. Beneath the barbute helm, the Automata's cuirass torso was pierced through and then wrapped around with thick chain-link tentacles. It had no arms. It stood balanced upon a single jointed leg and clawed foot. Its iron thigh bristled with spikes.

The tentacle undulated lazily, curling and uncurling around the space where a man would have ribs. When it flexed, scythe-sharp iron talons opened and closed like flower petals responding to subtle changes in daylight.

Metal scraped when the Automata looked down on Mal. Witch-light burned in the barbute's eye slit. It did not speak.

"Get up," Mal croaked in Baldebert's direction. The prince of Roue ignored him.

"Up!" Mal repeated, louder. His head whirled and he braced a hand on the ferric soldier to keep from falling. The Automata was icy to the touch. "Baldebert! Attend me!"

Baldebert raised himself from the ground unto his elbows. His cheeks were wet with tears.

"You'll have to come to me," he confessed. "If I were a lesser man I'd be long gone over the hills by now. I cannot come closer; if you held a blade to my throat I would not."

Mal staggered toward the man. Baldebert wrapped

him in a trembling embrace and dragged him, not into the barn, but around the corner and out of the Automata's eye line. There they collapsed again. Baldebert rolled onto his back and stared sightlessly at the darkening sky. Mal pressed his cheek against grass and listened to the sound of the two Automata breathing.

"Well," Baldebert managed after a time of silence. "I didn't believe you'd manage it, in truth."

"Nor I," admitted Mal after another timeless lull. "It takes . . . *more* . . . than I expected. I'm afraid we'll need quite a lot of source material."

Baldebert choked on hysteria. "You mean angry ghosts."

"Aye." Mal rolled onto his side. He held up a hand, studied the dying fire in the stone on his ring. "Angry ghosts seem to work quite well."

CHAPTER 16

Avani dropped her bag with a cry. Liam, busy polishing Morgan's armor with handfuls of scrubbing sand, looked around in dismay.

"My lady?"

She didn't reply. Standing rigid a few steps from the young earl's tent, she appeared not to notice Liam or the dropped bag. Her mouth worked silently; she pressed fingers against her closed eyes.

Liam set aside the sand and rose to his feet. He didn't want to jar Avani from whatever vision gripped her. Since they'd ridden out from the city five days earlier she was struck often with unexpected fits of what the Widow used to call augury, though as far as Liam could tell Avani wasn't seeing into the future, but back in the direction of Wilhaiim and Mal.

He'd surprised her once, the very first time it hap-

pened, when she'd been in danger of spilling hot porridge down her front. She'd startled, alarmed, from
her waking dream and brought her wards up in a wall
of silver fire at the same time, nearly setting Liam's
sleeve alight. After that they'd agreed he wouldn't
touch her but instead call out until she revived. It
seemed to Liam a weak plan, especially as the fits were
coming upon her more frequently as days passed.

"My lady," he cajoled, taking another stride in
Avani's direction. "Wake up, now. You're here with
me and the rest of the royal cavalry, my lady, atop
the white cliffs amongst scrub and heather, remember?" He snuck forward a second step. "Listen, hear
the Maiden crashing below us, can't you? And look,
here comes his lordship, red in the face and riled. I
suppose the constable's given him another tongue
lashing, the third in two days, innit it?"

"Liam!" Morgan rasped, abruptly stopping his
forward march into camp. He was indeed red in the
face, although Liam couldn't be certain that was the
constable's fault. Morgan, a sensitive sort, was easily
vexed by the simplest criticism. The young earl's men
were kind to his face but condescending when they
thought he wasn't listening. It was evident to everyone involved, especially Morgan, that they would
have preferred his dead brother in his stead.

"What are you doing?" Morgan demanded. "We
agreed it was safest to let Lady Avani alone when she
was caught out of body!"

Out of body seemed an odd fancy to Liam who could clearly see the clench of Avani's hands against her thighs and the roll of her eyes behind her lids. He squatted, picked up a medium-sized stone, and sent it whizzing through the air. He had astonishingly fine aim—the lancer in charge of their most recent training had remarked on Liam's keenness many times already—and the stone hit Avani square on the shoulder exactly as he'd planned.

"Sir!" Morgan yelped, aghast. He launched himself in Liam's direction as Liam reached for a second stone. For such a slight lad Morgan was surprisingly solid. He tackled Liam around the middle, employing one of Riggins's favorite grappling holds. They tussled in the dirt, more for the excitement of their new station as Kingsmen than any real quarrel. Liam choked on giggles. Morgan, trying to land an elbow on Liam's ribs and still avoid his damaged leg, socked him in the gut instead. Liam, whooping, bit his wrist hard enough to draw blood. Morgan's curses turned salty as any sailor's.

Bear, until then dozing in the shadow of the earl's tent, roused and began to bark.

"*Ai*, Liam! My lord!" Tepid water drenched them both head to neck. As one they froze and lay still, afraid to look around. "What mischief is this?"

"Not mischief." Liam swiped wet hair from his face. He prodded Morgan with his foot before sitting up. If they were about to have their ears blistered, he intended they'd do so together. "Practice. We're supposed to practice every chance we get."

"Aye, shooting and riding and throwing the lance," retorted Avani, setting aside the water skin she had used to douse their enthusiasm. "Not rolling about hissing and biting like two pups." She crossed her arms, looking down her nose at the both of them. Her eyes were clear again, her expression shrewd.

"My lady . . ." Morgan hopped to his feet. "Apologies. Only," he continued hastily, "you were suffering one of your visions, understand, and Liam threw a stone even though we both expressly gave our word not to disturb you during augury." He flicked an admonishing finger Liam's way. "My *squire* needs to learn that word given is binding. He cannot just ignore direction as he sees fit."

"He has a bad habit of doing just that," Avani said. "You're unlikely to break him of it any time soon." But she winked Liam's way as she retrieved her pack and slung it over her shoulders. "I'm going down the hill to check with Brother Absen at the healer's tent. Unless you've need of me, my lord?"

Morgan demurred. The young earl had yet to relax around Avani; Liam wasn't sure he ever would. The old houses hadn't forgotten the magi's betrayal and Wythe was one of the oldest still standing. Morgan had confessed to Liam that his grandsire, on the day Andrew had been installed as Renault's vocent, had ridden all the way from Wythe to Wilhaiim for the express purpose of begging the young king to put the magus to the sword. The audience had ended badly, Morgan's grandsire had not again set foot inside the white walls, and Wythe had been Renault's most grudging subject ever since, obedient only insofar as to not give undue offense.

Avani whistled. Jacob stuck his head through the flap of Morgan's tent where he'd taken to sleeping the days away as his wing slowly healed. Though Morgan claimed the raven muttered at night in his dreaming, Jacob had not spoken a word in public since the cavalry had left Wilhaiim, and Liam was glad of it. If a black-feathered bird was considered ill luck in battle, how much worse a black-feathered bird screaming broken king's lingua?

Jacob hopped out of the tent and made his way awkwardly to Avani's shoulder. She scratched his neck in greeting before arching a brow in Liam's direction.

"My lord's armor won't scrub itself clean," she reminded him. "The stew pot's empty and we're low on kindling. Either get yourself to the quartermaster for rations or find us some rabbit while you're foraging wood."

"Yes'm."

She ruffled his hair as she left camp. Liam took the gesture of affection with better grace than usual. He watched after as she made her way down the hill through Wythe's strictly ordered tent garrison. A few men and women called out in acknowledgement as she passed. Many more did not. Wythe's prejudices were not confined to the countess and her son.

"Are we to now pretend it's not happening?" Morgan asked when Avani was safely out of earshot. "Pick up and carry on just like she's not gone all stiff midconversation?"

"Avani's been struck with visions since I was a wee lad." Resigned, Liam glowered into the empty stew pot. "Why, before the *sidhe* burned Stonehill she was having them fast and regular-like. She knows better than you and me how to handle them. My lord."

"Before the *sidhe* burned Stonehill," Morgan ground out. "Are you listening to yourself? Don't you think it's worrisome they're coming fast and regular-like *now*, again?"

"Nay," Liam lied. "I told you, she can handle them. I'm going to check our snares. Bear, *stay*, guard!"

The brindled hound, curled nose to tail again near the earl's tent, opened one eye in lazy agreement.

"I'm coming with you," Morgan decided. Liam refrained from sighing. It wasn't that he disdained the lad's company. It was that lately Morgan couldn't seem to decide whether he was coming or going. Absent Arthur's blunt companionship, Morgan's anxious nature had turned high-strung as one of the cavalry's overbred coursers.

"As you like," Liam replied. "Just . . . try to keep up, my lord. I've plenty left to do before midday."

The white cliffs, while steep and unsurmountable to Wilhaiim's north where they abutted the Maiden Gate, at their heights sloped gradually further northward until the incline collapsed into prairie near the verge of the king's red woods. At their summit on a clear day the cliffs provided unobstructed views of countryside west of the forest as far as the eye could see; the King's Highway snaked on past Wilhaiim toward sandy Whitcomb where brilliant blue sea merged with the skyline beyond. Low Port, further to the west and north, was too distant for even Liam with his lauded eyesight to glimpse, but he'd taken to looking that way first thing in the morning when he woke, as if somehow the horizon would look different once Roue's small navy had arrived.

The highway was busy from dawn to dusk and often into the night with refugees come from farm and cottage to shelter within Wilhaiim's walls. The old keeps—and thanks to Mal's drilling Liam could list all fifteen houses by device and by title—were protected from invasion by even older bone magic, wards set into their walls tuned to repel even the most determined enemy, but the keeps were not large enough to contain every surrounding farm family, tinker's brood, or traveling merchant. Wilhaiim was meant to accommodate the overflow, and Kingsmen were busy up and down the flatlands spreading word that the time had come to seek the castle.

Liam couldn't help but marvel at the crowd below on the highway as he and Morgan walked the edge of the cliff nearest their campsite. He wondered how many families had come with children. He worried at the sheer number of mouths to feed, and whether Wilhaiim's food stores would hold out in the face of war. He hoped many of those men and women, come at Renault's call, would willingly stand in defense of the city alongside career soldiers, even once the royal armory was emptied.

Mostly, Liam wondered if they were afraid.

There were ground squirrels living in holes in the face of the cliff: fat, happy creatures with short whiskers and long, bushy tails. They were shy around men and difficult to catch but they were tasty in a stew and plentiful, and Liam had spent the first years of his life surviving off small game and determination. Squirrels on the Downs dugs their homes in the ground, which made for easier snaring, but Liam enjoyed a challenge and the puzzle of trapping dinner on a sheer, vertical surface kept his mind occupied during what was beginning to seem a ceaseless wait.

Like any lad, Morgan knew how to construct a simple noose snare out of strong leather cord and was eager to put his knowledge to the test. But without horizontal space to scatter bait, a basic lariat at first seemed of no purpose. Gorse, heather, and flowering scrub grew in abundance above the cliff face but the squirrels appeared to shun the plants, ignoring an array of bright red berries in favor of the nuts on a single, stunted oak growing halfway down the cliff.

After some time wasted exploring back and forth along the edge of the cliff and an evening spent gnawing tasteless jerky while trying to think like a squirrel, Liam finally worked it out.

"Water," he explained to Morgan their second morning at camp. "Surely they don't drink from the Maiden below—it's foul. They must come *up* to drink, I'm sure of it. Somewhere close to the edge, somewhere sheltered, somewhere they're not easily picked off by bird or fox."

"The only fresh water is all the way down the hill," Morgan argued, "in the old well."

"The arrowroot pool," Avani suggested from where she sat near Bear, ripping strips of cloth from a pile of embroidered petticoats and rolling the strips into bandages. Liam was certain she hadn't ridden out of the city with court fancy dress bundled in her journey pack. "*Ai*, it's more of a puddle than a pool, but it's close to the cliff and surrounded all around by old heather."

Morgan had run off to look and reported back that although the ground around the puddle was too marshy for tracks, it seemed a fine solution for a colony of thirsty squirrels, so Liam had taught the young earl the trick of anchoring a line of snares to a heavy piece of broken lance pole borrowed from a refuse pile, and the secret of anise seed for bait. Avani carried plenty of anise and the broken lance was solid enough to stay put in the mud near the arrowroot pool.

Morgan and Liam set the trap before dark and on their third day on the hill they had an abundance of squirrel meat for their cook pot and extra for Bear.

But on the fifth day, their snares were empty. Morgan, already in a pother over Avani's visions, with Liam's tooth marks still healing on his wrist, took the empty traps as a personal affront.

"By the Aug," the lad complained, stomping in the mud. "Someone's been about thieving our catch. Dammit all, my mother will hear about this. Wythe makes no allowance for theft. This is treachery!"

"A few stolen squirrels are not treachery. And I don't expect Wythe makes allowance for a tattling earl, either," Liam said mildly, squatting to examine the trap. "You'll never make a good commander if you run down to mum every time something goes awry. You didn't used to grouse so much before His Majesty pinned the bar to your breast. What's changed?"

Morgan didn't reply. Liam, without looking around, could feel the young earl tensing to spring.

"Do it, my lord," he said, "and this time I'll box your ears. It's not 'practice' if you deserve a thrashing." He rolled the lance pole over in the mud. The snares had been carefully loosened which meant Morgan was correct in assuming thievery.

"Sir," Morgan said, gone abruptly somber, "look."

He'd wandered away from the drinking hole and was peering at something in the heather. Curious, Liam joined him. What he saw there made him reach for the knife on his belt and wheel around, staring about, though he knew better. If Cleena had meant to be seen, she'd be standing before him, not leaving prettily wrapped gifts in the heather where she must have known he would find them.

Cleena, for it must have been she, had spread a patchwork kerchief in the mud beneath a large gorse, and weighted it down with an assortment of stoppered pots. Liam counted seven of the familiar jars, each decorated with a sprig of flowering herb. He'd seen their like many a time in her stall at the Fair when he'd stopped by to sample her sweetmeats.

"She took our squirrels and left us honey," Morgan said, baffled. Although he'd not heard the whole of Liam's wild Hunt, he knew enough to reach for his own blade and cast a nervous glance around the cliff edge. "What does it mean?"

"A game, I'm supposing." Liam wished the sight of those little pots didn't make his heart constrict behind his ribs. The wounds in his leg were barely scabbed over. He kept Faolan's torque hidden in his bedroll with the few other precious things he could call his own. He hadn't expected to mourn the *aes si* so deeply; he'd met Faolan just twice, he was for every purpose a stranger.

But Faolan had been kind to him, as much as any *sidhe* knew kindness. In welcoming Liam into the Hunt, he'd offered up a chance at belonging.

"Some sort of barrowman jape," Liam said. Still, he bundled the pots together, knotting the kerchief into a neat bag. "Or warning. She doesn't like me much."

Morgan looked doubtful. "Is it poisoned, do you think? The honey, I mean? Because it seems a fair trade to me, and she did save you from dying, so I don't know why you insist she dislikes you, and I wouldn't mind having something sweet to eat with our supper."

"Avani can tell us, I imagine," Liam said.

"No squirrel for the pot." Sighing, Morgan reset the snares. "Best visit the quartermaster after all."

"Avani first," Liam decided. "If the honey's good, we might trade some for extra rations."

"Oh, aye." For the first time in days the young earl brightened. "But not all of it. If the world's to end soon I'll enjoy a pot of honey first."

The walk down the hill to the healer's tent meant they had to pass through the center of Wythe's make-shift garrison. While the king's constable administered to the royal cavalry as a whole, it was Morgan's duty to directly marshal those mounted troops put forth by house Wythe. There were near one hundred tents flying Wythe's proud green-and-gray pennant beneath Wilhaiim's scarlet and silver, making house Wythe one of the largest and oldest divisions of the cavalry. Wythe took singular pride in the horses bred and raised on their land for service to the throne. Similarly the men and women sent to serve as Kingsmen were by custom drafted into the cavalry for their dexterity in the saddle.

During the day, the garrison was mostly empty of Kingsmen. Horses, hobbled near individual tents at night, needed exercise and distraction during the day to keep sound. Some were ridden out on scouting assignments. No one knew for certain from which direction the desert would emerge and a soldier on a horse could survey surrounding terrain much more efficiently than any foot infantryman. The rest were ridden in practice or in recreation. Every animal was meticulously groomed morning and evening to check for signs of illness or injury. A soldier's horse was more than just a livelihood; a cavalryman without a mount was infantry.

Servants and squires tended to the fitness of the camp while their betters tended to the safety of the kingdom. Water for soldier and horse had to be carried up in buckets from the stone well at the base of the hill. Meat, bread, fruit, and ale from the quartermaster's tent also needed to be refreshed daily. Armor and tack required mending and maintenance. A Kingsman's battle readiness, Morgan liked to lecture Liam, depended on the comfort of his temporary home.

In the wake of the Red Worm, Wythe's squires were grown men and women, farm folk better suited to battle than servitude drafted to replace lost children. When the time came, they would be expected to fight alongside their commissioned champion instead of keeping back and out of direct danger as a young squire might.

They were kind to Liam despite the rumors attached to his scars. He fretted over their own battle readiness after days of backbreaking work but found small consolation in the knowledge that, because they worked for the cavalry, they would at least be provided a good horse while their less fortunate counterparts in the infantry would not.

They paused in their work to bow in Morgan's direction as he and Liam made their way through the garrison. Morgan accepted their recognition with a congenial word here and a stiff nod there, but it was obvious from the growing color in his cheeks that he was unhappy with the attention. That he was uncomfortable was impossible to miss; servants and squires muttered amongst themselves as he passed.

"You might at least pretend you're pleased to see them," Liam said under his breath. "Instead of walking like you've a stick shoved up your arse. My lord. They're looking to you for courage."

"I'll ask for your advice," Morgan responded out of the corner of his mouth, "once you've commanded one hundred and eight soldiers to take futile stand. Sir."

"Futile?" Liam lengthened his step until they walked side by side, though tradition dictated a squire walk a perfect two paces behind his master. "Bit glum, don't you think? His Majesty wouldn't send out soldiers on a hopeless cause."

Morgan snorted. "Of course he would. He has to." He leaned close. "By all reports the odds are six to one, and if they have access to *sidhe* tunnels they could appear anywhere at all—or several places at once. I'm leading my brother's men to their deaths, Liam, and they must resent me for it."

"They're your men now," Liam reminded him, "and they'd resent you less if you pretended some pride. A soldier going to his or her death—why, I imagine they'd feel better about the job for some gratitude. I know I'd feel better about dying at your side if I thought you loved me more for it."

Morgan chewed his lip. "They'll be dying for Renault."

"It's not the king walking amongst them now," Liam retorted. "It's you."

"I'm frightened," Morgan confessed, voice cracking. "This wasn't *supposed* to be me. It was supposed to be Michael, and me the squire scrubbing his gear. I'm not old enough. I don't know how to be a man, much less an earl."

A squire, lugging two buckets of water past them on the track, stopped to gape their way. Morgan awarded her a frozen smile. Liam shook his head and waved her on. Water splashed over the sides of her buckets as she hurried up the hill.

"They're not meant to know that," Liam argued, drawing Morgan on. "And it's your job to see that they don't. What did Riggins say about the Kingsmen who took a last stand against the barrowmen and in the end drove them to ground?"

One corner of Morgan's mouth turned up. "He said, 'It wasn't their might nor even their steel nor even the horrific Automata that made the *sidhe* believe the war was lost. It was that they baffled the *sidhe* host with sheer bullshit, and made the world entire believe humankind had triumphed.'"

"Aye, good advice for a young commander facing his first test at warring, don't you think?"

"Baffle them with bullshit?" Morgan enquired archly, but some of the hectic color had left his cheeks.

"Seems like a sound plan to me," Liam proclaimed, and was delighted by Morgan's honest mirth.

The quartermaster's tent squatted at the bottom of the hill within sight of the red woods. It was a lively place during daylight hours, crowded with members of house Wythe vying for the choicest portions of meat, the newest pieces of fruit, and the least moldy bread and cheese. Rations of uncooked oat porridge and barley ale were passed out each morning for breakfast. In the evening there was wine for those who had their own coin to spend and more ale for those who did not. The tent closed at twilight. The quartermaster and his family slept in a covered wagon close by and rose again with the sun to start all over again. He was a florid man, but heavily muscled beneath his fat and by all accounts handy with the broadsword, while his two adult sons professed loudly and often their allegiance to the short bow's deadly accuracy. If ever any person thought to rob the tent after sunset, they were quickly brought to their senses by the sound of the quartermaster's hearty snore issuing from the bowels of his wagon.

The king's constable spent her days riding the garrison line from east to west, checking in with her commanders and making sure the cavalry was in order, but at night she slept with Wythe in a private pavilion near the quartermaster. A Kingsman stood watch on her doorstep whenever she was away, minding whatever royal secrets she kept secured behind the tent flap, and accepting the frequent missives sent up the highway from the castle. Several times Liam had seen a message arrive by wing instead of by hoof, sent by falcon over the white walls. He'd goggled at the beauty of the hawk, her noble head and her ruddy feathers, awestruck.

Wythe's priests lived beneath an open-air baldachin erected between the constable's tent and the garrison well. The baldachin, a raised timber roof supported at four corners by gray stone pillars, was spacious enough to bed down patients and healers alike while also providing for a basic stone altar for garrison worship. It, and the well, were remnants from war with the *sidhe*; they came as a pair and were duplicated fourteen more times throughout the countryside in an expanding half circle around Wilhaiim's flank.

Before, Liam had paid the ancient buildings little attention; the flatland was dusted with crumbling relics of time past. But now that he'd seen the garrison stations at work he couldn't help but admire the arrangement. Organized by house and by station, the cavalry stretched in an unbroken line encircling city and farmland together, the initial band of defense before infantry and white wall. Against overland *sidhe* the borderline of mounted lancers carrying iron spear and sword must have provided matchless defense.

If the barrowmen had not in their exile wormed the earth with tunnels, the line might still be to Wilhaiim's advantage. But a mostly immovable barrier would do no good against an enemy unfettered by the usual terrain. The sand snakes were equally as likely to erupt behind or within the line as they were in front of it. And in indiscriminate attack, Liam worried, it was possible the cavalry would break apart and fail.

It relied upon the Countess Wythe and her seconds to keep the line from falling into disorder no matter the threat. Liam did not envy her that task. It seemed to him an impossible one.

"Baffle 'em with bullshit," he muttered, glancing gravely in the direction of the constable's secured pavilion. "Bet your mum's quite good at that, hey, my lord?"

"Excruciatingly so," agreed Morgan, laughing again. "Are you suggesting I keep my mother in mind as I ride into battle? I'm told most men prefer a lover's token on their sleeve for inspiration."

"A lover!" Liam smothered a snort. "You've not yet grown chin hair, my lord. No self-respecting lass would have you."

"You're a bastard," Morgan said. "I should have you whipped for insolence."

But he said it with a grin and looked lighter of heart than he had for days, if not weeks. He lifted a cheerful hand to the men and women tending their horses in the shade of the red wood, and called hallo to another group galloping past. Pleasantly surprised, they all returned his hail with matching exuberance. Silently, Liam congratulated himself on a job well done. Mayhap, he thought, with a little encouragement the young earl would yet settle in to his role.

CHAPTER 17

Avani appreciated Brother Absen for his unflappable kindness and for his practical competency. He was soft spoken, yet firm. Skinny as a fence post, yet strong enough to hold a skittish soldier in place as he examined her badly dislocated shoulder, he had more gray in his tonsured hair than black. He did not seem at all put off by a foreigner in his ward, nor even by the raven that accompanied her on her daily visits.

"I know Deval," he explained when she introduced herself that first day on the hill. "Some days, when I've visited Wilhaiim for research and he's working late in the temple library, we taker supper together. He's an interesting man. He speaks highly of your character and your many talents. I'm not so foolish as to turn assistance away no matter what strange form it takes."

"They call me witch," she'd confessed then. She planned to make herself useful even if he turned her away for being magus, but it seemed considerate to give him a chance at cooperation. "And sometimes they used to call me vocent. The king's discharged me from that service for being lenient when wickedness might better further his cause."

"Even as far as Wythe we heard how you did in the city, battling the Red Worm," he returned, unruffled. "And I daresay I've heard all the rumors: it was because of you Stonehill burned to the ground, and because of you His Majesty consents to take a foreign wife. You make consort with barrowmen kept in the royal catacombs, you killed Armswoman Lane with a fiery hand, you take counsel from the dead, you drove Lord Malachi mad and then into your bed. Yon raven speaks your goddess's commands aloud and you can heal a man's putrid leg with a handful of grubs."

Avani bit the inside of her mouth. "Jacob has lately and inexplicably mastered the king's lingua," she said. "And if a healer doesn't recognize the value of maggots in an infected wound, she doesn't know her trade."

Absen narrowed his eyes at Jacob where the bird crouched on the grass in a spot of sunshine. Then he blinked. "How are you at sutures?"

"I have a steady hand."

"Good." He placed a sponge and a shallow bowl filled with tepid water in her hand. "Go and tend Laurence, there. He's gashed his hand badly on a splintered lance, and is not pleased about it. Once the bleeding's staunched and he's clean, come back and I'll show you where I keep the needle and catgut."

Absen was not the only theist come from Wythe to work the garrison baldachin, but he was the eldest of the three men who had and as such the most senior. He led worship sunrise and sunset at the low, east-facing altar, and in between times he ran his sickroom with the zeal of a person who knew and accepted his calling. Absen's priestly companions looked to him always for advice and leadership, and as such they put aside any quarrel they might have otherwise had with Avani or her heretical beliefs.

"The raven must keep his distance," Absen decided when Avani and Jacob arrived for their second day in the baldachin. "Brother Shin couldn't sleep last night for worry and Brother Cenwin woke badly disconcerted from dreams of black-feathered birds."

To keep the peace, Avani consented. She sent Jacob away to the edge of the red-flowered forest where he kept watch from the branches of a stout evergreen. He still preferred the comfort of a ride on her shoulder over flying, but he could take to the air again when necessary and seemed to enjoy judging the garrison from new heights. She thought he had forgiven her whatever wrongdoing had sent him from her side. Sometimes when they walked the hill, he still muttered complaints in her ear—*Cast him out! Cast him out!*—and she knew he must mean Mal.

War, even a war that had not yet quite begun, was a dangerous sport. The priests were kept busy all hours by patients in need of everything from the simplest spell to cure a squire's nervous constipation to more complicated healings worked on broken bones taken in practice or burns taken over the cook fire. Numerous unexplained rashes and the more common chafing caused by ill-fitting padding were treated with salves instead of spells. Slices and gashing, a daily occurrence, were also left to heal on their own, but more serious afflictions often needed tending. Avani and her needle and catgut were rarely separated for long.

Although she went home to her own bedroll in the evening, Absen and his priests continued working through all hours, snatching sleep on the floor of the baldachin as deep night grew finally quiet. They rested peacefully without guard or weapons of their own at hand, secure in the grace of their god. Avani, who found violence as distasteful as any theist did, nevertheless believed the Goddess helped those who looked after themselves. When she quizzed Brother Absen about the doubtful wisdom of going unarmed into war, he shrugged away her concern.

"The one god shelters and provides," he said. "And in return he expects his priests to eschew brute force. For us, it's not a matter of choice. It's a way of life."

Absen could not know, of course, that his brothers in Wilhaiim's temple were in a large part responsible for bringing brute force under the mountain divide. Avani wondered if he would change his stance were she to tell him. She thought he would not, any more than she would abandon her own Goddess because of another's irreverence.

He must have glimpsed concern on her face, because he patted her arm with a wrinkled, blue-veined hand. "I would prefer to die in righteous enterprise than out of harm's way and idle," he said. "Wythe has been good to me; I am not afraid to die in service if that is god's plan. Neither should you be, although I do not think for you it will come to that."

"Oh, aye?"

"I feel the world is not done with you yet, witch," Brother Absen promised with visible glee. "Whether you should find that a comfort or a torment, I cannot say."

Avani, watching the old priest chortle over his blood-letting bowl and, willing to accept any crumb of encouragement cast her way, decided to settle on comfort. She set her mind to her work in the baldachin and concentrated on the righteous enterprise of tending hurts great and small. In doing so, in honoring her Goddess and her ancestors, she reclaimed for a time a measure of peace.

"**A**i, it's Cleena's honey," she diagnosed, wrinkling her nose at the litter of stoppered crocks spread atop

Brother Absen's medicine chest. "I'd know her work anywhere." She took the hem of the kerchief between two fingers, testing the fabric. "I had hoped we'd seen the last of her."

The baldachin was uncommonly quiet, the morning's patients sent home with ointment for saddle sores or tea to settled an apprehensive gut, and the usual parade of cuts and scrapes not yet begun. A Kingsman come from Wilhaiim on foot with a message from the temple was napping on an unoccupied camp bed, shaking the baldachin with his snores. Brother Shin had gone into the forest for mushrooms while Brother Cenwin, an excitable man who had spent the first half of his life as a docks man in Low Port, was employed at the altar in snipping candle wicks. There was a sleepy quality to the morning; even the lancers and their coursers seemed subdued.

"There's no *sidhe* spell on these," she continued, choosing a jar and breaking the seal. She sniffed first, then scooped a dollop free and licked it off her fingertip, ignoring Morgan's squeaking protest. "Only rosemary in this one. To match the herbal sprig she's attached. But you're right to be chary," she said, "as honey is a knotty thing. A bee may drink of a flower poisonous to humans, and make of it a deadly nectar. On Shellshale there was a grandmother who nursed her bees on rhododendron and gathered from their combs a red, vicious honey that, when eaten, would make a person giddy and light-headed. She claimed her red honey ambrosia could make a man more virile and also cure the grippe."

"Mad honey." Brother Absen nodded. "We have it off the Black Coast ships to use in the temples for ailments of the heart. But there is none here." He waved a hand over the collection. "I would recognize it. As for other poisons, I've a sigil I use on the afflicted to spot a perversion of the system that will work just as well on these, my lord. Let me just retrieve my grimoire . . ." Glancing at Morgan first for permission, the theist hurried off on bare feet.

"Bit of an odd fellow," Liam murmured, staring after. "Do you suppose he realizes he's got dried vomit down the front of his robes? Are you certain he knows what he's about?"

"Absen presided over my nativity," Morgan sputtered. "And might have made Masterhealer in Wilhaiim if my father hadn't insisted on keeping him close. He's an accomplished physicker."

"He does fine work," Avani allowed, "and makes the most difficult patients smile while he's about it. I trust his appraisal." She capped the rosemary tincture. "I think we'll find these are safe, an honest exchange made for fresh meat." Bothered, she shook her head. "I mislike her continued interference. Even if it's curiosity driving her and not malice, her presence can only be construed as misfortune."

"The keening hag." Liam glanced out the baldachin at Kingsmen and horses. "Harbinger of death."

"You don't believe that?" The young earl shook his head. "It's superstitious nonsense, that's all. She's *sidhe*. An adversary, certainly, but no more terrifying than any barrowman."

"You might change your mind if you met her," Liam muttered. Avani couldn't help but agree.

"Superstition is rooted in truth," proclaimed Brother Absen, returning with a heavy, leather-bound book in hand. "According to our histories, the *sidhe* often sent out their womenfolk ahead of incursion, to scout the lay of the land and signal when the time for attack was ripe." He settled on his knees on the ground, opening the book on his lap. "They were indeed the harbingers of death, though mayhap not quite as your squire assumes, my lord."

Brother Cenwin, completing his work at the altar, drifted close. "Move back," he told Avani and Liam, "enchantment is dangerous work. You, too, my lord." He shooed them away from Absen and his book.

Avani was certain she saw Absen roll his eyes. He walked gnarled fingers down the page of his book, bypassing inked sketches, diagrams, and phrases. Words wavered on the page like fog over still water, making them impossible for Avani to read. Absen appeared to have no such difficulty.

"Ha, here it is," he said, pleased. "A seal for drawing out poisons. Haven't had much need for it lately, not since the countess's father ordered a hunt on Wythe's venomous moles. Nasty critters, those, but blind in sunlight and easily lured from their holes. We don't have them in Wythe anymore."

He recited words off the page, and like the letters the syllables refused to arrange themselves sensibly in Avani's ears. Andrew's ring warmed against her breastbone. Her skin itched in response to magic rising. When Brother Absen discharged the spell, tracing a shining spiral in the air above the honey pots with one finger, she felt the jolt of it in her back teeth.

The sigil hovered in the air for a brief, contemplative moment, then burned itself out in a flash of yellow, falling over the honey and the kerchief in a shower of ash.

Brother Absen wagged his chin. "They are completely safe, as I supposed. In fact, there's no ill intent secured to the gifting at all." He rose, joints creaking, and passed his grimoire to Cenwin. "A truth for which I cannot help but be grateful. If I'm to assume the flower corresponds to the tincture, these three here are a white myrtle concoction, and especially curative when painted on an open wound." He looked expectantly in Morgan's direction. "The rest would certainly make some of our healing tinctures more palatable. Why, even the kerchief, boiled and dried, could be cut into bandages."

"Or course, Brother Absen," Morgan replied. "Take them all, as my gift to the temple."

Beaming, the old theist bundled the pots in the kerchief. Liam muttered under his breath. Avani poked him in the spine.

"Brother Shin has been gone a long time in the red wood," she said. "Too soon the day will grow busy again and we'll need the extra hands. My lord, will you lend me Liam for a short while?"

"Certainly he will," Absen said before Morgan could speak. "My lord will keep me company here until you return or he's needed elsewhere. It will do the garrison good to see you doing the one god's work, young Morgan."

"Of course," Morgan repeated but with less enthusiasm. "Don't be long, Liam. We've still to pay that visit to the quartermaster."

"Shin never wanders far," Absen reassured the lad. "But he does tend to lose track of time in the forest. Consummate herbalist, that man, may the one god keep him safe."

"You're walking better," Avani ventured, pleased, as she and Liam crossed beneath the forest canopy. A grouping of Kingsmen, chattering quietly as they grazed their horses in the shade, grew silent as they passed. She supposed they were an odd pair, the witch and the scarred man, and tried not to resent those covert glances. "How is your knee?"

"Mending quickly." Liam grinned. His hand rested on the pommel of his knife, vigilant. Avani suffered a burst of bittersweet affection. He'd come a long way in a short time from the orphaned lad she'd first loved on the Downs.

"There's some magic in your healings now, is there, my lady?" he suggested. "When before it was learning and practice that made you so capable. You're taking what Malachi taught you and making it your own."

Sparrows twittered angrily above their heads. Jacob, having left his post in the evergreen near the baldachin, fluttered indolently from branch to branch in Avani and Liam's wake, disturbing the smaller birds. Avani could sense the raven's hilarity as he chased them from their roosts.

The tiny red flowers were fading as summer waned, turning the carpet on the forest floor from scarlet to rust. The forest ferns, too, were turning to yellow, their giant fronds becoming brittle as nights grew colder. Mabon was only weeks away; winter was not far off. But the sunlight filtering through the canopy was warm instead of scorching on the top of Avani's head and she was glad to see summer's end.

"One way or another it was always mine," she replied after a moment's thought. "Flatlander magic, bone magic, necromancy. Theist enchantments, ensorcelled sigils drawn in the air over pots of honey." She hopped over a narrow stream dividing two moss-draped banks. "Even the *sidhe* spells, *ai*? They're related, I think, sides of the same deep-rooted hardwood." She indicated an ancient sycamore growing near the stream. White lichen obscured bark on one quarter of the trunk, making it appear ghostly and withered in the shade, while the rest of the sycamore, favored with morning sun, appeared gray and gold and healthy. "The view changes depending upon where one is standing. Absen thinks the power comes from his god, I believe it's a gift from my Goddess, the magi prefer to believe it's a gift from the dead and the *sidhe*—"

"Earth magic," Liam said, kicking up a clod of forest soil with his toe. It spun over the ground then broke apart against a sapling. "Sometimes I dream the taste of it in my mouth, from when they used it to bring me back from death. Like mud and moldy leaves." He grimaced. "If they're all parts of the same thing, my lady—the healers, the necromancers, the *aes si*, what do you suppose it means?"

"I haven't walked all the way around that old hardwood yet," Avani confessed. "Nor seen it from every angle. But I suspect it means just what you said: the view is what we make of it."

Spoken aloud, it seemed a simple truth.

"What about on the other side of the mountains? Will there be desert magi come to kill us with spells, do you think?" Liam wondered, as they paused to take stock of their surroundings. On the far side of the stream someone had trampled yellow ferns in a straight track further into the trees. Avani assumed it was Shin, heading directly to his mushroom patch.

"I think," replied Avani, recalling what she'd gleaned of Desma from Mal, "that magic as we know it doesn't root well there."

"Well, that's good, innit?" Liam puffed a relieved breath. "Mayhap we'll have some small advantage."

Somewhere in the trees not far away someone was singing, quietly, and then with more force, and then quietly again. Avani put a finger to her lips. Liam froze, head turned toward the sound. Jacob dropped from the sky onto Avani's shoulder.

"That can't be Shin," Liam murmured. "I know that lay from Whore's Street. It would make even Riggins blush. Besides, it sounds like a woman."

"Whore's Street, is it?" Avani awarded her lad a narrow glare before shaking her head. "Never you mind. I'd rather not know. Wait a moment." She closed her eyes and sent a curl of questing power outward. What she discovered made her scowl and draw her sword and prime her wards.

"What is it?" Liam whispered, knife in hand.

"This way," Avani said. "No need for stealth. I imagine she knows we're coming." She set off along the trail in the ferns, Jacob bobbing on her shoulder, Liam steps behind.

They didn't have far to walk. The tavern lay sounded clearer as they drew closer; the refrain was indeed bawdy enough to make a soldier blush. Any other time Avani might have suspected a lancer wandered off from the garrison for a slice of solitude.

Garrison living was crowded in more ways the just the physical, and although a Kingsman could be drummed out for wandering off, most commanders would look the other way so long as a soldier returned in a timely manner.

But no lancer sang with such beauty, voice like silver bells, heartbreaking in its purity. And it was too much of a coincidence, not with the honey just now in Absen's care.

"Oh," said Liam, understanding late. "Avani. Should I go back for help?"

"Nay. She's not worth the panic it would cause." They'd reached a break in the trees, not quite a clearing but a notch of blue sky and grass free of flowers and fern. A knee-high wall of bramble blocked most of the narrow lea from sight. Shin's track passed through the bush, though thorny branches had closed again behind. Avani used her sword to part the tangle and saw that it was not so deep as she thought, easily passable.

She went through first, Jacob gone still, his claws scoring through her salwar to flesh long ago calloused by his company. Liam followed, moving through the brush without sound of footfall or leaf snap, as unnatural in the hunt as the one they hunted. Faolan, she thought fleetingly, must have been proud.

Cleena was waiting, sitting on her haunches in a patch of grass and mushroom, Shin's head cradled on her thigh. His blood stained her patchwork skirts. His bag, half full with picked produce, was clutched in his hands.

The priest wasn't yet dead, but he was very close. He'd been taken by three arrows, one in each eye and the last through his throat. Iridescent fletching shimmered beneath a spray of gore.

Cleena stopped singing when Avani and Liam stepped out of the bramble. She showed her pointed teeth in a grimace as Shin breathed his last breath, coughing a burst of blood onto her hands.

"You're too late," she said. "Poor man." She growled low as Avani reached for silver fire. "I didn't kill him, you fool. I found him dying amongst my lace caps and kept him company while he did."

"Then who?" Liam demanded.

But Avani already knew the answer. She'd seen variegated fletching in Desma's past. Heart pounding, she wheeled on Liam—"We have to go back!"— but too late. Garrison horns sounded in increasing alarm from the west, a precipitous clarion call. She thought she could hear a hound's angry barking.

"Bear!" Liam crashed headlong back through the bramble. "Morgan! Avani, the garrison!"

At once Mal was in her head, holding her limbs immobile as he tried to assess the situation, using her eyes and her ears and then her magic, summoning wards with such violence that Cleena hissed and cowered.

Jacob bounced and screamed on Avani's shoulder. He bit her earlobe, drawing blood. Mal snarled and used Avani's fist to try to knock the raven away.

"Stop it!" She fought them both, the bird on her shoulder and the magus in her head. "Get out!" Against all wisdom Cleena was crawling closer on hands and knees, dark eyes intent. Where the wards touched ground, grass smoked. Where Andrew's ring brushed salwar, silk began to smolder.

"So much potential," the banshee murmured, watching avidly as Avani struggled to regain control. Mal was insistent Avani walk at once deeper into the forest, away from danger. Jacob thought she belonged with Liam and Morgan. Both necromancer and Goddess desired to keep her safe. Neither gave a second's thought to free will.

They warred within her head and heart, through her blood and bones. She knew she would die of it.

"So much potential," Cleena repeated. She raised a hand, palm flat. "Why don't you *use* it?" And she shoved, hard, against the gleaming silver-green surface of Avani's wards.

It was lightning flashing in Avani's veins and behind her eyes. It was fire burning back along every nerve. It was exhilaration arcing through bone and blood and heart and head, purging. And when it was over she was alone in her skull as she hadn't been for years, wards burning clear and silver behind closed eyelids, an all-encompassing, pliant lattice in her head, guarding her very core, where she'd been trying and failing for so long to instead build adamant walls.

Jacob hunched on a nearby branch, silent but for the gnash of his beak. Mal was gone. Cleena clutched her palm against her breast, her grin pained.

"Now run," she said. "And save your friends."

CHAPTER 18

The *dullahan* wore a barrow gate key on a twist of tanned leather wrapped several times around his wrist. Everin had not so long ago found a similar key concealed in a dead man's coffin. Avani wore one on a chain around her neck, side by side with her vocent's ring. Stonehill's Widow had kept one on a bronze ring with passkeys in her vegetable shed. And Faolan had kept one on his belt.

The bronze barrow keys were not large, but they were unusual. The blade was sharply pointed, the bow and haft filigreed. Like the grille work across flatland *sidhe* tunnel openings, the keys were mortal made, crafted by blacksmith and magi together in attempt to keep the barrowmen contained. They were meant to be scarce and closely guarded and they had been, until the throne began to hunt necromancer instead of *sidhe*. After the magi were lost, so, too, were their barrow keys, scattered or destroyed.

Mal's jealous wife had used one to set hungry barrowmen free on the Downs. Everin had used Faolan's, deftly stolen and later returned, to escape the mounts with the *dullahan*. And now the *dullahan* wore one around his wrist on a strip of tanned skin cut from the back of a human priest.

"He meant to change his mind, in the end," Crom Dubh confessed as he walked the perimeter of the desert gate, Everin at his side, Drem three paces behind and Pelagius two more behind Drem. Drem's Desma disguise was fraying, whether because the lesser *sidhe* had been too long amongst desert steel or because Faolan was dead. An impression of Drem's shorter form danced beneath Desma's longer limbs and Desma's yellow desert eyes had gone dark. Everin thought the addition of the Aug's iron sword strapped on Drem's back for safekeeping was probably not improving the *sidhe*'s situation.

"He was hardly a stupid man," Crom Dubh said of the dead theist. "An obedient lap dog, until it came down to completing his master's task. He was willing to do as the Masterhealer ordered, up to a point. The horses were no obstacle. But when it came time to relinquish the barrow key he balked." The *dullahan* stopped to gaze upon the portal and inhale the perfume of pink-budded saplings. "I had no choice then but to kill him, of course. I'd come too far to let something so fragile as piety get in my way."

The guards stationed around the gate moved aside to let the *dullahan* through. Crom Dubh's feet were bare; he flexed toes gratefully on impossibly green grass. The rose-gold dawn spilling from the portal outlined a spread of otherwise invisible wings sweeping lazily back and forth in the night.

"I need but a short time underground to regain what strength the iron draws," he said. "Drem, also, will come and rest. It has grown meager with too much time spent amongst mortals. Bring the blade, Drem. I do not believe Everin is yet resigned to his fate."

Drem said nothing, shoulders hunched beneath the weight of the sword, face turned toward the gate.

"Nicanor is looking forward to your presence again in his lodge." The *dullahan* turned and strode toward the stone arch. Drem followed more slowly. "He will feed you up and find you a horse and proper armor. When we ride, you will lead the charge."

"And your geis?" Everin demanded. He could feel the weight of it now doubling, a shadow across his heart, that desperate pledge made against better judgment.

"Lead my army safely under the mountain," Crom Dubh replied, "and I will discharge it." He stepped beneath the gray stone arch and disappeared, there one instant and gone the next. The gate framed Drem briefly in rose-gold and then the lesser *sidhe*, too, vanished.

"This way," Pelagius said. "Nicanor is expecting you, *Erastos*." His tone said Everin had no choice in the matter, as did his cold grimace.

"I liked you better as a love-sick fool," he said.

"I like you not at all," answered Pelagius. "That way." He pointed past the gate at Nicanor's lodge.

Obviously, he believed Everin, unarmed, was not a threat. Everin was tempted to prove him wrong. Even with the newly roused geis heavy on his heart, he might have attempted flight, if only for a chance at smashing the dour expression from Pelagius's mouth. But even if he survived the tussle, escape now would do Wilhaiim little good; Everin did not doubt the *dullahan* would find its way back through the tunnels with or without him. Of a certain Drem knew the flatland gates as well as any barrowman.

He knew the Crom Dubh kept him alive purely for reasons of entertainment. Everin didn't mind playing *sidhe* games, so long as he came out ahead in the end. And he meant to.

He gripped Pelagius's shoulder in a friendly manner as he passed him. "Keep smirking, you bastard," he suggested hoarsely in the man's ear, squeezing flesh. "I owe you a bruise or six, and my time will come."

Nicanor welcomed Erastos with open arms, kissing Everin on each cheek and embracing him like a brother. The older man had grown frail in Everin's absence, but not so fragile that he could not lead his tribe into battle. The tattoos on his chest and thighs were faded, but the number of feathers in his long hair and on his sleeves had multiplied exponentially. He wore Rouen gold on his fingers and toes. The feathers and gold, and the proximity of his tribe to Crom Dubh's lodge, meant the sand lord was still prospering.

"The war to end all wars," he proclaimed, settling Everin in a nest of sand-colored cushions and pouring him clean water to drink. More even than his embrace, the water was an indication of Nicanor's joy over his friend's safe return. "I do not think I will miss this arid land, Erastos, though it nourished my family for longer than any living man can recall. It has grown stingy, unfruitful, bitter. For generations we have watered it with our blood and not regretted a drop spilled, but now even our most generous sacrifices are ignored. There are too many of us, or not enough desert, and we are all stretched thin."

Everin, looking openly around Nicanor's lodge as he sipped water, could see the other man spoke truthfully. The tent was full to bursting with members of Nicanor's tribe. The children playing quietly in one corner were small and skinny, visibly malnourished. Their mothers and sisters, wrapped in diaphanous white chitons, were sharp-boned and listless. Even the warriors moving unobtrusively in and out of the lodge were too lean, their bare chests verging on sunken. Nicanor's tribe had always been wealthy, and from the feathers in their hair and the embroidery on scabbard and kilt, they still were, but now they were also starving.

Camel roasted on two spits outside Nicanor's tent, and outside every nearby lodge, scenting the air deliciously. Soon enough there would be plenty of meat to go around, at least for a short time.

"You look well." Nicanor lowered himself groaning onto a large cushion. His goblet brimmed to spilling with beer. "But for the welts tarnishing your pretty face." He glanced Pelagius's way from under lowered lids. Pelagius, standing patient guard by the tent flap, did not appear to notice. "Crom Dubh said only that you came over the mountains from the west with a tinker's brood. I never thought to see you again, much less learn you'd left us for the mercenary life."

"I grew tired of making bricks and killing snakes." Everin set down his goblet, water half drunk. He was expected to finish the cup entire lest he give offense, but it was difficult to lie with that most tangible confirmation of Nicanor's affections in hand. "It was good pay for easy work. Besides, I wanted to see what was on the other side."

"I paid you well," accused Nicanor mildly. He sighed, took a drink, then set down his own cup. "So, then. What is it like, on the other side? Rolling hills, green as the grass surrounding the demon gate? Rain as often as sunshine? Rivers of all sizes flooding the land? And plentiful game, I'm told, so plentiful a man can throw his spear with eyes closed and always take down a gazelle or mountain lion."

As Nicanor leaned forward in curiosity so did the women and children of his tribe drift close, captivated. Even the most attentive guardsmen turned their heads to listen as they walked the lodge's inner perimeter. In their regard Everin recognized more than a passing interest; he saw desperation. Nicanor, noticing the fresh tension in the room, extended an arm. The children, all ten of them, came at once, dashing over the sisal rugs to sit at his knee. Lads and lasses of all ages, their yellow desert eyes round with excitement.

"I've told you tales of Erastos and his bravery," Nicanor said. "Now Erastos will tell us tales of our new home on the other side of the divide."

Pelagius, standing in the doorway, made a low sound of derision.

"Pelagius," Lord Nicanor said calmly as he settled the youngest child in his lap. "This is a family gathering. You may wait outside."

"But, my lord, I am here on Crom Dubh's orders to see that Erastos is kept safe."

"And who would do Erastos harm here in my lodge?" Nicanor looked not at Pelagius but at Everin, and Everin, shocked, realized many years too late that Nicanor had never been fooled—from the very beginning had always guessed that Erastos was not completely the desert warrior he pretended—and Nicanor had welcomed him into his home nonetheless, given the exiled king a chance to be something more.

"He is tribe," Nicanor said. "I will see to his safety myself. Step outside, Pelagius, and leave us to celebrate Erastos's happy return amongst ourselves."

Pelagius left the tent without another word. Everin, stricken, finished his water gift in one swallow.

"Go on, then, Erastos," Nicanor urged, "tell how it is on the other side of the mountain, what fortunes await us once our victory is satisfied." He stroked his chin thoughtfully, making the children laugh. "Tell us true, does every tree bear delicious fruit, and every cock pheasant lay a golden egg?"

Everin made a show of clearing his ruined throat. "Apples and pears," he began. "Worth more than any golden egg for their sweetness. As for golden eggs, what needs you gold, Lord Nicanor, when you can drink your fill of clear water for free?" He lifted his empty goblet in silent toast.

Afterward, when the candles were snuffed and the children asleep, Nicanor withdrew a pouch from the folds of his chiton. Taking a pinch of black opion gum from within, he tucked the drug between his lower lip and teeth.

"Today is for resting and eating, perhaps our last chance before Crom Dubh returns." He offered Everin a pinch and shook his head when Everin declined.

"You never were one for the small pleasures in life," Nicanor said. "Perhaps to your advantage. Since Khorit Dard's defeat opion has been harder to come by." He yawned and stretched, indolent, and lay back on his cushion. "Though Crom Dubh has promised us Roue again, once this western business is finished. There are tribes already massing on their border. Khorit Dard was an old man, and gone soft. Roue will not find Crom Dubh so easily chased off."

Everin grunted. "I'll admit I never thought to see the desert united in allegiance, much less tribe lodges settled peacefully together in one place. It goes against the tribe's very nature."

Nicanor's eyes gleamed amber in the candlelight. "Starvation will turn even the boldest wolf docile. Desperation makes for strange bedfellows."

"And afterward?" Everin wondered. "When the flatlands are won and every man's belly is full again, desperation forgotten? The desert is a vast place, the flatland one quarter its size. We will be one million sand fleas fighting over a single pheasant's carcass. Peace won't hold. Tribe will turn on tribe once again. What then?"

But Nicanor's expression had gone unfocused, his mouth slack. The opion was working upon his senses, blunting his edges, softening his wit. Everin suppressed a shudder. That any man would so willingly dull his own intelligence seemed abhorrent, but Nicanor had always preferred indolence to rumination, and how very tempting forgetfulness must be on the eve of war.

"Black Crom is no upstart chieftain chasing dominance," Nicanor assured Everin. "He's proved himself many times over these long years. His foes fall always before him and his allies rise to greater heights. He makes the proper blood sacrifices, and in doing so has tamed the demon gate. He has guaranteed our success. So long as he holds sway, no tribe will step out of line."

"I imagine the same was said of Khorit Dard," said Everin, "while the opion was flowing freely."

Nicanor, dreaming already with his eyes open, didn't reply. Everin, resigned, stretched out on the rug alongside and sought sleep. The rose-gold brilliance thrown off by the *sidhe* gate turned the tent's white canvas to pink even in the daylight. Pelagius's shadow loomed outside the door. The desert beyond was loud with industrious noise as men and women prepared to break camp. Everin rolled onto his back and covered his face with his forearm, blocking the light. The bruises on his face and ribs ached. His body was old and overused. He expected he would die in the next day or three, pierced by a flatland spear as he led the desert charge, or cut down by a warrior's scimitar from behind.

Surely the *dullahan* didn't intend to let him live even after the geis was broken, no more than the *dullahan* intended to let this game of mortal against mortal go on much longer. *Sidhe* grew bored very quickly and soon after boredom, broke their playthings.

The healing scar on Everin's throat itched. It made him think of Faolan.

He came back to himself with Desma's cold hand on his shoulder. Already up and on his knees before waking fully, Everin reached for his sword, forgetting it was in Drem's care.

"You're wanted," the *sidhe* said. It stood taller for time spent in the barrows but the Desma disguise still flickered dangerously.

"I should kill you," Everin snarled. "For being a sneak and a liar. Faolan trusted you."

"To keep you safe, little king," Drem agreed. "And here you stand, battered but breathing. Safer, I think, under Crom Dubh's nose than Pelagius's fists. Twice I've rescued you from your own stupidity." Pivoting, it strode from Nicanor's lodge.

Everin had fallen into the sleep of the exhausted, and more time had passed than he liked. Outside the tent it was deep night, although the *sidhe* gate kept darkness at bay. Nicanor's tribe sat beneath the open sky, sharing meat and beer. The children, faces greasy, giggled and pointed at Everin as he skirted the cook fire. Nicanor, sitting in place of honor nearest the spit, called out in greeting.

"Erastos! Come and eat! I've saved you a plate. Tonight we feast!" He clapped his hands and his family around him whooped excitement. "Tomorrow we ride!"

A surge of unexpected affection made Everin hesitate. But Drem was waiting and not patiently.

"Soon," Everin replied. "Save it for me a while longer."

Nicanor nodded and turned away to speak to a near companion. Everin took a long look around at the happy gathering, memorizing faces as he had not thought to do when last he parted company with Nicanor and his family. Now he knew better.

"Will I see him again?" he asked Drem quietly as they crossed between lodges. The wind was picking up again, battering tents and pennants and threatening to throw sand.

"From the back of your horse in the morning. For the rest, who am I to say?" Drem executed one of its cryptic shrugs. "Does it matter?"

"For a time he was kin," Everin explained. "So, aye."

"Kin is always kin," returned Drem coolly. "You

cannot say that he was and then he was not. He is or he is not."

"He is," said Everin as they approached the door of the *dullahan*'s tent. "And if I do not see him again after tomorrow, I will miss him." As he missed Avani and Liam and now Faolan. It shamed him that he'd chosen a solitary life over affinity. He was realizing too late that, like Nicanor with the opion, he'd taken refuge in apathy.

Pelagius, stone-faced, waited for them outside the *dullahan*'s lodge. He parted the tent flap with his hand and preceded them inside. Crom Dubh waited within, alone, absorbed in his own thoughts. Smoke from the opion brazier wreathed the tent, stinging Everin's eyes.

"Crom Dubh," Pelagius said, drawing the *dullahan*'s attention.

"Ah, good." He brightened. "Come and see." When he beckoned, unseen pinions rustled. Like Drem and Desma, the *dullahan*'s human guise was also suffering, blurring at the boundaries. When it smiled at Everin, that affable mien turned cloudy, like ink dropped in water, before recoalescing once again.

A rectangular, multicolored rug lay unrolled on sisal beneath the *dullahan*'s feet. At first Everin assumed it was a peculiarly patterned carpet, but as he reached the *dullahan*'s side, he saw it was a map made tapestry, colorful thread turned topography.

"I'm told it's a fine likeness. There were not so many stone edifices when the *Tuath Dé* still walked free, nor do I recall the forest being quite so thin. But the coastline is the same, and the southern flowing cataracts."

It was a fussy likeness: the flatlands recreated in cotton and wool and silk. Wilhaiim, picked out in silver ribbon, shone against floss-white cliffs. Royal keeps north and west were labeled with their corresponding devices done out in the most delicate cord. The Mors was a froth of blue braid and white lace, as was the sea. Crimson pin-flowers demarked the king's red woods. And around the whole, in a repeating pattern of knots and knit, ran the temple's spear and chalice.

Avani, Everin suspected, would have found it in bad taste.

"It is mostly to scale," he acknowledged. "But I've never been overly fond of ribbon."

Crom Dubh pushed a basket into Everin's hands. His breath stank of places under the earth. Everin peered into the basket so he didn't have to witness the monster under the grinning disguise. The basket, sisal like the rug under his feet, was filled with large, bronze-headed pushpins. They rattled, betraying the quiver in his hands.

"It's time to scheme," the *dullahan* proclaimed happily. "Mark the gates. Every gate, don't leave out even one." He scrubbed hands together, mimicking mortal glee, and Everin heard scales scraping. "Take your time but don't dawdle. Pelagius gets easily bored. Isn't that so, Pelagius?"

"Yes, Crom Dubh," Pelagius deadpanned. Everyone in the room knew it wasn't Pelagius's boredom Everin need fear.

His joints cracked complaint as he dropped to his knees. The air was cleaner near the lodge floor, the opion smoke rising to collect beneath the peaked roof. Drem squatted to join him. Pelagius leaned on his spear. The *dullahan*, gone preternaturally still, waited. One by one Everin began to stick bronze pins into the map. Gate by gate he made his way from corner to corner, north to south, east to west. Eyes half closed against haze, he struggled to recall Faolan's secrets. Drem watched without comment. Drem who, with its kin Bail, had run Faolan's most furtive errands beneath the flatlands.

"You're more suitable than I for this," Everin muttered as he stuck a pin into the brown ribbon swale that was Stonehill Downs.

"Drem will tell me if you place one awry," agreed the Crom Dubh. "I prefer it this way. Your mouth goes tight every time you set a pin, each time you betray your kind. There are grooves alongside your nose from the strength of your rage. And you are weeping, did you know?" It dipped all at once, curled a finger beneath Everin's chin, and scooped his regret into its mouth, sucking eagerly. "Different tears than those you shed when you rode on my back, I think. Those were relief. This is—"

"Opion smoke," retorted Everin as he placed the last pin. "The drug makes my eyes burn. There. Are we finished?"

"So many." The *dullahan* bent to get a better look. The smoke eddied in circles around him, briefly obscuring the tapestry. Pelagius waved the haze away, squinting. Outside the wind shook the tent, tossing sand against the canvas.

"Scores of them," Pelagius said, awed. "Worse than beetles in a cactus."

"Some are sealed," Drem said. "Around the cities and near the sea. Faolan closed many by the coast. The island witch barred others nearest their king with her spells. The barrow key is nothing against her sorcery."

Crom Dubh glowered. "I've not the time or the strength to pit magic against magic. I've given too much of myself already. This is meant to be disport, the contest of mortal against mortal, a culling of our enemies, before I sleep again." He turned his back on the tapestry map and stalked across the tent, pausing to pour beer into a cup from a silver pitcher. "Tell me. Which are open? Which can I make use of without undue effort?"

"There are two just east of the forest," Drem mused, leaning over the map. "But difficult to take an army through those woods. Six more that, last I knew, were still undiscovered and within several leagues of their white city. The safest are further west, between their city and the sea." It glanced under Desma's long eyelashes at the *dullahan*. "Into how many fragments will you divide your army?"

"Two, no more," Pelagius replied. He reached past Everin, pointing. "Our might is in our numbers. Stretch too far and we're no more fortunate going under the mountain than over."

Another volley of wind shook the lodge. Outside, guardsmen called back and forth as they hurried to secure tent poles and miscellaneous belongings in the face of the storm. A horse squealed terror. Camels were built to withstand even the most vicious duster. Coastal ponies were not.

The *dullahan* made a show of deep consideration before he answered.

"We'll make use of Drem's eight gates," it said. "Erastos, Nicanor, Myron. Hypatia of tribe cockerel. Panteleon, Sophus, and Lino. And my Pelagius. Eight bold commanders to make me proud."

Pelagius shifted uneasily. "And you, Crom Dubh?" he asked. "Where will you ride?"

"Oh, behind," the *dullahan* replied, returning to the brazier and warming his hands. "I'll provide the impetus."

"The impetus?" Pelagius's ever-present scowl deepened. "We are wolves, not cowardly flatland sheep."

"The tunnels affect some mortals badly," said the

dullahan, greedily inhaling smoke. "I expect a few will shy away, once the time comes. It's important no one is left behind."

"And why's that?" Everin asked from below the opion haze. "Hungry *sidhe* mouths to feed?"

"What?" snapped the *dullahan*, whirling in Everin's direction and almost overturning the brazier in the process. "What did you say?"

"It seems to me you've contrived a mass exodus. Straight into the mounds. You're right in that Faolan trusted me with his secrets." Everin glanced in Pelagius's direction. "Your people aren't the only folk starving. While the elders sleep, the barrowmen go hungry. How long have you served Crom Dubh? Surely you can't be ignorant. Drem, tell Pelagius: What's your favorite snack?"

"Fish is first," Drem answered promptly. Then it grinned at Pelagius, running its thick white tongue lewdly across Desma's lips. "But second, human flesh."

Pelagius had a scimitar in each hand. His eyes were reddened by opion smoke, his face a rictus of horrified realization. He had just enough sense left to back away toward the tent flap instead of challenging the *dullahan* head-on. As he turned to run, Crom Dubh groaned in mock dismay.

"Kill him," he said.

In one fluid motion Drem sprang across the tent. It muffled Pelagius's shout with Desma's hand. Pelagius dropped one blade in shock, swung wildly with the other. But even diminished by iron, Drem was faster, stronger—an innate killer. It locked an arm around Pelagius's chin and twisted. Neck bones cracked. When Drem released him, Pelagius fell, limp, on the sisal rug. The smell of fresh urine mingled with opion perfume.

"His death is on your hands," the *dullahan* told Everin. "Do not suppose I am unaware of your own contrivances." It glowered. "He was a droll companion, if dull-witted. Of course we can't eat them, not while they bristle steel. Bad enough they'll be bringing iron through the barrows—I fear the taint will linger, but worth it in the end."

"He was too free with his fists," Everin replied. Pelagius's crumpled body was a relief. "This isn't war," he continued, gesturing at the tapestry. "This is a farce. You're not setting them up to win. You're evening the odds."

"Mutual destruction," the *dullahan* agreed. He meandered to Pelagius's side, kicked the curved blades away into the corner of the lodge, then prodded the cooling corpse with his foot. "Might opposite magic. Steel opposite iron. Two very different cultures set to clash, and as many of each dead at the end as I can manage." He shifted Pelagius from back to belly with a kick, then stepped carelessly on the dead man's spine. More bones snapped. "And after, when beneath *our* blue skies *our* soil is drinking *their* red blood—why, then, certainly, we will feast."

Everin felt sick. "I'll kill you."

"I doubt you can," replied Crom Dubh, smug. "You set this in motion, when you woke me from slumber. You'll stay and watch it play out. Because I enjoy the amusing, anguished faces you make when you think no one's looking. They're almost as satisfying as vengeance taken." It stepped once more on Pelagius, this time breaking hipbones. "Almost."

CHAPTER 19

The desert scout was dead, cut down by a lancer, but not before he put more arrows through the eyes and throats of five Kingsmen and Brother Absen. Their deaths were instantaneous; Avani arrived too late to save them.

Morgan dispatched a messenger to the king's constable who was said to be riding somewhere near Wilhaiim's westmost line. The dead Kingsmen and Absen and Shin were loaded with grim ceremony into a cart for burial in the city. At Morgan's command their killer was quartered and his head mounted atop the baldachin. Afterward his ghost paced back and forth between the baldachin and the forest, blue eyes tilted always toward the top of the baldachin and his severed head. The theists and three of the soldiers returned to their god without Avani's assistance. Two lingered, either confused by the suddenness of their deaths or frightened by what might lie beyond. Avani used a banishing cant to send them on.

She let the desert haunt be in the hopes that he might decide to speak anything of interest, but he seemed to care only for his head and the indignity of that display. Avani didn't blame him for it.

"Can't you interrogate it?" Morgan appealed when she mentioned the spirit's restless misery. "Make it tell us if more are coming, and from where?"

"Mal could," she said. "I won't. And I promise you more are coming. Ramp up your guard patrols, my lord, night and day. I expect we won't have much longer to wait."

"Can you use his bones," Liam suggested, "to set further wards around the garrison?" He rested one hand protectively on Bear's wedge head. The brindled hound, first to sound alarm when the scout breeched the garrison, now refused to leave her master's side for any length of time.

"Only if he's willing, and I very much doubt he would be." Grim, Avani shook her head. "*Ai*, mayhap the poor dead soldiers, or even Absen, but I did not think and now it's too late."

"You did not think. I did not think." Morgan knuckled his eyes. He had not rested or eaten since the morning attack. Avani caught him looking often down the cliff in the direction of Whitcomb, as if by staring he could will his mother more quickly to his side. But the day was coming to close and there was as yet no sign of Wythe. "What good are you and I, then, if we don't stop to think?"

"Sit and sup, my lord," Liam coaxed, ladling boiled oats from their cookpot into a bowl. In all the commotion, they'd forgotten supplies at the quartermaster's tent and now they hadn't the heart, any of them, to wander back down the hill and in sight of the baldachin where Brother Cenwin grieved, prostrate, in front of his altar. "I've added honey."

"Honey." Morgan walked from the cliff's edge and snatched up the bowl, scowling. "This is the banshee's fault, I think, lurking about. Bringing ill luck to my garrison. I imagine she's laughing right now, believing us fools." He made a motion as if to toss the bowl and oats both over the edge of the cliff but Avani stayed his hand.

"If you won't eat it," she said. "I will. I'm tired and hungry and sorrowing. I knew Absen only a short time, but he was a good man. I think he would not like to see you blaming yourself. And I do not believe Cleena brought us ill luck, any more than Jacob has. It's only superstition, to explain away the misgivings that keep us awake at night."

Jacob, nested comfortably again inside Morgan's tent, grumbled loud agreement.

Thusly admonished, Morgan sat on the ground to eat. "I know it," he said after a silence. "We should have expected this—the flatland has been rife with wandering sand snakes since early summer. Only, my mother set the guards and I assumed they were sufficient."

"They were sufficient." Liam filled another bowl and placed it in Avani's hands. The steaming oats warmed her fingers through the pottery. "Against a man on horseback. Mayhap not one sneaking about on foot through the undergrowth, bow in hand and with better aim even than I."

"I've doubled the watch," Morgan said around a mouthful of honey and oats. "We'll have word from Wilhaiim before dark, I imagine. And mother soon after." He scraped his spoon on the bottom of his bowl. "This is good."

It was good. Avani's stomach, forgotten for most of the day, woke to sharp hunger. She ate slowly, savoring each bite. Cleena's honey turned otherwise bland oats sweet. When she was finished, she let Bear lick around the bowl, then rose and wandered to the cliff edge, hoping to catch the beginnings of sunset over Whitcomb.

"Riders on the highway," she reported before Morgan could ask. "Bearing Renault's device. Word from the king on the matter, I expect." She squinted. "Nothing from the coast, that I can tell. The road looks empty." It had been clearing in the past hour or so, as those who had not already made refuge in the city retreated to hidden places near farm or keep. There was a new sense of urgency in the air, a hastening of preparation. Fires were lit all along the Wilhaiim's wall-walk; she could see watchmen at work along the barbican and above the northern gate.

"Murder hole," Morgan said, appearing at her elbow. He sounded reluctantly impressed. "A gap above the gateway from which they send spears, and arrows, and worse. Smell the boiling tar? Pots of it, waiting to be turned over any enemy who comes close. There's a murder hole over every gate. They haven't been uncovered since the *sidhe* wars, I imagine. It's a wonder they remembered how to light the pots. They'll have brought the tar up from Low Port weeks ago, I suppose. His Majesty knows his duty. He'll do whatever it takes to keep us safe."

"He will," Avani agreed. She could not yet think on Renault without an uncomfortable mix of sympathy and resentment. She imagined the king standing in his oriel, waiting upon news of invasion while listening to Brother Tillion decry royal immorality from the street below.

"Oi, look!" Morgan pointed at the western horizon. "White smoke on the coast, there, can you see? The sea lords will be preparing their defenses, as well, kindling their watch fires." He bounced on his toes. "It's really happening, isn't it?"

"Aye, my lord, it is." Avani watched faraway smoke billow in front of the setting sun. It was a pretty picture: the blue sea, the orange sunset, and the white smoke scudding between.

"Come and rest," Liam called from the cook fire. "While things are quiet. You've been standing on your feet all day."

Morgan's expression turned petulant. "You're meant to be my squire, not my nursemaid."

"Beg pardon, my lord, but I was speaking to Lady Avani," retorted Liam, meeting Avani's eye over the top of Morgan's head. "Though you look as if you could do with some shut-eye yourself, and I'll not pretend otherwise."

"Turn around is fair play." Avani winked at Morgan. He was a good lad, and terribly earnest, and she could see his mother's determination in the set of his jaw. "I've sent that one to bed too many times to count when he was your age and more interested in playing hide-and-seek with the stars. I am weary," she confessed, turning toward her bedroll. "So should you be. Will you rest a time, my lord?"

She thought he would consent, but then that stubborn jaw grew firm as he remembered duty. "Not quite yet," the young earl demurred. "I should speak again to Brother Cenwin, see if there's aught he needs in his grief. And I want to check the horses another time before dark, to make sure they're well-guarded. The king's message may contain new orders; I'll meet the riders as they come, I think. And mother—" he peered again at the highway below "—will expect me to be on hand when she arrives."

"As you will, my lord." Her heart broke for his

conviction. Liam, too, had been a resolute child, but Liam had never been taxed with the responsibilities of an earldom.

She left Morgan standing lookout and unrolled her bedding on a level spot near the earl's tent with the cook fire to warm her back. Liam hummed under his breath as he banked the flames and scrubbed the pot and laid out Morgan's nightshirt for later. She realized, with some surprise, that he sounded happy. Bear snuggled up along Avani's front, laying her heavy head on Avani's thigh. Jacob, preferring the shelter of the tent, pretended not to hear when she whistled invitation.

The sky was the color of good red weaver's dye when she closed her eyes. Bear was snoring. And thanks to Cleena she was still blissfully alone in her own skull, warded inwardly against intrusion.

Nevertheless, she dreamed.

She dreamed she was crawling again in the barrows beneath Stonehill, Jacob hopping on the muddy ground a few paces ahead. She followed the raven down and down through the tunnel, hastening when she lost track of black feathers. The space was uncomfortably tight, as it had been when she'd first wriggled through Faolan's hidden gate. Dangling root and glowing moss ticked the back of her head, making her shudder. Thin streams of water ran down the tunnel walls, miniature waterfalls. She lacked a mage-light but she wasn't blind. Minuscule fragments of silver rock caught in the mud reflected a sourceless white glow, turning night to day.

The scrollwork gate at the end of the tunnel was cracked open. She could see the chamber beyond. Following Jacob, she crawled over the threshold. Once through she had enough room to stand. The ceilings were high, the old cavern at least as large as the village above. Moss and more vine dripped from the ceiling. Stone teeth grew out of the ceiling and the floor. The organic pillars were covered all around in carvings: *sidhe* sigils made for the purpose of protection and illumination. The chamber walls shone a diffuse white. The *sidhe*, who no longer walked beneath a natural sun, were forced to conjure light of their own.

"This light," agreed Mal, walking now at her side. "Not so different than that in the old laboratories. And the sigils—" he walked dark fingers along limestone "—not so different than those in the theist spell books. Mayhap you're more right than you know. Mayhap it all comes from the same source."

"There are no gods but the *sidhe*?" Avani grimaced. "Jacob would disagree." The raven flew in circles over their heads, neatly avoiding tangle with root and vine. His wingspan seemed to shrink and then swell as he circled, sending strangely shaped shadows onto the damp floor.

"Look," Mal insisted. He scraped a nail against stone then held up his finger. A minuscule amber pebble glittered on the tip. "The jewel in your ring. Khorit Dard's Heart. The magestone set in the doors of the Rani's palace. And the yellow gem set in Faolan's torque. Why have we never thought to wonder from whence the amber came?"

"Every stone comes first from the earth, Mal." Impatient, Avani hurried after Jacob. "He wants me to go that way. The river tunnel."

At the cavern's westmost curve were four arched doorways, their mouths dark against the cavern's glow. Once gates had secured the openings; large bronze hinges still hung in places from the limestone. More littered the ground around the old portals where, torn from the wall, they lay rusting in the mud and damp. *Sidhe* marks decorated the stone above each opening. Some of the sigils she knew as well as the freckles on her arms and legs—the same decoration had been carved with *sidhe* knives into Liam's flesh in the very same chamber.

Jacob, now the size of a small dog, crouched in front of the left-most opening, wings half extended. He clicked his beak impatiently.

"What's down there?" Mal asked, sniffing suspiciously at the air beyond. "Smells dank."

"*Ai*, I said, the *river* tunnel." She shook her head as she followed Jacob through the opening. "Why are you here? You're not supposed to be here. I've locked you out."

"I'm not here," he said, pacing once more at her

side. "You're dreaming. That was a tidy cheat, turning your wards inside out like that. I had no idea it was possible, and if I had, I certainly wouldn't have tried it for fear of melting my midbrain in the reversal. All that energy, cracking about near your cerebellum."

Avani paused midstride. She shot him a narrow look. "*Cerebellum.* I don't know that word. Why would my dream you know a word that I don't?"

"We've spent a lot of time in each other's heads," Mal replied cheerfully. He looked young and carefree in the diffuse tunnel light. His hair was long again, and he smiled easily as he hadn't since before Roue. He was dressed, not in vocent black, but in a plain linen tunic and trousers. She couldn't be sure but she thought there was the faintest scruff of black beard on his face. "You know what I know even if you don't, as do I you."

"You're talking nonsense."

"You're the dreamer," Mal pointed out, making Avani laugh despite her distrust. Then he gripped her wrist. "Listen. What's that?"

"It's only the river."

The path soon turned steep and slick, cutting straight down into the mountain. Avani put her hand on the tunnel wall for balance. Water rained in droplets from overhead, spattering her head and shoulders. It was icy cold. Jacob, being Jacob, managed to stay dream-dry even as he splashed through mud and shallow puddles.

The tunnel twisted sharply to the right once, and then again, and yet once more. Soon they were walking in tight circles, descending at a precipitous rate. The sound of the river grew loud, like many voices whispering at once, or an angry storm rifling countless leafy tree tops. The tunnel wall trembled beneath her hand. The tunnel floor became a muddy stream, catching at her ankles.

"I don't think that's the river you're hearing," said Mal as the ground abruptly evened out, flat and straight, now more tributary than tunnel.

Avani had been that way once before, and not in a dreaming. She'd explored the tunnel all on her own, out of curiosity, and not because a black-feathered bird insisted on drawing her through vision space. She remembered the twisty decent, the fear when she thought she'd missed the correct turning in her haste, the water rising from ankle to waist. She remembered the second cavern down below the river, flooded but for an island of limestone at the very center.

The island was there, and the ice-cold flood. But it wasn't the Mors River rushing above and around that she heard after all: on the island gathered a population of barrowmen, so many they were forced to stand shoulder-to-shoulder or crouch knee to knee. Corpse-white, flat-eyed, too thin, they were naked or dressed in fur or pieces of mismatched fabric. Many held sticks, or bronze knives, or pieces of sharpened bone. Some had covered their heads with tattered scarves or wide-brimmed villein's caps. One wore a noblewoman's stained silken gown over stockings made of old lace.

They were whispering amongst themselves. Their voices, sibilant and strange, shook the walls. When at last they noticed Avani, they fell immediately silent.

Jacob, circling again overhead, threw a shadow large enough to blacken the island entire. They barrowmen stood unmoving beneath that penumbra, faces upturned and afraid.

"Cast him out," ordered Avani's Goddess through Jacob, as the raven's shadow spread over water and limestone, blotting diffuse *sidhe* light to black. Avani, guilty, looked around at Mal where he stood thigh-deep in water, brows lifted in mute confusion, but it was not Mal the Goddess meant.

"Make a chalice of his head bones," the barrowmen agreed, voices mingled to one roar. "Bring the torches!" They straightened, gripping knives and bone in long-fingered hands, regaining courage. "He's coming! Cast him out!" They cavorted in place, a battle dance, and all around them the cavern shook until chunks of rock and mud thundered into the lake from the ceiling above.

"He's coming," warned the Goddess.

And "Cast him out!" screamed Jacob from his perch on Avani's chest where she slept atop the cliffs. Bear reared upright, alarmed, growling. Avani sat up, dislodging Jacob, almost breaking her forehead on Liam's as he bent to shake her.

"Wake up," Liam said. "I smell smoke on the wind, and not the good, clean sort. It's started."

Clouds obscured the moon. Wind rattled the balda-chin's roof and chased sparks from torches. Wythe was preparing for battle. Kingsmen strapped on armor with the help of squires. The coursers, too, wore plate over quilted blankets to guard their sides and haunches, and stiff leather masks called shaffrons to guard their faces. The shaffrons were adorned on the cheek pieces with Wythe's willow-tree device, and made the animals look quite fierce. They stamped their hooves and switched their tails as mail was tucked and tied and belted into place, snorting at the stench of char on the wind.

Avani made herself useful near the baldachin, steadying Brother Cenwin when he had need of it, keeping busy in between. Groundwork at night was a hazardous thing without nerves running high. Soldiers and servants were stepped upon by excited horses, or sliced on a mail edge, or recovering from too much drink the evening before. Avani handed out ginger to the gut-sick and willow bark for the aching heads. She bandaged sliced flesh and splinted broken bones. She had a stern word with Brother Cenwin when he faltered in the face of Absen's lack, and another with the desert scout's ghost when it walked straight through a gelding mid-tackup, making the horse kick and squeal.

The king's constable had not yet returned from the western curve of the line. Messages coming fast by wing or by rider from Wilhaiim suggested that attack had come first from that direction. Red and orange flame leapt high into the night sky where last sunset they'd been able to see Whitcomb's white clapboard. The wind blew a vague, anguished din eastward with the smoke; sometimes Avani knew the screams were human distress, but other times she assured herself it was only the shrieks of coastal gulls disturbed in the night by smoke and fire.

By tradition Morgan was the last man to sit his horse. Avani held Wilde's head as the lad reached for his stirrup, making soothing noises though the bay gelding stood quietly. The noises were for Morgan and for Liam. The young earl shivered in his mail and tried twice before he made the saddle from the mounting block. In the light of the torches Liam's smile, meant to be reassuring, was ghastly under his helm as he handed up Morgan's lance.

"I think you're meant to give a speech, say something bracing," he counseled. "I'll be two ticks behind you, my lord."

Morgan gathered the reins. Wilde bobbed his head, quiet as a lamb.

"I know what to do," he said. "Liam, don't dawdle. My lady, keep safe."

Then he snapped his visor to, wheeled the gelding around, and cantered away to address his waiting men.

As soon as Morgan was gone, Liam put his hands on his knees and breathed at the ground. Avani, recognizing an onset of panic when she saw one, resisted the urge to pat his shoulders and instead waited quietly. He didn't faint, but she thought it was a close thing.

"The infantry's come up the hill and settled behind our line to wait," he said thickly after a moment. "That's a burned city on the wind—you and I both know it. Everyone knows it." He straightened. He wore a battered cuirass, scrubbed to gleaming, over pieces of leather scavenged from the barracks, and a kettle helm with a leather strap to keep it snug. "It's happening now."

She did touch him then, a light brush of fingers to his set face.

"Morgan's not ready," he said. "I didn't have time to make him ready. He's always hated the quintain because he falls off every time and he'll never say it out loud but I think he's afraid of blood."

"I didn't have time to make you ready, either, but you've done well for yourself," she said, which made him grimace before he turned toward his own horse, a large gray with kind eyes beneath its shaffron. "I'm proud of you. Goddess protect you this day, Liam."

He swung quickly into the saddle to hide threatening tears. In a moment he was gone, trotting down the slope toward the gathering army in search of his lord. Bear, bouncing out of the night, ran after.

Avani hugged her ribs and listened the wind rattle the baldachin, briefly at a loss as to what to do next. The camp was emptied out, even the servants and tradesmen—those fit enough to hold a weapon—had gone down the hill to join the infantry rallying behind the cavalry. The quartermaster's tent was left unguarded, the man and his wife and his two grown sons departed to serve the king.

"Will you be wanting a horse, my lady?" Brother Cenwin asked, coming around the baldachin with a fat coastal pony in tow. He had a pack over his shoulder and a fat spell pouch tied to his belt and his book of healing spells under one arm. She was glad to see he had the sense to cover his tonsured head with a kettle helm, twin to Liam's. "There's Absen's mare or Shin's old gelding if you prefer."

"Nay," Avani replied. "But thank you. I'll go on foot."

He nodded sagely. "It's the infantry that takes the brunt of it, or so I've read. None of us alive this day have seen war to know for sure, god save us." He swung into saddle, agile, then tossed her a salute before hurrying on, the pony's short strides making him bounce.

And then she was alone, but for the ghost pacing

in front of the baldachin and a few scattered chickens startled from sleep and come to peck cautiously around the stone well. She glanced at the sky, trying to gauge the time by the stars, but smoke and clouds obscured the sky.

She had a helmet of her own, a barbute from Morgan's war chest, cut with a wide, Y-shaped opening for her eyes and mouth. She'd declined the matching visor, disliking the constriction. When she tugged it on, the helm caught on the felt skull cap she'd pinned over her hair until she wiggled the helmet side to side. The barbute muffled the wind and the disturbing sounds it carried, for which she was grateful. She wore no other armor—metal was heavy and she relied on her wards inside and out.

She carried her sword, a gift from Mal tempered to her hand when she'd accepted the office of vocent, and a belt knife for cutting bandages. Her own medicinal pouch was not as plump as Cenwin's, but she wore two full skins of water mixed with strong wine on her belt, which she believed might be far more valuable on the battlefield than the priest's supply of willow bark for fever or valerian leaf for sleep.

When she whistled for Jacob, he came, flapping clumsily from the roof of the baldachin. Remembering the raven's grace in her dreaming she suffered a pang of sympathy. He rebuked her concern with a chop of his beak against the top of her helm before settling in on her shoulder, head tucked low.

"*Ai*, then," she declared, reconciled. "This is not what I imagined for us the day I found a lonely cottage in a quiet village on the most isolated hills in the kingdom. Nor even the day we took rooms in the palace and I put on vocent black."

"Tricks," grumbled Jacob in agreement, pecking at the metal over her right ear. "Cast him out."

"I dare say we're giving it our best shot," retorted Avani as she began to pick her way down the hill. "Mayhap let the Goddess know that for me, just in case she hasn't noticed, aye?"

The Wythe cavalry line curved from the base of the cliff southwest along Wilhaiim's eastern flank, one hundred and fifteen lancers deep, stirrup pressed against stirrup. North of the first soldier in line, the forest and jagged mountain met where the white cliffs reached toward the foothills of the northern steppes. South of the final Wythe lancer another cavalryman sat his horse as a garrison line began anew. He wore House Grennich's device on his shield and on his cape. The mounted Kingsmen each had shield and lance in hand. They were meant to function as a living wall, preventing enemy intrusion while at the same time protecting the infantry massed behind. Armed with sword, lance, and short bow, and dressed in mail head to toe, and mounted on coursers trained to kick and bite, the cavalry was Wilhaiim's pride and joy. Their predecessors had put down the *sidhe*, and later protected the city from necromancy gone rogue. Any family with a member in the cavalry had pride of place in unspoken flatland hierarchy, whether that family be tenant farmer or of noble blood. So long as each garrison line worked in kind and did not break, Wilhaiim's cavalry was a powerful force indeed.

Less so the infantry. Avani, walking amongst the waiting foot soldiers behind the Wythe's wall of lancers, understood why young Parsnip had hope for a role in the cavalry. The infantry was a ragtag bunch, made up in large part by men and women whose experience on horseback was the family draft horse ridden from farm to market, and who hadn't the education needed to win an officer's medal. Some were Kingsmen in truth, trained to the sword in the royal barracks, and kitted out in bits and pieces of armor on the throne's indulgence. They knew how to use blade and fists and carried the light, round wooden bucklers more suitable to ground war. They wore good leather boots, also at the throne's indulgence, and simple metal sallets to protect their heads, and their weapons were in good repair. The officers amongst them wore a tunic fashioned in the king's scarlet over their jerkins.

The rest of the infantry, and as far as Avani could tell the vast majority, was made up of villeins drafted from Wythe's fields and surrounding hamlets. They had farmers' clogs if they had any shoes at all, and held pitchforks, cleavers, boning knives, and small swords for weapons. Some still wore the wide-brimmed straw hats used for working in the fields under a summer sun. Others had donned makeshift armor tacked together out of pieces of leather and fur and even burlap. A few had sacrificed dignity for safety and wore iron cook pots on their head to cover their vulnerable skulls.

They were a disparate lot but resigned to their fate, standing silently except for the occasional cough or mutter as they waited for battle to come their way. Avani stood with them, between a farmer with a long skinning knife clutched in her hand and a grandfather with a rusted scythe gripped in his, and tried to see anything past the horse and riders ranged ahead. In the dark and the smoke with the helmet to muffle her ears, it seemed the most helpless of choices, watching and waiting for danger that was yet only distant flame and voices carried on the wind. She marveled at the courage of the men and women ranged around her; her heart was in her throat, her sword drawn though she'd meant to use her wards for defense and her hands only for healing.

Death came from the west with trumpets and drums, the horns sounding from far too near and then one hundred and fifteen soldiers away, at the garrison next door. Wythe heralds blew an answering call, and the Kingsman in front of Avani stood in his stirrups to get a better look, leather creaking. He was a large man made larger by mail and shield.

"Bloody buggering Skald," he reported as calmly as if he were sighting a sudden rain cloud on an otherwise sunny day, "bastards shooting fire off their horses. No wonder the countryside went up overnight like Mabon festival come early." He sat again in his saddle, adjusted his shield and settled his lance across his forearm. "Ready up, lads and lasses, it's time to prove your mettle. Here they come!"

Avani thought she could hear Morgan's shrill voice over the groan and creak of cavalry preparing. Jacob bounced on her shoulder, croaking excitement. The grandfather on her right side kissed the blade of his scythe, tears streaming down his wrinkled cheeks, catching the orange flash of flaming arrows loosed in a volley over their heads. Someone in the crowd screamed. Someone else began to laugh nervously. The woman with the skinning knife howled, "For the king! For Wilhaiim! For Wythe!" and her call was quickly taken up on either side. Another blast of trumpets, a second volley of deadly arrows in the night sky, and then the cavalry plunged ahead, a first feint.

The infantry, more screaming mob than organized contingent, hurtled after, dragging Avani and Jacob along.

CHAPTER 20

"Knotcreek, Selkirk, Black Abbey—their fields and hamlets are burning all about, my lord, they're pinned between fire and water."

Mal, perched on one of the wide steps beneath Renault's throne, rose to pour wine into one of the silver goblets always at hand. He passed the goblet over.

"Drink up, Russel," he ordered. "And sit, before you collapse. The steps are not so comfortable as the throne, but they'll do for the likes of you and me."

Russel cupped the chalice in both hands and gulped wine. She stank of death and smoke. Her leather armor was pocked in places with new burns and her face was reddened as if she'd stood too long outside in a midsummer heat. Splashes of blood were drying on her boots and thighs. She wore a hastily knotted bandage on her sword arm.

As she drank she stared over the edge of the chalice at the oriel where Renault waited for the sun to rise on his kingdom and better reveal their losses. Brother Tillion knelt near the king, quietly praying. Despite Mal's misgivings Renault refused to send Tillion away. Oddly, the theist's presence seemed to comfort Renault.

Arthur and Parsnip, curled together, slept on the floor near one of the throne room's gigantic hearthstones. The grate was cold. Renault had ordered the fires put out as the flames on the midnight horizon grew in size and number.

Runners had stopped coming in from the coast hours earlier, unable to make it past flame or around the constantly moving influx of invaders. Until recently messenger birds had managed to find the castle despite desert arrows but as dawn approached the wind had grown in force until the city shook and sighed and any winged creature would surely need to find shelter out of the storm.

"You're a marvel, Corporal." Mal dipped his head in grudging acknowledgement. "Were I you, I would have gone to ground as soon as I realized I was trapped behind enemy lines."

"That's just it." She spoke to Mal but continued to look Renault's way. "There isn't any enemy line, so to speak. As far as I can tell they hit the ground hard and scattered, one by one or in small groups. They're there and then gone and leaving fire behind."

She indicated the bandage on her arm. "Some sort of resin, my lord, sticky and flammable and difficult to stomp out. If you ask me, the sea lords are in finer place, safe behind their walls and the water close at hand. They'll not burn so long as they can keep the bucket brigades going. It's the rest of us I'm worried about. Up in a gout of fire like Whitcomb and the sea too far away to save us."

She sat down suddenly, taking the lowest step on the dais, and stretched out her legs. Her hands trembled. Mal retrieved her cup and filled it again, but only halfway. He doubted she had thought to eat since she'd ridden west with Lory and Martin a day earlier. She wouldn't thank him for getting her wine-drunk.

"Whitcomb was brick and clapboard," said Renault from the oriel. "We are stone and mortar. There are two thousand good soldiers between us and conflagration."

"From what I've heard the sand snakes are five times that, Majesty," Russel replied. "They don't intend to fight honorably, if the desert even has notion of virtue on the battleground. And there's more." She hesitated, frowning at something only she could see.

"Speak," prompted Mal.

"A creature in the air." Russel's scowl deepened. "On the wing, flying above the smoke. A monster with a colossal serpent's tail. Black as the night sky and difficult to know for sure, but I think—" Now she did look at Mal, a quick, speculative glance "—it plucked soldiers randomly off the ground, Kingsmen and kilted warriors alike, ripped them to bits with no rhyme nor reason nor allegiance that I could tell."

"Wyvern," suggested Arthur, sitting up all at once. Parsnip sighed and snuffled. "A dragon, my lord!" His eyes shone.

"There are no such things as dragons." Renault left the darkened oriel for the brighter light near his throne. "A wyvern is only a fanciful creature used by mothers and fathers to frighten young lads and lasses into good behavior, like the basilisk or the unicorn."

Arthur's face fell. Russel rose to greet her king.

"Even so, Your Majesty," she said. "I saw it with mine own eyes, whatever it was, tearing men to gristle and tossing their parts at the fires." She swallowed. "The *things*, of late, in the forest—the reports of wolves and giant owls and six-legged hogs—"

"*Sidhe* beasts grown daring," agreed Mal. His heart sank. "Mayhap wakened by the sounds of war. Too much to hope we'd escape their attention, what with the desert riding rampant through their realm." A half-remembered dream surfaced suddenly, a recollection of barrowmen standing on an island beneath the earth, surrounded by a dark lake, and overhead a ceiling of false amber stars.

"Am I to fight *sidhe* and the desert both?" demanded Renault. "If so, we are indeed lost. It took a company of magi and a continent of iron to beat the barrowmen into the ground. Mayhap, if we were not already divided by sand snakes, but even then, Mal is only one man." He pulled at his beard, distracted.

"The one god will provide." Brother Tillion limped around the side of the throne. He walked tall, Mal noticed, and did not make use of his heavy staff for balance, though his step was short and uneven. "One way or another." He smiled at Mal, thin-lipped and solemn. "So long as the correct sacrifices are made."

Mal wished Baldebert was not already gone to battle with his band of bloodthirsty sailors. The infantry would improve for having the admiral and his cohorts on hand, but Baldebert knew how to cow the temple's overt xenophobia with a sharp word or snide grin. Mal, who would very much have liked to knock the theist off his pedestal, real or imaginary, was constrained by court protocol.

Renault dropped onto his throne, knocking both fists restlessly on the gray stone seat. "Send for Masterhealer Orat," he decided. "If he thinks the one god can yet save us, I'm willing to listen." He lifted a finger, forestalling Mal's protest. "Roue has become a moot point. If Orat truly believes our survival depends upon my choice of bride, I am desperate enough to be convinced."

"You will break your word?" Mal demanded. "Does not your god counsel equally against faithlessness, Brother Tillion?"

"His Majesty's faith is between himself and the

god," Tillion returned smoothly, ignoring Mal's snarl of disbelief. "I will send for the Masterhealer. He will gladly hear your concerns, Majesty." He descended the dais slowly, smiling again as he passed Mal.

"Malachi," Renault cautioned Mal. "Attend me. Russel. To bed with you, until dawn. In the morning, I'll have need of you again."

Mal stood one step below the throne, head bowed, as Russel trailed Tillion from the room. He spread his gloved hands before him in the air, flexing fingers one after another in a bid for patience until the heavy doors boomed shut and liveried Kingsmen took up their places in front of the double portal. But for the guards ranged about the long room, and the two children on the hearth, the king and his vocent were alone.

"Speak to me about faithlessness, brother," Renault said after a beat of silence. "Specifically, yours."

Mal caught his breath, lifting his head. He'd not expected discovery so soon; he and Baldebert had been careful and clever, and the one flaw in his plan—the capricious link he and Avani had forged, her window into his head—seemed to have been solved for him, if without his consent. He both resented and admired the cage Avani had woven around her mind and heart. It was not dissimilar to the wards conjured to protect physical body or royal keep, a sparkling net around the core of her that kept invaders out and her private self contained. Reaching across the link now was like grasping a hot coal with bare hands; he was allowed an instant of connection before pain struck. He knew that she was alive and well and yet with Wythe, but more than that was denied to him.

Not once in all Mal's study had he any indication that external wards could be made internal, nor that the stolid protection cants Andrew so relied upon to shield his mind from angry, intrusive dead were but ineffective, primitive fencing compared to Avani's silver net. Given the chance, he very much would have liked to learn the way of it.

That chance, he knew, had passed.

"Mal," Renault prompted. "Do not pretend ignorance. I know you too well. Confess—" He leaned forward in the throne, elbows on knees. "You intend to break faith with me the moment my back is turned."

"I—" Mouth dry, Mal cleared his throat. Renault did not look as though he intended to have Mal's head immediately on a pike for the treason of reviving ferric soldiers. Instead his expression was one of profound regret. "I would not—"

"I understand you would far prefer a chance at proving yourself as my champion on the field," Renault continued quietly. "That as my vocent you suppose you belong on the front line. I can see how you chafe at this confinement. But, brother, if Baldebert has taught us anything, it's how easily you can be snatched away. I will not lose my most precious asset to death or, worse, captivity. If we outlive these sand snakes and their ambition, Wilhaiim will need your particular faculties." He sat back. "Even more so now that Avani has refused allegiance."

Mal bowed his head for fear Renault would glimpse his anguish. "It is true, Majesty," he said. A lie spoken seemed crueler than a lie of omission. "That I believe a magus may indeed be more useful amongst the troops than in the palace."

"And if I had more than one at hand I would send you out," Renault assured him. "But you are, despite my best efforts, still the last of your kind. Like Parsnip and Arthur, you are most valuable here, at my side. I, also, would prefer to ride to glory, sword in hand and Kingsmen in my wake. And if I had an heir, mayhap—" He shook his head. "I expect we, the four of us, have the most difficult job of it, the waiting and wondering." He rose. "Join me before the windows. The sun will rise soon enough. Shall we watch and wait together? Would you like that?"

"Aye, Majesty," Mal replied, "I would like that very much."

With the dawn came a messenger bird, a black-beaked peregrine from the west. Renault and Mal watched the falcon fight the wind, skewing this way and that as it strove to reach the royal mews. Behind it the sky was gray and orange with soot, storm, and sunrise. Wilhaiim's white walls were smudged black in the falling ash. It was a grim panorama. Renault stood with his hands clenched at his sides as he had for most of the night. Arthur and Parsnip had left the hearth for an apple shared out between them near the throne. Brother Orat was yet to pay His Majesty a visit. Mal wondered, cynically, whether the man was in deep communion with his god or if he was afraid to leave the temple's shelter for fumy streets.

"If not for your assurances," Renault said as the peregrine found its way out of the wind and into the mews. "I would believe we were the last living things in an inferno."

"Nay," replied Mal. If he let his concentration slip only a hairsbreadth he could see them all in his head, flashpoints of life struggling to continue, the ordered stars that meant most of Wilhaiim's lines still held, and the less disciplined swirl and strike of some ten thousand warriors rampaging between coast and forest. A map of vitality, it was more efficient even than being midst-war, and more dangerous. Each time he took stock it was harder to come back without first sampling that bright energy.

If he swallowed the desert army in one gulp, he wondered, would he survive the experience? Would he be raised to godhood in the consuming, or be scorched in gluttony and fall, yet more gray ash, from the sky?

"What losses do you see?" Renault pressed. "What numbers? What do you *see*?"

"At this distance I cannot count the dead," Mal

confessed. "Only the living. And there is no way to differentiate Kingsman from sand snake. One mortal life is as beautiful as the next." He licked his lips, parched, and turned abruptly away. "Too many to know for sure even if they would consent to stay still for me to enumerate."

"What about the wyvern?" Parsnip asked around a mouthful of apple. "Is it there?"

"If there is such a thing," Mal said, "I cannot sense it."

"Here comes a man from the mews." Renault left the windows for his throne but did not sit. "I don't expect it will be good news."

They waited without speaking until the double portal split and the runner burst through, out of breath, eyes streaming from the smoke. Ash dulled the man's dark hair and scarlet livery. He clutched a scroll. He barely had the time to essay a bow before Renault snatched it from his hand. Breaking the seal—black wax stamped with Knotcreek's Three-Masted Ship—the king unrolled the message and began to read.

"Whitcomb is destroyed, as we feared," he reported. "Michaelmas writes that the first wave came up out of a hole in the ground near Bracken Keep and decamped east and south from there, lighting fires as they went. The grape fields are gone, the town leveled. God willing our people were safely evacuated in time. Michaelmas has some thirty survivors in hand

and hopes that Bracken has the rest, but there's been no word yet from Kingsmen Weatherford who holds it yet for the throne." He crumpled the missive in his hand, regarded the runner. "Nothing from my more southern holds?"

The runner, down on one knee, was still trying to catch his breath. "Not yet, my liege. But the wind is dying, some. The birds will have a better time of it. My mistress has sent up more just this morning, to Wythe and Burl, and the rest."

The king nodded. He walked another circuit from his throne and around the oriel, before making his decision.

"I mean to go and inspect the battlements until those birds return with news," he said. "From there, at least, I'll have a better grasp of whether the tide turns with us or against. And it will do the infantry good to see me; mayhap I'll walk amongst them if there is an ebb in battle."

Mal refrained from chastising his king in front of children and soldiers, but with effort. Renault grimaced in his direction as he descended the steps.

"I will avoid flaming arrows and well-thrown pikes and even Russel's flying monster," he promised. "Will you walk with me, brother, or stay?"

"Go," Mal hedged, "I have other things to attend."

"Do not wander far," His Majesty advised. As he crossed the long room Kingsmen peeled from the walls and fell behind all in a row. "I will have need of you once I've seen how things stand. Tell Orat when he comes to meet me on the battlements."

Mal, who knew very well how things stood, bowed from the waist. Renault took the obeisance as expected. Mal meant it as farewell.

Mal left Parsnip and Arthur sitting on the steps beneath the throne after extracting promises of good behavior. Parsnip was not as easily fooled as Renault.

"You can take my ax, if you like, my lord," she offered quietly. "I don't expect it will do you much good against dragons, but it's got a strong iron blade and that's all a soldier needs against man or *sidhe*."

"Thank you." He gave her suggestion the same serious consideration she'd taken before making it. "But I hope to stay out of range of man or *sidhe*."

"His Majesty will be very angry, my lord, once he realizes you've run off."

"He will," confirmed Mal. "But only because he's a good man who confuses heartache with temper."

"Shall we tell him you're sorry?" Arthur wondered.

"Nay. Never lie to your king," Mal said. "Not even to save his pride."

In his room, he dressed for war, though in truth he did think he would have no need of sword or helm or iron cuirass over Hennish leather. For practical reasons, he eschewed the vocent's cloak. He tucked a capsule of Curcas seed up his sleeve in case he survived long enough to see his own execution and courage failed him at the end. Until recently he had not thought of himself as a coward, but Holder's burned magus had struck him to the core, and he could not quite shake a creeping horror of his own death.

Baldebert's sapphire-and-bone pin was on his mantel. Mal picked it up, turned it over, then set it back in place. Baldebert had no need of the brooch any longer and eventually, when Renault thought to search the tower, he would find it there. He left it on the mantel next to the jeweled knife that was a wedding gift from Siobahn and a single inky raven's feather.

He snuffed the candles in the colored glass lanterns he'd carried with him all the way from childhood, then took one last look around the tower room: the four-poster bed with its green hangings beckoned, the old wooden desk and his beloved leather chair. His journal sat, closed, next to the silver inkwell and ebony stylus he'd used to record a life spent in the service of the throne. There was a letter for Avani there, too, written in the loneliest hours when sleep was elusive. He expected she knew his sentiments as well as her own, no matter how she pretended ignorance, but selfishly he hoped she would keep his words by her always after, and think of him fondly.

At the last moment, he eschewed the helm, disliking the way it constrained his line of sight, and left it on the desk.

The corridor outside was quiet. He locked the chamber door with a key instead of the usual cant. His boots made no sound on thick carpet as he walked the empty hall. The tower stairwell was cold and filled with haze blown in through the loopholes. He could hear the clash and cry of battle outside the city. War did not stop with the sunrise.

He stopped outside the throne room to deliver his key to the Kingsman on guard.

"See that His Majesty gets this when he returns from his walk," he told her.

"Yes, my lord." She was too well trained to ask questions and for that he was grateful. She folded the key into her sleeve, awarding him a bow. "Of course, my lord."

The great hall was deserted except for a handful of servants left behind to care for the king and those members of his court too elderly or infirm to take up sword. They stopped to gawp as Mal swept past, unused to seeing their magus in armor. He exited the palace by way of the front doors. The men and women standing guard outside clicked their heels together in his wake. The haze in the bailey was not yet so bad as it had been during the Red Worm plague when for days the temple had burned corpses right outside the city walls, but it would soon become worse, he thought, if the wind did not let up and fields and flatland continued to burn.

As Mal walked desolate castle streets in the direction of the Maiden Gate, archers aligned on the battlements let loose red-fletched missiles into the horizon or called down encouragement to their compatriots below. From their jovial shouts and friendly taunting he guessed that the brunt of the battle had not yet reached Wilhaiim proper and that the cavalry line continued, for the moment, to hold. If the sand snakes had come up all together west of Whitcomb and through only the one gate, then the flatlanders had enjoyed a stroke of luck beyond any Mal could hope for.

Too good, he surmised, to be true. The day was only beginning. Mayhap the enemy was waiting on better light to begin anew.

He crossed in front of the royal temple. Its louvered roof was closed, its doors shut tight. A group of refugees from outside the city huddled against the building, seeking relief from biting wind and the raining ash. They looked down on Mal and, recognizing his face, called frantic questions.

"My lord, Lord Malachi! The temple is full to bursting, my lord, and every tavern and inn! Where are we to go when the walls come down? My lord, who will protect us if not the god and his theists?"

They were only a small group, lately arrived. Vineyard workers, he deduced, from the dark stains on their hands evident even from a distance. Five men and six women, they were soot stained and frightened, and by all appearances had come into Wilhaiim with only the clothes on their backs.

"Have you come from the coast?" he asked, lifting his voice to be heard over the shouts from the wall and the scrape of the wind. "How goes it, there?"

"Badly." One of the men came down the temple steps, rolling the edge of his tunic nervously in both hands. "The keeps still stand, god willing, but the rest is gone, razed or looted or both. They came out of the night on foot and on ponies, ponies of our own breeding, my lord—good, sturdy animals—and slaughtered people in their beds, my lord." He rubbed his eyes, knuckling away moisture. "All of Whitcomb, gone, blood in the streets and on the dunes."

"You escaped." Another stroke of luck, Mal thought, too good to be true. "How?"

"The king's constable, my lord," the man replied, awestruck. "She came for us into Whitcomb, herself and a troop of good horsemen, scooped up those of us still standing and ran us back to the western gate."

"Countess Wythe broke the line," Mal repeated coldly.

"Aye, my lord, and we're grateful for it." The man indicated his companions where they cowered against the temple wall. "It was a near thing. All eleven of us would be dead but for her courage. We owe her our lives."

"She risked all of Wilhaiim for the sake of eleven Whitcomb vineyard workers."

The man winced. "Aye, my lord. Though I suppose she hoped there were more than eleven of us still alive when she thought of it."

"She should not be thinking past the wall she guards," retorted Mal. The wind gusted in reply, sending billows of ash across the temple steps. "Find your way to the Royal Gardens, all eleven of you. There is a refugee camp set up there, near the barracks tower. There you will be fed and armed, if there are weapons left."

"But, my lord, what if they breach the gates? Will we not be safer inside the temple?"

"They will not breach the gates," snapped Mal, glowering at the man. "The wards bound into the stanchion are strong still. I've made sure of it. So long as every person does his part as required, including the bloody Countess Wythe, the city will hold."

"Aye, my lord," the farmer answered, although with a dubious shake of his head, before running back up the steps to join his companions in good fortune. Unexpected fury made the tips of Mal's fingers smart. He buried them in his armpits, tight fists, to smother sparks. Turning his back on the temple, he marched on.

The Maiden Gate was locked down, the portcullis lowered, the murder hatch open to the battlement above. A band of infantrymen stood just inside the portcullis, blocking egress. Through the bars Mal could see the backs of soldiers and horses—the eastern line standing in wait. He could hear the hiss of missiles let go all at once from the battlements and then the blast of trumpets. The captain at the gate drew his sword as Mal approached then puffed out a breath in relief.

"Lord Vocent." He saluted in lieu of a bow. "We've just had word. There's another lot come up from the south near the wood; they'll be on us any minute now, Skald take them and break them." The man grinned, revealing gaps where his front teeth had at some point in his career been knocked out. "But don't fret. We're ready."

"Excellent," replied Mal, dry as blowing soot. "I'm going out."

The captain's grin wobbled. "We've orders to keep everyone *in*. Come direct from the throne, my lord."

Mal drew murk from the crevices under the gate and used it to grow tall. "I'm going out."

It was basic showmanship, but the guard took a step back. Mal could smell the metallic tang of his distress. Whatever he saw in Mal's eyes or in the cape of roiling, angry shadows changed his mind. He sheathed his sword.

"Through the guard tower, then, my lord. I canna open the portcullis. This way."

He led Mal past the infantrymen and into the right-side tower. There another guardsman, standing at attention between stacked barrels of Low Port tar, kept watch over the winch used to open the gate. The captain made straight for a thick wooden door, twin to the one they'd just come through and barred three times with padlocked iron. He wrapped his fist on the wood, loud enough to be heard on the other side of the wall.

"Coming through! Georges!" he hollered as he opened the padlocks. "Do you hear me, man? One to come through! Move out of the way!"

The door cracked open. A soldier in ash-dusted infantry togs thrust his head through the gap. Behind him in the morning horses danced anticipation and soldiers cursed roundly at less bold farm folk who wavered in the face of rising wind and smoke.

"What's all this, Pietre? You know we're not to let anyone out or in." The infantryman spat his displeasure in a wad of dark spittle onto the floor of the guardroom. When he saw Mal, he froze, aghast.

"Opion." Mal regarded the tainted spittle by his boot with loathing before studying the pin and badge on the man's breast: Black Abbey. "I should have your commission for indulging on duty."

"Opion's no offense, no more'n ale in a flask to make a long night tolerable, my lord. The priests hand it out to help with pain and the nerves, and thank the god for that." Pupils turned to pinpoints, Georges was too far gone to realize his danger. The drug blunted his senses and loosened his tongue, allowing for indiscretion. "You won't take back my commission, not today—you can't spare even one swordsman against odds like these."

Khorit Dard had used opion to turn fierce desert mercenaries into slaves willing and eager to die for the sake of Roue's flower fields. The poppy flowers, while reputedly beautiful to look upon and worth their weight in true gold, had nearly put an end to Roue. If not for the Rani's determination, Baldebert's initiative, and Mal's talents as an assassin, the small kingdom would surely have fallen to sand lords and opion traders.

While he'd long suspected that the theists eased their most difficult patients with the drug, and had turned a blind eye to the practice for the sake of compassion, Mal did not intend to let the poisonous habit spread throughout Wilhaiim. As far as he was concerned opion, while not so quick to kill, was in the end just as deadly as Curcas seed.

Mal widened the crack between door and threshold with a swift kick, reached through the opening, and ripped pin and badge from the Georges' breast, tearing fabric. With the medals, he stole the far more valuable honor of the fellow's remaining years, syphoning life until the soldier, mouth working in mute astonishment, collapsed to his knees, falling through the door into the tower. Georges was still alive, but barely. His poached vitality fizzed through Mal, a heady rush.

"One way or another, opion will kill a man." He gazed down at gap-toothed Pietre where he knelt on the floor, chafing Georges's wrists. "Were I you, I'd stick to ale." He stepped across the fallen man. "Pull him through and bar the door."

Pietre, white-faced, had the sense to do as he was told. Mal waited until he heard the thunk of iron dropped into place on the other side of the door before confronting the line. Wielding still his cloak of shadows, Georges's energy flushing his cheeks and turning his insides giddy, he scanned the mass of stinking humanity charged with defending Wilhaiim's walls.

They were Black Abbey infantry: Kingsmen, villein, tradesmen, and tinkers. A hardy people used to subsisting off a sometimes-fickle farmland. They were away from home, enduring hardship and facing mortality. What they knew of Wilhaiim's magus they'd heard, for the most part, third-hand. They were prepared for awe. If any realized they'd just observed murder they were prepared to give the most powerful man in the kingdom the benefit of doubt.

The looks turned his way were equal parts quiet adulation and fear. He let them stare, allowing himself one last moment of vanity before it all went to pieces. While Black Abbey ogled, he took a moment to observe the state of their garrison, the cavalry on their horses, the archers on the battlements above his head, the wind plucking at plumes and pennants and making the sounds of battle seem at first near and then far. He could not determine for certain from which direction the smoke came, if it was only from the west as expected, or if the situation had changed overnight.

"What's the word?" he shouted up at the wall.

A Kingsman peered down, pike in hand.

"Within the hour, my lord," she shouted back. "Wind's making it difficult to get news, or see anything past the highway. But Wythe's sent a runner— more of the bastards have come up along the edge of the wood, through another hole in the ground. They'll be heading our way anytime. We're ready. Black Abbey won't break."

Her confidence made the eavesdropping infantry whoop and stamp their feet. Mal nodded, pleased. He left the protection of the wall for the cavalry blockade— "Let me through, thank you, make way"—speaking softly to courser and lancer as he slipped between stirrups, patting withers as he squeezed through the barricade of horseflesh and mail. They opened around him and then closed immediately after.

Once free of the line he was alone, exposed, the highway under his boots. Haze obscured the horizon but for a few feet in either direction. He held out a hand, checking for ash, but the wind had shifted and he did not think the western fires were yet close.

"Hold your fire!" Someone cautioned from the battlements. "By the Virgin! That's our man, you fool. Don't shoot!"

Which recalled Mal to the present danger. He let go the shadows and conjured wards instead, silver-green in the smoke. He unsheathed his sword though he had not lied to Parsnip—he did not plan to get so close to anyone as to put it to use. He closed his eyes just briefly, reviewing the constellation in his head. A new cluster of stars expanded to the east, the enemy increasing. East was where Earl Wythe was stationed and Liam and Avani. He resisted the temptation to follow the link in that direction. She blocked him still.

Always? he wondered bitterly, but she did not relent or let him peek through her eyes.

It did not matter. She could look after herself, and his business was south.

He walked for a while along the highway a nose length in front of the cavalry. If they could see him, the archers on the wall would not waste precious artillery. The horses snorted in his direction, no doubt thinking Mal a ghost come out of the morning. If he closed his eyes the lancers were an incandescence in their saddles. Pride swelled behind his breastbone. They were beautiful.

Squatter's row was gone, crushed beneath the line, hovels scattered. He hoped its residents were safely inside the city walls and not winding down their final frail hours with makeshift weapons in hand. But for Gerald Doyle's kindness in taking a broken boy in from the Rose Keep, Mal thought, he might have ended up in a similar situation: homeless and hopeless, often out of his mind—if he had managed to live so long.

He found his way through the haze to Flossy Creek, leaving Wilhaiim behind. On the other side of the merry water Rowan stepped out of a fallow field and walked at his side.

"You're worse," Mal said without rancor. "Than Siobahn ever was."

"I know you've begun to worry she might have been like me," Rowan replied. He walked with his hands folded behind his back, barefoot, a furrow between his eyes. "Madness personified and not a dead thing walking."

"Avani saw her," argued Mal. "Spoke to her. And the *sidhe*."

Rowan grunted. "What's to say they wouldn't me, if you wanted it? You were odd even as a child, Mal. Talking to people that weren't there. Pretending to play games with lads and lasses I couldn't see."

"Ghosts," retorted Mal. "Just ghosts."

"Mebbe. But you're worried."

"It hardly matters now, I think."

"Aye." Rowan blew out through his nose. "Are you sure you want this? Absolutely sure—"

"Quiet!" snapped Mal. "Listen!"

The wind, capricious, blew now from the north-east, and with it came increasing sounds of combat. The noise of horses and soldiers in distress, the clash of blade on blade, screams of triumph and despair. One second he thought the battle was upon him, the next, wind and smoke made it difficult to tell. He crouched in the road to check the ground for vibration and in doing so avoided a flock of iridescent arrows come out of the murk. Their tips burned a pungent flame and where they landed tiny fires struck up.

"Fuck me," gasped Rowan, squatting beside Mal. "That was close."

"Don't move," said Mal, forgetting for a heartbeat that Rowan was just a symptom of his deterioration. He pressed his hand to the ground. "They're here."

The desert blew out of the smoke on a gust of wind, more than one hundred kilted warriors thundering across the field on coastal ponies. The sand snakes nocked arrow after arrow as they surged toward the Maiden Gate, kindling fires as they went. They were silent as they rode, yellow eyes fierce. The cacophony came from those giving chase, soldiers on foot and on coursers, racing in pursuit. Few of the cavalrymen still held their lances; most chased with sword in hand. They flew Wythe's ragged pennant.

The men and women on foot were struggling, bloodied and wild faced. One man loped past, badly burned and wheezing, pitchfork in hand. He blinked to see Mal squatting in the dirt.

"Don't just sit there pissing yerself," he said. "Wythe's gone and Black Abbey's next. Make yourself useful, man. Die like you mean it."

"Fuck me," Rowan said again, with more spirit.

He waited for a break in the charge then grabbed at Mal's sleeve. "Let's go."

"Wait. One moment." Shaking Rowan off, Mal clapped palms over his ears to block out his surroundings.

Wythe's gone. Black Abbey's next.

It was a terrible gamble, snuffing lives without first being sure of his choices, and he knew there would be mistakes made. But there wasn't time to be certain. He wouldn't second-guess intuition. He had, after all, just seen them ride past. He should be able to get it mostly right.

He found them in his head, a clot of one hundred or more vivid arid suns, lives well spent, lives wasted, lives hardly begun and those near their ending. He flexed his fingers over his ears, a clenching of power.

They extinguished all at once.

But not gone, oh not gone. He swallowed them whole and they filled him to brimming, knocking him over in the dirt where he lay curled, breathing through bliss.

When it was over Rowan gave him a hand up.

"Aye, that's that," Rowan said, reaching out to brush broken wheat from Mal's curls. "Now you've sealed it. Even Renault won't be able to look past that display."

"Keep the Curcas handy." Mal bit his tongue to keep back an inappropriate snort of laughter. "Terror makes good men do bad things. I suspect by the time I'm finished, the court will be ready to do their worst."

CHAPTER 21

From the beginning Avani had assumed Wythe would hold the line until the last. Wythe were the best of the best, bred from infancy to fight in the saddle, the boldest lancers with the finest armor on the strongest mounts, as well prepared as any garrison could be. For the infantry as well as the cavalry courage was a matter of personal honor. Their countess was constable to the king. Thus, their bravery could not be called into question.

Every man and woman in the garrison intended to die a hero, to make king, countess, and family proud.

Their mettle held through the endless, hazy hours before dawn. It held even as the sun rose and the countess did not return at first light. It held when the wind became a gale, sending smoke and dark clouds scuttling overhead, blowing apart tents on the hill behind their line. Lancers shifted in the saddle to keep from going numb. Horses dozed in place and then started again when the wind sent soot in their direction. The foot soldiers did the same. Avani wove her way back and forth through the unit, offering a kind word to those who looked as if they needed comfort, chatting quietly with those who were in danger of growing bored. She heard Morgan's voice as he conversed with his commanders, but couldn't see him past the horses. Once she thought she heard Liam's laughter and her heart was lighter for it.

With the sunrise came a rider up the highway from the castle and her heart was gladder yet to see Russel's earnest form. She stood on tiptoe with the rest of the infantry and strained to catch a glimpse of Morgan's face when Russel gave her report. She couldn't quite, but it didn't matter. Word spread quickly down the cavalry line and through the infantry.

Whitcomb was destroyed and the west flank was burning, and by all accounts lousy with sand snakes. There had been no word from Countess Wythe overnight, and none again when, with the dawn, messenger birds had arrived in the city. For the time being His Majesty was presuming his constable lost. Wythe was without its most seasoned commander as the battle spread from west to east. His Majesty thought it prudent the young earl step aside and let one of Wythe's more practiced lancers call the charge.

But if Morgan meant to concede the king's wisdom

he was not given the chance. Two more riders came around the hill, not from Wilhaiim, but from the southern slant of the red wood. Their horses were stretched to a gallop, the riders pressed low against their necks as they flew across the ground. Avani saw only the tops of their heads as they reined up in front of the earl, but their shouts rang out, audible to everyone in the garrison.

"My lord! My lord! They've come up just near the wood, my lord! A whole passel of snakes, armed to the teeth! Coming now, my lord! Just this way!"

The infantry let out cries of relief and anticipation. The wait was over. The cavalry kicked their horses to wakefulness, adjusted their helms and raised their lances. Wilde's hooves pounded on grass as Morgan rode up and down the garrison line, preparing for the push. Avani watched the pointed top of his barbute, bobbing as he shouted. She could not see Liam. More ash fell from the sky. On her shoulder Jacob shuddered, rattling his feathers in the wind. The man in front of her turned suddenly and coughed up bile onto his neighbor's clogs.

"Aye, son," his neighbor said. "That's it. Get it out now and you'll fight better for it later."

All at once Morgan lifted his sword in and then brought it down in signal. Trumpets blew. The cavalry surged forward as one, voices lifted in a roar. Hooves pounding, equipment rattling, shields raised.

"Stay!" Russel said, materializing at Avani's side.

Her visor was down and her sword in hand. Her uniform was burned through in several places. Her voice through the grille of her helm was a rasp. "They'll be back and forth a few more times before there's need of infantry. Also," she added, "breathe or you'll pass out."

Avani gasped air, embarrassed to be caught holding her breath. A Kingsman not far down the line called hallo Russel's way.

"Is it bad?" he asked. "It smells bad. Like the whole world's burning."

"Wilhaiim's not," replied Russel. "And that's all the matters."

"What are they like?" the man with the rebellious stomach asked. "The sand snakes? Have you seen any?"

"They're like us," Russel reported grimly. "Wanting to win this war. They advance and retreat and ride in spirals so they're difficult to hit. Don't follow them out; they mean to separate and slaughter. Stay together."

The cavalry returned in a crash, a tidal wave rolling back from deeper waters, wheeling around just in time to keep from trampling their foot soldiers. Morgan rode with them, and Avani saw Liam at his side. She took a quick head count and was relieved to see they had returned entire. One Kingsman had blood on his lance and on his cuirass. Three had arrows sticking like iridescent thorns in their shields.

"Again!" screamed Morgan, and off they went.

The second charge seemed to last three times as long, but Avani thought they hadn't ridden so far out as they had on the first because now she could hear the noise of nearby skirmish. She wiped sweat from her sword hand with her salwar then adjusted the kettle helm where it chafed her skull through her hair. Russel shifted her pommel from hand to hand, and rocked from foot to foot.

"You're not meant to be here," Avani realized belatedly. "Renault will be waiting for your report."

"Don't like my chances getting back," Russel confessed. "They're coming 'round the city like a hangman's noose and they're not lacking arrows. They'll know by now. Yon funny Wythe priest sent a bird as soon as Roberts and Fin made their report. Besides—" she danced again in place "—where safer than next to you and your wicked little blade, magus?"

Avani shook her head. "I don't mean to fight."

Russel laughed. "You will," she predicted. "Everyone does."

A riderless horse, wounded and trembling, came suddenly out of the smoke, galloping in the direction of camp, almost trampling infantry in its panic. Another followed immediately after, and then another. The last carried its rider still in the saddle, helm lost and head drooping on his breast. A shattered lance dangled from his lifeless hand, slapping the horse's belly, urging it on in flight. A desert arrow protruded from the back of his neck above the curve of his cuirass, an impossible shot made. Blood stained his front.

Behind the dead man on the horse the living cavalry returned, several less and some wounded yet upright still on their mounts. They barely had time to wheel and regroup before trumpets blew once more.

"Again!" screamed Morgan around the groan of soldiers and their horses and the agitated breathing of the men and woman waiting on foot.

"Next time," Russel said, "it'll be us. They're losing too many too soon. The one god help that lad."

She was right. The cavalry came back ragged and faltering. Morgan had an arrow in his arm, yet still he managed to lift his sword, up and down. And this time, the Kingsmen on the ground blew their trumpets in signal also. The infantry gave chase.

The grass beneath her feet was torn up. Horses and soldiers lay broken on the ground in every direction, forcing her to pick her way forward for fear of stepping on corpses. She'd never been bothered by carcasses before, not when they'd bobbed alongside her in the sea as she'd struggled to survive another day before rescue, not when they'd walked on the Downs, animated by angry *sidhe*, and not when she'd tended dying children during the Red Worm plague and later watched as priests and parents stacked their tiny bodies for burning.

She was afraid, now. Afraid not of the dead but of the dying, lest she step on someone still grasping to life and exacerbate their suffering. For suffering they certainly were, bleeding their last onto crop they'd tended, struck down by arrow, iron, and scimitar. There were an equal number of desert corpses amongst the flatlanders. The sand snakes wore little in the way of armor. Once caught, they were far more vulnerable than a Kingsman in even the lightest mail. But they were very difficult to catch, and there were many more sand snakes than there were flatlanders.

"Head down," said Russel, as a flight of arrows hissed by. Avani ducked automatically, though her wards would protect her from impact. The arrows struck the ground, starting tiny fires wherever they landed.

Avani quelled the fires with a cant, a reversal of the basic spell she used to kindle fire in her hearth at home or light a taper in the night when she needed the chamber pot.

"One to your right," Russel said, meaning not the fire but a man still living. Avani turned and saw him there, pinned beneath his dead horse, yellow eyes wide, mouth gaping. She squatted, touching his brow. His back was surely broken and there was a sluggishly bleeding wound on his brow. The wound wouldn't kill him, but the broken back she didn't know how to fix. There were tattoos on his chest and down his arms: long-eared rabbits marching beneath a many-rayed sun.

He said something quietly in his desert tongue. She shook her head. He was in pain, but he wasn't afraid of Avani nor, she thought, of death. He shuddered, gasping for air. She closed his eyes with her fingers before he could see Russel.

"I can't save him," she said.

For answer, Russel put her sword neatly through his heart. He died without a sound. Avani staggered to her feet.

Somehow in the smoke and the fury they'd gotten separated from the garrison, if the garrison still existed, and Avani was not at all sure it did. They were making their way in what they hoped was a westerly direction, toward Wilhaiim, but the wind and smoke made it almost impossible to be certain. Sounds of battle came and went. They pursued a cry only to get turned around again when the wind blew the shout away. She did not think, from the number of dead they came upon, that they were very far from the center of battle, but she was also not certain that center didn't continue to break and reform.

Four times they'd come upon the living: kilted warriors on foot wielding scimitars, one to each hand, and in each case looking quite as benumbed as Avani felt. Russel dispatched them without difficulty, mostly because Avani had encircled Russel also with her wards, allowing for an unfair advantage. The sand snakes couldn't land a single blow, nor could they outrun Russel. Avani might have felt sorry for them but she'd stopped feeling anything at all about the same time she stopped counting Wythe badges on the dead.

Jacob had left her shoulder for the ground where the haze was less thick. He hopped and flapped on the periphery of her awareness, cackling softly when he came upon a piece of shiny treasure pinned to a corpse's uniform. He ignored Avani's scolding, dodging Russel when she tried to boot him away from an infantryman's bloody chest. To Jacob dead was dead, meat on the ground, and unattended baubles were his for the taking.

"I hope you don't think I'll carry that for you," Avani said as Jacob struggled to pluck an embroidered cord off the hilt of a scimitar. "*Ai*, leave it be."

"Menace," Russel whispered. "Worse than a carrion crow."

Jacob squawked indignation through a beak full of cord. Russel held up a finger and tilted her head, straining to make sense of the clamor on the wind. Avani looked at the sky, hoping for a glimpse of the sun for orientation, but everything was sickly gray. Soot made her eyes water. She scrubbed them with the back of her hand and when they cleared she saw a dead man standing in the smoke.

He was hardly the first ghost they had encountered. Spirits were as plentiful on the battlefield as arrow-kindled fires. They sat by their corpses or wandered in the crop or stood at attention as if waiting for direction. At first she'd sent them on their way with a murmured blessing or a word of consolation. But as the morning wore on and regret became horror and then stupor, the banishing cant—like the spell used to quench desert arrows—came to her lips automatically and without emotion.

There were many more kilted spirits than flatlander ghosts. She was not fooled into thinking this was a good sign for Wilhaiim. Instead she remembered her own island people, almost entirely eradicated by cataclysm. War, she'd come to realize, was a cataclysm of another sort. And stumbling through an endless smoky vista was a lot like drowning.

"Avani. Are you with me?"

"Aye." Avani blinked back and forth between Russel and the dead man. "Aye, just. There's another one. Let me—"

She started to speak the banishing cant but the desert ghost walked away before she could finish, striding purposefully into the haze.

"Skald's balls!" Fury surprised her. Fuming, she trotted after his disappearing form. "Come back here! You'll get lost in this blight!" He wasn't far ahead. She could see the edge of his kilt fluttering in the wind.

"Avani!" Russel paced after, squinting right and left. "Don't be stupid. You can't chase down every spirit in need of—oh." She stopped behind Avani, peering at the ground ahead. "Oh, shit. What's this?"

They lay where they'd fallen, like Ceilidh marionettes with their strings cut. Animals and men, flatlanders and desert people, coursers and coastal ponies. They lay nose to nose and limb to limb, as if they'd been within a hairsbreadth of battle when instead they'd just . . . stopped. Impossibly, the smoke and wind refused to touch them; they lay beneath clouds and faint sunlight, a bubble of unnatural peace amidst the storm of war.

"Shit," Russel repeated with more emphasis. "Are they all—"

"Dead? Aye." Before Russel could stop her, Avani walked out of the smoke and into the clear air. She had to step carefully for fear of treading upon a corpse. The desert ghost, standing now amongst the fallen bodies, watched her approach, blue eyes flaring. As far as she could tell, he was the only spirit near. When she reached his side, he pointed at a body on the ground, speaking quickly and angrily.

"I don't understand," Avani apologized. "I'm sorry, I don't understand."

"Gone," the ghost said, switching to accented king's lingua. "My tribe. I can't find them. They're gone, every one."

"This one hasn't a wound on her," Russel reported. "Nor most of the horses. Whatever killed them, it wasn't the sort of weapon a soldier expects."

"It was Mal." Liam limped out from the wall of smoke, frightening Russel into a defensive squat. Morgan walked at his side. The young lord was without a helm and wore a bloodied rag wrapped around his crown, another around his arm. He led his rawboned horse on a loose rein and carried a curved scimitar instead of his own blade. His horse, like Liam, was badly hobbled.

Jacob rode Liam's shoulder, puffed up and proud. Bear stood at Liam's knee, tail slowly wagging.

"This one found us in the smoke," Liam said, wry, reaching up to pet Jacob's feathers. "A lucky thing. We've been wandering in circles, I fear."

He accepted Avani's fierce embrace with fortitude and pretended not to hear her tearful snuffles. Morgan awarded her a half bow, face bloodied, muddied, and grim.

"You're hurt," Avani said, reaching for her flask. "Your head, my lord."

"It's nothing." Morgan scratched at the bandage where dried blood stuck linen to his skin. "Wilde's worse off. Lady Avani, can you help him?"

"I lost mine own horse early on, after the third go," Liam said as Avani stroked Wilde's damp withers and ran her hands down his sides. "And right after that my knee blew." He grimaced. "Mayhap not as sound as I'd hoped."

"I wheeled 'round to pull him up," Morgan said. "And right then a passel of snakes came out of the smoke. One of them took Wilde in the front with his sword. We went down and I hit my head." He frowned. "I don't remember much for a while after that."

"Had his head rattled some," Liam concluded. "Dazed and muzzy but I kept him walking. Is that water?" He seized the flask.

"Only a wee bit for you, my lord," Avani cautioned Morgan. "It's laced with wine and if you're concussed I'd rather you abstained." Her fingers were sticky with Wilde's blood. The horse quivered as she examined the gash across his chest. The slice wasn't deep, but it was long, continuing under the horse's belly past his right foreleg.

"Good lad." Avani smiled at Morgan. "He'll be fine. It's only a shallow wound. He's sore, and it needs cleaning to keep back infection, but now's not the time."

"Obviously." Russel turned in a small circle, eyeing the sky overhead. "This place feels like a curse. Let's not linger. Difficult to be certain, with the clouds, but I think the city's that way."

"Why don't you ask Jacob?" Liam wondered around a mouthful of drink. "He led us right to you, without any trouble. Besides, he always knows which way is where. Even at sea. It's like he's got a compass in his head."

Throwing up one hand, Russel made a sound of deep disgust. Avani, feeling the fool, pinned Jacob with a stare. The raven bobbed his head up and down, self-satisfied.

"Tricks," he said.

"You black-feathered bastard," Russel snarled. "Do you mean to say he let us stumble about without direction all for the sake of looting the dead?"

"Mayhap." Liam flashed a weary smile. "Or mayhap he was just waiting for us."

"That one's Wythe," Morgan said quietly as they walked the periphery of the dead. "And that one. He's mine. That one's Black Abbey. She must have come up from their garrison. Should we collect the arrows? There are so many. Mother always said collect the arrows."

"I'm better with a blade," growled Russel. "And I'm not wasting strength carrying arrows or raven hoard, begging your pardon, my lord. I need my hands for fighting."

"I dropped my sword when I fell." Morgan scanned the ground as they skirted the odd clearing, noting faces. Avani did not doubt he was committing each Wythe corpse to memory.

"That scimitar will do you fine," Liam said. "It's light and strong. I think they must have skilled smiths in the desert."

"They don't fight fair," complained Morgan. "Running away and then popping up behind. Worse than barrowmen."

"War's not meant to be fair," Russel said. "If Riggins led you to believe it is, then he needs some sense knocked into him."

"He didn't want to frighten my lord, is all," said Liam.

"I'm not frightened," Morgan replied. "I'm angry. That one's mine. She wished me luck before we mounted. Twenty-five Kingsmen I've counted in this spot. A good chunk of my garrison and hardly any of them bleeding from more than a scratch."

Avani had noticed the same thing, although she'd been counting desert corpses alongside the Kingsmen and thought the Kingsmen would have soon met their deaths in a wave of iridescent arrows. Instead the desert had taken much greater losses, felled midrout.

At the edge of the bubble she turned and looked back. The ghost loitered amongst the corpses, searching. He saw her watching and bristled. He did not want her interference, so she let him be.

"What did you mean?" Russel asked Liam, low, as they followed Jacob back into the haze. The raven hopped across the ground with purpose. Corpses were fewer now, though the soil was torn up and trampled, pock-marked where arrows had struck but not caught. "When you said Mal did that, what did you mean?"

Avani felt Liam's eyes on the back of her head.

"It's fine," she said, although it wasn't. "He's not here. I've . . . got rid of him." She tested her wards, inside and out, and they were still strong.

"Of course he's not here," Russel said. "I left Malachi only hours ago, sitting attendance upon the king, under strict orders not to leave the castle."

"Mayhap. But he's done *that* before. I've seen it, in Roue, and on Baldebert's ship. He tried to do it to me, suck me dry, like." Avani felt rather than saw Liam's convulsive shudder. "He takes it from you, the energy that keeps you going, and he thrives on it. Like a tick on a sheep only much worse." Morgan put his hands over his mouth, stifling a nervous giggle.

"Bone magic," Avani agreed quietly. "Necromancy. Only, he works it upon the living. Steals away the spirit before the body is finished with it. It is—" now she did meet Liam's worried gaze "—I think, worse than murder."

Liam's shoulders slumped in relief.

"Did you think I would excuse him?" she asked sadly. "I left Wilhaiim as soon as I realized."

"I think you love him," her lad answered with a grown man's wisdom, "or at least you love what he might have been."

"*Might have beens* are eroded with the turning tide," Avani retorted. If she could convince Liam, mayhap she could convince herself. "Now is what we have."

"You're not listening, either of you," Russel groused.

Exhaustion slowed her strides. "I say, I left your necromancer ensconced in the castle just before dawn."

"And how long ago was dawn?" Morgan asked wearily. "I've lost track."

"Fire!" screeched Jacob, a breath before the wind tossed a blast of heat on Avani's face. "Bring the torches!"

They might have walked straight into it but for Jacob's warning: a crofter's cottage still smoldering, naught but charred stone and blackened earth. Sluggish flames still crackled. Another, larger hot spot smoked a few feet away in the near field. Avani quenched them both and then had to sit down suddenly in the crop, head spinning. Her reserves, she realized, were beginning to run dry. Bear crouched protectively by her side.

"Drink," Liam ordered, handing her her own flask. "It helps."

She did, watching as Russel kicked through the coals. The water cleared the taste of ash from her mouth. "I can't keep putting out fires if you expect me to keep wards up," she said.

"Can you wrap us all in those wards?"

"Russel—*Ai*, mayhap. If we stand close. Not the horse. I'm sorry, my lord, but Wilde will need to fend for himself."

"Good." Russel nodded once. "Because I recognize this cottage, or what's left of it. Maiden Gate's that way. And that corpse, in the crop, that's Black Abbey.

Black Abbey infantry, this far out, which means Black Abbey garrison broke just like Wythe. We're almost home. But things are about to get hairy. If the lines are broken, west and east, I cannot but assume by now the city's under siege."

CHAPTER 22

Either Crom Dubh had not counted on an uprising beneath the skin of the earth, or he hadn't paused to care. And if Everin had guessed the barrowmen hadn't consented to an influx of steel-wielding mortals through their tunnels, even the *dullahan*'s ferocity would not have convinced him to lead unsuspecting tribesmen through the gate. But he hadn't guessed or, like the *dullahan*, he hadn't stopped to think, even though afterward he knew Drem's conspicuous silence on the matter should have been warning enough.

The desert braved the rose-gold gate in the deep night, hours before the sun rose on white sands. Everin rode at Nicanor's stirrup as promised. The sand lords knew well how to whip fanfare into a frenzy. Spear clashed against spear, tribe shouted down tribe, much was made of each family's bravery and loyalty.

"We ride to victory!" Nicanor howled, shaking his spear at the sky. "We ride to prosperity!" Everin, sitting his stout coastal pony at the foot of the gate, looked out across the sand. The city had turned itself into an army. Those things precious enough to pack were carried. The rest was left behind. The men and women and children on ponies and on foot did not intend to return under the mountain. They were finished with privation. They meant to make the flatland their new home or die trying.

Fear and tenderness tangled together on Everin's tongue. He was selfishly grateful the injury to his throat prevented his voice from carrying. He might have begged them all to stay.

The *dullahan*, in human form still, had disappeared early into the crowd with vague promises about guarding the army from behind and joining the battle later. Everin searched for sign of him in the crowd but was disappointed. *Sidhe* did not break their promises. Nevertheless, they delighted in twisting a vow to cracking, and Crom Dubh's absence did not sit well in Everin's gut.

"May your enemies fall beneath you!" Nicanor screamed. The desert returned his adulation fourfold, roaring at the night. "And if they do not—may you find god's cradle in good time!" He wheeled his horse toward the gate. The rose-gold light turned his eyes to fire. "Myron! Hypatia! With me! Erastos, you must show us the way!"

Crossing into the barrows was little different than stepping through any door. The *sidhe* light was a muted yellow glow once inside the tunnel mouth. And because it was *sidhe* made, and outside of mortal time, the tunnel stretched to encompass their need, expanding until five men could ride abreast and still not scrape boot or head on curved, muddy walls.

The ponies were not pleased. Probably, the tunnel smelled distinctly of *sidhe*. Possibly they did not like the confined space, the dearth of fresh air, the diffused light. The first tribesmen through were not any more pleased. Sand lords and proficient warriors all, still they muttered amongst themselves, starting at every echoing hoofbeat or sound of dripping water. They were no more used to the underground than the animals they forced ahead along the tunnel.

Drem wore Crom Dubh's bronze barrow key on Desma's wrist and the Aug's sword on her back. The lesser *sidhe* rode ahead of Erastos and Nicanor, choosing each turning whenever the passage branched. If Erastos was the desert's ceremonial guide through the earth, Drem was their guide in truth. Everin hoped he would notice if the barrowman led them awry. He'd studied the tapestry map until he could see it with his eyes closed, and centuries of imprisonment had instilled a necessary sense of direction without stars or sun to guide him, but Drem had proved itself clever and Everin did not wholly trust it to steer them true.

There were sounds in the tunnels, faraway pops and whistles, whispers and mutters seemingly come from the walls. The sounds of the earth shifting, of underwater rivers pooling in the depths, of a clandestine kingdom waking to invasion.

Everin's pulse began to pound in his ears. Nodding stiffly Nicanor's way, he kicked his reluctant pony ahead to Drem's side.

"Tell me the *dullahan* gave them some warning."

"And whom do you suppose Crom Dubh would warn?" Drem replied, gaze fixed on the passage ahead. "The elders sleep on and my kin, as always, are beneath his notice."

"Not beneath mine." The hair on the back of Everin's neck rose. "I was right, wasn't I? This is a travesty. Like lambs to a slaughter—are we even meant to reach the surface?"

"Erastos!" Nicanor called, too loud. His voice bounced along the tunnel and came back mixed with sibilant, inhuman laughter. Drem flinched. The ponies, valiant animals, dripped foam and pinned their ears.

"Quiet!" Drem warned the sand lords. The Desma disguise wavered, showing Everin fangs and dark eyes beneath. That sorcery, he thought, would not last much longer.

"I carry the key," Drem said to Everin. "And while I cannot guess Crom Dubh's game to the end, *I* intend to reach the surface. Of late I've grown weary of living forever in the dark."

More mutters along the tunnel, a susurrus of rising dismay through the soil, making clots of mud fall. Nicanor cursed. Myron, turned frail without Pelagius's comfort, nearly came off his horse. Hypatia drew her bow though Everin did not think she could use it effectively in such a tight space.

"Drem," he said. "Give me my sword."

"Not yet."

"He isn't here to know. Give me my sword!"

"Not," repeated Drem, "yet."

Somewhere behind them in the tunnel a man screamed.

Everin stood in his stirrups and reached for his weapon. Drem snarled, threatening. And a host of barrowmen came out of the walls, teeth and claws shining, sharp bone and bronze knives and pointed sticks in hand. Nicanor and Myron, screaming, were overrun at once. Hypatia abandoned her bow and drew her curved sword instead. A barrowman dropped from the tunnel roof onto her back and bit into her shoulder, spraying blood. Hypatia shrieked. The barrowman pulled her from her horse. The pony plunged between Drem and Everin, dividing them, before galloping away down the tunnel. Everin came away with his blade in hand and Drem's toothmarks on his arm. Drem, gasping, raised a hand to block Everin's strike.

"*Stad!*" it cried, to Everin and the barrowman together. Drem ripped Faolan's spelled thread from around its wrist, at last abandoning the Desma illusion. "*Tá ceart pasáiste againn!* We have right of way!"

"By whose authority?" whispered the tunnel walls in a language older than time. Behind Everin he heard the noise of barrowman feeding and the muffled moans of terrified tribesmen. Grief rose like bile in the back of his throat.

"By Faolan's right!" shouted Drem and then, sharply, to Everin. "Show them your face!" It stood tall in its stirrups and addressed the barrows. "We are returning the exiled king to his cell in the ground, renewing Faolan's bargain! Let us pass!"

"Do you suppose us fools?" A barrowman with a scar instead of a nose appeared suddenly in front of Everin, clinging to the tunnel ceiling, and thrust its face in his own. "I know you, Drem," it said. "And I know Faolan's pet. But Faolan is dead and you've brought sweet meat and poisonous iron both into our home. What manner of disport is this? We have not been so diverted since before the Unseelie elders lay down to sleep."

"It is as it is," Drem insisted. "For Faolan's sake, let us through. We will not tarry long."

The noseless barrowman smiled at Everin, dark eyes canny. "It is true that Faolan's pet, escaped, brought woe upon our heads." The creature's breath was foul. There was red human blood on its tongue.

"If not for his meddling above we might have continued as we were, forgotten. Now the mortals have increased their defenses against us, the elders stir in their dreaming, and we suffer dearly for both. Why should I not have his head as recompense?"

"There is geis upon my head yet," Everin answered. Gripping the reins of his twitching mount with one hand, he used the other to press the flat of his sword against the barrowman's torso, shoving. "Will you contest it?" The iron made the *sidhe* flinch but it did not retreat, bolder than Everin liked to see. Pale face screwed in concentration, it sniffed at Everin before growling dismay.

"Crom Dubh," it hissed. "*Dullahan*. The dark serpent, roused. Accursed human, you have brought disaster upon us indeed."

"Cast him out!" The tunnel walls seethed and shuddered, inhuman voices lifted in rage. Behind Everin the sand snakes gasped and wept but stood their ground. "Crom Dubh! Cast him out!"

"He's coming," said Drem. "This is the *dullahan's* game we play. Faolan died for it. Will *you* stand in his way?"

"Would that we could." The Aug's sword against the barrowman's chest was leaving a welt but still it would not back away. Clinging to the ceiling with fingers and toes, it peered along the tunnel.

"For Faolan's sake I will give you and yours free passage, Drem," it said at last. "For fear of Crom

Dubh's ire, we will not block your way. But by our laws for the offense of iron you must pay a price. We are hungry. Those that we can catch, we keep. Crom Dubh will not begrudge us a meal."

"Drem!" protested Everin, knocking the noseless *sidhe* aside with his blade. "That is no bargain!" But he knew it for what it was: *sidhe* justice.

"Cast him out!" The ground quaked. "He is coming!"

Drem would not look Everin's way. "Forward," it shouted, hollow as a tomb. "Forward, children of the desert, or die!" And then it suited words to action, spurring its pony ahead down the tunnel. The desert surged after, pushing Everin ahead in its path.

They burst out of the earth into sea-salt air. A blast of chill wind made Everin choke. He had an impression of moonlight on clapboard and brick as he fought to stop a mount gone wild with terror. He hauled on one rein, turning the poor animal's nose into his stirrup. The pony stumbled but didn't fall. It stopped at last, flanks heaving, nostrils flaring pink.

Everin swiveled in the saddle and looked back at the flatland gate.

They poured out of a gaping hole in the ground, a terrified river of survivors, more on foot than on horseback, many bleeding, some dying as they fled. He thought they would slow to a trickle and then cease, and his cheeks were wet with expected sorrow at the loss, but they kept coming: young and old, dignified, determined, desperate. They'd faced the demons in the depths and come out the other side.

"You discounted the iron they carry," Drem said. "And their resolve. The situation was not so grave as you assumed."

"You told a lie," marveled Everin, watching in disbelief as the desert emerged, mostly whole, onto flatland dunes. "To win us passage."

"I did not." Drem showed its teeth. "I intend to keep you again beneath the earth, as per Faolan's bargain. Carn was not wrong; we have suffered for your absence." Drem licked its lips. It shrugged. "Only, I did not say to Carn when I would deliver you." It inhaled deeply of chill sea air, nostrils flaring much like Everin's winded pony, then dismounted gracefully, landing on its toes in the sand, a pale figure with too-long limbs and dark, discerning eyes in a thin face. "What is this place? Are we west?"

Everin glanced around. "Whitcomb. Aye, west. Where are you going?" he demanded when Drem smiled and turned away.

"Back below," Drem replied. "I have a barrow key. I will use it." It slunk forward then paused and glanced back. "What will you do, little king?"

Everin showed his own teeth in a feral smile. "I have a fine iron sword," he said. "And I intend to use it on that black winged, cold-hearted, meddling *sidhe* bastard. Just as soon as he shows his ugly face."

"You will not have long to wait," Drem predicted. "He is coming." It scuttled away, vanishing between one blink and the next.

Wind drying the sweat and tears on his face, Everin dismounted. He pulled the saddle from the pony's back and dropped the bit. Then he slapped the poor beast on the rear and sent it away into the night before taking a second look around. Whitcomb was quiet, picket fences and peaked roofs a haven against gusty wind. The torches burning alongside every door guttered in the weather but did not go out. North beyond the village white dunes reflected moonlight and past the dunes Wilhaiim's favorite vineyards slept.

"Erastos! Erastos! Are we safe? What is that stink?"

He had no special fondness for Whitcomb. He'd stopped there many times in the year he had worked for Renault as a runner, carrying messages between village and keep and the city while learning for himself what sort of king his grandson made. He'd not allowed sentiment to enter into it for fear that if he became too attached to his flatland people he would someday believe he could do better on their throne than the current king. He was not a man who dreamed beyond his station. He was not a man who dreamed at all.

He had no special fondness for Whitcomb, but he would grieve its destruction.

"That is the sea you smell," he said, spinning to confront gathering desert tribes. They surrounded him in growing numbers, shaken and frightened, but as Drem had pointed out, resolved. Red starburst on a white background flew over their heads, banners twisting in the gale. The *sidhe* gate spat forth more survivors, though the exodus was slowing. He shivered to think of those who, like Nicanor, had not made it through the barrows, and then sighed for those who had eluded fang and claw but would fall to flatland soldiers.

"And the green, growing things," he continued hoarsely. "Fresh water. Rain on the wind. Hearth smoke and meat roasting. This is your future, if you take it."

"And what of you, Erastos?" The sand lord's name was Lino. He'd shared camel meat with Everin and Nicanor in the *dullahan*'s lodge. He was not blessed with Nicanor's wisdom but neither was he rash. He'd seen Everin send his mount away. Mayhap he'd seen him also exchanging words with Drem, mayhap he knew enough to question Everin's purpose. His bow was in his hand and an arrow set loosely to the string.

"I have business of my own," Everin replied evenly. "I have led you safely through the tunnels, as I promised Crom Dubh I would. The rest is up to you, my lord."

"Safely?" Lino laughed without mirth, but he did not nock his arrow. "Half of my tribe is murdered, dragged by demons away into the earth. Nicanor is *dead.*"

"May he find the god's cradle quickly. Victory does not come without a price, prosperity without sacrifice." Sheathing his blade, Everin pushed his way through the watching crowd. If Lino loosed an arrow he would be dead before he knew it. The geis that protected him from the *sidhe's* wrath would not save him from Lino's.

"My lord, look! Light in the village! My lord, leave Erastos to his business, we have our own to begin!"

Everin did not dare glance over his shoulder. He didn't need to. The wind brought with it the sound of voices raised in inquiry. Whitcomb was waking to alarm. He walked faster, moving blindly past horse and man in the direction of the barrow gate. No one moved to stop him. The desert kindled their arrows and drew their swords, preparing for war. Everin broke into a run. If anyone paid him notice, they pretended not to see his cowardice. He hastened over dunes, tripping on soft Whitcomb sand, the sea in his nostrils. He ran until he was within a stone's throw of the barrow hole, then fumbled about in the moonlight until he found a clump of late-blooming gorse behind which he could hide. The desert staggered from the tunnels to either side of him, most now on foot, struck wide-eyed and mute, the old and the infirm climbing over each other in a bid for escape. He saw on their faces that he would not have to wait much longer.

It was not barrowmen that pursued them. It was Crom Dubh driving them so cruelly through the earth, lashing at their feet and shoulders with a coiled chitinous whip, snapping again at their heads with the tip of his serpent tail. He erupted out of the earth in a storm of ebony feathers and mud and wheeled straight up into the night sky. As he swooped past Everin, the weight of the geis upon him cracked, a promise kept, and he was free.

He waited a breath and then rose from concealment, head tilted to the sky, tracking the monster as it flitted between cloud and moon, riding the wind. He did not suppose a shout would draw its attention. He needed something more.

While he pondered, a crack split the air and Whitcomb went up in flame.

The *dullahan* was not easy prey. Everin tracked him, undaunted, while the world around them burned. Desert arrows, dipped in myrrh, set fires wherever they touched down. The flatland, coming to the end of a hot, dry summer, was tinder waiting to go up. The wind only made things worse. The conflagration in Whitcomb spread, sparks leaping from roof to roof, then into the vineyards where the grape vines sizzled and spat. The dunes might have kept the burn contained but for the tornado of sparks chased this way and that in the squall. Clumps of gorse exploded into flame, sending a pungent smoke up into the night sky, joining the black plume from the enkindled village. Soon a dank haze obscured the moon and made it difficult to see more than an arm's length to either side.

Crom Dubh kept close to Whitcomb, darting in and out of the smoke, alighting to snatch a victim at random before returning to the sky. He did not distinguish between flatlander or tribesman. He plucked away villagers as they fled from burning buildings, tearing off their heads before throwing their flailing bodies back into the fire. He seized warriors from their ponies, ripping free their spines before dropping them again from great heights. Whitcomb's white sands turned red beneath him. The smoke in the air reeked of immolation.

Everin hunted Crom Dubh by the screams of his victims. On hands and knees beneath the smoke, or crouched to peer at the sky when a singular gust briefly cleared the haze overhead, he crept in pursuit. He had no strategy in mind other than to get as close as possible and then somehow draw the monster's ire. He stopped once to change out of desert garb and into a villager's togs, once again stripping a dead man of his garb. He drank water from a vineyard aqueduct running in a ditch toward the sea; it tasted of salt and made him gag. He was wondering if he dared climb to the top of one of Whitcomb's ancient pine trees despite their proximity to the fire when the solution came within an arm's length of running him down. Through the wind and screams he didn't hear the riders until they were on him.

"Blood of the Virgin!"

"Look out, soldier!"

"Fuck me, another one! Friend or foe?"

They halted about him in a circle, six Kingsmen astride six gigantic coursers, lance and shield pointed his direction. Their faces were guarded by helm and visor, their armor dusty with soot. He rose slowly upright, hands up, pommel loose in his fingers.

"Friend," he said clearly.

He could guess what he must look like, yellow desert eyes above a flatlander's sharp nose. But yellow eyes were not exclusive to the desert—that blood had mingled long ago. Silently he thanked the dead villager for the gift of his clothes. If he'd still been wearing kilt and snakeskin, they would have cut him down immediately.

"Are you escaped from Whitcomb, man?" One of the soldiers leaned in for a closer look, lifting her visor. The device on her shield and breastplate belonged to Wythe, though her five companions wore Low Port's cresting wave. Everin recognized her stern features and the king's favor glittering below Wythe's insignia.

"Aye, Countess."

"You're one of just twelve, then," the king's constable replied grimly. "The rest, as far as we can determine, are dead. What are you doing away out here on the dunes? Get back toward the garrison if you want to live."

"I'm tracking the monster." Everin jerked his head at the sky. He thought dawn must be near by the change in the smoke from black to gray. "I mean to kill him."

The Kingsmen laughed.

"Fine chance that," one said, bitterness plain even through his closed helm. "It eludes our best archers and steals our lancers from the ground. My infantry, bless them, broke and ran before it. Wyrms are meant to stay in nursery rhymes. I did not expect a live one to come ahead of the desert on a cold wind."

"No wyrm, that," Everin told the constable. "That's *sidhe*. The *dullahan*, called Crom Dubh, Black Crom for his black heart. Iron will kill him, if only I can tempt him close." He looked pointedly at her lance. "A strong, iron-tipped spear through the flank might drop him."

He'd piqued her interest. "*Sidhe*, is it? *Sidhe* do not frighten me, even though they sham a wyrm's form. *Sidhe* are killable." She smiled, fierce. "I have impeccable aim with the lance. I'll do better than the flank, I'll take the murderous bastard through its breast."

"I fear even impeccable aim will do little good unless I can draw him close."

The constable's fine brows rose beneath her visor. "And how," she asked, "do you plan to do that?"

"I had not decided," Everin confessed. "Before you near ran me over, I thought to climb that tree." He indicated the old pine. The needles on its lower branches were beginning to smoke. The soldiers, following the direction of his gaze, chortled. Any moment and it would go up like a torch. He sighed. "I'll admit I'm not at my best, my lady. Nevertheless, I need to draw his attention."

Wythe's expression softened. "Neither are we at our best, man. And we have not immediately suffered the loss of our home." She crossed herself, shoulder to shoulder and brow to groin. "The people of Whitcomb will not be forgotten. What are you called, dragon slayer?"

"Everin, my lady. After the king that never was."

"Well, Everin," the king's constable said, looking around at her companions. "As luck would have it, I believe we have just the thing you need." She reached down a gloved hand. "Come aboard. Keep your head down. The sand snakes are generous with their arrows."

"**E**lephant gun." Countess Wythe walked a circle around the wagon, removing her helm as she did so. "Roue's first ship, *Fine Lady*, made port yesterday. The wind blew it in ahead of its sisters. Unfortunately, the wind also keeps it from tacking into the bay, what with waves tossing to and fro. Lapin and Chama managed to get this one on dry land by use of a fisherman's barge."

Lapin and Chama, Everin assumed, were either the two sober soldiers guarding the gun or the large oxen tethered near the garrison's well some few feet away. The soldiers were Roue men, wearing brightly colored enameled armor and true gold around their wrists and in their ears. On his back one carried a tightly woven, narrow lidded basket. The oxen also wore gold—on the tips of their pointed horns.

"There were two," one of the men told Everin in, precise, unaccented king's lingua. "Two guns, two barges. The waves took the second barge down into the bay, the crate of cannon shot and my tools. Lapin was fleet enough to retain his." He indicated the basket on his companion's back. "Captain Shal, she decided better to wait until the wind passes rather than risk sinking another. The admiral, he will be quite angry as it is."

"There are more coming," Lapin added quickly. "Two more ships, five guns. And soldiers." He shifted, peering past the garrison, abandoned but for three stone-faced Low Port infantrymen keeping guard over the wagon and its contents, at the growing inferno beyond. "We are too late, I am afraid."

"Or mayhap just in time," Wythe said, tapping her fingers on her thigh. She gestured Everin close. "Well, what do you think?"

Excitement ignited Everin's grin. He paced his own circle around the wagon, admiring the gun. It was much larger than the small cannons ranged on Wilhaiim's battlements, bigger even than those he'd seen shipboard in Low Port. The cannon had one long iron barrel, secured by way of great metal bolts to the cart and then bound together four times with bands of copper and more iron. The cascabel at the rear was as wide in diameter as a wine cask, and opened by way of a complicated set of levers.

"Powerful, is it?" Everin asked, daring to stroke his hand along one side of the barrel.

"She would shoot down the moon, if we asked," Chama agreed. Beneath his enameled breastplate his chest puffed in pride. "Had we cannon fodder at hand, this one gun alone might clear your kingdom of rebels."

"If I contrive the cannon fodder," Wythe said. "You'll need not reach quite so far." She pointed over Whitcomb at the killing shadow coiling in and out of cloud and smoke. "There."

The two soldiers appeared unimpressed by Crom Dubh's bloody rampage. "Wyrm," said Lapin. "Not since my grandmother's time has a wyrm dared plague Roue. The smoke," he added regretfully, "will make it difficult. To kill a wyrm, one must pierce its eye."

"Just bring it down," Wythe said. "Leave the killing to us," she barked at the watching infantrymen. "Iron shot! Now! Spear head, dirk, the meat knives from your belts. Bundle and bind all you can find, tight, with the leather from my stirrups."

"Scrapshot, Constable?"

"Exactly! Be quick!" Somberly, she eyed the standing oxen. "We'll need to be right beneath the ugly thing. Will yon fancy oxen pull toward fire?"

"Of course. They are trained to battle, the finest from the Rani's stables."

"Bless her." Wythe clapped her hands together. "Chama, hook them up. Let's go! I want Black Crom's black heart for my trophy room!"

Everin wondered what Drem would have made of their gambit. The *dullahan* was hardly a beloved figure in barrowman history. Crom Dubh, like most of elders, spared no kindness on his lesser cousins. He did not think Drem and its kin would mourn the *dullahan's* loss. Far from it. He suspected rather that they would dance on the monster's corpse, given half the chance.

Lapin and Chama were not braggarts. Once harnessed to the front of the wagon the oxen plodded placidly forward, pulling the elephant gun out from the relative safety of Low Port's garrison into chaos. Wythe and the remnants of her cavalry rode in a loose oval about the wagon while Lapin and Chama stood balanced on the running boards. The blades they wielded were long and thin, more rapier than broadsword, and enameled on the pommels.

Everin crouched in the wagon behind them, hastily securing what sharp iron the soldiers had managed to collect into a solid bundle.

"Not much larger than that," warned Chama. "Divide it into two, I think. Two barrels, two missiles. One load, at least, will hit him."

"The god willing," said Wythe as she struck out with her lance, smacking a tribesman on the side of the head as he came barreling their direction out of the smoke. The sand snake tumbled from his pony. A Low Port lancer finished her off as she fell, deftly driving his spear through her ribs. Everin recoiled. His regret was short lived. Four more warriors followed her out of the haze, howling as they fell upon the wagon. Flaming arrows struck the running boards, bounced off Lapin's armor, broke beneath wagon wheels, and struck one of the Kingsmen in his shoulder.

Everin stamped out flame before the wagon could catch. The oxen lowed unhappily but did not stop their forward momentum. Chama left the wagon for the ground, blocking scimitar with rapier, feinting sideways and around and down, ducking another flock of iridescent stingers. A tribesman leapt from his pony onto the back of the wagon, swinging in Everin's direction. Everin had his blade in his hand before he thought. The warrior lunged, scimitar flashing. Everin blocked the cut with the flat of his blade and pressed forward, backing the man toward the rear of the wagon. Smoke wreathed them both.

Beside the wagon a gorse bush went up with a whoosh, limning them both in orange light and a blast of heat.

"Erastos!" The tribesman gasped in recognition. "What are you doing?" He faltered in his surprise just long enough to catch Lapin's rapier through his arm pit. Lapin, breathing hard, booted the dying man onto the dunes.

"Friend of yours?" he inquired.

"Nay," Everin replied. But it felt as if it was his own heart Lapin had pierced.

A shadow fell across the wagon from above and for the first time the oxen wavered in their path.

"'Ware!" Wythe shouted. "There he is! Here, stop here! Prepare the gun!"

Everin looked up. The *dullahan* dipped and dove overhead, playing hide-and-seek with the smoke. Crom Dubh's hands and restless whip rained blood onto Whitcomb below, making flames spit. His empty-eyed helm turned this way and that, seeking, while his wings beat against the wind. He held a still-struggling Kingsman gripped in the squeezing coils of his tail.

Lapin and Chama prepared the elephant gun, retrieving their tools from the basket still on Lapin's back. Emptying black powder from a heavy pouch into the butt of the gun, they added a quantity of wadded, dry grass and then Wythe's scrapshot bundle. Together they rammed their provisional fodder into the bore, using a long, bronze, bulbous-nosed stick that had come out of Lapin's basket in four pieces hastily screwed together to make the whole. Wythe and her Low Port lancers fought to keep an increasing number of tribesmen from the wagon. Everin stepped up onto the running boards and hammered the pommel of his sword against the muzzle of the cannon while Lapin used a flint and fuse from his basket to start the cannon's vent, shielding the spark with his hands from the wind.

"Dullahan!" Everin screamed. "Crom Dubh!"

He did not expect to be heard over the sounds of battle, over the fire's blistering draft or the wind's ferocious tempest. He'd spent his long life overlooked and forgotten. He did not suppose that would change only because the world was burning.

But Crom Dubh hesitated midflight, rolled around, and swooped back across the pyre that had been Whitcomb. Behind Everin metal groaned as Lapin and Chama adjusted levers and cranked gears, aiming the gun. One of the Low Port lancers was sobbing as he lay beneath the wagon, a scimitar lodged in his thigh, his courser fled. Another plucked an arrow from his visor as he rode down a fleeing tribesman. Wythe clung to her saddle and her sword, breathing out curse words instead of air.

The *dullahan* swooped lower. His vacant gaze unerringly found Everin amidst the fray.

Little king, Crom Dubh said, silver bells in his head. *Tell me, why should I spare you any more of my attention?*

"Dullahan," Everin said, and this time he did not bother to lift his voice. *"You and I have a score to settle."*

The elephant gun went off, jolting the wagon backward, knocking Everin to his knees on the running board. The oxen braced against the recoil, bowing their heads, ears flicking back and forth as they waited for a signal to move again. Everin feared for a moment the cannon's concussion had struck him deaf. Wythe bent over him, mouth moving, but he could not hear a word she said.

Chama discharged the cannon's second barrel. Wythe yanked Everin off the wagon and forward over the supine bodies of sand snakes and Kingsmen. He stumbled, dizzy. Then his ears popped and sound and balance returned together.

". . . saw it fall!" Wythe was shouting. "The second round, I think. Aug save you, man, don't drop your sword now." They were dangerously close to Whitcomb. He could feel the heat of the fire starting blisters on his face. Most of the burning buildings had fallen in on themselves; flames licked brick and stone and jumped from fence to tree to hedge. The smoke near the village was so thick they were forced to drop to their hands and knees and crawl in the sand to save their lungs. Charred corpses littered the ground but no other living thing dared come so near the pyre.

Everin and Wythe met Crom Dubh on their hands and knees, found him waiting behind the burning village with the sea at his back. Shrapnel from the elephant gun had taken him several times through one wing, and several more across his muscular flank. *Sidhe* ichor fountained from his wounds, poisoning white sand. Where iron had pierced his body, dark scales folded inward, peeling away from flesh below. The scales dropped off, one by one, leaving ulcers behind. The contagion was spreading in fits and starts, down his long tail and up his broad belly.

The monster's serpent-like body coiled and uncoiled painfully when he breathed. In the fall Crom Dubh had lost his chitinous black whip; he gripped instead a tasseled desert spear, made tiny in his sharp-clawed hand. As Everin crawled close, he saw that what he had taken for black armor on the *aes si*'s torso and arms and hands was in fact scaling, and what he had taken in the confusion of his wild ride so long ago for an empty champion's helm atop Crom Dubh's powerful shoulders was instead ridges of obsidian bone and chitinous flesh, part of his body.

The *dullahan* looked down on them, exhaling dry, pained amusement. He slapped the sand with his tail, tossing up grit and pieces of burned gorse.

"*Well,*" he said, out loud and in Everin's skull. "*Don't sit there, choking on smoke and flame. Come and play. Together you make a gratifying entertainment. For that mayhap I'll kill you quick above the ground, and you'll be glad of it."*

Sighing, the king's constable rose to her feet, lance pulled back over her shoulder as she took aim.

"Aye, then," she said pleasantly, grinning all the while. "Let's play."

CHAPTER 23

Wilhaiim's walls were breached. Mal could not see the rift from where he'd climbed atop the ruins of the Bone Cave. The smoke was too thick. But with his eyes closed he watched the encroachment unfold, an onrush of life over the northern walls. In his head the desert invaders were a luminous watercourse, pressed so close together he could hardly tell one individual from the next. They massed against gray stone in ever increasing numbers. He could not tell how exactly it happened, whether they went over or somehow through, but all at once they were in, Wilhaiim's winding streets and open bailey over-whelmed, the castle engulfed.

His eyes snapped open. A chill gust of wind threatened to topple him from his perch. It smelled of autumn and of winter damp, and it whipped the smoke around him into an army of minuscule cyclones. The Automata gathered about the Bone Cave paid the weather no mind. Mal could not tell for certain whether they noticed it at all, whether they cared for anything beyond his next command.

In the end, he and Baldebert had managed only five ferric soldiers, but not for lack of trying. Their kindling took more bone and strength than Mal had first assumed. In the night he'd ravaged the lich yard, depleting every sack he'd found under the grass of its contents. But the charging of each Automata, even with the benefit of powerful lich bones, had left Mal shaken and feeble for hours after. Despite growing urgency, he'd been forced to rest between kindling, and the desert had come too soon—in the end Mal had simply run out of time.

He wished now that he had given in to necessity and stolen the strength he needed to birth all seven Automata. The rush of their creation had bolstered his pride even as it drained his body. But that incredulous satisfaction was nothing compared to the rush of potential he'd gained in subsuming the lives of one hundred warriors in their prime.

Remembering that rapture, he quivered. The luminous watercourse was a nagging temptation, even with his eyes wide open, and more difficult to resist now he'd had a healthy swallow. Another sip, he thought, would go unnoticed. And Wilhaiim would only profit from his strength.

The wind suddenly dropped to stillness. The sounds of a city toppling reached his ears: the grind of stone upon stone, the clash of spear against armor, the bellows of men and beast. Renault was there, barricaded inside the palace, safe for the moment; Mal would know if the wards worked into the palace wall failed. He could sense Avani, their link an arrested thread between them, expanding and contracting as the distance between them shifted. But he could not know her thoughts to guess how Liam fared, and he could not guess which amongst those bright pinpricks might belong to Baldebert and his crew, to Peter Shean who had been Siobahn's friend, to the last of Wilhaiim's children, or to stalwart Russel whom he had come, grudgingly, to respect. He would not let himself assume they had fallen to battle and he would not risk ending them by mistake merely to quiet his trembling hands or to fill the new hollow yawning at his center.

The dying of the wind did nothing to improve visibility. Mal could not wait any longer. He jumped from his perch and ran a calculating gaze over his walking machines. Anyone else would think the malformed creatures grotesque—Baldebert certainly had, refusing to come near the Automata after that second kindling—but Mal adored them with a fondness usually reserved for his small circle of self-made family.

None of the five were the same. Lane's creation,

even with its long, restless tail and profusion of spikes, was the least strange. Its barbute head was set atop its shoulders in a distinctly manlike semblance and its torso, pelvis, and limbs were all attached as a seamstress might attach a doll's: loosely but in all the right places. Lane's Automata reflected Holder's vision—it was straw man made iron.

The lich machines were a different species. Either because the dead magi recalled the original Automata from life, or because more powerful spirits made for more varied personalities, the final four Automata were far from humanoid. One sported too many arms sprouting from its upper spine, each arm reinforced with a long chain-and-cog flail. Another had chosen to eschew a torso altogether and had instead set its helm atop a bulky pelvis bristling all around with a multitude of round, rotating blades on metal stalks. The third was a mountain of piston and gears, and had chosen for its foot one gigantic cylinder studded over and under with thick spikes. Its waist was narrow, a ladder of crooked cogs, and around its stubby neck it wore a collar of chain tentacles.

They were each at least three times as tall as Mal, except for Sensha's proud monster, which topped them all by half a man again. She—for Mal thought of her so despite the fact she had not been a living woman for centuries and would not be again—was the most magnificent of them all, with her writhing appendages and her one strong leg, and for the not small matter that she was his first.

Her very existence, that Mal had invoked magnificence from naught but bone magic and detritus, was worth the certain cost. If she could save Wilhaiim, she was worth his sacrifice ten times more.

He conjured wards to keep out distraction, pulled smoke all about to replace the shadows that had disappeared midday along with Rowan, and led the way.

"Now," he ordered out loud, though he hardly need say the words, for the Automata worked in sync with the agitated beat of his heart. "Let us begin."

The Automata approached Wilhaiim with single-minded enterprise. They loped, they hopped, they rolled, and they crushed: field, fire, corpses, and soldiers. They threw no shadow in the midday haze, but those with eyes yet to see and sense yet to understand who came within their periphery soon dropped, gibbering, to the ground. They butchered anyone within easy reach so long as they were the enemy, and some who got in the way who were not. Mal could not prevent himself from supping on the ghosts left, stunned, in their wake. He gorged until his wards grew too bright to look upon, energy suffused his eyes and his fingertips, and bliss made him reckless. He saw terror all around, he could not tell flatlander from desert dweller, and he did not much care to think deeply on their differences. The battle-field fractured into further chaos near the Automata. Those that had the fortitude to turn and run did so. Those already shattered by fire and smoke and the terrors of war lay on their faces in the charred crop, foes forgotten.

It was easier, much easier than Mal had foreseen. And it felt very, very good.

Wilhaiim's northern wall gaped where gray stone had toppled, the battlements above were collapsed. Broken bodies lay all about, buried beneath rubble or fallen in piles around the breach. Angry flies buzzed already around the dead. Mal took the flies, and the mournful dead, and swallowed them all as he advanced through the hole. The Automata followed, crushing rubble further with limb and tentacle.

Mal staggered when his foot hit cobblestone. The press of life inside the city was almost too much. He shaded his eyes against their brilliance; Kingsmen, sand snakes, refugees, the wealthy nobility and the dirtiest squatter's-row drifters. He steadied himself with a hand against a fallen stone to keep from gorging.

A fly buzzed his ears. He brushed it away. Blinking, he looked about.

An equal number of the living and the dead filled the street. The living who were able fled. The rest Mal consumed. The Automata arranged themselves in the narrow road, waiting. Their bulk broke cobblestones and crushed anything beneath their iron-clad feet.

The fly buzzed around Mal's head again. Groggy, he slapped at the sound. It was not a fly, after all, but a fat honeybee within the protection of his wards. Impossible. He took its tiny, indomitable spirit. Its corpse fell on his boot. But another replaced it, circling his crown. And another. He stumbled, baffled. Each time he ended one yellow-and-black marauder another appeared. One had the temerity to sting him on the neck, sacrificing its own life before he could snatch it away.

The impossible honeybee were a puzzle and a distraction, so much so that he forgot for a moment where he stood, so much so that he didn't see Brother Tillion step out of the smoke in front of him, dangerously close to Mal's spitting wards.

"Necromancer," the theist said. "You and yours are not welcome here."

Mal froze. A bee landed on his swatting hand but did not sting. Another orbited his chest. The Sensha Automata, sensing his indecision, twitched a tentacle in Tillion's direction.

"Nay," Mal ordered, and she stilled. Tillion leaned on his staff, regarding Mal sourly. Mal could not separate his star from the city's too-bright constellation.

"This is my home," Mal said, regarding the theist in kind. The buzzing around his head increased but he dared not glance away from Tillion. He could not fathom how the bees had breached his wards. He could not fathom their presence at all. "I've come to keep it safe; I'm the only one who can."

"So you have," Tillion said. "But at what price? The enemy retreats before you, aye. And so, too, do the good people of Wilhaiim, and you have barely stepped inside our walls. If you come further there will be mass terror, rioting, further loss of life. Appetite has blinded you, I think." He held his staff in both hands, turning it into a weapon. "I did warn you. You cannot be allowed to continue."

Mal laughed. "How bold you are now." He took one step forward. Tillion retreated a stride before his wards. "Stronger than ever. Hardly the palsied man I've come to know. Is it opion?" He let disgust shade his smile. "I did not think so, not at first, but I've since discovered the temple has become very free with its curatives."

"I've no need of opion. My god is my only curative. He delivers unto me strength." Tillion struck at Mal with his staff. The wards sputtered angrily. Tillion blanched but struck again. "You continue to discount him."

Bitterly amused, Mal extinguished a swarm of stinging bees. "And did he send these to torment me also, as if you, Brother Tillion, were not enough?" He stepped forward until the curve of his wards brushed Tillion's bare foot. Tillion gasped, jerking away, but held his ground.

"Nay, the priest is not responsible for your stings. Those would be *my* darlings you're ending."

It was Mal's turn to blanch. Cleena detached herself from the smoke. The *sidheog*'s lovely mouth was set in a flat line, her dark eyes snapping angrily.

"This human king said we were to keep you from dwelling too long on the hunger in your heart, necromancer. The little stings, the buzzing, they are working, I think." She showed him pointed teeth and hatred. He extinguished another handful of her bees in retribution. Sensha took a grating hop forward. Tillion groaned but held firm. Cleena shuddered and cursed him roundly.

But Mal had forgotten them both, and even the bees and their stings, as his brain caught up with his ears.

"'This human king said,'" he repeated, aghast, rocking on his heels.

"Brother."

It was the thing he did not expect and should have. He knew Renault, loved him, had served him since boyhood. The king was not the sort who would willingly hide away in safety while his kingdom struggled, no matter that he'd insisted his vocent do the same. Of course he would be out in war, sword in hand, clad only in the ease of light armor, and Mal's blue-and-silver brooch on his sleeve to keep him hidden when need be.

Renault was not alone. Baldebert clung to his sleeve, pale and sick in the presence of the Automata, but upright, knuckles white around familiar ivory manacles.

"You great fool," Mal growled, pressing the heels of his hands against his eyes to keep back incandescence. "You could be killed."

"Do you mean to do so, then?" Renault replied. Despite the ferric soldiers, he sounded very calm. "Are you past the point where you care who lives and who dies? I cannot be sure. You are laying waste to my city, Malachi, as surely as any desert wolf."

Mal flexed his hands. The remaining bees in his circle fell. Only Tillion's quick flying staff kept Cleena from clawing at Mal's wards.

"You told him, did you?" Ignoring the *sidhe*'s rage, Mal speared Baldebert with his glare. "When did you tell him? When first I asked for your help? Did you betray me from the beginning?"

Baldebert was beyond speaking. Renault shook his head.

"You would not be standing here had I known before your machines began to walk," he said. "And even then, I could not credit it. This is treason, Malachi. I suspected you came back to me from Roue changed, and I grieved. I did not think I would have to grieve you in truth for sedition." He drew himself up, and looked down his nose. "Lord Vocent, let go your wards."

"Nay." Mal gritted his teeth. "I mean to save this city first."

"The city is saved, was well on its way before you interfered," Tillion retorted. "If you'd stayed where you were told, you would have known—word comes that the Rani's ships have docked. We need only hold out until reinforcements arrive."

"The wall was—there was a breach—" Mal's breath came hard and fast. All at once he could not think straight, could not get his bearings. Light seared his skull. Reflexively he reached for Avani. That refuge was closed to him. He groaned. "I watched them push inside. So many."

"Aye," replied Renault. "The desert pushed inside. And was neatly encircled by my battlements, by my archers and Brother Orat's deftly laid spells and sigils. The sand snakes know nothing of walls; they did not expect that within my city would be more treacherous than without. As Brother Tillion says—if you had listened to me and stayed where you were told . . . but I fear you were already well past comprehension. Drop your wards, Mal."

The stings on his hands and face throbbed. His eyes dazzled and ran. The Automata waited patiently; they would wait forever for his command. If he moved them forward, the city would be his. If he dropped his wards, he would die. He'd planned on the dying, though mayhap not so soon. He hadn't planned on the terror.

"I understand now," he told Baldebert. "Why you cannot look upon the Automata without dread."

Baldebert, still clinging to Renault, clenched his jaw and met Mal's gaze, though he could not look around at the walking machines. "I nigh pissed myself when they stepped into the city." He said, "But here I am, nonetheless, facing certain destruction because I know somewhere inside the madness you are the man who saved my sister and her people." He held up the ivory manacles; they rattled in his shaking fingers. "Let me help."

Mal laughed. Mirth felt like smoke in his throat. "There is no help for me now, friend. I am a dead man."

"You were that," said Brother Tillion, "from the first moment you denied the one god his due."

Mal shaded his watering eyes to better see his king's face because he could not separate that individual, beloved star, from the rest. Renault looked back, expectant. Grief furrowed his brow and dampened his beard.

"You have no choice," Renault said quietly. "Unless you mean to kill me."

Mal dropped his wards.

They sprang upon him as one, knocking him onto rubble as they sought containment. He bucked beneath them. There were the bravest of Kingsmen on the battlements above and arrows trained Mal's way in an attempt to shield their king from harm. He would have very much liked to end them, if only he could be sure he would not also swallow those he loved. He would have liked to rid the world of Tillion and his bruising staff. When Cleena sat on his chest and promised to tear out his throat if the Automata so much as twitched, he laughed and wrenched a hand free, grasping her fingers and *taking, taking, taking* because she'd been so stupid as to set herself apart from the others but that was only another *sidhe* snare. In Mal's distraction Baldebert snapped ivory cuffs around his wrists. The world dimmed, vitality snuffed out. Men were only men again; even Cleena, once as difficult to look upon as the sun, was dulled to flesh and bone.

He could no longer feel the Automata. Bereft of his guiding hand, they froze, waiting for a command he couldn't give.

Bereft, Mal wept and raged for the loss of light, the sundering of his magic. He snarled at Cleena and even at Renault, and that earned him a whack from Tillion's staff. The Sensha machine uncoiled a fretful feeler and that meant Tillion hit Mal again, harder and then again because Baldebert's fear was as catching as any spring plague, and after that unconsciousness was preferable to pain.

"... east, Your Majesty, into the woods. While some three hundred more are camped within our walls."

Mal came to himself reluctantly. His head hurt. His

eyes were stuck closed. His muscles were cramped from lying too long on a hard surface, and he was cold. He smelled rain in smoke and heard the faraway sound of thunder or cannon. He tried to lift his hands to rub the crust from his lids but encountered resistance. He lay without moving for several more heartbeats before he understood that he was bound.

"And the rest?"

"It's difficult to be sure how many yet live, Majesty. They won't come near Wilhaiim for fear of the walking machines. My men report small fires in the night, but there is no way to be certain whether those are camps gathering on the prairie or remnants of the greater inferno. When the sun rises, we will know better. Until then, Roue will stand defense."

That was Baldebert, no longer made mute by terror, sounding much more like the admiral and self-satisfied pirate prince he was. Mal forced his eyes open, tearing lashes in the process, a small price to pay for clarity. When he moved, metal grated on stone and his heart quailed. He was not sure what he had expected but it was not the indignity of iron shackles hand and foot, nor the absence of clothes but for a scanty wrap around his loins. He'd been stripped of Hennish leather, left to freeze in the oriel behind Renault's throne. Four somber Kingsmen stood his guard, front and back and either side. Baldebert's ivory cuffs clung still to his wrists. They chafed less than Renault's chain.

"Slowly," Avani cautioned, appearing in his periphery. "You've two great lumps on your skull courtesy of Brother Tillion and at least one broken rib that I can tell."

He inhaled sharply and that hurt his ribs and made the vertigo worse.

"You're here," he said.

"I am." She helped him uncurl from the floor and let him lean against her shoulder. He sat, shivering, and tried to make sense of the tableau in the throne room below.

Renault, standing beside the throne, hands clasped tightly behind his back, hair tussled beneath his crown, new bruises beneath reddened eyes. Orat and Tillion and Baldebert arranged in a row beneath the steps, all three soot blackened and battered. Orat's robes were torn and spattered with blood; a vicious-looking scratch bisected the bridge of his nose. Tillion's back was hunched, his weight again on his staff, weary and in obvious pain. His gaze darted about the room, from Renault to Orat to Mal and Avani crouched in the oriel and back again.

Mal shuddered.

"*Ai*, you're freezing." Avani chafed Mal's bare arms. Her touch inflamed the bee stings on his flesh. The pain cleared some of the muzziness from his head but vertigo made his stomach heave. "They insisted on stripping you down. I could not stop them, though I tried."

"Liam." Like bubbles in a murky pond rising to the surface, Mal's anxieties burst behind his eyes. "Is our lad yet living? Did he take any hurt? Russel? What about—"

"Silence!" Renault whirled away from the throne. He snapped two fingers and the Kingsmen raised their spears; iron points kissed Mal's bare skin. "Keep silent or you will force me to call for gag as well as chains!" His cheeks were livid. A vein above his eye pulsed distress.

"Cut out his tongue," Tillion suggested, "before he uses it to worm his way back into your graces, Majesty."

"Be still," the Masterhealer ordered his priest. "Remember kindness in adversity."

Baldebert did not trouble to hide his derisive snort. Renault took the steps down from the dais one at a time, boot heels echoing in the chamber. In front of Orat, he stopped, and placed one hand coolly atop the pommel of the sword he wore on his hip.

"The one god and I are even, I think," he said.

"Aye, Majesty." Orat had the grace to bow his head. "It was the necromancer's trespasses all along that so enraged the god and not, after all, Roue's interference."

"You made a mistake," Renault said, "in interpreting your god?"

"Paul made the mistake." Orat regrouped, drawing his tattered robes close. "One more of many questionable decisions that man made. Mayhap, in his new avarice, our brother stopped listening clearly. Or mayhap the magus clouded his mind. There was dissent between Paul and Malachi from the beginning; we all saw it. Tillion saw it most clear. Would that we had listened to him sooner."

Mal might have laughed but for the spear points still pressing his flesh. Avani squeezed his knee, an admonishment. He closed his eyes to blot out her anguished expression and lessen the vertigo. It was cold and dark inside his skull, a constellation abolished. He mourned the loss of light and wondered how he had ever wished it gone.

"I begin to distrust this flatland god, Majesty," Baldebert said. "His moods seem to wax and wane with the turning of the season or, if I may be so pointed, the changing of the temple guard. When my sister comes at last to meet her husband—what then? I daresay I fear Brother Orat's further vacillation."

"Nay," replied Orat. "You have my word, Majesty. The Rani will be feted as she deserves, hero and queen. So long as the necromancer meets his fate as required by the old laws."

"**W**ine," Mal begged after the two priests were ushered away. "Please."

"The spells in my bracelets wreak havoc upon his

system," Baldebert murmured. "Wine will settle his stomach and his head."

"Nay," said Renault evenly. "Water, to wet his throat, but nothing more. He's had too much of wine, lately."

Spear points fell away. The warmth that was Avani left Mal's side. After a moment, she returned and pressed a goblet to his mouth. He sipped, then gulped. She took it away before he could drink his fill.

"Lay your head in my lap," she said, settling again on the floor. "Rest if you can."

"Liam?" Forgetting dignity, he accepted her comfort, cuddling close to the heat of her.

"Alive and well as any of us." Her fingers soothed his curls.

"How much time do I have left?"

"Enough," she said, but he thought she lied. "Close your eyes."

He must have dozed, the rain a comforting rhythm outside the oriel. Someone started a fire in the hearth; it crackled and he dreamed restlessly of flames. He woke, gasping, rolled onto his side and wretched up bile. He knew without opening his eyes that Avani had left the dais. The ivory manacles dulled their link to nonexistence but he did not need that thread to find her in the chamber.

"Let him go with Everin, back over the mountains." Her voice cracked. Mal thought she had been weeping. Carefully he sat up, blinking the chamber into rough focus.

They gathered around the hearth, the arbiters of his fate. The king, the witch, the admiral, and to Mal's greater surprised, Everin and Cleena. The *sidhe* he might have expected—Renault always paid his debts. But he had not supposed Everin would come willingly before the throne that by all rights belonged first to him.

Everin dissented, his voice a rough whisper. "I came to beg your mercy for the desert, Majesty, not Malachi. I fear he is beyond saving. The desert tribes are decimated but not exterminated. I beg of you, stay your hand."

"The desert attacked me." Renault was taller than Everin. Stronger. He loomed. Everin endured the king's posturing with aplomb. "And this is not the first time they've overstepped. Baldebert has no love for the sand snakes. My forefathers built watch-towers to keep them at bay. Why should I not water my fields with their blood?"

"They were misled," argued Everin, "by Khorit Dard, by Crom Dubh, by your Brother Paul. They are starving. *Will* you walk the footsteps of your forefathers? The *sidhe*, the magi, and now the desert, who are your cousins in truth. And if you had listened to your priests, why not Roue?" He did not falter beneath Renault's indignation. "I regret to see a penchant for extermination plagues the bloodline."

"Do not pretend you would have done better." Renault bristled. "Oh, aye, I know who you are, grand-sire. I guessed when first you showed your face in Wilhaiim, looking for a job as courier. You very much resemble your mother, Elodie, whose paintings are relegated to back halls for her betrayal. Oh, I see. You supposed you were never mourned amongst your family in the quiet hours when regrets come home to roost? We spoke of you often, your name whispered in the nursery as a cautionary tale."

"The Virgin King," Everin replied coldly. "You made mockery."

"Legend made mockery," snapped Renault. "Virgin, aye. Unsullied, undefiled, untouched by the weight of the crown. Amongst your family it was not mockery. It was reverence. We owed you our continuance, our gratitude."

"I don't want your gratitude. I want the desert."

"So, what?" Renault paced a circle. In doing so he glanced Mal's direction, seeking counsel, before he recalled circumstances and pivoted away. "In another decade you will lead them across the divide against me again?"

"Nay. There will be no divide. These people need your help, Majesty. They will not survive without Wilhaiim to blunt their hunger, and in return they have much to offer. They are hardly the savages history has led you to believe. Under the right cir-cumstances, the desert might cease to be the enemy knocking always at your door."

"Do you suppose so? That is a very large boon you ask, all for ridding my skies of Crom Dubh." Renault turned his growl on Cleena. "And you, also, have come seeking a boon for your service?"

"Aye," the beekeeper answered, smiling. "I've come for Crom Dubh's head as proof to my people that he is gone. Surely that is not too much." Her smirk turned venomous. "I sacrificed my swarm for the sake of your city."

"Bees." Renault shook his head. "Recompense for bees."

"Wisest to comply, Majesty," Everin said. "Amongst the *sidhe* a single honeybee is far more precious than an entire kingdom of mortals. Cleena did you honor indeed."

"Why?" Renault wondered, regarding the *sidheog*, "Did you? Are you intending, like Everin and his sand snakes, to broker peace between barrowman and flatlander?"

Cleena spat into the fire. The flames jumped. "Nay," she said. "We are not interested in peace, nor ever will we be. This is our land—you took it from us. Someday we will have it again and make chair and table of your bones. Nay," she continued, "I did it for the lad. The brave, bonny lad with the scars on his hands and face. So the necromancer would not swallow his splendor with the rest."

"Liam?" Avani said, disbelieving. "You loathe Liam."

"I loathe that he is not anymore the babe I brought

to term, cradled in my arms, and called mine own. I loathe that he was murdered in the mounds for the sake of a trivial dispute, and I loathe that when the *aes si* brought him back he was different, no longer the son I loved. Aye, witch, I loathe him and I love him together." She shrugged. "Nevertheless, in the doing I earned Crom Dubh's head. That is the boon I ask."

"Wythe guards the monster's corpse still," Renault said after a terrible silence. "Tomorrow you may go to her and ask, in my name. If she doesn't kill you for the temerity of claiming her prize, I will not stand in your way."

"And?" Everin pressed. "What of the desert? Their time is running out. Roue's troops will advance with the dawn, slaughter any survivors by your order."

Renault glanced once more Mal's way. Mal raised his brows. It hurt badly, the pull of his flesh over his too-sensitive skull and also Renault's bleak resignation.

"Come into my war room," the king ordered Everin. "It seems we have much to discuss."

"**W**hy are you still here?" Mal asked Avani when the rain had stopped and sunrise turned the panes of the king's oriel silver. They were alone in the throne room but for some fifteen watchful Kingsmen and Jacob, who sat perched on the back of the throne muttering to himself about the dawn.

They sat back to back because it was easier for Mal to stay upright that way. Avani, like Jacob, looked out the window panes. Mal, when he could keep his eyes open, watched the fire in the hearth. Baldebert, against Renault's wishes, had smuggled in a blanket and a large flask of red wine.

"I'm sorry," the pirate prince had said, meaning the ivory manacles. "Would that I could have taken you cleanly through the heart with my sword instead."

"Not a chance," Mal said. And then in gruff surprise when, in shuffling beneath the blanket, he discovered the Curcas hidden in its folds. "Thank you."

"Where else would I be?" Avani asked now. They passed the goblet of wine between them, though Mal's shackles made the sharing difficult. She took a sip, then rolled her shoulders against his spine. "Besides which, Renault promised if I left this chamber, he'd lock me in the catacombs until he decided whether I'm to stay or go." She huffed amusement. "Yesterday he begged me to serve him as magus, today he's terrified I will."

"It's not Renault's decision, nor mine, but if you'll take advice from a friend—"

"Aye."

"—run far and fast away from this place. Sooner or later they will look at you and think of me."

"So Deval also counseled. I'm inclined to agree."

Mal felt something poignantly close to relief. "When the time comes, then, mayhap I'll think of you on the Downs again, with your sheep and your loom."

"If you like," Avani agreed.

"Tricks," muttered Jacob from Renault's throne. "Tricks!"

"I didn't know you taught him to speak." Mal squinted at ebony feathers.

"Ai, well. I didn't. I expect it's the Goddess's idea of a joke."

"You don't find it amusing, I think."

"Nay," Avani agreed, pointedly not looking Jacob's way. "I don't."

It was Avani's turn to sleep. She did not stir when Renault returned to the throne room, nor even when he climbed the steps into the oriel.

"Brother," the king said. "I was promised the ivories would prevent your conjuring. Whence came the blanket and the drink, then, for surely no one in this castle would disdain my express command?"

"Brother," replied Mal, well in his cups but not yet so drunk as to use the Curcas seed, "lack of sleep has you imagining things. There is no blanket or drink here."

Renault squatted to better see Mal's face. "When you are gone, will the Automata . . . stop? They ruin my city just by standing in one place; very few have the courage to endure their glance without collapsing."

"Say not when I am gone but when I die. We've never been delicate with each other, Majesty."

"When you are executed," Renault said evenly, "will the Automata cease their twitching and staring?"

"In truth, I am surprised to hear they have not yet stopped," Mal confessed. "Baldebert's bloody bracelets are worse than death." Despite a grief like oil sloshing in his belly, or because of the wine, he giggled.

Renault snatched the goblet from the flagstones and drank. Wine beaded on his lower lip. He wiped it away with the back of his hand.

"My grandsire desires all of the east, to make a kingdom of his own. Though he will not admit ambition, of course, and claims only to have the best of intentions."

Mal laughed harder. Avani sighed in her sleep, but did not wake.

"Your Majesty, I wish you luck. I fear where that one is concerned, you'll need it. I expect it's his hard-headedness bred true through generations that makes you Wilhaiim's finest king."

He'd only seen Renault weep openly once before, when they'd found Kate Shean murdered in the royal herb garden. Mal wished he did not have to see it again.

"I do not want you dead. Damn you, Mal, I will not forgive you for this though I live another fifty years."

"I do not want to die," replied Mal. And then, "I forgive you."

They came for him before evening fell again, armored head to toe as if he could smite them on the way to his pyre, as if iron was an antidote to bone magic. By the time they seized his blanket, he had the Curcas tucked in his loin cloth. Russel met his eye from beneath her helm; his heart broke a little that she showed no remorse. Avani was stiff and silent at his side, one hand a vise around his chains.

"My lady," Russel said gently. "He's to come with us, now."

"Where is Renault?" Avani demanded. "Surely the king will not let him go to his death alone!"

"He's not alone, my lady. He has us. The king is in the bailey, waiting."

Avani nodded stiffly, let go the chains to touch Mal's cheek, then turned her back on his disgrace. The Kingsmen ushered him down the steps and through the chamber. He stumbled, vertigo making his legs useless. Two of the soldiers hauled him roughly upright. Jacob left the throne and flapped overhead, lurching from rafter to rafter, shrieking. Mal, lightheaded and dazed, could not tell whether the raven's noise was celebration or indignation.

The court had turned out in the main hall, clothed in all their finery as if Mabon had come early. They applauded his nakedness and his dishonor. The bravest amongst them spat in his face and on his bare chest. He remembered how bright they had appeared when they were stars instead of people. He'd loved them then, for their potential and their shine. Now they appeared dark and dingy, muted and self-absorbed. He couldn't remember why he'd thought it reasonable to sacrifice his life for theirs.

To his distant surprise, they took the servant's stairs instead of parading him through the palace's front doors. Through an arrow slit Mal could see the bailey was cleared but for Renault and Tillion, and a tree trunk driven into the ground where Tillion had once made his pedestal, and kindling piled all around the base. Despite the rain the air stank still of fire and battle. Mal was glad. At least they would not be able to tell the smell of his own cooked flesh from the rest.

"Careful," Russel said when he swayed, near to fainting. He thought her rough edges had softened. "Almost there."

Brother Orat met them on the steps, dressed in clean, white robes, a mug in his hand.

"Yet more wine?" Mal's tongue had grown thick. He was not sure they would understand him.

"Laced with a sleeping draft," Orat said. "Quick acting. Even for all your trespasses, Malachi, the king does not wish for you to suffer." He held the mug to Mal's lips. "Swallow it down—God willing you'll dream sweetly into death and spare us your angry haunt."

Better than painful Curcas poison, far better than the agony of suffocation and flame. Mal let his heavy lids fall shut. He imagined for himself a garden, a beloved pocket of spring, grass growing as thick as a rug, and brilliant flowers climbing invisible walls. He populated it with marble benches, and glistening fountains, and rolling hedges sporting violet berries, and a three-tiered fountain frothing beneath blue skies. Siobahn sat there, in her blue wedding garb, the Siobahn he remembered from youth, before his ambition had ruined her. Rowan lingered near the hedgerow, head tilted, mouth curved in a welcoming smile.

"Swallow," urged the Masterhealer, tilting the mug so liquid flowed across Mal's tongue.

Mal drank.

SURRENDER

A bonfire burned in the Rose Keep's bailey. Flames made blue and orange by damp driftwood popped merrily. The keep's housecarl, an extraordinarily tall man called Biaz, fed sea grass and pieces of evergreen to the large brazier, encouraging the blaze. Mabon was not Mabon without a good, hot fire and the Lady Selkirk had guests to impress.

She needn't have tried so hard. The Lady Selkirk had won Avani over the day she'd sent word to the Downs that she meant to hold funeral rites for her disgraced youngest son, the court's opinion be damned.

"Look at the colors of the sunset," Parsnip breathed. The lass craned her neck to see past the bonfire. "I've never seen one so pretty."

"It's because we're so near the sea." Arthur, sitting

on his haunches, wrapped his arms around Bear's neck, cuddling the brindled hound close for warmth. The days had become cold and even so near the coast snow had fallen, covering the keep's famous rose brambles with a dusting of white.

"Hush, now," warned Liam. "Here they come."

Seamen and merchants stood in a loose crowd around the bonfire. Joseph, the keep's Masterhealer, passed amongst them, dressed in mourning kit, a shawl emblazoned with embroidered roses wrapped about his sloped shoulders. Selkirk's guard stood on the battlements, ringing the courtyard. They looked down on the funerary fire, their backs set, resolute, to the sea. The Selkirk's cook, a stout woman with strands of silver in her hair, was weeping loudly into a kerchief pressed against her nose and mouth. Her honest grief made the lump always in Avani's throat grow painful. She coughed to keep from choking.

Seamen, merchants, and servants bent the knee when Lady Selkirk descended the stairs from the lighthouse tower. Avani, Liam, and the three pages stayed properly upright. It was apparent Mal had gotten his diminutive height from his mother. A compact, dour woman, she wore the seaman's uniform of trousers and tunic, and the Rose badge on her arm. A simple silver circlet rested on her curls; wind burn and age spots freckled her face and hands. She carried an orange-needled branch in her arms—a gift from Wilhaiim's king for Mabon. When she tossed it onto the fire, the flames hissed, snapping. She watched the branch burn, then gestured to her priest.

When Brother Joseph rose, creaking, to his feet, the servants, merchants, and seamen followed. He took three strong men with him into the temple keep.

"Red sky at night," murmured Liam as they waited. He sounded bemused.

"Sailor's delight," Morgan finished quietly. The young earl was dressed in lavish velvet and silk according to his station. He'd come to the coast to pay his respects, and of all of them Lady Selkirk appeared to appreciate his presence the most. Wythe was an old and respected house; Morgan was the first of his family to visit the Rose Keep.

Brother Joseph and his three companions returned, a corpse swathed in a sigil-painted sail cloth balanced on their shoulders. It was not a corpse, of course, but an effigy of bundled sweet grass. That it was not her son's body in truth did not seem to bother Lady Selkirk.

"It's not unusual. Sailors often die at sea. That my lady lost Malachi to burning instead of drowning makes little difference."

It was Biaz, returned from feeding the bonfire. The housecarl's cheeks were wet with tears. "For all their faults they were good lads, Rowan and Malachi both," he said. "She's lost them all now, her husband and her sons. Though she hides it well, I fear her heart is broken."

"I'm so sorry," Avani said. "If there's aught I can do to help—"

Biaz shook his head. "It's enough that you made the journey. If you'll follow me, my lady, my lord. It's time we'll be taking him to the beach."

Brother Joseph and his attendants with their burden preceded them to the keep's west gate, the Lady Selkirk on their heels. As soon as she passed without, the rest of the keep followed. Avani and Liam and Parsnip and the two lads took up the rear of the procession, boot heels crunching on the oyster shell spread over sand.

Brother Joseph began to sing the high, thin burial chant reserved for lords of desert and sea and plain. Avani had heard the lay once before, at Kate Shean's funeral. She had not thought to hear it at Mal's. As the priest sang, the sigils painted on Selkirk's burial shroud glowed first indigo and then star-shine pale. Theist magic throbbed in Avani's bones. The priest's chant grew loud and sweet, and the shroud burned brighter, illuminating the steep stairs that led to sand and wave below the keep.

Selkirk perched upon a natural stack of rock. The peninsula jutted in crags and cliffs over the water. There were ordered steps cut into the rock made slippery by snow and sea spray. Thick rope was bolted into the stone for ease of climbing. Avani clutched at the guide ropes with one hand as they descended, eyeing the sheer drop with misgiving, and exhaled relief when at last they stepped from stone to sand.

A long pier braved the restless sea at the foot of the stairs. Fingerling waves, turned pink by the sunset, lapped at the beach. Two tall ships were moored at the end of the pier; the bay, Avani thought, must grow deep quickly to allow for such large vessels. One of the ships wore ink-black sails instead of the usual white.

When the front of the procession touched sand, it broke in two, spreading a single line north and south along the shore. Mal's mother followed Brother Joseph onto to the pier. The Masterhealer's song softened. In response the burial shroud dimmed to half-light.

As those on the shore watched silently, the crew of the black-sailed ship disembarked one by one. They walked the pier, and took the bundled effigy on their own shoulders. The sky was the color of blood as they carried their burden onto the funeral ship. Lady Selkirk stood motionless on the plank while the ship was freed from its moorings. Gulls cried in the evening. The black sails were raised though there was no wind to fill them. Oars splashed in the cold, dark sea.

The ship moved slowly into the bay, and it was done.

"This way," Liam said. "Only a little further."

The sun had set and the stars come up. Avani's

mage-light bobbed over their heads, lighting the stretch of northern beach. Bear frolicked in and out of the water, chasing imaginary prey. Jacob, less inclined to endure sea foam, scolded the hound from atop Parsnip's shoulder. Avani was glad of the new wool cloak she'd brought with her from Stonehill. The wool kept the damp from her skin and from the contents of the pack she wore over one shoulder. She was doubly glad of the sword on her hip when she glimpsed the barrowman waiting for them at the base of the old monkey wood monument.

"*Ai*, you've taken to keeping odd companions indeed." She greeted Everin with an embrace, ducking to avoid the torch he carried for light. "Sand snakes and *sidhe* are more to your taste than good flatland stock?"

He'd grown a beard again and wore an embroidered scarf in the desert manner to hide the scar on his throat. He smiled to see her and hugged her tight.

"You are to my taste, black eyes," he said. "I've missed you. When will you come to visit?"

"Across the mountain divide?" she scoffed, amused. "I'm done with traveling, for the nonce. But I'm eager to hear tales of your new oasis in the desert."

Bear was growling at the barrowman. The barrowman was growling back. Jacob laughed from Parsnip's shoulder.

"Drem," snapped Everin, releasing Avani. "Let the hound be." He shook his head when Avani lifted her brows in inquiry. "*Sidhe* morality is not flatland morality. That one thought it was doing me a favor in keeping a promise made to Faolan."

"In keeping you alive," Avani said. "No matter the cost to you or to others. And you understand its choices?" Watching the lesser *sidhe* and the brindled hound cavort, almost she also could understand.

"Aye," Everin agreed. "Drem loved Faolan, in its own way. As I did. And I spent too many years in the barrows to discount *sidhe* logic. I might have done the same, were our roles reversed."

"Nay," Avani said gently. "I know you would not."

"Avani," interrupted Liam with a shout, pointedly ignoring both barrowman and hound, "come and look!"

The beam had been part of an island dwelling, before cataclysm brought Shellshale down into the ocean. Avani rapped her knuckles on monkey wood; it was solid as stone but she knew also that it would be buoyant in the water. A trestle not dissimilar had kept her afloat as a child, saving her life as others drowned.

"There's a plaque," Arthur cried. "Set in the wood. May I borrow your light, Lady Avani? I'd like to read what it says."

Avani sent her witch-light spinning near the lad but she needn't have bothered.

"'All life springs from the waves. All life returns to

the sea,'" Liam quoted from memory, looking not at the bronze plaque but out across the water.

"I'm sorry, my lady," Morgan said quietly. "For your loss."

"It was a long time ago." Avani patted monkey wood as if it was Jacob in need of soothing. "I hardly remember who they were." The realization didn't hurt as much as she expected.

"Kin is kin," said the barrowman, creeping up against Avani's side. The lesser *sidhe*'s nearness made the stone in Andrew's ring flare amber. "We honor their bones in the dark places, even after we forget their names."

"That's grim," retorted Parsnip, glowering. The lass did not seem at all disturbed by Drem's proximity. Which suggested Everin was not the only one spending time in the company of new friends. For all her barking, Bear seemed less impressed with the barrowman than the new smells around the base of the monkey wood beam. Nor had Avani missed the crock of honey Liam had left with Lady Selkirk as a Mabon gift.

"Where's Baldebert?" she asked, peering into the darkness. "We can't do this without him."

"Late as usual," Everin replied. "Granted it's a bit of a ride from Low Port. We'll wait. I have beer and Drem has caught us a brace of fish. Come and sup, and we'll celebrate the end of this day as we should, in quiet companionship."

Baldebert did not arrive until well after sunrise the next day, but Avani found she did not mind the wait. Less Drem, who entertained itself by stalking night crabs in the tide, they huddled together high up on the beach, sharing bedding and drink and roasting fish over a fire much smaller than the one they had left behind in Selkirk. While they ate, Everin explained to them the complications of building trade between the desert and the flatlands, of teaching sand lords the intricacies of flatland etiquette and flatland merchants the importance of clean water in desert custom, and the difficulty of wiping out generations of prejudice and enmity on both sides of the divide.

"But not impossible," he mused. "Skerrit's Pass proves my point. Sixty days the tower's been staffed by Kingsmen and tribespeople together, and only the one instance of fisticuffs to speak of. It helps that the tinkers are eager to resume business on both sides of the mountain."

"What does the desert have of value?" Arthur wondered doubtfully. "Sand and cactus ain't worth much to Wilhaiim."

"Steel," Everin said. "Lighter than iron yet still useful against the *sidhe*. Textiles. Their needlework rivals even Roue's. And mesquite beer. Whitcomb's vineyards are gone. It will be years before the wine trade rises from the ash, if ever. Wilhaiim's court will soon suffer the lack." He winked in Arthur's direction. "Already our mesquite beer is finding favor in a few prominent taverns; it's far less costly now than Whitcomb wine."

Avani fell asleep smiling, the perfume of salt in her nose and the laughter of her companions a joyful noise in her ears. She slept deeply and without dreaming and roused midday to Baldebert's shout as he galloped the stretch of beach between Selkirk and the monkey wood monument, waving a feathered cap in greeting. It was low tide, the sea retreated away across gleaming sand. Baldebert's arrival stirred the children to excitement. They broke camp quickly while Everin admired Baldebert's Low Port courser. Liam and Bear scouted ahead along the beach. By the time bedding was returned to journey packs and the last of the fish consumed, they'd returned, the dog filthy with sand and the young man looking hopeful.

"It's there," he reported, "exactly as Russel said it would be. An old fisherman's cottage, more driftwood than plank and grown all over with Selkirk rose but the thatching on the roof looks new and there's the smell of smoked meat. Someone's about the place."

"*Someone*." Baldebert pursed his mouth. "We well know who." He slanted a glance in Avani's direction. "Will we be welcome?"

She shrugged. "Your ivories make it impossible to tell." Settling her pack more comfortably on her back, she grabbed up a length of driftwood from the beach to use as a staff, testing the weight of it in her fist.

"There's only one way to find out, *ai*. Jacob's lit off. I imagine we'll find him there ahead of us."

The raven waited for them on the roof of the fisherman's cottage in a tangle of thorny vine and black rose hips. He called out raucously as they approached. The man standing with him outside the cottage snarled a rebuke.

He did not look at all as he used to, and though Avani expected the change, it was disconcerting. Cleena's spell had added the illusion of height and bulk to delicate bones, turned green eyes to brown, repaired the broken nose. His hair was disconcertingly straight, pulled back in a knot at his neck. Gray bristles roughened his cheeks and chin. He wore fisherman's togs beneath a tattered red Kingsman's cloak and desert sandals on his feet.

He watched them approach without speaking. Bear, barking again, raced to meet him, then circled eagerly about the cottage. Everin put his hand on his sword but knew better than to insult Avani by drawing it. Liam whistled, a thrush's call, and to Avani's relief Mal whistled back.

"In his right mind, mayhap," Baldebert murmured. "Here, lad." He tossed Arthur his mare's reins and jumped from the saddle into the sand, landing lightly on his toes. "Where's the barrowman?"

"Here." Drem appeared as if out of thin air, carrying a spear and a length of bulbous seaweed. The horse spooked. Arthur cursed roundly but managed not to let go. Drem grinned.

"More trouble than it's worth," Baldebert told Everin. "You should have killed it when it showed up again in the desert." He flapped his hat in the air, an invitation. "By all means, you first, my lady."

But Avani was already striding ahead. In her eagerness she wanted to run but, for fear of frightening the man turned hermit, she measured her steps carefully, as casually as a beach comber spending a pleasant afternoon searching for treasure on the sand. Drem capered at her side. Baldebert followed at a slug's pace.

"Hello," Mal said when she reached the cottage. His voice was the same, but rough with disuse, more broken even than Everin's hoarse whisper. "I didn't expect you or I'd have put water to boil for tea."

She laughed, made light-headed with joy. "Do you really have tea?" she asked, wiping tears from her cheeks.

That unfamiliar mouth curved upward at one corner. "Nay. But I have water and a pot and I'm handy with the flint. And I imagine you've brought leaf with you." He arched thick brows at the heavy pack on her back, then turned his attention to Drem and Baldebert. "You're my first guests," he confessed. "It's close inside but you're welcome." He lifted his gaze, considering Everin and Liam and the children. "Afraid to come too near, are they?"

"Not afraid," Avani said. "It's only caution. Until we can be sure—"

"That I'm safe?" Mal guessed. "Ah, well. Come inside and we'll see."

"Not inside," Drem said, baring fangs. "Here. I'll do it here. It stinks of iron inside."

"As you wish." Mal inclined his head, waiting.

Drem scuttled across the sand. The lesser *sidhe* sniffed about Mal with the same enthusiasm Bear had shown the cottage moments earlier.

"*Sidheog* are very clever," it said, prodding Mal with its claws, peeking beneath the red cloak, poking fisherman's togs. "And Cleena more than most. She would have hidden it where you cannot find it for your sake and for ours—ah." It paused, pointed chin buried in the back of Mal's neck, beneath his hair. Avani shuddered in sympathy but Mal did not seem disturbed, although it was difficult to read illusionary features. Drem walked its fingers beneath the knot of bundled hair on the nape of Mal's neck, then yanked viciously. Mal grunted. Drem came away with a broken length of colorful thread.

The glamour dissolved as the thread snapped. Mal as Avani knew him stood there instead in the fisherman's togs. Without the disguise they were too baggy about his bony hips and shrunken torso. His dark curls were a riot of tangles and salt. The bristle on his face was dark, patchy. She was surprised he'd managed to shave at all; his body shook all over with fine tremors. Baldebert's ivory manacled his wrists. He stank of Whitcomb wine and sour sweat. He had the reddened eyes of a man who hadn't seen sobriety for much too long, but his irises were vivid green once again.

"Thank you," he said. "Whoever he was, I'd grown deeply sick of living in his homely skin."

"A Whitcomb refugee who didn't survive the breaching of Wilhaiim's walls," Baldebert said while Drem dug a hole in the sand with one foot and dropped the bit of thread within. "It was his corpse, in your guise, that Tillion and Renault burned as magus in Wilhaiim's bailey. So mayhap show the man a little gratitude, for saving your life."

"Cleena did that," said Mal. He swayed and set a hand on Avani's shoulder for balance. "And Russel and mayhap even Orat. Why?"

"Because Renault asked them to, you stupid man," said Avani. She tilted her head at Baldebert. "We can finish the rest of it inside."

"Finish," agreed Jacob irritably from a nest of thorns and rose hips.

"It was Rowan's cottage, before he died," Mal said as they settled on a floor of old rugs and older pelts. "My brother. He built it when he was a boy. No one dares come near it now for fear of his haunt. There's no ghost here," he added when Avani glanced around.

"There never has been. He died at sea, went down with his ship. My mother blamed me for his death. As the eldest, he was supposed to take the title. It was supposed to be me on the sea. I was meant for the merchant fleet. Until they discovered I was magus."

Avani contented herself with looking about the square room as Mal fought vertigo and Baldebert battled misgivings. It was comfortable, if sparse. A large fishing net hung on one wall, a pile of heavy iron weighs on the ground beneath it. A barrel of fresh water sat in one corner next to a large Whitcomb cask. There was no bed for sleeping and as far as she could tell no chamber pot for pissing, but the rugs and pelts were comfortable and she'd not used a chamber pot on the Downs, either. There were advantages to living alone on a stretch of desolate land.

"You can't go back," Baldebert said. "You can't ever go back, to Wilhaiim or anywhere near. In fact, I wouldn't show your face in any keep or hamlet were I you, for Renault's sake if not your own. Roue's out, for the sea journey, but Everin says you'd be welcome in the desert. The Black Coast—no one would know you that far south. Or mayhap Stonehill—only Avani lives there willingly."

"I like it here," Mal said mildly. "No one comes down this stretch of beach willingly, either. If the monument doesn't turn them away, my brother's cottage will." He looked, not at Baldebert, but at Avani. "Russel said you would come to take them off, but

I did not believe her. You know what I am without the ivories. In all good faith, I should not allow it. In fact, I'm certain it would be a bad idea. They make me weak and sick, lesser than I was. Given the opportunity, I do not think I could resist . . ." He flushed slightly. "I've a hollowness needs filling."

"I cannot help you with that," agreed Avani. "You must learn to live with that emptiness—you owe Renault that." Her heart broke a little at his stricken expression. Did he still hope he could be magus again? "There is another option, a prison still, but one less invasive than ensorcelled ivory."

He narrowed his eyes, understanding already. "The wards," he guessed. "The shining cage that kept me from your head even before these bloody bangles. I never taught you that. I did not know it could be done."

"Not so much a cage as a net. I think I can do the same for you, if you consent. Internal wards, to keep you in and temptation out." Determined to be forthright, she added, "My spell in your head, not so different from Baldebert's bracelets around your wrists, although I am hoping the side effects will be less painful."

"Your wards in my head, constraining my power and my freedom. Keeping me from mischief, is that it? Side effects or no, my dignity will suffer." He gazed down at old ivory. "A prison without walls, no end in sight."

"Ah, drama! You still have the Curcas seeds," retorted Baldebert. "I know Russel left that poison with you here. You haven't used it. Mayhap life alone in your head is not so bad as you pretend. After all, most of the world gets on just fine trapped in our own skulls and with no more than the usual side effects of loneliness and self-absorption. And I expect Avani will be a sympathetic jailer."

Mal said nothing.

"By your own consent," Avani reminded him. "I'll not force it on you. And I'll not tolerate reproach after."

His lips curled again, but this time without mirth.

"If I consent now," he said after a short silence, "I may forget acquiescence the moment you remove the cuffs. What of the ferric soldiers, waiting still on my command?"

"They are gone," Baldebert pronounced with more than a little smugness. "Dismantled piece by piece, melted to slag. They did not move claw or chain to prevent their own destruction, although it was deuced hard to find men and women stout enough of heart to do the job." He shrugged minutely. "Be that as it may, the Automata no longer wait for your direction. They are abolished."

"As I suspect I will be," Mal muttered. If he grieved the lost Automata he did not let it show on his face. "If this experiment goes wrong."

"It will not go wrong," Avani said. "I've been

practicing moving the spell from my head, person to person, back and forth, like flame between two candles."

He snorted. "On whom? Not Liam. No young man wants his mother in his head."

"On Parsnip," Avani replied with dignity. "She has an interest in all things preternatural, and she's not afraid to visit the Downs. And Morgan because he wants to impress Arthur with his daring."

"Avani's safe," Mal warned Baldebert after a short silence, "but you're risking your life in this. The instant I'm free, it will be your light I reach for."

"I'm flattered," the pirate prince replied, deadpan, "but I trust Avani when she says she can do it. I'm willing to try."

"The others stay down the beach till we finish. Just in case."

"Aye," agreed Avani. "Just in case."

In the end it was simpler than even she expected. Baldebert broke apart the cuffs with one hand before jerking away out of Mal's reach. Unhindered by the ivories, the link between Avani and Mal burst back into life. It was a matter of two heartbeats to transfer the wards in her head through that intersection and into Mal. He struggled briefly against the caging of his power, but he did not have time to learn the secret of that strange sorcery before she locked him away from the world, from the living and the dead and even herself. Once in place the silver net dulled their connection again to a whisper. She felt the loss like a blow. She'd grown used to missing him, but that briefest of mingling inflamed longing once again.

"Alone in our heads," she murmured, facing the pain of loss and then setting it aside again. "No end in sight."

Mal lay on his back on the floor, eyes closed. The tremors in his body were easing, but his chest rose and fell in bursts as he gulped air.

"So?" Baldebert crept close. "Did it work? Is he contained?"

"Aye," answered Avani softly. Her own head felt raw as an open wound, newly exposed. Once she felt strong enough she would have to replace the warding spell she'd pushed on Mal with a new conjuring; she did not intend to leave herself unprotected. "He's only now grieving what was lost, I think. Come outside. Give him time."

Later, after Baldebert said his farewells, while Everin and Liam and the children explored the beach and Drem chased Bear through the rising tide, Avani unpacked her bag. From Stonehill she'd brought folds of good undyed wool and fine shears and her best needle and thread for making Mal new winter clothes. From Wilhaiim she'd gathered fruit, fresh and dried, and all her medicines plus spices for hot cider and Rouen leaves for tea. She had three interesting books on Black Coast piracy loaned to her by Deval and also Mal's volume of Selkirk poetry for reading when the snow fell, and several pairs of thick socks purchased at the Fair at the last minute. She carried also a sealed letter from the king and another from Russel. She set those beside Mal as he slept.

Her Goddess she placed in the corner near the fishing weights and added an offering of snipped seaweed and a handful of rose hips gathered from the vine outside. Then, satisfied, she went out into the fresh air to watch her small family frolic. Eventually, Mal joined her there.

"You're staying," he said, blinking in the sunlight.

"Aye. They'll go tomorrow; they each have burdens waiting in the city, or over the mountains. But I'm staying."

"I don't want to be your burden."

Avani smiled. "I'm staying because I've been too long away from the sea, and I miss it." She nudged his bony shoulder with her own. "Also, I've missed you. I'd like a winter of rest, holed up in your brother's cottage, safe from snow and storm but with the water a stone's throw away. I'd like that very much."

"I'm not a restful person. You know that." He sighed. "Lately I've developed a penchant for too much red wine and too little self-discipline."

"I don't mind." She took his hand. It was strong in

hers, fingers warm. It trembled, but not from vertigo or illness. She'd surprised him. Her smile widened.

"I can teach you to fish from a line and hook," Avani offered. "And how to make a fine mussel broth."

"I'd like that." Mal squeezed her fingers. He cleared his throat. "I'd like that very much indeed."

ACKNOWLEDGMENTS

Thanks as always to Paul, Katherine, and Aidan for ignoring dust bunnies while I'm on deadline. To the Hobblings, for being family. Fandom, for the distraction. And extra special thanks to my editor, Priyanka, for her encouragement and hard work.